# THE UNICORN

Tony Salter

ETS Limited
16 Beech Avenue, Chichester, PO19 3DR

First published in Great Britain in 2021 by ETS Limited



ISBN: 978-0-9957977-9-6

# THE UNICORN

*Time is running out ...*

---

Ibrahim Abdel Hak is the Unicorn.

Lost in the mists and shadows of urban legend, he waits and builds his plans in the cold darkness.

Each time Ibrahim attacks, he leaves a trail of very real death and destruction in his wake.

The world's intelligence services know he is planning the worst atrocity yet. They know it will be soon. But they have no idea where or when the Unicorn will strike.

---

Tony Salter is the bestselling author of four previous novels, His previous novel, Sixty Minutes, is a prequel to The Unicorn.

Tony is currently working on a series of illustrated children's books set in Norway.

He lives in Chichester with his Norwegian wife.

*ALSO BY TONY SALTER*

*Best Eaten Cold*
*The Old Orchard*
*Cold Intent (Sequel to Best Eaten Cold)*
*Sixty Minutes*

For my wife, Gro, who has always been by my side.

In good times and in bad.

# *Prologue*

*The young woman walked up the grand stone staircase. Each step was slow, measured and precise; she took exaggerated care as though she'd become an eighty-year-old version of herself, unsure of her balance and terrified by the consequences of falling.*

*She was tall and slim, dressed in jeans and a light leather jacket. On another day, she would have been pretty, but her lips were tightly pressed together and the white bandage over her right eye threw her features out of balance.*

*Aside from the armed police at the door, the Natural History Museum was empty; the last of the forensics teams had left a few hours earlier and the restoration specialists weren't due to arrive until the end of the day. The woman had used all her persuasive talent and every ounce of remaining goodwill to convince her boss to allow this visit. She flashed her ID badge, did her best to smile, and stepped into the great hall, her footfalls echoing in the silent space.*

*Microscopic particles of pulverised sandstone still floated in the air, leaving a bile-bitter taste on the back of her tongue. The bombing had taken place more than a week before, but for her, it may as well have been just a few seconds earlier. Stuck in a hospital bed, all her dreams and waking thoughts had been filled with the time before the explosion, constantly playing and replaying the final minutes and seconds, wondering whether she could have done something more, anything to change the course of events.*

*After less than a dozen paces, she came to a massive stone column and stretched up, using one finger to trace a pocked crater in the polished stone. That was where she'd been standing, half-sheltered behind the pillar, when the world had fallen apart. That was where her memories stopped, though it didn't take much to imagine the steel ball-bearing striking like a bullet, shattering the stone and propelling that single pointed shard of marble through her temple and into the back of her left eye.*

*The woman took her dust-covered finger and probed the coarse fabric of her dressing, feeling the sharp ache of the still-knitting bone underneath. She leant against the cold stone, waiting until the red waves of pain, anger and guilt had passed. She should have been faster or, what scared her even more, she should have been smarter and more professional.*

*Taking three deep breaths, she moved forward towards the centre of the huge hall where a dark circle scarred the tiled floor, charcoal-black streaks radiating outwards like a macabre drawing of the sun. Beyond that, there was little obvious damage to be seen, although the absence of the famous dinosaur skeleton left a gaping hole in the empty air above her head – as though a ghost image was still there, just on the edge of sight.*

*The woman stood in respectful silence, head bowed and staring at the centre of the black sun as she replayed those final moments once again; the vulnerable young man coming to his senses and lifting his hands in surrender; the two brave men leaning over him, and then … nothing. The next thing she remembered was waking up in hospital, head wrapped in bandages and the sound of the Niagara Falls thundering in her ears.*

# 1

Another cleaning job?

Really?

Nadia had only just come out of a six month cleaning assignment at the Birmingham Mosque and David had promised he'd find her something less grim to make up for it.

So much for promises.

She sighed theatrically, snorting air through both nostrils as she watched the first hints of morning appear through the squeaky-clean, plate-glass windows. It was always hard to pin down the moment when night started to slip away, but there was definitely a pale glow picking out the silhouette of the Shard. Another grey cloudy day on the way; no stars – except for Venus – were bright enough to burn through the Autumn murk.

Venus wasn't strictly a star, of course – then why was it called the Morning Star? At the end of a mind-numbing ten-hour shift, Nadia often found her mind wandering down such strange and pointless cul-de-sacs. Who cared what the stupid planet was called?

That had been the subject of her first argument with James. Nadia had insisted Venus was the Morning Star, and he'd been certain it was known as the Evening Star. Before she'd had time to explain why she was definitely right, he'd Googled it. She could still remember the taste of dissatisfaction when he'd explained that it was actually both.

How dull was that? She couldn't decide which was more disappointing – the fact that they were both right, or that he'd looked up the answer before they'd had the chance to disagree properly. Outside work, Nadia made a point of never checking facts on her phone, but she couldn't prevent other people ruining the fun.

The windows were finished and so was she. She trudged back to the utility room, feeling the weight of the heavy bucket on her tired arms. At five in the morning, the offices were empty, long rows of desks and drab dividing screens waiting for the day's activity. As she reached the swing doors, her phone vibrated in her pocket.

There was a single message from a familiar number. 'See you later' had a very particular pre-agreed meaning which meant Nadia's day wasn't quite over. She lifted the bucket, straightened up and half-ran towards the lift. The first shift would be arriving in less than ten minutes and someone might be early.

Nadia's swipe card shouldn't have allowed her to access the forty-second floor, but she wasn't an ordinary cleaner and her card wasn't an ordinary card. The lift was moving unbearably slowly, but eventually gave a soft cheery ping as the doors opened onto the executive level.

Nadia left her bucket in the doorway and ran out. She could hear the sound of less-than-happy lift pings behind her as the doors failed to close. She had two minutes before the blockage would trigger an alarm, but she'd be quicker than that.

It took her thirty seconds to replace the two USB computer leads with apparently identical copies from her tunic pocket and she was on her way back to the lifts. Another thirty seconds and the lift doors were closing. She tucked the swapped leads carefully away, holding her breath as she watched the floors counting down. Life would be much easier if no one saw her coming out of the lift. Why did Anthea always have to cut it so fine?

It was close. The lift doors had barely shut behind her when she spotted one of the senior execs walking down the corridor flanked by two young women. It was Liu Janlin, the VP in charge of the controversial 5G roll-out and a nasty piece of work by all accounts. Nadia let her shoulders slump forward, dipped her head and walked towards them. She wasn't going to forgive David for giving her another cleaner assignment, but she had to admit it was effective; most people didn't even register her existence – especially people wearing Armani suits who could still remember their peasant-farmer parents shuffling bent-backed through the paddy fields.

The locker room was empty and Nadia managed to tidy up and change in less than five minutes. The *'see you later'* protocol also included a handover right across town and she needed to miss the morning rush hour to stand a chance of making it there in time. She span the numbers on her combination lock and was turning to leave when a shadow loomed behind the glass door.

Nadia took a step backwards reflexively as a massive woman pushed her way into the room.

'All right, luv?' said Donna, her shift supervisor. 'Working unpaid overtime, are we?'

'Nah. I was just struggling with those bloody windows,' said Nadia. 'You should have seen the state they were in.' She laughed, but her heart sank. She could really do without a conversation with Donna – who had no family to go home to, and could talk for England.

'So … What you up to?' said Donna. 'Fancy a cuppa?'

Nadia was already pushing past her and through the door. 'Love to,' she said. 'But I gotta get back for me mum. She'll be climbing the walls after a night with my two … I'll see you tonight. Right?'

'Yeah … Right,' said Donna. 'I forgot you had kids.'

'See ya,' said Nadia, shouting over her shoulder, unsure if Donna was annoyed about being brushed aside. The bloody woman had a chip on her shoulder a mile wide and was quite capable of moving Nadia back to cleaning toilets out of spite.

The street was already busy as she made her way down to the tube. Once she was lost in the crowds, she took off her headscarf, allowed herself to stand more upright and forced a smile back onto her face. Her undercover character might have two little monsters waiting at home and driving their grannie mad, but Nadia didn't. She wasn't actually struggling to pay the rent and provide food for her family, weighed down by the effort of simply making it through another day. It felt good to be herself again – even if only for a few hours.

She found herself jealous of the imaginary children, though. When she was younger, she'd always believed her future would have kids in it – a girl and a boy. Nappies, first steps, first words, school uniforms, traumatic teenage years – Nadia had never doubted that she would have her own family. The normal happy family she'd liked to have had herself.

Life wasn't that straightforward, though. After joining the service and moving up the ranks, the conflicts with normal life were becoming more and more pronounced. She was still holding onto her dreams of family, but she loved her job. It had become an integral part of who she was.

Could she really find a way to reconcile those two lives without tearing herself apart?

Waterloo station was humming by the time she got there, buzzing with that unique noise-scape only found in old railway stations, each individual sound multiplied and merged by cavernous echos from the soaring glass and steel. It was quite different from a football stadium or a big hotel atrium. Almost as though the rushing crowd had a voice of its own. Even the motionless ones, patient commuters waiting transfixed by the departure boards, added a soft bass murmur of expectation which cut under everything else.

Stations were great places to meet. You could lose yourself in the bustle and commotion while still maintaining good sight lines to check for possible tails. The apparently random movement of a busy commuter was surprisingly difficult to replicate, and unusual activity tended to stand out.

Anthea was already there, sitting in a corner table at Starbucks, two flat whites and an almond croissant in front of her. The croissant was pointing away from the doorway – a signal that there were no issues – and Nadia half lifted her hand in greeting before walking over and sitting down in the wicker armchair. Before even saying hello, she tore off a big chunk of the pastry and pushed it into her mouth. Part of a signalling protocol or not, it would have been a shame to waste it.

'That is so good,' she said, swallowing. 'I was famished.'

Anthea pushed the plate towards her. 'Not surprised,' she said. 'Those are long shifts. Take your time. We can catch up in a minute.' Nadia could feel Anthea watching her as she demolished the croissant and then proceeded to hoover up the final loose almond flakes. When she was sure there was nothing left, she picked up her coffee and leant back in the chair, subconsciously scanning the busy crowd for anything out of the ordinary.

'Don't worry,' said Anthea. 'That new techie guy – the hot one – is on the cameras. He's good.'

'Why?' said Nadia. This was a routine handler meeting as part of a routine assignment. There would normally be no need to have extra CCTV monitoring eating into already-stretched budgets. Something was going on.

'I'll explain in a minute,' said Anthea. 'Have you got something for me?'

Nadia took out the two neatly coiled computer leads and passed them under the table. 'What's with the last-minute panic?' she asked. 'I almost got tangled up with Liu Janlin.'

'Sorry. We only got the intel an hour ago. The Chinese have called for a full company-wide security sweep this morning. Orders coming in from Shenzhen.' Anthea took the leads and slid them into her bag. 'They probably wouldn't have spotted these, but the powers-that-be decided it wasn't worth the risk.'

Nadia nodded. It was the right call, even if it had put her on the spot.

'So. What's with the extra security today?' she said.

'Mr McAllister will be joining you,' whispered Anthea, leaning towards Nadia and covering her mouth with one hand. 'He'll be here in a few minutes.'

Nadia bit back the smile before it reached her lips. Anthea was clearly very excited to be part of any activity involving the big boss, even if it was just setting up a field meeting with Nadia. The poor girl was only a year into the job and, despite her two first-class honours degrees, she was probably still only working very basic admin and support jobs – a long way down the food chain from David McAllister who was, to all intents and purposes, the *powers-*

*that-be.*

Nadia tucked a loose hair behind her ear and straightened her blouse. She'd been working for MI5 for nine years already and had been promoted to senior intelligence officer three years earlier – the youngest woman ever. She wasn't going to get starry eyed at the thought of meeting David, but that didn't mean she took his good nature for granted. He hadn't risen to the top of one of the world's most respected security services just by being a nice guy.

Anthea checked her watch before standing and picking up her bag. 'I'm supposed to leave now,' she said. 'Mr McAllister will be joining you in a few minutes. Good luck.' And with that, she walked off.

Nadia checked her phone for messages and sipped her coffee. That explained the extra video surveillance, but the reasons why David wanted to meet her so urgently were about as clear as the milky-brown sludge in the bottom of her coffee cup. Why not simply call her into the office?

Still. She hadn't seen him for months and was looking forward to catching up. David had been a mentor for her right from the beginning and she'd come to see him as almost a surrogate father-figure. Maybe she was going to be reassigned early?

There was only one message on her phone – a WhatsApp from James, wanting to confirm they were still seeing each other for a drink later that afternoon. It would be their first meeting since he'd dumped her, and she wasn't holding out much hope for a reconciliation – the poor guy had plenty of justification, after all. Nadia had to accept that he had a point, even though it hadn't really been her fault, and she'd never been given the chance to explain herself properly. After months of trying, she was desperate to set the record straight.

She rubbed the tiny scar at the edge of her left eye. So small, yet so close to taking her sight or worse. Life was packed with those seemingly insignificant 'what-if' moments, any one of which could lead to such hugely different outcomes. She was halfway through a novel which played with the idea of infinite parallel universes – where every possible scenario, every fork in the road since the dawn of time has played out. She'd enjoyed the concept at the beginning, but was finding it more and more stressful to read. No-one could get their head around those infinite possibilities. People weren't made that way.

The easiest – and only – option was to accept the reality of the universe you were living in and do the best you could. There was no point in either believing in an 'everything will happen' multiverse, nor sinking into a dull and pointless fatalism whereby each action is pre-ordained and there is nothing anyone can do to change what happens. Nadia was also coming to the conclusion that it was best not to think too deeply about these things.

She'd been feeling increasingly ill-at-ease over the past few months. It wasn't only because of everything that had happened in the museum and all the loose ends – although those never stopped fluttering at the back of her mind. Her nagging worries were also linked to her upcoming big birthday and a growing sense that life was slipping through her fingers like grains of rice.

She yawned – the idea of bed was becoming very appealing – finished her coffee and drafted a short reply to James. As she hit the send arrow, she saw David moving through the crowd towards her, his approach surprisingly unobtrusive for a man of his size. If she hadn't been looking out for him, she wouldn't have spotted him until he was right in front of her.

David looked at the table as he approached. 'No croissant?' he asked.

'I thought I'd better eat the evidence,' said Nadia, smiling. 'Coffee?'

'I took the liberty of ordering us cappuccinos,' said David, looking over his shoulder. 'Looks like they're ready.' He put his leather folder on the chair and turned round. 'Back in a mo.'

How had he done that? Nadia had watched him walk out of the crowd. There was no way he could have slipped past her to order coffee and back out again without her seeing him, even though she'd been using her phone. She shook her head slowly. He was the director of A Division, almost sixty years old, and still felt the need to show off his fieldcraft tricks. Well, one thing was absolutely certain – there was no way she was going to indulge him in his silly schoolboy games.

'What's going on?' said Nadia as soon as David had sat down.

'Hang on,' he said. 'Let me have a sip of my coffee first. I'm not normally up at this hour.'

'… And you haven't just come off a ten-hour shift cleaning the Shan-ding building, have you?'

'Fair enough,' said David. 'Although a little more respect for your superiors might be in order.'

Nadia looked at him and raised her eyebrows. He'd broken his promise and she had no intention of letting him forget it.

'All right. All right. Point made.' David waved his hand as though that was enough to brush the issue away, before opening his folder and taking out an A4-sized photograph.

A city. Probably in America. Probably New York. A man was walking between two parked cars – slim, bearded, but he was wearing a baseball cap which made it difficult to see his face. Even so, Nadia felt a tremor of excitement run through her.

David took out another photo. It was the same location, the same man, but zoomed in and catching him just as he was looking up to check for oncoming cars. Nadia sucked in air and brought her hand up to cover her mouth.

'It's him, isn't it?' she said. 'It's Unicorn.'

David nodded.

The two of them sat in silence as Nadia stared at the close-up photo. Those piercing green eyes weren't visible, but there was no mistaking his face. Since the Natural History Museum bombing, he'd been in the top ten of the global most-wanted lists, but there hadn't been a single report or sighting of him. Unicorn had detonated the bomber's suicide vest remotely using a burner phone, taken an Uber to White City, walked calmly into the Westfield shopping centre and vanished from the face of the earth.

Nadia leant forward, adrenaline banishing all thoughts of bed and sleep.

'What are we going to do?' she said.

David looked at her. '*We're* not going to do anything. Six are on this and I'll be staying close to them. I need you where you are. The Chinese are our top priority for now.'

Nadia felt the rush of excitement evaporate as fast as it had arrived and sagged into her chair.

'So why bother to come here and tell me, then?' she said. 'I could have been in bed by now.'

'I thought you'd want to know,' he said. The noise and bustle of the booming hall seemed to fade away as David leant forward and lowered his voice. 'Look, Nadia. You've been in the field long enough to know how it works. You're one of our best, but you need to trust me and remember it's my job to decide what's a priority, not yours. Something big is happening, and it's tech-related. The Chinese government might not have been controlling Shan-ding at the beginning, but that's changed. The company lost more than half of its market value when our esteemed American cousins decided to hamstring their phones, which left them extremely vulnerable. It's become "us and them" and we have reliable intel that something is going to happen very soon. I know you have strong feelings about Unicorn, but your personal vendetta will have to wait. I need you right where you are.'

Nadia felt all her frustration and impatience bubbling up like boiling water. She fought to keep control – David was her boss, and she needed to stay professional. But she might as well have been Canute trying to push back the waves.

'Shit, David. It's not a vendetta,' she snapped, the angry words flying out as the pressure valve burst open. 'You know me better than that!' The vein in her right temple was pounding, and she noticed a handful of people turning towards them.

David didn't respond. The look on his face told her all she needed to know. He was worried about her – not only as a friend and mentor – but as a manager. He was probably thinking she might not be fully recovered, that she wasn't ready to be back on active service. Had he been testing her in some way by showing her the photo? Dangling the information in front of her then holding her back. The last thing Nadia needed was to be put back on sick leave.

'I'm sorry, David,' she said, once the silence between them had stretched to breaking point. 'That was out of order. I'm just tired … and, yes, I do still think about Unicorn, and it does make me angry, but it's not a vendetta and it's not an obsession. I'm fine. I'm really fine.'

David smiled and patted her on the shoulder as he stood up. 'I need to go,' he said. 'You go and get some sleep and I'll see you for the debrief meeting next week.' He picked up his leather folder. '… And don't worry. I'll keep you posted if I hear anything more about our friend.'

And then he was gone, melting back into the crowd. Nadia counted slowly to a hundred before standing up herself, feeling the aches in her hips and knees. That was ridiculous – she was only twenty-nine, but felt like an old woman. She pushed her way through the crowds as quickly as possible. Her drink with James was at five-thirty. A quick shower and six hours sleep would make all the difference.

As she squeezed into the crowded tube, Nadia realised she was still struggling to unclench her fists. Was David right? Was she obsessed with Unicorn? She did see those eyes glaring down at her every night in her dreams, but that was surely just a reminder of her failure. But the attack had also been a failure for him; the casualties had been limited and the subsequent publicity had, if anything, helped to defuse the anti-Muslim sentiment which had been growing for the previous decade.

Perversely, that didn't make her feel better – there had been casualties and consequences and Nadia could still picture the look on that young man's face, the moment when he came to his senses. He'd become Unicorn's puppet, he'd worn the suicide vest, but at the critical moment, he'd not been prepared to squeeze the trigger. She'd known all along he wouldn't go through with it. She'd got it right. It should have been a good day.

It would have been a good day if it hadn't been for Unicorn. Nadia had watched the CCTV footage a thousand times. The slim figure standing in the shadow of a small tree outside the museum, waiting for sixty seconds with eyes closed before shaking his head, taking out his mobile phone and dialling a number. Half a second later, the CCTV footage showed cars stopping and every other pedestrian flinching like startled rabbits before turning towards the clouds of dust already billowing out of the museum entrance.

Not Unicorn. He hadn't even turned to look. He'd simply walked away at a steady pace, dropping the mobile phone into a black bin on his way. There was something inhuman about that coldness and Nadia wanted him brought to justice more than anything she'd ever wanted.

New York. What was he doing in New York?

# 2

Ibrahim looked out over the blue-black sea. A wind was whipping white tops on the waves, but the afternoon heat was still oppressive and he found himself feeling grateful for the air conditioning. Was he getting soft? When all of this was over, he would take a trip alone to the desert for a few weeks, go back to basics and remember what was important. He wasn't an old man yet and the days of lying on soft cushions and eating dates were years ahead of him, whether in this world or the next.

On the street below a different kind of sea shouted up to him, swaying bodies waving flags and posters. An ocean of red and white, dotted with green cedars. The passion and love of country were very real – 'It's now or never', 'In unity there's strength' and 'You have stolen my dreams'. Every word screamed from the heart with the certainty of youth. The protesters were right, of course, but did they really believe the thieves in Lebanon's government had any intention of handing those dreams back? That wasn't how it worked.

He opened his laptop and started up the virtual private network application. It was no ordinary VPN; this piece of software could lay a false trail that no-one – not even the NSA – could distinguish from the real thing. His brother was an extremely talented programmer.

On the launch page there was a long list of IP addresses hacked from around the world. All he needed to do was to choose one as the dummy source and the software would then lay a trail across the internet – a trail which would end at the chosen place, but give the impression that he was trying to conceal it. All traces of his actual physical location were removed.

He selected an option which belonged to a router on the fifth floor of an apartment building on the corner of Barrow and Bedford Streets in Greenwich Village. The American spies already knew he had been in New York. Why not let them think he was still there? There were no lifts in the apartment. In fact, most of his decoy routers were on the upper floors of buildings without lifts. If they traced his call, it amused Ibrahim to imagine the overweight, lazy FBI operatives panting their way up those stairs. And then the surprise on the innocent occupants' faces when the door burst open …

He had invested a lot of time finding Frank. Unless Ibrahim could keep tabs on what Homeland Security knew about him, there was always a risk of a surprise … and Ibrahim didn't believe in surprises. That meant not hiding his identity from Frank, but as long as the weak fool didn't have any idea where Ibrahim actually was, it was a small price to pay … and one day, Frank would have another role to play.

Frank picked up the fresh burner phone on the third ring.

'Ibrahim,' he said. 'Right on time, as always.'

'What news, Frank?' said Ibrahim, wondering if Frank assumed subconsciously that people from the Middle East were incapable of punctuality.

'Not much,' said Frank. 'As you know, the people looking for you aren't in my department. I don't want to raise flags by asking too many questions.'

‘Find a way,’ said Ibrahim. ‘I need to know what they know.’

‘Don’t worry. I will,’ said Frank. ‘I’m seeing one of my guys in a couple of weeks. I should have more then … I told you they got an image of you in New York, didn’t I? I’m hoping for some follow-up on that. Where are you now, anyway?’

Ibrahim often felt an urge to slap Frank. An open-handed slap, as though he were a woman, but hard enough to split his lip and knock him to the floor. He was a necessary evil, but could test the patience of an angel. Although he suspected the man’s incessant babbling was only a sign of nerves, which would indicate that he wasn’t entirely stupid.

‘Yeah. OK. Whatever,’ Frank said, breaking the silence at last. ‘The British are calling you the Unicorn. Did you know that?’

‘Yes. I first heard that name six months ago,’ said Ibrahim, thinking back to the bombing at London’s Natural History Museum. ‘I am named after a mythical creature which exists only in the hidden places, never actually seen except in rumours and small girls’ fairy tales. It is a good name, don’t you think?’

‘I guess. People do talk as though you’re a myth, that’s for sure. Sometimes I doubt you’re real myself.’

Ibrahim hardened his voice. ‘… And you wish I wasn’t. I know that, Frank. But never doubt that I exist. I am very real and, if you need any confirmation of that, it can be arranged.’

‘No. No. That’s not what I meant.’ Frank moved so quickly between cowboy bluster and effeminate grovelling, it was sickening. ‘I get it and I’ll do what you ask, but when this is over, we’re done, right? You gave me your word.’

Ibrahim smiled. ‘… And I am a man of honour,’ he said. ‘When this is over, I will not ask any more of you.’ Was Frank stupid enough to believe he would ever be free? Either he would continue to be of use, or he would have an accident. Ibrahim was a man of honour, but there was no issue of honour where people like Frank were concerned.

He looked at his watch. Even with the VPN, he didn't want the call to be traced. There was a chance they might triangulate Frank's location. 'Tell me more about the photograph,' he said.

'I only saw it for a second,' said Frank. 'You're crossing a road in Brooklyn. You turn your head to the CCTV for just a second, but it's enough. They have a confirmed match.'

'And what will they do now?'

'They have your clothing and a starting point. They'll use other cameras to track you back to where you came from and follow you to where you ended up.'

'I wish them luck. They will find no traces at the apartment I stayed in … and as for where I went … I think they will find that the Unicorn is truly a magical beast with the ability to appear or disappear at will.'

'You've been doing this for a long while and we haven't got close yet.'

'Indeed,' said Ibrahim, looking at his watch again. 'We must end for today. We will speak in four weeks at the usual time. Buy a new burner phone and post the number in the usual place.'

'OK,' said Frank. 'Just one more thing though …'

The voice disappeared as Ibrahim hung up. Enough was enough.

The October sun beat down on his bare head as he walked along the road which, if he was honest, was as much pothole as road. A kilometre from the sea it was as if the city centre protest marches didn't exist. Two rough street dogs stopped scrabbling through a pile of plastic rubbish bags and stared at him, teeth bared and eyes hungry. It was as though they were sizing him up, deciding whether he was a viable alternative to the uninspiring rubbish. Ibrahim glared back and, after a few seconds, the larger of the two dogs gave a small whimper and they turned their attention back to the pile of sacks.

He stopped walking and sniffed the air. A slow, deep inhalation, like a bloodhound. Behind the bitter tang of tarmac and cement dust, he could still pick out the rich greenness of orange trees as he turned the corner and started to walk up the hill. The familiar smell was faint though – the bass note of a once-rich perfume – and it wasn't enough; each time he came home, the town seemed smaller and dirtier; the reality of Sidon had become a poor shadow of his memories.

The people were more or less the same, but the laughter and teasing appeared a little too bright, a little too forced. Firm embraces and loud voices were matched by furtive looks and were no more than masks for fear and resignation. Ibrahim had seen these changes before in other places; he knew the signs.

Omar should move away from here before the past was lost forever, but he was stubborn and no-one, not even Baba, had ever been able to push him into anything. He would see sense this time – especially now they were so close to the end.

At the top of the hill, the clean black metal gates and freshly painted white wall stood in sharp contrast to every other building on the streets, as did the two security guards, sharply dressed in black uniforms and fully alert. The beautiful modern villa at the end of the long drive was clearly not somewhere to visit unless a welcome was expected.

The taller of the two guards watched as Ibrahim approached,

fingers never far from the Uzi sub-machine gun at his waist. He signalled to his colleague to watch the street, before pushing open the side gate and stepping out, smiling and lifting his arms in welcome.

'*Masa al kheir, Haji*,' he said, as Ibrahim approached.

The two men had been childhood friends and, a few years after the Israeli invasion of 1982, they had both taken their anger and left the Lebanon together, joining the Afghan Mujahideen to fight the Russians. At that time, neither of them had cared who they fought – they simply wanted to fight. Mohammed had lost all of his family, Ibrahim all of his apart from one. Ibrahim had been sixteen, Mohammed a year younger.

'*Masa al noor, Habibi*,' said Ibrahim, leaning forward to kiss his friend three times on alternate cheeks. 'It's been too long, Mohammed.'

The two boys had left home as friends and equals, but, as they embraced in the Sidon sun forty years later, the relationship was anything but equal. They both understood that reality deep in their bones. Mohammed was still the foot soldier he'd been from the start, while Ibrahim had risen through the ranks without pause. Mohammed no longer understood what Ibrahim actually did, but knew enough to respect the man he had become.

'Much too long,' said Mohammed. 'Every time you come, I am somewhere else, but now I have seen you at last, *hamdullah*.'

'*Al hamdulillah*,' said Ibrahim, draping an arm loosely over Mohammed's shoulder as they walked towards the villa. 'Tell me. How is my brother?'

'Omar is well enough,' said Mohammed, 'but I worry for him. He spends his days sitting in front of his computers or playing those children's video games. I try to talk with him, but he isn't interested.

He is lonely and still so angry.'

'Can you blame him?' snapped Ibrahim, bristling in defence of his younger brother, although he knew his friend meant well. 'And what would you have him do?'

'I don't know,' said Mohammed, avoiding Ibrahim's eyes. 'I don't know.'

# 3

After working night shifts for months, Nadia's body clock had become comfortable with the upside-down rhythm of her days. She woke peacefully at four o'clock, twenty minutes before her alarm was due to go off. Gossamer threads of a half-remembered dream fluttered just out of reach, each tantalising strand brushing her fingertips and giving her a warm feeling in the pit of her stomach. It must have been a very good dream indeed, and she lay on her back smiling as she tried to put a face on the shadowy figure who knew exactly where she wanted to be touched – when, where and how.

She drifted back into a half sleep and saw his face at last, cheeky-boy grin and tousled sandy-blond hair hanging over her. He leant down to kiss her, and she actually imagined her toes curling …

Nadia snapped awake and sat up, hands clasped in front of her eyes. That wasn't right. Her dream man was Ed Bailey, the MI6 analyst who'd been studying Unicorn for years. Why was she suddenly having soft porn fantasy dreams about Ed? They'd only worked together for an hour and he'd visited her in hospital twice. That was it. He'd not been in touch since and had probably gone back to Karachi … or moved quietly back to his analyst's desk at GCHQ.

She smiled as she remembered Ed's reactions when they'd set off on their mad chase around London. He might know all there was to know about Unicorn, but he'd been scared witless in the car and then when he'd seen her checking her pistol …

He definitely wasn't cut out for the field, but most people weren't and he'd turned out to be brave enough when it came to it. She smiled again. There was something about Ed … hidden inner depths … which intrigued her. But so what? The last thing she needed before seeing James was any sort of romantic confusion. Their situation was messy enough as it was.

She ran the shower colder than usual; it had always been her way of exorcising bad dreams and demons, ever since she was a girl. Cold enough to cause an involuntary intake of breath and to bring out goosebumps on her shoulders and breasts, cold enough to focus her mind on what lay ahead, rather than what might have been.

She smiled to herself as the icy water worked its magic. It hadn't been such a bad dream …

Nadia double-locked the black door behind her and reached up to brush a tiny thread across the gap between door and jamb. Even though her flat was packed with technology and any unwelcome visitors would trigger alerts both on her phone and the office, she'd been trained in the old ways.

In any case, technology wasn't always as reliable as it was cracked up to be. The guys back in the office claimed they could block or loop every surveillance or alarm system in existence – they bragged that they could go in and out of any room without leaving a trace. They called themselves 'The Ninjas', but most people just thought they were cocky techies.

She would have needed a healthy dose of blindness and arrogance to assume that other agencies, or even terrorist organisations, weren't able to access their own ninja skills and Nadia was neither blind, nor arrogant. She shivered as she remembered how close she'd been to actually being blinded – or rather half-blinded – just a few months earlier. Life was so fragile.

It never hurt to have real world back-ups and Nadia's job still relied mostly on human skills – maintaining a constant, almost sub-conscious state of alert, observing and recording your surroundings at all times, noticing anything which was out of place and, most of all, never appearing out of place yourself. It could be exhausting, but eventually became second nature. After the first few years, those habits became as natural as picking up a glass of wine or putting one foot in front of the other.

As she strode down Childebert Road towards Tooting Bec, she could feel a tightness in her calves from the previous day's run. She'd matched her personal 10K record even though her body had been running on empty for the final kilometre. Ever since the bombing, she'd been even more driven than usual – pushing herself to her limits and beyond. Part of the motivation was completely understandable – she was very aware that things might have turned out differently – but there was something else, that nagging sense of unfinished business which wouldn't leave her alone.

Much as she hated to admit he was right – David could be so frustrating at times – of course she was still thinking about Unicorn. That was normal enough, wasn't it? Objectively, she probably couldn't have done anything to stop the bomb going off, but the whole disaster still felt like a personal failure and, as for those long black hours when she was waiting to learn if she would recover her eyesight ...

The tube station was crowded, but there was nothing out of the ordinary and Nadia felt strangely alone as the escalator drew her smoothly into the underworld. There were so many aspects of her job which she would have loved to be able to share with a partner, but would never be able to. And how could an outsider appreciate the unique stresses and strains she was expected to manage? The contrast between the hours and days of mindless tedium involved in undercover work and the explosive, adrenaline-fuelled activity which could come at any time. It wasn't surprising that field officers went a little crazy now and then.

Working as a cleaner at the Birmingham Mosque had actually been even more boring than her current assignment at Shan-ding. She'd been investigating Snowflake, or rather Hassan Qureishi, for months and, while the few dribs and drabs of relevant intel had painted a picture of an unfortunate and impressionable young man, there had been nothing to indicate that he was involved in anything significant or sinister. Just like her current assignment at Shan-ding, the whole thing had felt like a complete waste of time.

Her only respite had been every other weekend when she'd been given two days off and could escape back to London to her real life. Even then she hadn't been able to see her partner, James, who'd been told she was in Melbourne on a six-month secondment.

Until suddenly it transpired she hadn't been wasting her time; Snowflake disappeared, and two independent sources confirmed online chatter that he was about to launch a suicide bomb attack somewhere in London.

Nadia hadn't been able to imagine him being capable of such a thing, but the intel had been red hot and she'd been pulled back to London and embroiled in a nerve-shattering race against time to stop the attack. Arriving at the Natural History Museum just minutes too late to intervene, she'd watched the young man stop under the huge dinosaur head and reach into his jacket pocket.

Why was she always too slow? She could still remember holding her breath while time ground to a halt, before Snowflake's shoulders had suddenly slumped forward, and he'd dropped to his knees, both hands on the floor, surrendering to the museum guard who was walking towards him, talking calmly and slowly as he approached. The foolish young man's better angels had prevailed and Nadia could still remember her feelings of elation and vindication – she'd been right about him after all.

… And then the bomb had exploded anyway. From what she'd been told, the guard and another old man had miraculously absorbed most of the shrapnel, but not all. Nadia's own memories were still a confused jumble. For her, there had been a blinding light, a shock wave and she'd woken up in hospital with bandages wrapped tightly around her eyes.

But she'd survived, unlike Snowflake and those two brave men. And Unicorn had been one step ahead as he always seemed to be.

David was right, it was personal. She wanted to stop him and something inside her knew she was the right person to bring him down.

Maybe David was also right about Shan-ding being important, but she couldn't see why it was such an urgent priority. Unicorn was up to something big or he wouldn't have risked going to New York. That was where the real danger lay. Immediate risk, unlike all the political bullshit about China's influence over 5G systems. As far as she could see that was mostly part of the trade posturing coming out of the US, and the UK was just tagging along like an obedient poodle as always.

David had probably been right about her going to see a shrink after the injury, though. Nadia hated the idea of that sort of thing and had dug her heels in, but she had to admit she still wasn't quite back to normal; the images and memories of that day were elbowing their way into her thoughts too often and with too much clarity. And there was no real sense that things were improving. She wasn't used to uncertainty and as for feeling afraid …

Maybe confirmation that her eye was fully healed would help draw a line under that mess and allow her to move on.

The tube pulled into Old Street station. She would normally always take the stairs, but allowed herself the luxury of standing on the escalator. If all went to plan, her appointment at Moorfields Eye Hospital would be short and she would never need to go back. If all went to plan.

'Good morning, Nadia,' said the tall man in the white coat, his straight back and rich plummy voice leaving no doubt of his position in society. 'Please take a seat.'

Nadia was almost certain the scan would show a full recovery. She felt fine. She was as fit as she'd ever been. The headaches were gone. Everything would be fine … except … except … She couldn't get rid of those nagging doubts at the back of her mind; there was something about the hospital environment, the faceless corridors, the quiet smiles of the nurses and the total unquestioned authority of the white coat. Doctors were the final guardians of the truth and there was always the possibility that the truth could be bad.

'Good morning, Mr Wilson,' she replied, feeling the cold hard plastic of the chair press into her back as she sat. She wasn't going to make the mistake of calling him Dr Wilson again – not after the look he'd given her the last time. 'One never refers to a surgeon as "Doctor", my dear,' he'd explained with a condescending smile. 'A simple "Mister" will do just nicely, thank you very much.'

Once Nadia was settled, he opened a scuffed brown folder and pushed his glasses to the end of his nose, each action slow and methodical. That was the other thing about hospitals and doctors, especially surgeons – they seemed to love playing for dramatic effect, revelling in that moment of power. He ran his finger down the page, lips moving silently, before closing the folder and laying it on the table.

'This all looks fine, Miss Laroche,' he said. 'As you know, even after the operation, we couldn't be one hundred per cent sure the optic nerve hadn't been damaged … but if that had been the case, we would have seen cell dieback by now and there is no indication of that. The bone has healed nicely as we would have expected and the scan confirms we didn't miss any of the stone fragments. I'm assuming the headaches have stopped?'

Nadia nodded.

'Then I don't think we'll need to see you again.' He leant back in his chair. 'You're a very lucky woman, you know? When you were admitted and I saw the first scan, I thought it was highly unlikely we'd be able to save the sight in your right eye. A fraction of a millimetre to one side or the other …' He stood up, smiled and reached out his hand. 'God seems to have been smiling on you that day.'

Nadia shook his hand, thanked him and made her escape, hardly breathing until she was out in the fresh air. She'd been irritated by his talk of God's grace but, as she stepped out into the weak sunlight, she felt a huge weight lifting from her shoulders and was almost tempted to look for somewhere to thank God for her lucky escape. But which God? Was one any better than the other? The absurdity of that dilemma soon brought her normal agnostic cynicism flooding back. Much better to offer quiet thanks to both her parents for not trying to impose their faiths on her.

Nadia looked at her watch. There was no time for theological rumination – she was meeting James in fifteen minutes and had no intention of keeping him waiting.

James walked into the wine bar right on time, looking from side to side and then half lifting a hand as he saw Nadia tucked away in the furthest corner from the door. He looked tired. After two years together, Nadia knew him as well as she knew anyone; he'd never been a good sleeper when he was stressed. Maybe that meant there was a chance? If there wasn't even a tiny chink of light coming through the door, he wouldn't have been stressed … and he probably wouldn't have shown up at all.

He looked at the bottle of wine and two glasses on the table and sat down opposite her.

'Hi Hana,' he said. 'You look well.'

Nadia loved her job, but hearing that name was a shocking reminder of the price of undercover work. She'd been three other people since Hana Khoury, all of them quite different. Had it been Hana who'd loved James or had it been Nadia? She wasn't quite sure she could remember … And who had James fallen in love with?

She poured him a glass. Seeing James again was always going to be difficult, but the first five minutes together were harder than she could have imagined. It was impossible to imagine that either of them had ever liked each other, let alone been in love. She could feel an almost-physical barrier between them, pushing back against her and making the conversation painfully distant and formal. She tried, but could barely see past the wall and anyway there was no hint of warmth or affection on his waxwork face.

'So. You wanted to meet?' he said, once the mindless conversation had reached a point of banality that was making her teeth hurt. 'Why?'

'I wasn't prepared to leave it like that,' said Nadia. 'I thought we had something together … and you clearly did too.'

'Well. I guess I probably wouldn't have flown half way around the world to ask you to be my wife if I didn't,' he said, every word oozing bitterness and sarcasm.

'Do you remember when we went skating?' she said, determined to ignore the venom in his voice and to keep trying.

He nodded, lips pressing even more tightly together.

'You were rubbish,' she said. 'You fell over after ten seconds and then sat on the ice giggling while I skated around you. We gave up and went for cocktails at Harvey Nick's?'

James nodded again.

'And afterwards, we went back to yours,' said Nadia. 'That was when I knew I wanted to be with you. I still remember that feeling and I don't think it's right to throw it away because of something that had nothing to with us. Nothing directly to do with you and me.'

James was gripping the edge of the table, knuckles white with the effort.

'Nothing to do with us? Really? Tell that to the sad idiot standing outside an abandoned office in Melbourne waiting to propose to someone who wasn't even in Australia.' He breathed in and out through clenched teeth. 'Of course I remember the skating and of course I can remember how much I loved you, but now you're saying that the fact that you lied about absolutely everything, the fact that the person I fell in love with doesn't even actually exist … You're saying that's got nothing to do with us? I can't believe you've got the nerve.' He shifted in his chair as though about to stand up. 'I knew this was a mistake.'

Nadia reached across the table and put her hand on top of his. 'Wait,' she said. 'Let me finish. There are things – work things – which force me to keep certain facts confidential. I need approval from my boss before I can discuss them with anyone outside the office. When we first met I was working undercover as Hana Koury … and after that, I was stuck. I had no choice.'

'For two years?' said James. 'Surely there was time to speak to your boss in two bloody years?'

'I did. I applied for approval the day after we went skating – I finally got it around the time you decided to surprise me in Melbourne,' said Nadia. 'If you hadn't decided to make the big romantic gesture I would have told you the next time I saw you.' She looked across the table, willing him to see how sorry she was and how much she cared. 'But it was too late.'

She thought there might be something changing in his eyes. A softening? And then he jerked upright, eyes shining. 'Wait a minute,' he said, laughing nervously. 'Working undercover? Who do you work for then? Are you some sort of spy?'

Nadia said nothing, but raised one eyebrow.

'I don't believe it,' It was as though James had suddenly forgotten he was supposed to be coming across as hard and emotionless. 'That's what it is. Of course … I thought you must be a psychopath or a fraudster or just plain nasty … It's not as though you look like a spy, is it?'

'… And what exactly do spies look like?'

'Oh my God,' said James, staring intently into his wine glass, his brow furrowed in apparent concentration. 'You are, aren't you? … So are you planning on telling me the truth now?'

'Maybe,' said Nadia, '… but it depends.'

'On what?'

'On whether the two of us have a chance. I've got permission to tell you the truth, but it's probably better for you to stay blissfully ignorant if we don't have a future together. What you don't know … well, what you don't know, you don't know.'

'Ta-da. Talk about stating the obvious.' James looked at her, the waxwork pallor gone from his cheeks. He almost looked like himself again. 'I don't know, Hana – or whatever your name actually is. I've had a miserable few months, and I thought I was coming out the other side …' He sat staring into the distance for what seemed like minutes and Nadia glanced up at the big clock. She would need to leave for work in less than ten minutes and James had an amazing ability to drag things out.

'… James,' she jumped in. 'I've got an idea. I know you've been through a lot and, even if I didn't have a choice, I get that it's all my fault. Let's not rush into a snap decision. I finish nights next week. Why don't I take you out for dinner? We could go to the Riverside?'

He looked up at her, clearly annoyed she'd interrupted his train of thought. But she could see the cracks in his resolve showing.

'Give it a try,' she said, sensing the chance to press home her advantage. 'We'll have a fun evening, talk things over, and take it from there.'

Another long pause. She'd always loved watching James when he was lost in his thoughts. For a short while, he seemed totally unaware of his surroundings and then his head flicked up and he looked her in the eyes for the first time.

'OK. Let's do that,' he said, nodding and smiling. 'It sounds nice.'

Nadia got up and picked up her coat from the bench beside her.

'I'll book it and let you know,' she said, giving James a chaste kiss on the cheek before leaning further forward.

‘My name’s Nadia, by the way,’ she whispered.

James pulled his head back and stared at her, wide-eyed as a six-year-old boy who’d just been handed his Saturday sweets. Nadia made a quick exit, restraining the urge to skip, fist pump and squawk with delight all at the same time.

# 4

'Hi Nadia,' said David. 'Come in.' He got up from behind his desk and beckoned to the low glass table in the corner, which was surrounded by three black leather and chrome chairs.

They both sat down and David reached forward to squeeze Nadia's shoulder gently.

'It was good to see you the other day,' he said. 'I forgot to say how sorry I am not to have made time for you over the past few months. It's not that I'm pissed off with you for disobeying a direct order back then – although I am, of course.' He smiled. 'But that's old history, and the truth is that there's just so much going on and, what with you working night shifts …'

'… Yes, about that,' said Nadia. 'You promised.'

'I know,' said David. 'But circumstances can be a bitch sometimes and I needed you at Shan-ding.'

'Really,' said Nadia. 'From where I'm standing, it seems like there's something wrong with our priorities … especially now Unicorn has resurfaced.'

'That's one of the reasons I wanted to meet,' said David. 'I want to give you an update on our strategy for Shan-ding. I know you're up to speed on the basics, but Phil will be joining us in a few minutes to add some more context.'

Nadia rolled her eyes. Phil Castle was MI5's Senior Operations Director and a total creep. She couldn't forget the way he'd pushed her into a corner at a Christmas party five years earlier. Thinking about the smell of beer and whisky on his breath and the raw lust in his eyes still made her shiver. He wouldn't make the same mistake again, but for Nadia his card was permanently marked.

David laughed at Nadia's expression. 'Come on, Nadia. I know you think he's a jerk and I suspect you have your reasons, but Phil's my right hand guy and decent at heart. He's rock solid on strategy and the team would be a lot weaker without him. Just keep it professional and listen to what he has to say.'

Nadia thought about pointing out that Phil was the one who struggled with 'keeping it professional', but thought better of it. Although David was a good man, he would never understand how it felt to be on the wrong end of that kind of treatment.

'What was the other reason you wanted to meet?' she said.

'It's about Unicorn,' said David.

Nadia braced herself for a dressing down about her outburst at Waterloo Station. She hated appearing weak and uncontrolled in front of David. He could always see right through her.

'I understand why you reacted like you did,' he said. '… And I will keep you updated on future intel, but you are going to have to find a way to keep a lid on your emotions. Take a step back from it. It can't become personal. OK?'

Nadia breathed a sigh of relief. She hadn't blown it, after all.

'Of course, David. Fully understood. That was a one off and won't happen again. I doubt you'll change my mind about the level of threat he represents, but I'll keep it together from now on.'

'Good,' he said. 'Now let's get Phil in. If he's quick, you and I will have time for a quick coffee afterwards.'

As Phil walked into the office, Nadia was reminded of why everyone in the office called him Voldemort. He was a natural slimeball, even if he was good at his job.

'Hi Nadia,' he said. 'Nice to see you. You must be getting pretty good at cleaning offices by now.' He sniggered as he sat down opposite them and Nadia took a deep breath to compose herself. The thing was that Phil's attempts at camaraderie and office banter always missed the mark and came across as just bitchy and nasty. Maybe that wasn't his intention, but …

'Go and take a look at the third floor of the Shan-ding building,' she said. 'The cleanest windows in the City.'

'I'll make sure to do that,' he said, before leaning forward in his chair. 'Now. David wants me to update you on why we're still seeing Shan-ding as such a high priority.'

'And about time,' said Nadia. 'I understand it's important. I get the general issues and agree that many, if not all, future threats are sitting in the digital world. But I don't feel the balance has tipped away from the physical yet – bombs, knifings, shootings, they're still happening all the time … and, in the meantime, Unicorn is still out there, probably plotting the next 9-11.'

'No-one would disagree with that assessment,' said David. 'And that's probably a more clear and present danger than most of the digital risks.'

'Then wouldn't looking for Unicorn be a better use of my skills and background?' said Nadia. 'Let GCHQ keep tabs on Shan-ding and the other digital threats.'

'I said "probably",' said David. 'Let Phil explain what keeps us awake at nights.'

'OK. Sorry,' said Nadia. 'Go ahead, Phil.'

'Let me paint you a picture, Nadia,' said Phil. 'Imagine a world under the grip of a pandemic. It might be as a result of some sort of bio-warfare, but could just as well be a natural virus. We've had enough warnings since the first SARS virus, but no-one is really ready.'

'You're talking about another Spanish Flu?'

'Or worse,' he said. 'Anyway. Imagine that world. Stock markets crashing, borders closed, everyone forced to stay home.'

'One of life's great optimists, aren't you, Phil?'

Phil didn't respond, but the look he gave her was pure poison. 'In most scenarios,' he carried on. 'The system just about manages to hold things together until they find a vaccine. Hospitals barely cope, thousands die and there is some civil unrest. But a lot of people will be able to work from home and our social fabric would remain largely intact through virtual contact. We have a lot of advantages in today's world.'

'Yes. I remember your scenarios well enough,' said Nadia. 'It was only two years ago that you ran those pandemic war-games. You had me playing the role of the Home Secretary, organising mass burials and implementing martial law.'

Nadia remembered how shocked she'd been as the details of Phil's virtual pandemic had evolved. He was a sadistic arsehole, but she hadn't been able to pick holes in his maths nor in his assessment of human behaviour. The first few weeks had been fine – the media had a field day, invoking the spirit of the Blitz and, apart from a few idiots, most people had embraced the lockdown with good humour and patience. She would almost certainly be out in the field, but it hadn't been hard to picture someone just like herself alone in their flat, working on their laptop, watching Breaking Bad and Game of Thrones box sets and occasionally sharing a glass of wine with friends over video links.

In most of the scenarios, British society had emerged bruised and battered, but still in one piece. However, in the most extreme scenario, Phil's imaginary virus was persistent and the medical advisors refused to countenance an easing of restrictions. After ten months, behavioural analysts predicted the first signs of a breakdown of society and after a year, looting and rioting became widespread and the army took control of the streets.

'Good. So you weren't asleep like most of your colleagues,' said Phil. Nadia wondered, not for the first time, what it would feel like to slap that smug face. '… And you'll remember that, according to the behavioural scientists, most people would cope with the social isolation and many businesses would continue to function with remote workers.'

'… Because we've crossed a critical technological threshold.'

'Exactly. People can now replace physical interaction with virtual interaction … entertainment, social interaction, exercise classes, even school lessons. It allows a significant proportion of society to function – at least for a while – even when people can't leave their homes.'

Nadia looked at him, willing him to get to the point. To tell her something she didn't already know.

'Well, there's an additional scenario which we didn't present before. And it's a game changer,' said Phil, placing both hands, palm down on the table in front of him. Nadia counted five long seconds of dramatic pause before he continued.

'Imagine that, in the midst of a global pandemic like that, all mobile networks and all telecommunications go down. Bang. Everything stops working overnight. Isolation becomes something quite different and the social contract is ripped to shreds. We've got contingency systems for vital networks, Government, the NHS and the Armed Forces. But nothing for normal people. It's just not feasible.'

He paused again. 'A breakdown in digital communication would be difficult enough to manage at the best of times – even if we had normal face-to-face contact to fall back on. Combined with lockdown scenario, however …? None of our models look good if that were to happen. Someone with the ability to break our technology would hold all the cards, wouldn't they?'

Nadia sat grim-faced, the possible consequences of that combined one-two punch leaving her in stunned silence.

David turned to her. 'As you know, Shan-ding have an estimated forty per cent market share of mobile and internet network switching technology as well as twenty per cent of the smartphones in circulation. That theoretically exceeds the critical mass needed to force the entire system to crash and stay crashed. As you also know, we have good reason to suspect the company might be susceptible to Chinese government influence. Now do you understand why I need to keep my best officer focused on staying ahead of this?'

Nadia struggled to argue with the reasoning. Even though they were only discussing theoretical 'what ifs', the implications dwarfed any potential terrorist threat and there were plenty of warning signs that a pandemic could hit at any time. Phil took advantage of the silence to make his exit.

'I've got a call with MI6 and Homeland Security in five,' he said to David, before turning to Nadia. 'I hope that's clearer for you now, Nadia?'

She nodded and lifted a hand to acknowledge Phil's departure, still imagining the consequences of his words. All those people, living more or less happy lives and blissfully unaware of the potential tragedies which might be lurking in wait for them.

'These concerns sit at the top of the briefing notes for every COBRA meeting,' David continued. 'Learning more about Unicorn's next steps is also critical and I know our dear colleagues at MI6 are doing whatever is possible to track him down.' He looked up at Nadia. 'In the meantime, please don't imagine what you're doing at Shan-ding is any less important.'

'Shit,' said Nadia eventually. 'It just gets worse and worse, doesn't it? At least in the Cold War, there were rules.'

David smiled. 'Be careful what you wish for,' he said. 'Reminiscence is never what it's cracked up to be … Anyway, Armageddon aside, what else is going on with my best girl?'

'Leaving aside the joys of breathing in fumes from industrial cleaning fluids and working nights, I saw my ex-boyfriend for a drink yesterday.'

David raised his eyebrows.

'James,' said Nadia. 'The one who decided to pay me a surprise visit in Australia only to discover a fake office and a flat with someone else in residence. You remember my cover story for the Birmingham Mosque assignment was a six month transfer to Melbourne? I wrote you a breach report about the whole fiasco.'

'Ah. That one.' said David. 'Didn't he go out there to propose to you?'

'Yes,' said Nadia. 'It was all a bit of a train smash, really. He was understandably pissed off and decided I was some sort of mad, lying psycho bitch. I've been in touch a few times since, but he's refused to talk to me or listen to my explanations. Yesterday was a last-ditch attempt and I seem to have worn him down. He's agreed to have dinner on Sunday week.'

'We do our best to prepare you for these …'

'I know,' said Nadia. 'And I know it's tough to find a balance … But I think James is worth it. You already agreed I could let him know what I do and share my real identity.'

'I remember, but things have changed since then. Are you still sure about him? Can he be trusted?'

'I don't know. How can I be sure?' said Nadia, suddenly picturing James's cold angry face in the bar. Had he really needed to dump her so brutally with no opportunity to explain herself? She shifted in her seat as she felt David's gaze burning into her and forcing her to address concerns she'd rather have left buried.

She looked down at the table and took a few deep breaths. 'I do appreciate you worrying about me,' she said, smiling at David. 'But I'll see him for dinner and take it from there. He was obviously badly hurt and what we had may have been burned for ever, but I need to find that out for certain. One way or another I'll know before we get to the main course … and I won't tell him my full name or anything confidential if it's not worthwhile, or if I feel it might not be secure. He's been through all of the screenings and I know the drill.'

'As long as you've thought it through and understand the risks,' said David, standing up. Nadia followed suit and he stepped forward and wrapped her in his signature bear hug. 'Good luck,' he whispered in her ear. 'No-one can be good enough for you, but I hope he comes close.'

'Thanks David,' Nadia said as she broke free and turned to leave. 'It was good to see you.'

David looked her in the eye. 'One more thing,' he said. 'Make sure to tell him he'll have to answer to me if he hurts you in any way.'

# 5

Monday came too soon and Nadia groaned as she opened her locker and changed into her work clothes. Another week of night shifts was looming in front of her which filled her with dread. Monday was always the worst as she couldn't seem to get to sleep in the daytime, however much she knew she needed to dig deep, find her inner dormouse and store up energy.

She'd found it even more difficult to sleep after the meeting with David and Phil. The briefing had left her more comfortable with David's need to prioritise Shan-ding, but that didn't mean she actually agreed with him. Nadia still wasn't convinced that the information she was gathering would make any difference. Shan-ding was an obvious target, but if someone wanted to disrupt telecoms, they could always infiltrate or hack into one of the big Western firms. That's how she would do it, and those sorts of breaches were happening on a small scale every day. The whole Chinese government link still seemed a bit simplistic and she couldn't help feeling that European governments were just kowtowing to US global trade policies.

And, as always, probability needed to be factored into the equation. Phil had made the potential disaster sound very real but, if the odds of it happening were one in a hundred thousand and a major attack by Unicorn was running at fifty-fifty, the security services were still focusing their energies in the wrong place.

David and Phil were older and more experienced than she was, but that didn't make them right. Their seniority also trapped them in the wheel ruts of old habits and they were probably under continuous pressure from politicians who had no real idea about what went on behind the scenes. Still, David was her boss and she would do what she was assigned to do … at least until she found a better opportunity to change his mind.

The Monday night shift muddled along uneventfully until just after three-thirty. That was always the point in the night when she felt her eyelids sagging and the desire to curl up on the thin carpeting became almost overwhelming – just like the dormouse she'd failed to imitate earlier. She shook her head, feeling her pony tail slap against her cheeks and sucked deeply from her water bottle. Only three more hours.

Despite her frustrations about the Shan-ding assignment, Nadia was feeling much more positive. She couldn't stop herself from thinking about Unicorn, but at least David's briefing had made it clear she hadn't been shunted into some career-killing cul-de-sac. The USB data leads were safely out of harm's way and her supervisor, Donna, hadn't seemed put out by the previous week's brush off. Last, but not least, she was still flying high after the double whammy of her positive meetup with James and the all-clear from the eye surgeon.

All in all, her life was beginning to shape up again. She knew she'd made an error of judgement at the Natural History Museum and it was only blind luck that more people hadn't been killed and injured. Nadia wasn't used to doubting herself and had struggled to come to terms with it, but enough was enough. It was time to move on.

If she could only get out of this bloody cleaning job … and find a way to exorcise Unicorn from her dreams. How could she persuade David to reassign her, to let her help find him? Someone else could easily take over the Shan-ding assignment.

She'd almost finished hoovering the ground floor meeting rooms when she heard a door swing closed behind her. Nadia hadn't heard anyone approaching and jumped as though stung by a wasp, her muscles tensed and ready for action. Meanwhile, her brain fought desperately to override her reflexes – a struggling mother-of-two would react differently and she needed to stay in character.

There was no-one there, but, as she peered through the glass partitioning, she spotted a figure walking towards the lifts. The frosted glass blurred his features, but she could see he was carrying a large briefcase and wearing a suit. What was an executive doing wandering around the offices at four in the morning?

Nadia picked up her bucket – a useful prop – and inched closer. Then, as soon as the lift doors closed on the figure, she ran forward. The lift was going down to the basement which was even more unexpected. There was nothing on that floor except for the post room and some storage offices – and a cleaning supplies cupboard which could give her an excuse to be there.

She took the stairs and made her way down, easing the exit door open a crack and listening carefully. She poked her head out carefully – just in time to see the man disappear through the double swing doors which led into the post room. None of this made sense and Nadia felt the hairs prickling at the back of her neck as she moved slowly down the corridor. Something was clearly wrong and her well-known intuition was screaming that it might be important. And dangerous! She suddenly felt naked without her gun, and a plastic bucket wouldn't be much use.

The gap between the post room doors was just wide enough for her to see the man taking handfuls of small cellophane-wrapped packets out of his briefcase and packing carefully them into a large cardboard box. After taping the box closed, he pulled a printed label from his pocket and stuck it carefully to the top. He then picked up the box before suddenly dropping it and spinning around as though startled by a noise. Nadia struggled to suppress a gasp – it was Liu Janlin, the 5G vice president who'd almost caught her coming out of the lift. He was senior management and she was surprised he even knew where the post room was.

He stood silently, body tensed as he scanned his surroundings, before eventually picking up the box and walking towards the corner of the room, out of her sight-lines. Nadia guessed he was adding his secret package to the palette of ready-to-ship items. What could he need to send in such a clandestine way? As soon as he'd left, she had to get in there to take a look at that box.

Suddenly, with no warning, he stepped into her line of sight, just two metres from the door. Nadia turned and started walking slowly towards the cleaning cupboard, controlling her breathing and hunching her shoulders. She would be fine. After all, he was the one who was out of place at four in the morning. She was supposed to be there.

She heard the doors swing closed behind her and then nothing until there was a gentle tap on her shoulder. She leapt in surprise and yelped like a frightened puppy before turning around.

'Where d'you bloody spring from?' she shouted. 'You nearly gave me a bloody heart attack.'

Liu Janlin smiled and opened his hands in apology.

'I'm so sorry,' he said. 'I didn't mean to startle you.' Then his eyes narrowed and Nadia felt their focus drifting down her body. 'Ah. It's you,' he continued, once his appraisal was complete. 'I saw you before. Early one morning? Maybe two weeks ago?'

So much for the invisibility of cleaners. Nadia crossed her arms and hunched forwards – her mind was racing through ways to get past him and upstairs.

'I dunno,' she said. 'I just do the cleaning … And if I don't get finished, my supervisor will kill me.'

She was trying to walk past him and towards the lifts when she felt him grab her arm. His grip was strong, but with the benefit of hindsight, that would have been the time to pull free and make a run for it. Instead, Nadia froze, still unsure about what was happening and afraid of blowing her cover.

'Don't worry about Miss Donna,' he said. 'I will speak to her and there will be no problems.'

And then, in a single fluid movement, he pulled open the door to a small storage room and swung Nadia inside. By the time she'd regained her balance, he was inside with her, back to the door.

The room was small – not more than ten feet square, with a row of wooden cupboards on one side and a metal desk on the other. It had probably been someone's office at some point, but didn't appear to have been used for a while. Nadia felt the walls tighten around her and the weight of the huge building overhead. She'd trained hard for situations like this and had been in more than her share of tough corners, but, like everything else in life, each reality is unique and begs its own solution.

Maybe he had seen her follow him? If he were Chinese Intelligence, he might know who she really was. That wouldn't be good.

Liu Janlin walked towards her, smiling and with his hands held out as if to tell her that she had nothing to worry about. But he kept himself between her and the door, and he looked fit and strong. Nadia doubted she could overpower him, even if she got lucky.

'What d'you want?' she said. 'I've not done nothing wrong.'

'I know that,' he said. 'And I told you not to worry about your boss. I will tell Miss Donna I needed your help with some spilt wine in my office.'

'So. What am I doing here, then?' said Nadia, doing her best to appear calm. 'Shall I go clear it up?'

'No need,' he said. 'There isn't actually any wine.' His constant smiling was doing nothing to settle her suspicions, nor was the way he kept inching closer to her. 'I've noticed you around,' he continued, his almost-perfect English distorted by a strong accent. 'And when I saw you by the lifts, I thought you looked very beautiful … young and fresh.'

What was this? He was coming on to her like a creepy perv, not like an enemy agent.

Nadia stepped backwards as the truth hit her. She felt the cold metal of the table pressing against her thighs. Her cover wasn't blown. Liu Janlin was after something quite different. An unexpected fear and panic gripped her, and she frantically looked around the room again to see if she'd missed anything useful. But she knew what she would see – there was nothing to help her, no way out and nothing she could use as a weapon.

'Don't worry,' he said, over-whitened teeth shining in the fluorescent lights. 'If you're nice to me, I'll be nice to you.'

'I'll scream,' said Nadia, desperately trying to come up with a plan.

'And who is going to hear you?' he said. 'It is the middle of the night, after all.' That grin again. Did the man actually think he was going to charm her into submission? He reached forward and held Nadia by the chin, squeezing firmly. 'This will go much better if you co-operate.' She could feel the strength in his grip and the hard calluses on his hands – probably earned by training in some sort of martial art.

As she struggled to pull away, he grabbed her shoulder, span her around and pushed her over the desk, holding her with one arm as he pressed against her and reached forward to grope her breasts. He was strong. Even though Nadia was in the gym regularly and had been given advanced training in unarmed combat, she couldn't move.

'Don't worry,' he said. 'I like a little fight, too.'

Nadia felt the grip weaken slightly as he reached back with his free hand, presumably to undo his belt. She was only going to get one chance, and the timing needed to be perfect. She pushed herself back and away from the desk and, at the same time, let her body become a dead weight, dropping to a squat and pulling her attacker down with her.

As she'd expected, his response was lightning quick, instantly finding his balance and letting her fall away from him. That gap between them was a vital part of her plan and Nadia dropped her head to one side before launching herself upward, feeling a sharp pain in her shoulder as it connected with Liu Janlin's chin. She span around immediately, arms raised and body tensed in a fighter's crouch.

But there was no need. Shan-ding's Vice-President of 5G technology was lying in a crumpled heap on the floor, head twisted at a seemingly impossible angle. Nadia stayed in her crouch, breathing heavily as she allowed her thoughts to settle.

Was he dead? He looked dead.

Whether the bastard deserved it or not, that would not be good.

Nadia knew there was nothing in her locker which could be traced back to her. A rapid exit from an undercover assignment was always a possibility – although accidentally killing a Chinese senior executive had never come up in the textbook contingency scenarios. She pulled out her phone and sent a short text – 'going home early'.

Having wasted another thirty seconds checking in vain for signs of life, she straightened her clothes and inched the door open, aware of the adrenaline still coursing through her body and fighting back the urge to run. There was no-one in the corridor. Nadia crept out and took the lift up to the ground floor. As she stepped into the huge marble-floored lobby, the security guard on reception raised an eyebrow and beckoned to her. It was unusual for one of the cleaning staff to be leaving so early.

Nadia held both hands over her stomach, miming a grimace of pain as she ignored his instruction and continued to walk towards the exit. He nodded and shrugged his shoulders, the door lock buzzed and she pushed her way through and outside.

The icy morning air hit her like a slap in the face and the desire to move faster became almost unbearable. She fought back the urge, digging her nails hard into the flesh of her palms and understanding, once again, why her field training had been so prolonged and repetitive. Habits of control and discipline needed to be deeply ingrained if they were to cope with extreme and unexpected situations. The nearest safe house was two miles away and Nadia would have to appear calm and unexceptional as she mingled with the pre-dawn commuters along the way.

She hoped she was giving a passable impression of a tired cleaner on her way home after a night shift, but a line of sweat was running cold down her back and her knees were wobbling with every step. She'd just killed a man. A civilian. Whatever he might have been about to do to her, she'd taken his life. Maybe he had a wife and children? She should know that from the briefings, but her thoughts were jumbled and she couldn't remember. All she could manage was to focus on putting one foot in front of the other and to get to her destination.

By the time she reached the safe house – on the tenth floor of a faceless block of executive flats – her whole body was trembling and she fumbled the access code three times before the door finally opened. The place was empty, but she knew she'd have company soon enough. Debriefing sessions were unpleasant at the best of times and this one would be anything but routine. Even her relationship with David might not be enough to protect her.

# 6

'Have you seen my black jacket?' said Nadia. 'I left it on the sofa.'

'In the hall cupboard,' said James, walking out from the bathroom, a small white towel wrapped around his waist. 'I hung it up for you.'

As he stood in the doorway, looking decidedly gorgeous, Nadia was briefly tempted by the idea of being late for work … but it was the wrong day for that kind of irresponsibility. She had a meeting with David for the first time since the Shan-ding incident and had no intention of keeping him waiting.

Apart from being the big boss, David was the closest thing to family she had – the only person she could imagine talking to about the way she was feeling. Her Aunt Leila was all that was left of her real family and, aside from the unresolved issues between them, Leila had never known what Nadia really did for a living.

Even talking with David was highly complicated; he would be kind and understanding enough, but she couldn't afford to show signs of vulnerability and weakness in front of him. He always had to see the confident, strong Nadia if she wanted him to give her the punchy assignments.

The reality was that she would have to manage her issues alone. She'd always understood that, and her natural self-sufficiency and ability to compartmentalise were key to why she was such a good field officer.

In any case, David hadn't contacted her once in the weeks since she'd been attacked; hopefully his shoulder would still be a friendly one?

Personal relationships needed to be kept in another mental compartment and Nadia had pushed hard for permission to keep her dinner date with James, even though it was just a few days after the Liu Janlin debriefing. The dinner had turned out to be a much-needed relief and James now knew the truth – a partial truth, sanitised and whitewashed in line with company policy. It made for a fine line and Nadia knew their relationship was fragile. She would be walking on eggshells for quite a while and, in any case, James could never know anything about the big things – like the Unicorn or Liu Janlin.

'I enjoyed last night,' said James, leaning forward to kiss her while taking care not to drip water on her blouse. '… A lot, actually.'

Nadia smiled. They'd had a great evening – James was such wonderful company when he was on good form and she couldn't remember laughing so much in a long time. It was early days, but there was plenty of reason to hope their relationship would mend. They'd talked it through carefully and both of them understood it would take time; he was very bruised by the way they'd broken up, and she was equally bruised – physically and mentally – by what had happened to her.

For the time being, Nadia was treating the relationship as though it were brand new – there was something fresh and exciting about starting from scratch, and waking up next to a warm, strong, kind man eased the pain and panic of her frequent dreams.

The dreams were not unexpected.

It had been just two weeks since she'd been bundled out of the safe house and into a waiting van. The forty-eight hour intensive debrief which had followed had already taken on the cloudy soft-focus shape of a childhood memory. The interrogators' goal was to maintain the subject in a continuous state of disorientation while digging forensically into their mind to scrape out every last thought and memory, truth and untruth. From Nadia's almost-total inability to remember any details of those two days, they must have been good at their jobs.

The worst questions were the ones they repeated over and over. 'What was in the package?', 'Who was it addressed to?', 'Why didn't you check that before you left the building?' There was no good answer except that she'd panicked and behaved like an unprofessional new recruit. And that wasn't such a good answer.

When they'd finished with her, she'd been moved to another safe house in Ealing while they waited to see what would happen with the police investigation into Liu Janlin's death. Once she – or rather her office cleaner persona – became a suspect, the alternatives weren't promising. She'd left no traceable possessions, but she'd had a photo pass, there would be plenty of video footage – including some of her leaving early – and the police forensics teams would almost certainly be able to lift fingerprints and DNA from somewhere. Even with the best training, it was hard to hide in the twenty-first century.

She'd been given access to an in-house lawyer who'd almost convinced her it would be unusual for an officer to be hung out to dry … unless there was major political fallout. However, her career would almost certainly be over and she would probably need to take on another identity, most likely outside Europe and definitely outside the intelligence community. She'd given everything to the service and that would be her reward? It was too enormous to even think about.

She'd also been assigned a counsellor to help her through any shock or PTSD issues. Although Nadia wasn't convinced it would help, the sessions hadn't been optional, and she'd tried hard to engage. Her first priority had been to convince the psychiatrist that she needed to see James for dinner as planned – there was no doubt that cancelling that date would have meant the end of any hopes of reconciliation.

James could never be a true shoulder to cry on, but Nadia wasn't prepared to give up on him without a fight. The chasm between work and her dreams of a normal family life was opening wider and wider every day and she'd started to see her relationship with James as the final chance to bridge that gap. If she couldn't make that work, she would become a black widow, focused only on her career and living a childless, solitary life in a smart flat filled with modern art and designer furniture. There would be a few select friends to meet in restaurants and the occasional lover who would never know her real name. It wasn't such a terrible life … but it wasn't what she'd always dreamt of.

Of course if they fired her and shipped her abroad, the problem would solve itself, but leaving the service would be terrible and Nadia would much rather accept life as a solitary black widow.

Luckily her counsellor had felt that some normality would help to ground her and the office had approved her spending time with James … on condition that she agreed to have a sub-cutaneous tracking device inserted into the soft skin of her right armpit. So much for trust – or were they worried the Chinese might be looking for her?

She pushed the dripping James away using her fingertips.

'Yes,' she said. 'I had a wonderful time as well.' Then she reached out and cupped his cheek with the palm of her hand. 'I missed you, you know?'

James nodded. 'Me too,' he said. 'Thanks for not giving up on us.' He took her hand and kissed it. 'Will I see you tonight?'

'Tomorrow,' said Nadia, turning and opening the door. 'I've got that work review thing today and I need a quiet evening on my own to work through my options.'

James opened his mouth to speak, but flapped it closed like a goldfish as Nadia raised one finger and gave him her best stern stare.

'… And, no. I can't tell you anything about it.'

James grinned. 'OK. Tomorrow, then.' Nadia could feel his eyes on her as she left, tracking her out onto the street. It felt good to be wanted. Even during those difficult days, as the rest of the world seemed ready to collapse on top of her, James gave her something real and important to hold on to. She wouldn't make the mistake of losing him again.

Randolph Avenue was unusually quiet as she walked down to the bus stop and she was surprised to find herself humming random notes in time with her steps. She definitely approved of James's new flat choice. Little Venice was a charming mix of canal-side town houses and white stucco buildings set around a series of magical, hidden gardens. He must be a very good accountant if he could afford to live there. Nadia toyed briefly with the idea of checking his tax records at the office, but dismissed it immediately. Trust was important.

There was time for a quick, overpriced espresso at Raoul's before she jumped on the Number Six bus and made her way up the curling metal stairs. Looking down on London from the top of a double-decker bus was a unique experience, and she never tired of it. Well worth leaving home fifteen minutes earlier to avoid the sweaty mole-like claustrophobia of the underground.

She shifted along her seat as a man sat next to her, turning to give him the obligatory London half-smile of cautious acknowledgement. Her breath caught in her throat as she turned back to face the window, the bouncy, positive feelings draining from her like blood from a butchered goat. The man was Asian, probably Chinese, dressed in a smart suit and carrying a black leather briefcase. Nothing suspicious about him, but enough to shatter her bubble.

How could she pretend life was normal? Laughing and making love with James as though nothing had happened. What was wrong with her? She'd even managed to enjoy their dinner at the Riverside Cafe, just three days after she'd killed someone. It wasn't her first traumatic experience, but managing the consequences seemed to be becoming easier every time. Surely it wasn't normal to be able to hide all the terrible things away and feel pleasure and joy as though nothing had happened?

She took out her phone with trembling fingers and opened her Keep Notes. There was already a long list under the heading 'Shrink' and she added 'Why don't I feel anything any more?' at the bottom. At the very least, her counsellor sessions meant she had someone to talk to about these doubts – there was no-one else, not even David … especially not David.

She'd only been back to the office once since she'd started the Shanding assignment three months earlier and wasn't keen to cross paths with anyone she knew, although her work colleagues had always been slightly afraid of Nadia and now they would probably be even happier to keep their distance. Despite strict rules and compartmentalisation policies, gossip tended to tear through Thames House like an Australian bushfire and 'Little Miss Perfect' Nadia Laroche being almost raped and then killing a man was exceptionally juicy gossip.

Luckily the lobby was empty apart from a security guard she didn't recognise. Did he raise one eyebrow slightly as he looked at her security pass? Nadia didn't look back as she waited for the lift; she was being paranoid as usual – he'd probably just been checking her face against the photo. The steel doors opened like the jaws of a trap and she stepped inside, punching the button for the sixth floor while still not looking back at the guard.

The lift took forever – as lifts often do – and she had time to straighten her hair and pull down her jacket several times before the doors eventually opened. Why was she so nervous? David was her friend as well as her boss … and she'd done nothing wrong.

But walking down the long faceless corridor to David's office still felt almost like walking back to school to collect her A-level results. The terror and uncertainty of the build-up to a pivotal moment. With the luxury of retrospect, such key events are usually not as important and life-defining as they might appear, but at the time …

Nadia bit into the soft flesh at the back of her lower lip, focusing on breathing through her nose and fighting to control the anxiety which churned in her stomach as though she'd not eaten for a week. She'd had plenty of close calls before, and more than enough run-ins with David, but this was different. Her job was on the line and, as the next half-hour really might decide the course of the rest of her life, it was hard to ignore the dark thoughts which lurked at the back of her mind. What would she do if they kicked her out? The Service had become her life. She couldn't imagine being on the outside.

Nadia felt the sweat prickle on the palms of her hands and wiped them on the sides of her black trousers. There was only one way to find out.

David's assistant, Sue, was one of the few real friends Nadia had in the office, but she was on maternity leave and the strange young woman sitting at her desk looked up at Nadia with a blank questioning stare.

'Nadia Laroche,' said Nadia. 'To see David.'

'Oh yes,' said the temp with no hint of a smile – or a raised eyebrow for that matter. 'He's running a little late. Please take a seat.'

Thinking about how much David must be missing Sue was a welcome distraction – he'd definitely drawn the short straw with her maternity cover. David liked fun, charming, cheeky people and Nadia was surprised he hadn't found a way to reassign the sour-lipped woman in front of her.

The nerves were back by the time David's office door swung open and she saw him filling the doorframe.

'Nadia,' he said. 'Please come in.'

His expression was decidedly neutral – no sign of his usual warmth – and Nadia felt her fingers clenching into tight fists. She followed him inside and closed the door behind her.

It was only then that his face cracked into a broad smile and he spread his arms wide. He held her in a hug for an age and Nadia felt her body sag with relief.

'I've been worried about you,' he said, releasing her at last and looking her in the eyes. 'You understand why I couldn't make contact sooner?'

Nadia nodded.

'Come. Sit,' David said, waving at the low coffee table. 'I've only got half an hour, I'm afraid.'

They sat opposite each other and David pointed to a slim folder on the table.

'That's what we have so far,' he said. 'But, before we get down to it, tell me how things are going with this man of yours. I gather you insisted on seeing him. Is he treating you well?'

Nadia could feel the smile spreading across her face. 'It's good,' she said. 'We're not fully back to how we were before, but neither of us expected that and we both seem to be enjoying going through the first dates phase for a second time.' Nadia reached over the table and took David's hands between hers. 'Thank you for agreeing to let me see him, even after everything that happened. I really think it's going somewhere and …' Nadia lifted one hand, thumb and forefinger millimetres apart. '… I was this close to losing him completely.'

David smiled. 'I'm very pleased for you,' he said. 'If anyone deserves a break …' He leant back in his chair and took an expansive breath before pushing the folder towards Nadia. 'And now to business …'

It took her less than five minutes to skim the contents. 'But there's almost nothing here,' she said. 'Nothing's been reported to the authorities here or in China, there's no body, it's as though Liu Janlin never existed.'

David nodded and shrugged his shoulders.

'What about the package?' said Nadia. 'Did we manage to find out what was in it?' She looked up at David. 'I'm so sorry about that, David. There was definitely something dodgy going on. I had the chance to find out what it was, and I blew it.'

'It's one of those things,' said David. 'And your instincts were right to get out of there as quickly as possible. As for that box, we've managed to trace every shipment made that day and we think we've isolated the one you saw being packed.'

'And …'

'And we know it weighed just under two kilos and was couriered to a pick-up box in West Hampstead.'

'Do we know who picked it up?'

'We're working on that,' said David. 'But whoever collected it appears to have known where all the nearby CCTV cameras were located. It won't be easy.'

'Shit. Another dead end,' said Nadia. 'So where does all this leave me?'

'I need to continue the investigation,' said David. 'If nothing else, to make sure we avoid any future comeback, but if you ask me …'

He paused and Nadia leant forward, willing him to say the right thing.

'… If you ask me, nothing will ever come of it and you'll land on your feet again.'

Nadia sat silently, trying to process David's words. She realised she really had expected the worst – hours of pre-dawn circular thinking had consistently led to a disastrous outcome. And now it appeared that everything might be all right.

David wasn't smiling. 'But how many of those nine lives have you used up now, Nadia?' He took the folder from Nadia's frozen hands, reached back and put it on his desk. 'Six? Seven? I can think of five other close calls off the top of my head.' He raised both eyebrows. 'You know they actually only have seven in Spain? And in Turkey and some Arabic countries they run out after six! I'm too old for this … and if anything happened to you …'

Nadia saw his age then for the first time. Not in his face or his body, but in his fear for her. The certainty and immortality of youth was a distant memory for him.

But not for Nadia. Not yet. 'Don't worry,' she said. 'It's been a tough year, but I'll be fine. I'm not saying I'm finding it easy, but I'll figure it out.' She looked at her watch. 'So … Hopefully you're right and the whole thing disappears. What does that mean for me? What do I do while the investigation is running? And what about afterwards?'

David took another folder from his desk and handed it to her. Inside was a single one-page job description. Nadia read it three times, but the words refused to change.

'An analyst?' she said, desperately trying to keep a lid on her anger and frustration. 'I don't believe it. That's worse than being a cleaner.'

'It's just for a month or two,' said David, frowning. 'I need you to stay in the office … and I need someone with a brain to go through all the Shan-ding data you got for us.'

'It seems more like some sort of punishment,' said Nadia, pushing the sheet of paper back across the table. 'Making me pay for something I couldn't avoid. What else was I supposed to do? Let the bastard rape me?'

'I'm going to ignore that,' said David, glaring at her. 'I'm not punishing you. This is coming from legal and, apart from anything else, you won't be signed off as field-ready for at least a month.' He picked up the job description and handed it back to Nadia. '… And I want you to take a week's compassionate leave first. Somewhere abroad.'

'Fine,' said Nadia, quickly realising she was no longer talking to her friend and father figure and had no cards to play. 'I'll take the holiday and do the mindless analyst job. But what about afterwards? When the investigation's over and they say I'm OK to go back in the field.'

'Then we'll see,' he said, before leaning forward and resting a hand on her shoulder. 'You know I appreciate your drive and ambition, the fact that you're never satisfied, but you need to learn to be grateful for small mercies once in a while. This could have all gone very differently.'

Nadia swallowed back her response and stood up to leave before she said something she would regret. Despite the nerves, she had been looking forward to seeing David, and now she couldn't get away quickly enough.

He hadn't quite finished with her, however, and she'd not made it out of the door before she heard him call after her.

'And Nadia,' he said. 'You'll keep seeing the counsellor until she says otherwise. No discussion.'

# 7

As Nadia sat alone in her small flat later that evening, she found herself replaying the meeting with David's over and over . She sighed as she pushed the final piece of pasta from a pack of Tesco's Finest porcini ravioli around her plate. Why was she so demanding of herself and others? She knew her drive for perfection had tainted friendships and other relationships throughout her life. People found it either tedious or intimidating and either way, they kept their distance.

Could it be that she was still angry at her parents for dying in that car accident? Or at herself for failing to get help before the tide came in. What good could it do to dwell on ancient history which couldn't be changed? One way or the other, she wasn't the person she wanted to be. She wanted to be more grateful for the good things in her life. Even with everything that had happened, she was still so much luckier than most people. She needed to find a way to embrace that.

A week's holiday followed by a month or so doing stress-free work surrounded by colleagues. Most people would have been grateful.

She stabbed the ravioli dead centre, stuffed it in her mouth and threw the fork clattering back onto the plate. She would go to New

York. Why not? She had a good friend in the FBI and there was nothing to stop her asking him a few innocent questions while she was there.

David was wrong when he said she was obsessed with Unicorn. It wasn't an obsession, it was something different. Try as she might, Nadia couldn't shake off this persistent, niggling feeling that she needed to be a part of the operation to bring him to justice. A sense of destiny? Female intuition? Whatever it was, it wouldn't go away.

In any case, she had another perfectly good reason to visit New York. Leila, her mother's sister was there.

Leila – calling her Auntie Leila had always been strictly forbidden – was the younger of the two sisters, although it was difficult to imagine they came from the same family.

Nadia's mother hadn't been a strict Moslem – she'd married a Catholic Frenchman after all – but no-one would ever have accused her of being a rebel either; she'd been modest and sensible, well-educated without showing it, conservative with a small "c", full of fun without needing to be the life and soul of the party and devout without making it a big deal.

Leila couldn't have been more different. She was much too young to be a true child of the sixties, but that didn't stop her trying to be. Her frizzy hair hadn't seen a headscarf since the day she'd left Lebanon, and she wore her intellectual feminist credentials proudly on her sleeve. She smoked weed in front of teenage Nadia, probably took cocaine when her niece wasn't around and seemed to believe that the best way to get even with the patriarchy was to party harder than most men … and to sleep around more as well.

As for her faith, it seemed to Nadia that Leila was only really Moslem when it suited her. Religion for her was like an umbrella or one of the Burberry trench coats she loved so much. When the sun was shining, it would sit alone at the back of the cupboard, but when it rained …

Strip away all the over-intellectualised bullshit and Leila had been, even at forty, not much more than a self-centred child who loved to party. A million miles from the mother figure Nadia had missed and needed. That had been clearer than ever the last time they'd seen each other face-to-face.

Leila had flounced into Nadia's bedroom while she was knee deep in history revision.

'Nadia?' she'd said. 'Nadia, darling?'

Nadia had looked up and seen the make-up and excited eyes. Leila was off partying again by the looks of her … And then Nadia saw the two black suitcases in the hall behind her.

'What's going on, Leila?' she'd said, smelling the tension fill the room like ozone after a lightning storm. 'What's with the bags?'

'Well, sweetie. The thing is … the thing is … I know you've got your A-levels coming up and everything, but I've been offered this amazing job with Vogue in New York. I would have told you earlier, but you know how I hate a fuss.'

And then, as Nadia sat stunned and silent in her chair, it all came out. Leila had a black cab waiting for her outside and was leaving immediately. The Kensington flat was paid for until the end of the summer and Leila had transferred five hundred pounds to Nadia's bank account. After that, she would come into a small inheritance on her eighteenth birthday and would be, quite literally, on her own.

'But you can't just leave,' Nadia had said as reality started to bite. 'Who's going to look after me? You promised Mama that if anything happened to her …'

'… And I have looked after you,' said Leila. 'For seven years. I've done my best, but you're almost grown up now and I need to get on with my own life.'

'You can't,' sobbed Nadia, staring at the two bags looming behind her aunt like freshly polished tombstones. 'It's not right. It's not fair.'

Leila had walked over to her, taken her face in both hands and smiled. 'You're so much like your mother,' she'd said. 'Always looking for justice and honour.' She'd dropped her arms to her sides and stepped backwards. 'It's about time you learnt that life isn't fair. People are bastards and you have to step up and take what you want or you'll always be screwed over.'

And with that, she'd walked out and left Nadia alone in the flat, six weeks before her A-levels.

Nadia hadn't seen her since and, over the years, a few phone calls and the occasional expensive gift had done nothing to quench the anger which flared white-hot whenever Nadia thought about that selfish, cowardly betrayal.

Nadia couldn't remember what exactly had happened to change her mind. Maybe the offence had outlasted some sort of unspoken statute of limitations … or maybe she'd realised that family was too important to completely discard. One way or the other, in recent months she and her aunt had started to talk on the phone more often and she'd been doing her best to forgive Leila. Twelve years had passed and grudges only ate away at the soul. They never actually accomplished anything.

It was past time to look her aunt in the eyes and see if it was possible to take that forgiveness to the next level. She still wasn't convinced she was big enough to take that step, but there was only one way to find out.

The next morning, Nadia got up late, packed her laptop and went to her favourite coffee shop to make plans. She was confident that everything would slot into place – she could stay with Leila, set up a lunch with Danny – her friend from the FBI – and spend a few days wandering around the city. It would do her good to relax and take in a few galleries and museums. More importantly, assuming Danny helped her out, she could go to the part of the Lower East Side where Unicorn had been spotted.

Although Nadia was confident she was as good as any of the agents working on the Unicorn case, she knew the odds of her finding anything new were vanishingly small … from what David had told her there just wasn't enough of a trail to follow. She knew all those things, but the nagging voice in the back of her mind wouldn't stop reminding her that Unicorn was planning another attack. Maybe David was right to call it an obsession, after all. It made no difference; she wasn't minded to admit that and, in any case, the only way to muzzle her inner voice was to do whatever she could to try and stop the attack.

She settled into a corner seat, opened her laptop and checked the room, almost subconsciously, over the rim of her Flat White. Once comfortable there was nothing out of the ordinary, she emailed both Leila and Danny and logged onto Kayak, her favourite travel site. In spite of her frustrations with David – and the world in general – Nadia felt positive and energised. She was taking control of the situation and facing her concerns about the Unicorn's next steps head on. On top of that, a break would do her good – new scenery to distract her and time to think clearly about her life.

Unfortunately her coffee had barely turned lukewarm before her plans began to unravel, tearing her good mood into tiny pieces. Nadia was usually good at being a travel agent, always able to find the cheapest flights and the best places to go, but her streak of bad luck seemed to be following her like a wraith.

For some unknown reason, this was the week when everyone else had decided to go to New York – there were no cheap flights, and the best options she could find had her flying out via Orly on the Tuesday and coming back overnight on the Friday. It was a long way to go for only three days.

She slammed her coffee cup on the table, clenched her fists and leant forwards. Looking daggers at the laptop screen wasn't going to help and punching the screen would be even less constructive.

In a more rational frame of mind, she would have ignored the flashing messages telling her there were only two seats left on the outbound flight and that three other people were currently looking at them. She knew those warnings were nothing more than cheap sales techniques to fool suckers.

Unfortunately, Nadia was not at her most rational and she could easily see herself losing those final options – sitting frozen as the flashing text changed to 'No Seats Available'. Her fingers took on a life of their own and she found herself clicking through to the checkout and reaching in her bag for her passport and credit card. She'd decided to go to New York and that was what she would do.

As she stepped onto the plane, the dark memories of all her recent experiences seemed content to stay behind in London. The one exception was that photo of Unicorn. The one David had showed her at Waterloo Station. If only she'd seen the street name …

After booking her flights, she'd assumed that her luck couldn't get any worse, but it had. Leila was going to Colorado on a fashion shoot and wouldn't be back until the Friday and Danny could meet her for a lunchtime drink on the Friday, but not before. The flights couldn't be changed, she had nowhere to stay and no chance of grilling Danny until it was time to leave. Not what she'd been hoping for.

On her first day in the Big Apple, Nadia spent a few futile hours walking randomly around the Lower East Side which was where David had told her the photo was taken. Without any specific location to help, she knew she was wasting her time, but couldn't think of a better alternative. And it was cold. A biting cold wind funnelling down the dismal streets and knifing through her thin jeans.

Was Unicorn still in New York? At any moment, he could be walking past on the other side of the street and she wouldn't know. The photograph had been taken in early October when it was still warm and she was almost certain he would be long gone. She couldn't imagine him enjoying such icy temperatures.

On the positive side, a few hours of walking in that cold air cured any jet lag she might have had and convinced her to put that image of Unicorn aside and become the ultimate New York tourist – at least the galleries, museums and sandwich bars were warm.

The Unicorn was never far from her mind, though. Nadia knew his visit to New York must imply that he was planning something big and she couldn't shake the feeling that she was somehow connected to him. Apart from anything else, he'd grown up in her mother's home town which was bizarre and felt like a violation in some confusing way. Sidon wasn't such a big place and they might even have gone to the same school for all she knew. How did people from similar backgrounds develop so differently?

The AirBnB room she'd managed to find was tiny and overpriced – the sort of room that had featured in the classic television sitcoms she'd loved watching as a teenager – there was even a fold-down bed. In fact, everything about New York was like a TV show. It was only Nadia's second trip to the US, but she'd grown up with American TV and films and a part of her felt like she was stepping inside a familiar story, although one that wasn't quite real. At any moment she was expecting a wall or door to wobble and her surroundings to turn out to be nothing more than studio scenery.

By Friday morning, Nadia was ready to go home. She sat in the miserable room next to her already-packed bag looking at the yellowing wallpaper and the steamed-up window as she waited for her Uber to break free of the unrelenting New York traffic. She'd tried ringing James several times, but he had his phone off and she suddenly felt very alone. She'd achieved nothing and had run out of time. Even if Danny had something new to tell her about Unicorn, it would be too late to do anything about it. As for Leila, Nadia had started to wonder if seeing her again would turn out to be a huge mistake.

Until she'd learnt about the Colorado trip, Nadia realised she'd been imagining visiting her aunt as some sort of fairytale reconciliation – floating on a soft carpet of champagne bubbles from gallery to concert, from fashion shoot to society party. Leila would have pulled never-ending strings of designer outfits from her wardrobe and paraded her niece around town like an old-fashioned debutante. It was the foolish dream of an abandoned seventeen-year-old girl and had no place in the real world. Leila would be a self-centred as always and that seventeen-year-old girl had needed to grow up quickly many years earlier.

The fact that Leila was out of town for work wasn't a snub, but Nadia couldn't help feeling annoyed and let down. Again. After everything she'd done, Leila could at least have been around to look after her niece. A part of Nadia still felt there was an unpaid debt between them; Leila owed her something to compensate for her abysmal behaviour back then. Unfortunately, she knew Leila wasn't likely to see it that way and the only chance of bridging the divide was for Nadia to be the strong one and draw a line under the past.

At least they would be able to meet before Nadia's flight. Leila was taking her to lunch – at a posh restaurant called Portale – and then she'd be on her way back to the mind-numbing reality of an analyst's job on the second floor.

They were meeting at the restaurant at half past one but, before then, she had a date with Danny at Bar B on 7th Avenue.

Danny was already standing at the bar when Nadia arrived. He pointed at his glass of red wine and raised a finger. Nadia smiled and nodded before starting to push her way through the mass of bodies. Bar B was tiny and completely rammed full. On a Friday lunchtime. The owner must be doing something right.

By the time she'd fought through the mob, Danny had already got her glass of wine and found them a spot tucked away in the corner.

'Nadia,' he said, kissing her on both cheeks. 'Great to see you. It's been forever.'

They'd first met five years earlier while she was on a one-month course at the FBI training centre in Quantico. Danny had been one of the instructors and, even though he was married, they'd become close … a little inappropriate perhaps, but it had been fun. Like the best holiday romances, there had been a natural beginning, a thrilling middle and a natural end. They'd stayed friends, there hadn't been any complications and there wouldn't be – she wouldn't tell James about Danny, but he had nothing to worry about.

She did tell Danny about James, however.

'Are you serious?' he said, clearly trying not to laugh. 'The guy went to Australia to propose while you were skulking in a mosque an hour and half up the freeway?'

Nadia nodded, also finding herself tempted to laugh at the absurdity of it all.

'This job really can make personal life a bitch, can't it?' said Danny. '… And you've managed to patch things up with him?'

Nadia nodded again. 'It wasn't easy though …'

'I'll bet. That man deserves a medal.'

'That's for sure,' said Nadia. 'And I screwed up the operation anyway. It should have been obvious to anyone with half a brain that Unicorn would have a remote trigger. It wasn't his first rodeo.'

Danny shrugged. 'Sounds like the sort of scenario planning I teach. Maybe if you'd paid a bit more attention to the lectures and less to the lecturer, you'd have joined the dots.'

Nadia laughed. That was the thing she'd always liked about Danny. His sense of humour was almost English and he didn't pull punches.

She didn't bother to reply and they ordered more wine before spending an enjoyable half hour catching up on Danny's news. He'd just become a father for the first time and was clearly besotted. However, although his new son was beautiful and Nadia was very happy for him, she had an ulterior motive for their meeting and the clock was ticking.

'Danny,' she said, handing him back his phone after scrolling through an endless string of baby photos. 'You're working anti-terrorism with Homeland these days, aren't you?'

She saw his posture change, almost shrinking back into the corner. Was something wrong?

'Yeees …' he said. 'Why are you asking?'

'You know I was actually inside the Natural History Museum when the bomb went off?' she said.

'I heard,' he said. 'A bad business. Your eye seems fine now, though. No ill effects?'

'All good. Although it was half a millimetre away from being much worse,' said Nadia. 'Look. I'll get straight to it. I saw the photo you guys took of Unicorn on the street in New York and wondered what the latest was on that?'

Almost before the words left her mouth, Nadia realised she'd screwed up. Danny's eyes narrowed, his shoulders tensed and he turned away, refusing to look at her. Nadia had the feeling he would rather be anywhere else than in that bar with her. After a moment or two, he did his best to put on a smile, but she'd definitely crossed a line.

She put a hand on his shoulder. 'Hey. I didn't mean to speak out of turn,' she said. 'I just wanted to know if we're any closer to tracking him down.'

Danny stared deeply into his wine glass before looking up at Nadia. 'First off. I don't know how the hell you got eyes on that photo,' he said, suddenly sounding much more like a senior instructor than an ex-lover and friend. '... And you're the second unexpected person to be asking me about Unicorn in three days. This is not good.'

'I'm sorry,' said Nadia. 'I really didn't want ...'

'... We can't be having this conversation,' said Danny. 'You've put me in a tough position here.'

And that was that. A minimal amount of small talk, a splitting of the bill and they went their separate ways.

Heavy flakes of snow were falling as she started to walk the block and a half to the restaurant. The soft white blanket soon began to coat every surface and the noise and bustle of the city faded. Nadia felt herself disappearing into a silent bubble, suddenly on her own in a strange world.

Why had Danny reacted so strangely? Nadia could understand him refusing to discuss the operation with her – it wasn't her case, after all – but his reaction had been disproportionate. He knew she'd been involved in the museum bombing and he should have understood why she cared what happened to Unicorn.

Danny's reaction was wrong and there must be something else lurking in the background. Something she didn't understand.

In any case, Nadia was disappointed to have ended their catch-up on such a sour note. She shook her head to clear her thoughts, sending snow flurrying in all directions. It would be easy to fix – she would give him a call after a few days and everything would be fine.

Nadia loved eating out and had already looked up the restaurant online. The reviews were all five stars and on first impression Portale didn't disappoint. The unassuming sage-green door opened in front of her and she stepped from the snow-muffled silence of the street into brightness, warmth and the unmistakable sound of people having a good time.

As she handed her snow-covered coat to the receptionist, Nadia found herself smiling. All the fears and anxiety about seeing Leila again were washed away as she realised how the righteous anger she'd held on to for so long had actually been getting in the way of something much more fundamental. She loved her aunt, she was an interesting independent woman … and for all those years Nadia hadn't allowed herself to admit how much she'd missed her.

Leila waved to her from a corner table and stood up to greet her. Nadia had seen recent photos of her aunt online, but would have recognised her anyway. She didn't look so different from the woman who'd walked out on her over ten years earlier.

'You're covered in snow,' Leila said, kissing her flamboyantly on both cheeks. 'Aren't you cold?'

'No. I love it,' said Nadia. 'We almost never get fluffy snow like this in London. And it was only a block and a half from the bar.'

Leila seemed scandalised. Nadia suspected she never walked anywhere. She would probably be happy to run for miles on a treadmill at the gym, but walking on the street? In Louboutins? That was never going to happen. Wherever Leila was, day or night, a black town car would be lurking nearby.

'I ordered you a drink,' said Leila, brushing over Nadia's aberrant walking-in-the-snow behaviour. 'This place serves the best Negronis in New York.'

Over the previous days, Nadia had been reminded how Leila had always been more like an older sister than a replacement mother. Nothing had changed and, as Nadia was no longer an uncertain child, she liked it better that way.

'It's amazing to actually see you in the flesh,' said Nadia, raising her glass. 'I've missed you.'

'And I you,' said Leila, looking down at the table.

It was definitely the best Negroni Nadia had ever tasted. It was also the first, but she wasn't planning on letting her aunt know that. She was looking forward to having the quiet talk she'd planned on the flight over and didn't want Leila thinking her niece was uncultured.

'You haven't changed,' said Nadia. 'Not a bit. I guess those magic creams you advertise in Vogue really do work.'

'… And we get lots of free samples,' said Leila, laughing. 'But you have changed. I left behind an awkward teenager and now here you are – a gorgeous woman.' She leant forward. 'Anyway. It's been forever. Tell me everything. What's going on in my little Nadia's life? I want to know everything about this James of yours.'

'In a minute,' said Nadia. 'But before that, there's something I wanted to ask you while I remember.'

Leila shrugged. 'Fire away,' she said.

'Have you been back?' Nadia asked, as the last memories of snow slid from her hair and dripped onto the table.

'To Sidon?' replied Leila. 'No. Not since I left. Your mother and I talked about taking a trip together, but never got around to it. I suppose I always preferred to remember Lebanon as it was.'

Nadia smiled and nodded. She'd never known Lebanon 'as it was'.

'I wanted to ask you about someone who used to live there back in the day,' said Nadia

'In Sidon?' said Leila. 'It's a big town, you know.'

'I know,' said Nadia. 'But he would have been around the same age and you never know. His name is Ibrahim Abdel-Hak. Does that ring any bells?'

There was no hint of recognition in Leila's eyes. 'Sorry, sweetie,' she said. 'Like I said. It's a big town. Why do you ask?'

'Oh. It's nothing. A friend of a friend,' said Nadia. 'Never mind.' She was strangely disappointed. Had she really been expecting Leila to recognise the Unicorn's name? That would have been a ridiculous coincidence.

'You and your mother went back a few times when you were small, didn't you?' said Leila. 'To see your grandparents.'

Nadia struggled to know which of her childhood memories were real and which were recreated composites of stories and photographs. She thought she could remember looking up at her mother and grandmother huddled together at the kitchen table, bodies pressed together and laughing as they sliced and diced heaps of bright red tomatoes. And her grandfather, already close to the end, once-proud features collapsed in on themselves, each breath a rattling labour of defiance. Rage, rage, against the dying of the light. Was there any point?

'Yes. The last time we went was in ninety-six. After Mama died, there wasn't so much of a reason … and you weren't interested in taking me.'

'There was no one left to visit,' said Leila. 'Your grandmother only survived your grandfather by a few years and it wasn't safe to go back during that time.'

Each generation is fated to see the world from its own self-centred perspective and Nadia realised she'd never thought about the fact that Leila had not been able to go to her own mother's funeral. That must have been heart-breaking.

'Maybe things will change now?' said Nadia.

'Because of the protests?' Leila shook her head. 'You don't really believe anything will change, do you?'

Nadia shook her head. She'd been reading the MI5 internal briefings since the start, and it was hard to see how the uprising – however big, and however popular – would make anything better for ordinary Lebanese people.

'But don't you care?' she said.

'Not really,' said Leila. 'I have a wonderful life here and I mostly just worry about myself, I'm afraid.' She laughed. 'I've always been a selfish bitch – you know that better than anyone.'

Nadia held one hand over her chest. 'And what about me?'

'I care about you, of course,' said Leila. '… But I was a pretty useless substitute mother, wasn't I? I've always been this way. Since I was a girl. That's why I never wanted children.'

'You found yourself with a daughter whether you wanted her or not, though. Didn't you?'

'Yes. And I actually loved being with you most of the time … but

I was still relatively young and loving my work and my freedom. It was hard for me to make compromises.' Leila looked hard into Nadia's eyes. 'Would you actually be happy to drop your career – whatever it is you actually do – and choose to devote yourself to raising children for a couple of decades?'

So. Leila suspected Nadia's work cover story was fake, but had chosen to let it pass. Nadia would love to have known how she'd figured it out, but there was no good way to discover that without making the whole thing into a larger issue. The subject was best left alone.

'I think I'm different,' Nadia said, after a few moments. 'More like my mother, perhaps. When the time comes, I'll be happy to make that choice.' As the words left her mouth, they sounded lifeless and grey. She thought back to a few days earlier, when she'd been terrified she might be kicked out of the Service. Would those feelings of impending emptiness and loss be any different if she left of her own accord? Could she really just walk away from it all to play happy families?

'Well. I guess that makes you lucky,' said Leila, a strange half-smile, half-frown flickering across her face. 'I hope this James guy turns out to be the right one for you.' She poured two glasses from the open bottle of champagne which had miraculously appeared while they were talking. 'Still. An accountant? Are you sure?'

'I think so,' said Nadia. 'To be fair, he's really not dull at all. We've only been back together for a few weeks, but it feels right.'

'I'm happy for you,' said Leila. 'But don't rush into anything, Make sure you're sure. And you call me if you have any doubts.'

'You say I don't need to rush,' said Nadia. 'But my work makes it really hard to find the right man and I can't help thinking I'm running out of time to start a family.'

'Rubbish,' said Leila, nostrils flaring. 'You've got another ten years at least.'

'Maybe,' said Nadia. 'But I want more than one child and, by the time you meet someone new, build a relationship, decide they're right … you know how it works?'

She'd never talked about these fears before. Of course, Leila was right in theory, but Nadia couldn't just rationalise away that growing sense of urgency. The sense that, if things didn't work out with James, it would be too late. A door would close and the service would become her life – all of her life. And the worst part was that she was no longer entirely convinced she didn't want that to happen. Surely there was a way to have both?

Leila looked at her and took hold of her hand.

'I'm sorry,' she said. 'But I don't actually know how it works. My relationships last as long as they are destined to. I don't have any plans beforehand and generally no regrets afterwards. When I'm too old to meet attractive men, I'll probably get a dog.'

She let go of Nadia's hand and sat back in her chair.

'I wish I could be more helpful, but these are things you need to figure out for yourself, I'm afraid. It might have been easier if you'd had your mother with you growing up, but I don't think that me staying around with you in London would have helped. We're just too different.'

They sipped their champagne in silence while their waiter filleted a huge Dover sole with practised precision. Nadia suspected the previous five minutes of conversation represented the closest thing to an apology she was ever going to get from Leila. And that was fine. The angry seventeen-year-old Nadia was only a memory. Leila had done her best with a situation she hadn't asked for. It wasn't really her fault that her best had fallen way short.

'Leila,' she said, once the fish was filleted and served. 'Tell me about Mama. What was she like?'

Over the previous four or five years, Nadia's childhood memories had started to fade, and she'd realised she had no real sense of who her mother had been. Seeing Leila again was a chance to add some texture to that insubstantial framework.

'Ah,' said Leila. 'I figured you'd be asking me that at some point. Where do I start …?'

Leila took a deep breath but, before she'd had a chance to speak, Nadia's phone started to ring. She took it out of her bag and saw it was the office secure line.

'Sorry. I need to take this,' she said, standing and walking towards the cloakrooms.

'Nadia?' It was the last voice she'd expected to hear.

'David? What's wrong? I'm in a restaurant. I can't really talk.'

'Well, go somewhere where you bloody can.' She'd never known him sound so angry.

'OK. Give me a minute.' She opened the door and stood under the tiny porch. 'All right. I'm outside, but it's snowing and I haven't got my coat. What's the problem?'

'Did you meet with an FBI agent earlier today?'

'Yes. An old friend. Danny Carhew.' Nadia felt the Negroni and champagne curdling in her stomach.

'Just a friendly drink, was it?'

'Yes,' said Nadia. 'What's this all about?'

'Did you ask him about the Unicorn photo I showed you?' Nadia's heart sank. Danny must have called in the incident as suspicious behaviour. But that was ridiculous. All she'd done was to ask an old friend a question. His reaction was totally out of order.

'I might have mentioned it in passing,' she said. 'Is that so terrible?'

David's fury showed no sign of abating. 'I made it very clear that I wanted you to keep away from the Unicorn case, didn't I?'

'Well …'

'Didn't I?'

'Yes, David. You did.'

'I explained that I would keep you posted as and when we had new intel?'

'Yes.'

'Well. Now that we have that clear, I suggest you come home, get on with your bloody job, and keep your nose out of things which don't concern you. Is that understood?'

'Yes.'

'Good. Now I have to spend the rest of the day clearing up your mess. Enjoy your dinner.'

# 8

Nadia's flight from JFK landed at six in the morning. As it was a Saturday, she expected to breeze through immigration and baggage reclaim. But expectations were dangerous things, and she found herself standing at the end of an interminable, snaking queue for the passport scanners. There must have been thirty or forty scanners, lined up in expensive, high-tech rows. Less than ten of those were in service and even those were rejecting almost half the attempts. Nadia had slept a few hours on the plane, but flight sleep wasn't the same as normal sleep and had done nothing to make her feel less grungy.

It hadn't helped that her phone conversation with David kept replaying itself at the back of her mind. She bounced between being angry with him for the way he'd spoken to her and furious with herself for being such an impetuous, insubordinate idiot. She knew she was doomed to spend the entire weekend worrying what Monday morning might bring. Someone must have gone over David's head to make him that angry, but why? It wasn't such a big deal.

A triple-shot flat white followed by a steaming hot shower were the only things which might drag her back to the land of the living and, at the rate the passport queue was moving, she wasn't going to be home for hours.

She watched as a couple of passport officers – a man and a woman – strolled out from behind security, yawning and adjusting their uniforms. They'd probably been enjoying coffee and donuts. The woman pressed a button on the main console and ten more scanners lit up with green arrows. Was that really so difficult? The queue started to move faster immediately and Nadia felt the beginnings of hope. She'd be through in twenty minutes and surely her bag would be waiting? The flight had landed an hour and a half earlier, after all.

Twenty minutes was a good guess. The bag was there, and Nadia found herself walking out into the Arrivals hall just a few minutes later. If she was lucky with the Heathrow Express and the tube, she could be home in not much more than an hour – unless she gave up precious minutes to grab a coffee? She was standing blinking in a moment of decision paralysis when a face came into focus in front of her.

James? James?

'Hello, you beautiful woman,' he said, wrapping her in a big hug.

For some reason, Nadia felt tears in her eyes. She'd not considered the possibility of him coming to meet her. Apart from anything else, James was a world class aficionado of the Saturday morning lie-in. He'd turned it into an art-form. Getting up at five in the morning to come and meet her at the airport was a huge deal.

'Hi,' she said, looking into his eyes before kissing him. 'It's great to see you, but what are you doing here? You hate mornings.'

'I know. Impressive isn't it?' he said, laughing. 'Why I'm here is a surprise, but … first things first.' He handed her a cup of coffee and a plastic swipe card.

'What's this?' she asked, head still spinning from seeing him and from the long flight.

'Access to the Elemis Travel Spa,' he said. He pointed to the end of the hall. 'It's just down there. You can have a shower and I've booked you a half hour massage as well. I've got my book, so take your time. We've got about a two hour drive afterwards and you can get some more sleep in the car.'

'Where are we going?' said Nadia. Nothing James had said was making her any less confused.

'That's the surprise,' he said. 'Now off you go. Relax and enjoy yourself. You've had a long flight. I'll be just over here.' He pushed her gently in the direction of the spa and turned towards Costa Coffee.

Needless to say, the spa experience was amazing. Nadia had never been someone who pampered herself, and her experience of spas was limited to one visit to the Gellert Baths in Budapest during a hen weekend for an old schoolfriend. Inevitably her memories were hazy, although she could remember looking at the masseuses standing squat in their white coats and thinking that must be where Soviet Olympic shot-putters went to retire. They had been ten hens and not one of them had dared try a massage.

The Elemis staff were somewhat different – slim, beautiful, unfailingly polite and apparently from every corner of the globe. Maybe there was more to the idea of self-indulgence than she'd imagined. She already had a mental list of things to change in her thirties and treating herself to the occasional spa experience was quickly added – under the heading of 'be kinder to yourself'.

James spotted her walking towards him and got up to greet her.

'You look better,' he said. 'Not that you didn't look wonderful before, of course.'

'I feel better,' she said kissing him, before taking his arm. 'In fact, I feel great. Now where are we going?'

'Let's start with the car park and take it from there,' said James.

Nadia laughed as she realised he wasn't going to crumble. It was his surprise and his rules. At least this time she was where she was supposed to be. They'd agreed to spend the weekend together and she'd been looking forward to it. A great opportunity to forget about work and put Liu Janlin and Unicorn to the back of her mind. But she'd assumed they'd just hang out – walks in the park, a trip to Borough Market, normal London weekend activities. James clearly had other ideas.

'Come on then,' she said. 'The sooner we start, the sooner we get there.'

Nadia stayed awake for as long as she could. She remembered smiling as she realised they were going south, hopefully to the coast. It must have been over a year since she'd had the chance to stand by the sea, face the wind and suck in mouthfuls of salt sea air. Each time she and her parents had gone to their holiday cottage in Brittany when she was small, it had been her first act – to run down to the beach, stand facing the English Channel and just breathe. Both her parents had grown up close to the sea and she could still remember how often that had filled her with jealousy. Weekends at the beach were always over too soon and Paris held few charms for a small child with salt in her veins.

They sat in companionable silence as James turned onto the M3. He was tapping his fingers on the steering wheel and Nadia could tell he was feeling very pleased with himself – and so he should be, she was seriously impressed. It was also obvious how much he was enjoying spinning out his surprise.

She was happy just to sit there reminiscing about sunny salty days on the beach at Ploumananc'h with her parents. She would spend hours foraging and gathering dozens of small treasures, building a big collection in readiness for the moment – late in the afternoon – when her father would ask her to choose her three favourite items. Never more. The rest would be returned to the sea.

Brittany was beautiful and Ploumananc'h was exceptionally lovely. At high tide, there was nothing except for a smart hotel and a restaurant overlooking a water-filled bay. A few hours later, the bay would be transformed into a huge beach, ringed by the famous pink granite rock of the Cote d'Armor and little Nadia would be free to explore. She'd not been back since her parent's death; it didn't seem possible.

She remembered smiling at the memory of those wonderful holidays and then ... the ups and downs of the previous weeks combined with the rhythmic motion of the car and the soothing afterglow of the massage to fill her head with cotton wool. If she'd had a pillow, she would have been asleep before her head hit it. Her last thoughts were about asking James one last time if they were going to the coast – she would probably never know if she'd actually said it out loud.

Nadia couldn't remember ever sleeping that deeply. Waking up was like pulling herself hand over hand up a slippery mud-covered hill. Her head had been resting on the seatbelt and she could feel the way the weave of the material had printed itself into her face. She was alone in the car. The windows were open and the air was full of tangy salt air. The nagging clanking of ropes and stays against masts left her in no doubt she'd been right about their destination.

She opened her eyes slowly. Where was James? Why had he abandoned her in what seemed to be a marina car park?

Nadia looked around as she got out of the car and stretched. Not somewhere she'd ever been, but she had a good working knowledge of most UK ports from basic training. The Sunseeker sign was a big giveaway. They were in Poole. But why?

The key to answering her question was walking towards her, holding two old-school, soft ice-creams with chocolate flakes.

'You just left me,' she said, pretending to be annoyed whilst reaching out for the ice-cream.

'I didn't want to wake you and I needed to sort out a couple of things,' said James. 'You looked so angelic.'

'So,' said Nadia. 'A marina in Poole? Is it about time for you to share the surprise?'

'I've borrowed a yacht from a mate of mine. We're going sailing.'

'But I've never been in anything bigger than a dinghy,' said Nadia. 'Do you know how to sail?'

'As it turns out, yes,' said James. 'I went sailing in Greece for two weeks every year with my folks. My dad even had a yacht on the Hamble for a few years. We used to race most weekends. I even did my yachtmaster qualification a few years ago.'

How had Nadia not known that? This was the man she was considering settling down with. Getting married and having kids … and she didn't know the first thing about him.

'Come on. Grab a bag,' said James, opening the boot. 'I'll show you the boat.'

He locked the car, and they walked through a security gate and down to the end of a floating pontoon. Nadia had no idea what was in the bags, but had to assume there were suitable clothes for her. Apparently it didn't take long to turn into a sheep.

James walked over a narrow gangplank and onto a yacht.

'This?' said Nadia. 'But it's huge. Can you sail this thing on your own?'

'Not easily,' he replied. 'Although it's not that big – only thirty-seven foot. Anyway, you're going to help me. I'll show you the ropes … as it were.'

Nadia did her best to enjoy his wit, although she couldn't take her eyes off the fibreglass monster in front of her. She was used to picking up instructions quickly and had needed to learn to become extremely adaptable. That being said, there were a lot of ropes. Still, if James could do it, how hard could it be?

'Don't worry,' said James. 'We've lucked out with the weather. No rain and light winds. Perfect for a gentle cruise. I can't promise you warmth and sunshine, but it is December.'

He looked at Nadia, standing on the pontoon like a lemon, bag at her feet, and grinned.

'Come on,' he said. 'It'll take us half an hour to get out of the harbour and we don't want to miss the tide. Grab that bag and get on board. You can unpack and have a look around while we're motoring out.'

By the time they reached the harbour entrance, Nadia was kitted out in thermal underwear, a thick jumper and full oilskins.

'Do I really need all this?' she said. 'You know I'm warm blooded.'

'Yup,' said James. 'Trust me. Now give me a minute to get past the chain ferry and we'll teach you how to sail.'

Luckily Nadia didn't get seasick – the moment they passed the harbour entrance, the water changed from smooth and safe to lumpy and menacing and the boat lurched randomly in all directions.

'Don't worry,' said James. 'It'll feel better when we're sailing.'

James was a patient, confident teacher, but there was more to learn than she'd expected. All the ropes had names – you weren't actually allowed to call them ropes for some reason – each bit of the boat also had a strange name and a vital, often obscure, purpose and there were plenty of hazards with the potential to crush your fingers or knock you overboard.

It didn't take her long to pick up the basics and, after fifteen minutes, the sails were up and James declared they were ready to start sailing.

'OK. Nadia. Come in on the main,' he said, pointing at a winch. 'That one. Wind it in … and remember to keep your eyes on what it's connected to.'

Nadia bent over the winch and cranked the handle, watching the rope – no, the mainsheet – feeding through the pulleys. And then, without warning, it happened …

The wind caught the sails and tilted the boat over, the whole, massive craft picked up and surged forwards like a racehorse given its head and James switched the engine off, plunging them into an unfamiliar silence.

Nadia didn't believe she would ever forget that moment. The great fat plastic tub of a boat turned into a different, sleeker beast, gracefully carving its way through the water. A little like the way a seal or a penguin becomes transformed the moment they flop off the ice shelf and into the ocean.

She tilted her head back and laughed out loud.

'You get it,' said James, laughing with her.

'Oh, yes,' said Nadia. 'It's great. I never imagined.'

She looked up at James, standing tall at the wheel, his knees slightly bent, at one with the movement of the boat. He was strong and confident, more so than she'd ever seen him. This was a man to hold on to. It wasn't going to be easy, but they'd find a way.

'Thank you for this,' she said. 'It's incredible.' She twisted around and looked over the bow for a moment before slowly turning back. 'You know I love you, don't you?'

James nodded. 'And you're the best thing that's ever happened to me,' he said, voice cracking with emotion. He put one hand over his mouth as though trying to hold his feelings inside. 'Anyway. Just wait until you see where we're spending the night. It's one of my favourite places. You're going to love it.'

The winter sun was just brushing the horizon behind them as they motored along the north coast of the Isle of Wight. James turned the boat towards the shore, but there was nothing there. It was as though he planned to drive straight into the stony beach.

But they didn't. As they got closer, Nadia saw the narrow channel open up in front of them and they eased forward into a land that time seemed to have forgotten. Low marshes surrounded them, dotted with black half-petrified wooden timbers, many of which were acting as perches for white seabirds . They tied up to one of half a dozen waiting mooring buoys and switched off the engine. They were completely alone, the peace was overwhelming and, after a moment, Nadia realised she'd forgotten to breathe.

James stood behind her and wrapped his arms around her, kissing her on the back of the neck, lifting her hair and brushing his lips over the soft down just below her hairline. Nadia shuddered as she felt the warm glow spreading through her body.

She took his hand and pulled him gently towards the stairway.

'Come on,' she said. 'I've missed you.'

After a simple supper of cheese and red wine, they wrapped up in all their warm clothes and went to sit at the front of the boat. The night was clear, and the stars reflected on the black, oily water. There was no sound apart from the occasional plaintive cry of a lonely seabird.

Nadia lay on the deck with her head in James's lap as he pointed out the constellations one-by-one, adding little snippets of Greek mythology or ancient navigation tips as he worked his way across the sky. She felt good – protected and at peace.

James lifted her head in his hands and stretched his legs.

'I'm cold,' he said. 'Shall we go below?'

'Give me a minute,' said Nadia. 'I want to enjoy the stars a little longer.'

'OK. I'll see you very soon.' He kissed her and disappeared into the blackness.

Nadia got up and stood at the rail looking out. The tide was coming in and she could sense, rather than see, the marshland being eaten up by the rising sea. And, just like the encroaching waters, her fears insisted on creeping back, even in such a tranquil place. Even though she'd already been through plenty of tough times in both her career and her personal life, the memories of what happened with Liu Janlin were persistent and affected her ability to enjoy being intimate with James. Seeing the psychiatrist had helped, but even that process seemed to have reached a limit – the advice had become stuck like a stylus in a scratched vinyl record. 'These things take time. It will get better. You need to be patient.'

So much easier said than done. It was like telling herself to forget about Monday's upcoming conflict with David, or stopping worrying about Unicorn, who was still out there, plotting. Maybe other people were actually able to separate work and leisure, but she couldn't imagine it. Perhaps accountants or shop workers didn't feel the same way about their work as she did? If that were true, one of her problems would be solved – James could stay home and look after the kids and leave her to do what she did best.

She took one last look at the view before turning and making her way down below. James had given her one of the best days of her life. It wasn't right to leave him alone and cold in bed.

# 9

Ibrahim sat in the small cafe in Oslo's Grunerlokke district, sipping his third espresso and watching the people around him through half-closed eyes. Twenty or thirty years earlier, a man like him would have been a curiosity in that cafe – an exotic Asian outsider floating in a sea of blonde, red-cheeked Norwegians, each of them complacent and at ease in the cultural consistency of their remote frozen backwater. Foreigners and immigrants had little reason to go to Oslo.

What a difference a few decades – and some trillions of barrels of oil and gas – could make. His flight from Paris Charles de Gaulle might as easily have been a shuttle from Karachi to Dubai. He'd spotted a few Scandinavians, but the vast majority of passengers were from Asia, the Gulf or the sub-continent. And amongst them, the majority were people of the faith, dressed modestly and babbling away in a mix of heavily accented Norwegian and their native languages, many of which even Ibrahim struggled to identify.

His own path had been chosen for him many years earlier and he would always fight his battles head on, but these ordinary families were also unknowing foot-soldiers in an eternal conflict. Ibrahim had spent the long months between battles studying history and philosophy – no-one, not even Omar, would have suspected that he secretly dreamt of a peaceful world where all religions and cultures would find a way to live together side by side. He also believed that the families on the plane and the people in this cafe would be the ones to deliver that peace, not frontline shock troops like himself.

But Ibrahim was not a fool. He knew his utopian vision may never come to pass and, even if it did, it would be generations in the making. Before that, in the real world, he and Omar would make their mark ... and finally have their revenge.

He thought back to the time spent with his brother - just a month earlier. He always left his brother's house feeling guilty and ashamed, but also slightly afraid. Omar was filled with a righteous anger of such oozing intensity that it was easy to imagine he was possessed by an ifrit of the jinn. He was nothing of the sort of course, but as the day they had been planning for so long approached, Ibrahim found his imagination developing a will of its own.

The sun had been relentless as Ibrahim and Mohammed strolled, arm-in-arm, up the long drive, and it had been a joy to push open the ornately carved wooden doors and step into the cool embrace of Omar's marble-floored courtyard. The space inside was much larger than anyone would suspect, and the sickly sweet smell of jasmine was almost overpowering. Against the far wall, shimmering sheets of water trickled down a geometrically spaced series of sandstone slabs, each one carved with horizontal ridges to aerate the liquid and maximise the cooling effect. Omar had designed the villa himself, down to the tiniest detail; Ibrahim caught himself marvelling, not for the first time, at the uncontrollable genius of his younger brother.

Mohammed stepped back outside and closed the heavy doors behind him, leaving Ibrahim alone to drink in the cool freshness of the scented air.

'Omar,' he called, once the oppression of the midday heat began to leave him. 'I'm here.'

A whine of an electric motor from behind his left shoulder and there was Omar, deftly manoeuvring his wheelchair much too quickly down the narrow steel ramp. His brother looked thinner than Ibrahim remembered, hooked nose and bulging eyes standing out against the shadows of his sunken cheeks.

'Brother. You look well,' said Ibrahim, stepping forward and taking both of Omar's hands in his.

'You are kind, but I don't think so,' said Omar. 'The summer has left me weary.' As Ibrahim released his hands and stood back, he felt his brother's gaze bite into him. 'You, however …' Omar continued. '… Really are looking old and tired.' He span his chair around and moved towards the waterfalls.

Ibrahim laughed. For many years, no-one had dared to speak to him like that. No-one except for Omar.

'It's been a long week,' he said, following Omar's wheelchair past the sandstone slabs and down a narrow passage, half running to keep up.

At the end of the corridor, Omar pressed a button on his wheelchair console and a section of the blue-tiled wall swung open. The room beyond could not have been more different from the entrance courtyard. In place of the Ottoman or Mughal sense of sparse serenity, Omar's office was firmly set in the anxious chaos of the twenty-first century. Screens and keyboards were everywhere and banks of computer servers lined every wall, lights flashing and sprouting dozens of yellow cables like fields of spaghetti.

Ibrahim looked around him. 'Now I understand where the twenty thousand dollars went,' he said. 'You've been busy since I was last here.'

'You should come more often,' said Omar, eyes hardening.

Ibrahim imagined his mother looking down on them and shrugging her shoulders in agreement. Of course he should visit his little brother more often, but at least he'd always done his best to look after him, just as he'd promised to do. The guilt lived with him always, but how could he have known about the bombs when he left Omar playing alone …?

'You know it's risky for me to come here,' he said. 'The spies are on high alert after the museum bombing and I'm sitting on top of their wanted lists now.'

'A dubious honour,' said Omar. 'You should have cancelled that operation. It wasn't a great result and not worth putting everything else at risk.'

'You're probably right,' said Ibrahim, 'but what's done is done and there is too much at stake to let regrets stand in the way. When this is all over …'

'… When this is all over …' Omar was smiling again. 'How many times have I heard you say that over the last forty years? Is it time to accept that it will never be over for us?'

'Maybe?' said Ibrahim. 'But it never hurts to dream a little.' He leant forward over the desk where Omar was opening a small cardboard box. 'Now. What do you have to show me?'

Omar held out a black computer chip swaddled in its protective blanket of anti-static blue plastic.

'The prototype 5G chips have arrived,' he said. 'One hundred of them. I've run some initial tests and I'm ninety-five per cent certain they'll do exactly what we need them to do.' Omar looked up at his brother. 'How did you manage to source these? I can't believe there are more than two or three hundred in existence.'

That was the news Ibrahim had been waiting to hear. He'd tried to get shipment confirmation from his contact at Shan-ding, but the man had disappeared into the ether, taking the fifty thousand dollars with him. For several days, Ibrahim had been fearing the worst – that they'd caught his man and blocked the shipment. Without those chips, the operation would be set back months or even years.

'I found a man in the right place who needed money,' he said. 'You know what the Chinese are like with their gambling? It seems this man was either very unlucky or an exceptionally bad card player.'

He shared a look of disdain with his brother. Neither of them had ever considered any form of gambling; games of chance were not only forbidden, they were foolish and weak.

'And the other thing …?'

Omar had smiled the smile of a small boy coming home to his parents with perfect scores on every test.

'There, I'm even more confident,' he'd said. 'The three transponders you loaded for me worked perfectly. The tests needed to be short – a minute or two at most – but there were no issues. The system will work as planned. I'm certain of it.'

People finished work early in Oslo and the cafe was filling up. Ibrahim looked at his watch, an antique steel Rolex and his only concession to luxury. Four o'clock. Almost time to go and call Frank.

Throughout his life, he'd been proud of his ability to keep calm and stay patient, both essential qualities in a good soldier, but since that meeting with Omar, he'd found it more and more difficult to control his burgeoning excitement. The feelings had started while he was following his brother back down the corridor to the courtyard. Ibrahim could remember sensing an unfamiliar lightness in his step for the first time in many years. They were really going to do this;

the culmination of a life's work was only a few months away.

Once Ibrahim was comfortable that the phone chips had arrived and were working as expected, he and Omar had managed to take half an hour to talk about other things, sitting in the cool shade and sipping mint tea. It wasn't much, but better than nothing.

'Do you have everything you need?' he'd asked.

A shadow had flashed across Omar's face and Ibrahim had imagined him fighting back the impulse to snap back and vent his frustration. Of course, he didn't have everything he needed. There was no unfamiliar lightness in his step. All he needed was to get out of that chair and walk, to be free of that gilded prison, to laugh in the cafe with friends, to walk by the sea with a young wife. He needed the Israeli bombs to have fallen somewhere else, or never to have fallen at all.

'I'm fine,' Omar had said in a soft voice, studying the residue of tea at the bottom of his glass. 'Alia still comes in morning and night. She gets me up and helps me prepare for bed. Mohammed also checks the house a few times a day and makes me coffee. Otherwise I work.' He'd looked up at Ibrahim. 'There's still a lot to do and there has to be a point, doesn't there? Some purpose behind all of this. Otherwise, why bother?'

Ibrahim had leant forward and squeezed his brother's skinny shoulder. 'Of course there is. You know that. What we are doing will change everything.'

The two men looked at each other, each taking the moment to refuel their reserves of certainty and conviction.

'You said Alia still looks after you?' said Ibrahim.

Omar nodded.

'But she must be almost seventy?'

'Seventy-five, I think,' said Omar. 'She seems to be made of knotted thorn-tree wood, although she has been sick more often since last winter. When she can't come in, her daughter comes instead. You remember Dounia?'

Hearing that name had jolted Ibrahim back to a summer's evening four decades in the past. Standing shivering on the high rocks which loomed over the harbour, preparing to leap off into the sea, so scared he could actually imagine the pain of his legs snapping or the cold finality of salt water filling his lungs. The reasons why he would overcome that fear were sitting on the beach at the edge of the water, waiting for him to jump.

Amal, Dounia and Omar. The four of them had been inseparable since childhood – running, fighting, swimming, spending every waking moment together until, seemingly overnight, the two girls became women and were swept back into the protective shelter of their families. The friendship had continued, but the rules had changed, creating a new distance between them.

Then, that summer, two days before he found himself on the point of leaping to certain death, Amal had allowed him to kiss her. The memory of that kiss was still filling him at the moment he'd launched himself upward and outwards and, as the fifty-four-year-old hardened warrior sat in a coffee bar in Oslo, it filled him still.

Ibrahim used the teaspoon to scrape the sugary coffee from the bottom of his cup and stood up to leave the cafe. There was no time for self-indulgent reminiscences. He had a lot to do and his plans had many moving parts.

The days of keeping safe houses or sleeping on a friend's sofa were over for him. Those houses were never that safe in any case, and many of his friends were probably under surveillance. So much easier to use Airbnb. A different account every time. It allowed him to hide in plain sight and move quickly if required. The accounts were completely untraceable if set up using his magic VPN and a stolen credit card … and the accommodation wasn't damp and reeking of sweaty, nervous men.

A middle-aged Norwegian woman was coming out of the front door of the apartment block in Sverdrup's Gate. He stepped aside and gave her a polite smile, but she ignored him completely – perhaps the liberal, socialist Norwegians were beginning to regret their generous refugee policies. A little late for that, he thought as he entered the code and opened the door.

Setting up his VPN and dialling Frank's new number took less than a minute and, with Oslo's super fast cable network, it was as though Frank was sitting in the same room.

'Ibrahim,' said Frank, almost whispering. 'I'm sorry, but I haven't got long. A meeting came up and I've just stepped out to take your call.'

'Don't waste time then,' said Ibrahim. 'Tell me what you've found out.'

'It's what I thought,' said Frank. 'They tracked you back to the flat you were staying in. As you said, it was clean, but the forensic guys got a DNA match from skin particles inside the front door lock. They rub off when you take keys out of your pocket. They know for sure you were there.'

Ibrahim glared at the screen and clenched his fists. They were getting better all the time. Video feeds on every corner and now this. He might be a mythical beast from fairy tales, but the world was running out of secret glades to hide in.

Frank coughed. 'There's more,' he said. 'Because they knew the actual internet router you were using, they were able to track your internet history … and the phone numbers you dialled. They know you dialled a cell phone in Washington. Luckily it was a one-off burner, and I was nowhere near the office or my home.'

Not luck, thought Ibrahim. Just a reminder that covering all the bases and having back-ups was essential. He thought back to other calls he had made from New York and websites he had visited. There was nothing which could help them, except … except …

'Were there any other phone numbers?' he asked.

'Just one,' said Frank. 'In London. I couldn't find out more though. I was just out for a couple of beers with my buddy and he was already wondering why I was so interested in you.'

Ibrahim didn't bother to tell Frank to find out more. He knew what that number must be, and tracing it could have been a disaster if the Americans had been quicker. Everything might have been ruined because of a moment's lack of focus and a lucky face match. He exhaled slowly and relaxed his hands, turning them over and absentmindedly looking at the even row of angry red indentations his fingernails had made in both palms.

'Is that it?'

'Yes,' said Frank. 'I really need to get back inside. I'll see if I can find out more before our next call.'

'OK,' said Ibrahim as he flipped the lid of his laptop closed.

He was angry and disappointed with himself. He couldn't afford complacency. The world was changing at a breakneck pace – advances in technology had almost wiped out the concept of privacy, which only played into the hands of governments and their spy agencies. So many brave warriors for the faith were being traced, tracked and taken quietly before their plans came to fruition.

But Ibrahim wasn't just anybody, and with men like Frank on the other side, the odds were still in his favour for a while longer. What a feeble, spineless fool the man was. Ibrahim would have – and had –

let anyone go to the fire before he would consider betraying the cause – himself, his family, anyone. That was why he knew the weak idiots would lose in the end.

He just needed to keep them looking in the wrong direction a while longer. It would all be over soon enough …

# 10

'So, Nadia. How are you doing today?'

This was the tenth and (hopefully) final visit to Dr Pinker, the army psychiatrist in charge of assessing and managing her post-traumatic stress levels. Although Nadia had always been cynical of anything to do with psychiatry and counselling, after the first four or five visits, she'd been forced to admit the sessions were helping. Manning up and getting on with life was all very well and good, but it probably wasn't healthy to leave too many feelings of fear and guilt wrapped up inside. Dr Pinker had taught her to imagine those black thoughts sealed like pus in a cyst, never changing and waiting for the future moment when something unexpected would puncture the protective coating and allow the evil inside to burst out. Much better to lance them now … even if it was a painful process and, most importantly, David hadn't given her a choice in the matter.

As a bonus, Dr Pinker was great company and Nadia was being paid to sit back in a comfy chair and chat for an hour … and paid for the half hour travel time at either end of the session. It made a welcome break from being stuck in the office all day.

'I'm good, thanks, Sheila,' said Nadia, settling into the familiar leather armchair. She'd been offered a couch at the first session, but that would have been taking things a little far. 'I'm bored stiff at work, but it could be a lot worse.'

'No more bad dreams?'

'Not that I'm aware of,' said Nadia. 'I'm exercising a lot, eating well and generally feeling much more myself.'

'Have you heard from David?'

'No,' said Nadia. 'Not a word.' Even weeks later, she still found herself fuming about that New York phone call. The only explanation she could come up with was that something was going on with Unicorn and she was being shut out of it. Maybe there was intel about a planned attack, or they were coming close to tracking him down. If either of those were true, and she wasn't involved, it was reason to be angrier still.

She knew she'd been out of line, but it had just been one little question. David wanted to have his cake and to eat it. He was happy for her to be creatively insubordinate when things worked out – then all was forgotten even if there was a little collateral damage. He'd had no right to speak to her like that. None whatsoever … and, even worse, she'd missed the opportunity to have a proper conversation with Leila about her mother; it just wasn't the same over the phone.

'How does that make you feel?'

'How do you think it makes me feel?' said Nadia. 'Can we drop this one please. I don't think psychoanalysing the reasons why I'm pissed off with my boss is going to get us anywhere, do you?'

Sheila smiled. 'Fair enough,' she said. 'Let's talk about you and James then? How's that going?' Nadia noticed the way Sheila moved slightly forward in her chair. They'd talked in great detail about her relationship with James a few weeks earlier and it was clear that the doctor's interest had been piqued. Lots of room for Freudian psychobabble there, but she couldn't refuse to talk about every topic.

'Nothing new, really. Getting better all the time. I told you I went to New York?'

'Yes,' said Sheila. 'That was when you had the difficult call with David.'

'Well. I didn't tell you that James surprised me at the airport when I got back and took me on the most amazing sailing weekend. Since then we've been seeing each other three or four nights a week, working on getting back to where we were before. It's going better than I expected, although I can tell he still struggles with the fact that he didn't know I was lying to him. James fancies himself as a "people person" – a sensitive, thoughtful type, over-endowed with emotional intelligence. You know what I mean?'

Sheila laughed. 'I know exactly what you mean. And is he?'

'Is he what?'

'Is he such a great judge of people?'

It was Nadia's turn to laugh. 'Not so much,' she said. 'But there's no harm in letting him think he is, is there?'

Sheila smiled and raised her eyebrows. 'You, however, are a pretty good judge of people and situations,' she said. 'And you know perfectly well I was asking about something else.'

Nadia had, of course, been fully aware of the doctor's intention. Before her trip to visit Leila, she'd been stupid enough to mention that she was struggling to achieve orgasm when making love with James … and had been forced to start faking it.

'Yeah. I figured you wanted to dig elsewhere,' Nadia said. 'And, no. I still haven't been able to come when I'm with James, even though it was never a problem before. I get really close and then … then it's as though something in my head won't allow it. My thoughts just flick away and the moment's gone. I don't know if it's because of our break up or because of what happened at Shan-ding.' Nadia felt the anxiety building and sucked in a deep breath. 'How can I fix this if I don't know what's going on? I feel powerless and I really hate that.'

Sheila lifted one hand, fingers splayed. 'Don't be too hard on yourself, Nadia,' she said. 'These things are never black and white. You'll just need to be patient and matters will probably resolve themselves. We mental health professionals love to try to find explanations and solutions for everything, but it's not always possible and often not worth the effort. You're an experienced officer and this isn't the first time you've had to deal with issues which would prove too much to bear for most civilians. That being said, what happened at Shan-ding was an unusually traumatic experience and my opinion is that you're dealing with it extremely well. The final ten per cent will take time, I'm afraid.'

'Thanks, Sheila,' said Nadia, inwardly groaning at the pointless advice to just be patient. 'I know it will get better. And, as you say, it's early days. My major focus at the moment is getting operational again. I'm not built for a desk job and, as for the possibility of being put out to grass …'

'One bridge at a time,' said Sheila. 'That's beyond my pay grade and, although I'm happy to sign you off as mentally fit, there are other considerations … as you know well enough.'

Nadia was very aware of the 'other considerations'. Towering over them all was the fact that she could still become a murder suspect at any moment.

Six weeks on, there was still no sign of an investigation. Apparently, Shan-ding hadn't reported anything to the police. Two of her colleagues were trying to establish what had happened to the body without any success. As far as the records showed, Liu Janlin had flown back to Shanghai the day after he died, although the airport CCTV footage subsequently confirmed it was another, unidentified man using his passport. After arriving at Shanghai airport, the mystery man had disappeared.

Companies like Shan-ding were notoriously secretive, but it seemed unlikely they would hush up the murder of one of their key executives. They were an established global business, operating in thirty countries around the world. One possible explanation was that Liu had actually been Chinese Secret Service, but equally there was no evidence of that and there still hadn't been any of the usual back channel, tit-for-tat arrests or expulsions.

The other possibility was that he was being paid by one of Shan-ding's competitors and Nadia had caught him in the middle of some sort of industrial espionage. One of their officers in Beijing had passed on a rumour about some prototype 5G chips having gone missing. Perhaps they were what was in the package that Nadia had watched him pack up?

The long and short of the situation was that she might still end up being incredibly lucky but, until the investigation was formally concluded, nothing was certain – and that left Nadia stuck behind a desk doing basic analyst's work while trying to ignore the Sword of Damocles swinging above her head. It was driving her crazy.

Dr Pinker's comments stuck in Nadia's mind for the rest of the day, nagging away every few minutes like a faulty smoke alarm. In principle, she really didn't care much about having to fake it with James for a while, but she felt a burning need to understand what was going on.

They were meeting for dinner that evening and she wondered whether it would be worth bringing it up. He was always talking about being in touch with his feminine side. Maybe he would be able to get past his male pride and engage in a sensible, sensitive discussion about the problem?

She looked at a photo of James on her phone and tried to imagine his reaction. Whichever way she played it, she knew he would turn it into an accusation and leap into defensive mode. The conversation would end up being about him rather than her. And, let's face it, she was the one who wasn't being satisfied.

Nadia finished the last touch of mascara and stood back, contemplating her reflection in the bathroom mirror. Why was she being so demanding? It was wonderful to be back together with James and it was hardly his fault she couldn't tell him about the traumatic event which was almost certainly at the root of her problems. It was as though she was blaming him for not helping her deal with that dark knot of fear which still twisted in the base of her stomach. The weekend sailing had been one of the most wonderful experiences of her life, orgasm or no orgasm, and he actually managed to think of something special to do most weekends. James was a lovely man, and they had genuine uncomplicated fun together. A little patience was all that was required.

She'd never found patience easy. She remembered a time sitting on her father's knee when she was maybe five or six. He was holding a plate with a slice of *tart tropezienne* and was carefully cutting off small mouthfuls for her with the back of a fork, mouth set in concentration under his droopy French moustache. But she couldn't wait, wriggling and leaning forward as though to ram her face into the sugary, cream-filled delight. '*Il faut que tu sois patiente, ma petite*,' he said, laughing as he held the next mouthful away from her at arms length. 'Everything comes to those who wait.'

Well that was easier said than done and, if she didn't shape up, Nadia knew James would start to notice something was wrong. Was it fair to expect him to understand and respect her passionate belief in her job without knowing the most important details? Fair or not, was he able to do it? Nadia also harboured a tiny, hidden fear that James was more conservative than he pretended to be. When push came to shove, would his career always take priority?

The idea of derailing her recovering relationship with James was like looking down into a bottomless black well. If she messed things up again, her dreams of family and normality would fall silently and irrevocably into that sucking blackness. She thought back to her conversation with Leila. Patience alone wouldn't be enough. She needed to find a way of satisfying both her dreams of family and her love of the Service or she might end up losing them both.

She and James were supposed to be having a romantic date night – at their favourite Italian restaurant – and Nadia didn't want to ruin the evening. She gave her mirror-image a stern look. It would be good to put those worries aside for a while. She would behave herself and they would have a lovely time.

She arrived at the restaurant early, found a seat at the bar and ordered a dry martini with a twist – a proper spy drink if ever there was one, although she preferred hers stirred. It was beautifully dry, almost neat Tanqueray 10, and slipped down effortlessly. She checked the time and found herself, almost subconsciously, ordering a second.

With impeccable timing, James arrived just as she was draining the last drops of the first martini and the barman was sliding the second one across the smoked glass countertop. He bent down for a kiss and sat in the chair next to her.

'Is it a competition?' he said, pointing at the two glasses. 'Anything I should know?'

'I'm sorry,' said Nadia. 'I've had a crappy day at work. To be fair, I've had a pretty crappy week as well.'

'Well you won't find the solution at the bottom of a glass,' said James, whose parents were stalwarts of the local golf club and appeared to prefer gin to water.

'I know,' said Nadia, laughing. 'But the first one was so nice.' She passed the glass to James. 'Here. Have a taste.'

'Mmm. That is good,' said James, signalling to the barman for another. 'You won't be able to walk after two though.'

'I'll manage,' said Nadia, who normally stuck to a few glasses of wine. 'And anyway, you can carry me, can't you?'

James flexed his biceps. He wasn't a big man, but he was surprisingly strong. 'Always there to oblige, Milady.' He reached over and stroked Nadia's shoulder gently. 'You know I'd love to help you deal with your work issues,' said James. 'Be a shoulder for you to cry on.' He shrugged. 'But I still don't really know what you do.'

'I told you up front that there was only so much I could tell you. You said you understood why.'

'I do,' he said. 'It's just …' His wounded puppy-dog expression wasn't as charming as usual.

'Let's not get into that again,' she said. 'All I can say is that my day-to-day work has changed quite a lot recently and I'm not happy with it. I used to love my job, but there was a bit of an issue a couple of months ago – just before you and I got back together – and since then I've been stuck behind a desk doing routine analysis.'

'Still. It must be exciting,' said James. 'Saving the world and all that stuff?'

Nadia laughed. 'You would have thought so,' she said. 'But it's really nothing like that. I think I'd rather come and help you do a company audit.'

It was his turn to laugh. 'I really doubt it,' he said. 'You'd end up bankrupting every client I had … or killing them out of frustration

…'

Too close to the bone, unfortunately. She looked at his smiling face and fought back the urge to say something deeply inappropriate. The gin was kicking in and, in many ways, it was actually turning out to be more difficult to live a life of half-truths than one based on outright lies. She shouldn't have been surprised. Most water cooler conversations at the office ended up with somebody complaining about the impossibility of managing relationships with civilians, however much you might want to make them work.

'So, what kind of data are you analysing?' he said. 'Surely you can tell me that?'

Was he never going to let it go? He was like a persistent mosquito in a holiday hotel room. You allowed yourself to believe that it had gone away, the room silent and calm, and then the buzzing bastard was whining right next to your ear again.

She was drunk and getting worse by the second. Two Martinis on an empty stomach had been a schoolgirl error. She bit her tongue. Actually bit the tip of her tongue until it hurt, but it wasn't enough. 'I surely can't tell you that, James,' she snapped. 'Can you tell me how much profit each of your clients make? I don't think so.'

The puppy-dog now looked as though it had been beaten half to death and Nadia realised she'd gone too far. But how else was she going to make him understand?

Fortunately, the waiter chose that moment to appear. 'Ready to order?' he said, and Nadia was gifted some minutes to compose herself, finish her glass of water and to remember yet again that it wasn't James's fault her work situation was in such a mess. Unfortunately for him, he was a conveniently placed punchbag, primed to absorb the anger she wanted to point at David.

More than anything, she would have loved to be able to tell him what had happened with Liu Janlin, but it was never going to happen. James was a sensitive man and would surely have given her the patient love and support she needed … although the bit about killing someone might have stretched him a little. Who was she kidding? That could never be an option.

'I'm sorry, James,' she said, once the orders were taken, and the waiter was on his way back to the kitchen. 'I didn't mean to be so aggressive. I shouldn't have had that second Martini. And work really is driving me crazy at the moment.'

He reached across the table and held her hand. 'It's OK,' he said in a soft voice. 'I do understand. And you know I just want to be there for you when things aren't going well, don't you? I want us to be a team.'

Nadia nodded and put her other hand on top of his. With enough love and patience, they would find a way to work things out. They'd been through so much already. She lifted her drink. They clinked glasses and drank a silent toast.

'Maybe …?' said James, leaning towards her. 'Maybe …?' Nadia felt the last drops of gin turn acid in her mouth as she saw the expression on his face. Was he really not going to give up? 'Maybe if you give me an idea of what happened two months ago at work? No need to tell me names or details, but give me an outline so I can help?'

'Oh. For Christ's sake, James.' Nadia couldn't hide the anger and frustration in her voice. 'Can you just fucking drop it, please. Enough.'

The rest of the dinner passed in silence apart from the odd stilted platitude about the quality of the food and wine. It was hard work maintaining a forced smile for an hour when your insides were churning like an industrial washing machine. Nadia and James didn't have a history of fighting. They were generally both smart enough to know how and when to compromise, but for once there was no question of that. James looked as furious as Nadia felt.

No dessert or coffee and the bill came as a welcome relief; they split it fifty-fifty without any of the usual 'let me get this', 'no, it must be my turn' discussions. The waiter must have spotted the storm clouds looming over them and their coats appeared before they'd even got up from the table.

James held the door open for her and, when she stepped out into the street, Nadia wasn't surprised to see that a soft, wetting drizzle was falling. It matched her mood perfectly. Fire and fury had given way to a sinking sadness.

James turned to her. 'So. I'm guessing you don't want to come back to mine, then?'

Nadia felt her eyes widening. There was so much truth in that Mars-Venus, Man-Woman thing. Was he even considering the possibility that they might go and have make-up sex and then forget about everything? Not on her planet.

'I don't think that would be such a great idea,' she said, spitting out the words. 'Do you?'

'No. I guess not,' said James, head dropping forward. 'Do you want me to get you a cab?'

'No thanks. I'll walk.'

'All right. Goodnight, then.'

'Goodnight.'

And they turned away from each other and walked off into the dark and drizzle.

# 11

Nadia was still fuming when she arrived at Thames House the next morning. Why couldn't James accept things as they were? She knew he was only trying to help, but knowing that only made her feel guilty as well as annoyed. She didn't remember him having been so pig-headed before they broke up. Had he changed? Had she?

She plonked her backpack down on her chair and sighed. To be fair to James, she tended to find something to be irritate her most mornings as she arrived at work. Analyst work was so unbelievably dull … and as for the people who chose it as a career path …

Jenny, who sat at the desk next to her, was an exception. She was always laughing, had a wicked sense of humour and was often the only thing preventing Nadia from trying to commit ritual Japanese *seppuku* with a plastic ruler. Out of sheer boredom.

Jenny leant over her desk towards Nadia as soon as she sat down, cupping one hand over her mouth and talking in a stage whisper which could have been heard two floors above.

'Hey, Nadia. Someone told me you're wanted upstairs.' She added a wink and nod so filled with innuendo she would have put a music-hall comedian to shame. 'Who's been a naughty girl, then?'

'It won't be anything important,' said Nadia trying to hide the tremor of excitement which sent goosebumps all the way up to her shoulders. If Jenny was right, a call upstairs could mean her purgatory was coming to an end … and, although she still wasn't sure what that end would look like, anything was better than being stuck in a state of powerless limbo. She tucked her bag under the desk, put her phone in the drawer – mobiles didn't work in the office – and switched on her computer. 'They probably just want to tell me I'll be stuck down here with you for another three months.'

'Or …' said Jenny, ignoring Nadia's jibe and slicing a finger across her throat. 'It might be curtains. You never know.' She leant further over her desk and whispered. 'You do remember you killed someone, don't you?'

Jenny was an incorrigible wind-up artist and Nadia didn't bother to reply. She was watching their supervisor across the room, waiting to see if Jenny was right. Would she be called up to see David?

She hadn't spoken to him for almost a month – not since that horrible phone call. Her ill-advised meeting with the FBI probably wasn't the main reason he was avoiding her, though. Although she was now signed off as mission ready by the psychologist, the internal investigation was still ongoing and David was enough of a political operator to know when to keep a distance. He would wait until the dust settled and the jury came back with a verdict before being seen to take sides either way.

He'd be loyal as far as he could, but if it became necessary to hang her out to dry, Nadia was harbouring no delusions; he'd dump her without a second thought. For the time being she was dirty and that sort of dirt had a tendency to rub off. She knew he cared about her and would be sad and disappointed if the worst happened, but that wouldn't be allowed to stand in the way of business.

Things were bad enough with her fellow intelligence officers, let alone the analysts on the second floor. She already had a reputation from the time three years earlier when she'd been forced to shoot a friend and colleague through the shoulder. It had been the only way to save him from the crazy fascist standing behind him. The man had been holding a hunting knife to her fellow officer's neck ready to slit his throat … but that important contextual detail tended to be forgotten when the story was told. 'Oh, she's that Nadia – the one who shot Jim. Keep an eye out for her. They say his damaged nerve will never recover.'

Nadia wasn't being paranoid; she'd overheard that exact conversation a couple of years earlier. She could only imagine what people were saying about her now. The looks were enough – even though the Shan-ding incident was highly classified, everyone had known exactly what had happened before she even got back to work. Her co-workers expressions seemed to be screaming 'are you still here?' as though she were one of those 'dead men walking' on Americas's Death Row. Why else would an experienced senior intelligence officer be relegated to an analyst's desk job on the second floor? Every aspect of her current situation didn't bear thinking about, but they wouldn't get rid of her that easily. She wasn't in the habit of accepting defeat.

Jenny didn't appear to have any more useful information and Nadia's supervisor was tapping away furiously at her keyboard, seemingly unaware that Nadia was even in the office. It was probably a false alarm – nothing to get excited about and long past time to get back to those fascinating Shan-ding emails. After two months, she knew what she would find. Absolutely nothing. There was no pattern, hidden code or nefarious agenda. They were just hundreds of dull business emails about dull business things – supply issues, the consequences of being sanctioned by Trump, a new policy on travel allowances – the list went on. Meanwhile Unicorn was out there … still thinking and still planning.

Her hand felt heavy as she reached for the mouse. She knew she'd done nothing wrong, but holding on to all that righteous indignation was exhausting.

Jenny wanted them to go to lunch together, but Nadia felt like being alone. She wolfed down an egg mayonnaise sandwich and set off to walk along the river. The sky was grey and pregnant with rain, the Thames was dark and menacing, even the pigeons looked depressed. She'd told Dr Pinker that she was feeling good, but it wasn't true. Everything felt pointless, even though she knew her situation could have been so much worse. She'd escaped unharmed, it appeared as though she was literally going to get away with murder and, against the odds, she was back together with James.

So why was she so miserable?

Nadia had dealt with depression before. After her parents died, she'd struggled for over a year, and then again when her aunt had upped sticks for New York with no warning. Leila leaving her alone in London had been the worst. Nadia had only just started to come out of her adolescent ugly duckling phase when her life's foundations had been torn out from under her. She'd eventually figured out how to find a way to cope with tough times back then, and she knew she would manage again.

By the time she got back to her desk, the black clouds were already lifting – she wasn't happy, but felt more positive and ready to face the world.

'You look cheerier,' said Jenny. 'A brisk walk will always do the trick.'

'I guess,' said Nadia. 'And I've decided there's no point in getting depressed just because I'm stuck doing this stupid job.'

'Hey,' said Jenny, a sharp edge to her voice. 'Enough already. I like this work and it's about time you got off that high horse. Not everyone thinks being a field officer is so great.'

'Sorry,' said Nadia. 'That was out of order.'

'No worries.' Jenny didn't take offence easily. 'You can buy me a glass of wine later to make up for it.'

'Deal,' said Nadia. 'And I promise I won't moan about work.'

'You'd better not' said Jenny, before slapping her forehead and handing Nadia a folded piece of paper. 'I almost forgot. Someone left this for you.'

Nadia looked at the note and jumped to her feet. David did want to see her. There was light at the end of the tunnel, after all.

As Nadia stepped out of the lift on the sixth floor, she was almost back to her old self and could feel the heaviness leaching out of her body.

She was half way along the corridor when a familiar man's voice called out from one of the meeting rooms. 'Nadia?' he said. 'I was wondering how long you were going to take.'

She turned and peered into the room. 'Ed? Is that you?' He was the last person she'd expected to see, especially after his recent guest appearance in her dreams. Was she becoming psychic? After their brief time working together just before the Natural History Museum bombing, she'd assumed their paths would never cross again.

'Who else?' he said, stepping towards her.

Nadia didn't know why she was so pleased to see Ed, and he seemed equally happy to see her. They fumbled awkwardly in that no-man's land between handshake and peck-on-cheek, before settling for a proper hug. They barely knew each other, but they'd shared an intense and unforgettable experience which had left its mark on them both.

'It's great to see you,' she said, stepping back to look at him. 'You look well.' There was something different about him. A hardness or determination. She couldn't quite put her finger on it, but he seemed more solid. If you pushed against him, you'd find yourself bouncing off.

'I'm doing OK,' he said. '… Been working out a bit.' Nadia managed to keep a straight face. Men really were becoming more vain than women – but the changes in Ed ran deeper than just a few hours in the gym.

He squeezed her shoulder gently. 'I heard about what happened at Shan-ding, by the way. Must have been horrible. Nasty creep … and crazy bad luck.'

'Yeah,' said Nadia. 'Not that anyone in the office actually believes my story. They all think I snapped and overreacted.'

'What else were you supposed to do?'

'I couldn't see an alternative. And the fact that nothing was reported to the police speaks volumes.'

'Not easy to hide a body and keep the family quiet. They must have been terrified of a scandal. That would hit their share price even more than the US sanctions.'

'Which could indicate there were others before me … and they were afraid some of them might come forward?'

'It's a possibility,' said Ed.

'Or he was an industrial spy?' she said. 'Last I heard, that's still the theory over here. I always felt there was something extra dodgy about him and the fact that he was preparing secret shipments at four in the morning supports that.' Nadia wondered if Ed was getting fed up with the one-way conversation, but he seemed genuinely interested and sympathetic. 'And I can't tell my boyfriend, of course,' she continued. '"Oh I just accidentally killed a Chinese telecoms executive who was trying to rape me while I was working undercover as a cleaner.". You can imagine how that would go down.'

Ed laughed. 'I know it's not funny, but you should see the expression on your face.' He looked down to the floor. 'So, you managed to patch it up with that guy, then?'

'James? Yeah. We've been back together for a few weeks now. It was tough to begin with, but we're getting there.'

'That's great,' said Ed, still not meeting her eye. 'I'm really pleased for you.'

There was a long moment of awkward silence until Nadia turned towards the door. 'It was good to see you, Ed,' she said. 'But I'm late for a meeting.'

'Hang on a sec,' he said. 'David knows you're with me. He wanted us to talk before you went in.'

'Why?'

'You saw the photos of Unicorn in New York?'

Nadia nodded. Why was Ed talking to her about Unicorn? Was it a trick David was playing?

'Well, that was all we got,' said Ed. 'Five minutes after that they lost him again and there's been no sign of him since. Nothing.'

'… And you have no idea why he was in New York?' Nadia turned to the window to hide her excitement. Was she finally being allowed back in?

'Not really,' said Ed. 'It can't be good though. Our American cousins are getting very twitchy. They traced him back to a flat on the Lower East Side – empty of course – where they had some positive DNA and fingerprint matches, but nothing else.'

'And you?' said Nadia. 'D'you think he's planning something?'

'I think he's always planning something,' said Ed. 'But taking that trip to the States was a big risk for him and my gut tells me we should be very worried. That's why I wanted to see you.'

'Why?'

'You remember Unicorn was born in Lebanon? In Sidon?'

Nadia nodded. That awful coincidence had been etched in her mind since she'd first found out. She remembered the last time her mother took her back home – the taste of salt and dust mixing together on a warm breeze, the smell of jasmine, blurred images of a row of dusty green vines tied against a rust-stained concrete wall.

'We sent an officer there earlier in the year to try and find out more,' said Ed. 'Where Unicorn grew up, who he knew, what he was like as a kid. Anything really. They came back with a big fat zero. Most records were destroyed in the 80s, it's all a complete mess.' He shrugged. 'Either that or Unicorn's wiped his history.' He looked at Nadia. 'Sidon's where your family's from, isn't it?'

Nadia nodded again and smiled. The image of the vines still lingered – she could almost feel her grandmother's rough skin on hers as the old lady showed the seven-year-old Nadia how to water the tomato plants without wasting precious drops. And then, without warning, Unicorn's face appeared. More and more, her few remaining memories of those visits were being sullied by his presence.

Ed continued 'I'm taking a trip there to see if I can find out anything new about him. It's a bit of a long shot, but we've got nothing else.'

'That makes sense,' said Nadia, pushing those piercing green eyes out of her head. 'If we've got nothing else, it's worth a try and you know the man better than anyone.'

'Fancy coming along?' said Ed, unaware of the bittersweet

memories fighting for prominence in Nadia's mind. 'I've got a civilian contact down there – an old friend – but could use a fellow officer who'll "fit in" and you already know a little about Unicorn.'

'You know I'd love to,' said Nadia. 'And I'm always happy to be the token brown woman.'

She saw Ed's mouth sag and grinned. 'But seriously,' she said. 'I still have a couple of family contacts who might help, and I'll do anything I can do to stop that bastard …' She shrugged and looked down at the floor. 'There's no way it would be authorised, though. David's made it very clear he doesn't want me involved. Which leaves me stuck here, keeping my head down and going through this Shan-ding data. Mind-numbingly boring and almost certainly pointless.'

'Don't worry about approvals,' said Ed, a smug grin spreading over his face. 'My boss got involved and David's already given us the OK. They're closing your investigation – no body, no crime, no problem. But you're burned with the Chinese now and he agrees it would be good for you to make yourself scarce. When we mentioned Sidon and suggested a secondment to MI6, he nearly bit our hands off.'

'Oh, did he?' said Nadia, trying to look hurt, but unable to hide her smile. 'That keen to be rid of me? … And nice to find out from you about my investigation being closed.'

'Apparently there's something else,' said Ed, ignoring her attempts at sarcastic humour. 'But David was a bit tight-lipped about that. He wants to tell you himself.'

# 12

It turned out she and Ed were booked on a flight that same evening – by the time Nadia finished her meeting with David she had just over an hour to get home and pack.

Her mind was spinning cartwheels as she walked down the corridor. The information David had just shared with her had been made up of very few concrete facts and a lot of theories and assumptions, but if any of it were true … Nadia squeezed her hands into tight fists as a shiver ran through her. This was more like it. This was what she'd signed up for.

She was even almost prepared to forgive David for sitting on the bombshell for so long. She knew he was constantly trying to balance the pressures of politics and the law and … she stopped in her tracks as the truth hit her like a hammer between the eyes. He'd actually been planning to involve her since he'd first shown her the photo of Unicorn at Waterloo station. He'd teased her and played her like an over-excited puppy. Even the near disaster at Shan-ding had merely slowed him down. He could be a cold, manipulative bastard at times, but he knew what Nadia wanted, and he'd given it to her.

David had left it up to her to decide how much, if anything, to tell Ed, but there were so many individual strands which didn't yet make sense to Nadia. Apart from anything else, why hadn't Homeland Security officially updated all the UK agencies? She needed some quiet time to think, and to try to fit the pieces together. Then she'd decide what to share.

Ed was waiting for her in the lobby as she came out of the lift.

'Everything OK?' he asked, standing up and walking towards the exit. 'Come on. We've got a taxi waiting.'

Nadia nodded and followed him out.

They didn't speak in the taxi. Ed seemed to be working his way through issues of his own, or maybe he was smart enough to realise that Nadia was struggling with the unexpected change of direction and the brutal way she was being dragged back into active service. It was absolutely what she'd been hoping for, but half a day's notice would have been nice.

They arrived at her flat to find a huge bouquet of long-stemmed red roses leaning against the door.

'Someone's popular,' said Ed.

'So it seems,' said Nadia, picking up the flowers and looking at the handwriting on the attached envelope. James, of course. She opened the door, glancing up to check the telltale hair was still in place, and went inside.

'Come on in,' she said, putting the bouquet on the hall table. 'Make yourself at home. There's beer in the fridge. I'll only be ten minutes.'

She was back even quicker. Nadia always had a grab bag packed – careful long-term planning was all well and good, but most of the time intelligence officers were obliged to react quickly to unexpected new information and a changing environment. Being reactive rather than proactive demanded a constant state of readiness.

She put the bag by the door before picking up the bouquet,

arranging the flowers in an empty vase and separating the stems; there was no point in adding water – the roses would still be beautiful after they dried and she didn't have a better alternative. James's card went into the small leather backpack which had been given to her by her Leila – an expensive guilt-gift, sent from New York just in time for the first Christmas the teenage Nadia had spent alone.

She smiled as she touched the soft skin of the bag. It felt good to have finally spent some time with Leila. Taking the first steps towards forgiveness and understanding hadn't been as painful as she'd feared and there was nothing to match physical closeness – shared laughter and memories, interspersed with the clinking of a champagne flute or a touch of the hand. Nothing could match that.

'Come on. Let's go,' Nadia called to Ed, as soon as the flowers were just right.

He appeared from the kitchen, half-full glass of lager in hand.

'You don't mess about, do you?' he said, flicking his gaze from the packed bag to the precisely arranged roses.

'We've got a plane to catch,' she replied. 'You go ahead. I'll see you downstairs.'

Once Ed was out of sight, Nadia locked the door and carefully brushed the hair back in place. Better safe than sorry.

Ed was sitting in the waiting taxi; Nadia climbed in and sat next to him. She opened her backpack and took out the card from James.

'OK if read this and make a quick call?' she said.

'Knock yourself out,' he said, pulling a copy of The Economist from his bag and leaning back into the seat.

The card was as thoughtful and contrite as she'd expected. Hopefully James was feeling understanding enough to deal with her sudden departure as well. There was only one way to find out, she thought as she dialled his mobile number. He didn't pick up until the sixth ring.

'Hi. It's me,' said Nadia

'Nadia!' He was whispering and she could barely hear him. 'Could you hang on a minute? I just need to step out.' She heard the squeak of chairs and the bass rumble of muttered apologies. Hopefully he wasn't in the middle of a client meeting, although it sounded as though he might be. 'Hello darling,' he said, eventually. 'Did you get my flowers?'

'I did. They were beautiful. Is this an OK time to speak?'

'It is now,' he said. 'I'm back in my office. We're running a bit behind today.' He cleared his throat before continuing. 'I felt so awful about last night and it took me ages to find the right words. I really don't know what gets into me sometimes.' James sounded sad and desperate and Nadia wanted nothing more than to be hugging him tightly and stroking his hair. As long as she didn't miss her plane to Beirut. Nothing was going to stand in the way of getting back in the field.

'Well, you succeeded,' she said. 'The card was very sweet, and it made me feel a lot better.'

'I'm so relieved,' he said. 'Of course I understand why you can't tell me everything about your job and I promise I'll learn to keep my stupid mouth shut.'

Nadia smiled as she imagined how likely it was that he would keep that promise. 'Thank you,' she said. 'And I'm sorry too. I should be more patient … and more careful about how much I drink on an empty stomach. I know it isn't easy for you, especially after what happened in Melbourne. I've tried again and again to imagine how you would have felt standing outside that fake office. It must have been horrible … and, if I'm honest, I've been taking my work frustrations out on you and that's not fair.'

She could tell that James was getting emotional again as his voice was hoarse when he eventually spoke.

'I'm so happy we see things the same way,' he said. 'Can I see you tonight? We can start over … one more time.'

'I can't,' she said. 'I've got a work thing.'

'OK. Where are you anyway? You sound as though you're in a car.'

'I'm in a taxi on the way to Heathrow,' she said. 'My job has suddenly become much more interesting again.'

'Jeezus,' said James. 'They don't mess around, do they? When did you find out about the trip?'

'Earlier this afternoon. I ran home, packed a bag, and we came straight here.'

'Proper "International Woman of Mystery" stuff,' he said. 'Where are you going? … Sorry, sorry … I know you can't tell me. Can you say how long you'll be away?'

'I would if I knew, but it's all a bit last minute and up in the air. My best guess is a couple of weeks, but I'll let you know as soon as I have any more info.'

'OK,' he said, the resignation in his voice mixing seamlessly with a slight note of petulant resentment. 'You said "we came straight here". Are you travelling with someone?'

'Yes. I'm going out there with a colleague. He's a decent guy. We worked together for a short time a few months ago.'

'I'm jealous already.'

Nadia laughed. 'There's really no reason to be. He's not my type.'

'Not your type, eh?' said Ed, after Nadia had finished the call.

'Sorry,' said Nadia, laughing. 'What else was I supposed to say?'

She leant back and looked at Ed properly for the first time.

'To be fair, you've changed a lot in six months,' she said. 'You look more confident. Less like a nervous rabbit.'

'Thanks a lot,' he said. 'Is that really how I came across?'

Nadia smiled and shrugged her shoulders. When she'd met Ed six months earlier, he'd been the typical career techie – geeky, unfit and jumping at shadows.

'Well, maybe I have changed. After our last "experience", I finally accepted the offer of field training my boss had been pushing for.'

'You told me you weren't interested in becoming a field agent,' said Nadia. 'What made you change your mind?'

Ed turned away and covered his mouth with his hand. 'Personal stuff,' he said in a low voice. 'Maybe I'll tell you some day.' He turned back to face her. 'Anyway. I completed a bespoke course six weeks ago.'

Nadia felt her eyes widen. 'Hang on,' she said. 'That means you did it in … what? … four months?'

'Seventeen weeks,' said Ed. 'I've never been so physically and mentally exhausted. It was brutal.'

Nadia could see his eyes were glowing with pride. 'That's incredible,' she said. 'But why so intense?'

'They needed their Unicorn expert to be more mobile and effective quickly… And I was up for it.'

Nadia sat back in her seat. She'd taken almost twice as long for her basic training and that had been tough enough. There was more to Ed than she'd given him credit for – whatever had happened to him in his private life must have cut deep.

'I have to admit I'm impressed,' she said. 'But, most importantly for me, how did you do on the range?' Nadia was known to be the best shot in the combined services and the last time she'd seen Ed near a gun, he'd turned pale and started shivering.

'Pistol or rifle?'

'Pistol.'

The expression on his face was steadily migrating from proud to smug and Nadia had a moment of doubt. There was no way he could be as good as her. Surely not?

'By the end, I was shooting thirty-five or thirty-six.'

Nadia breathed a sigh of relief. 'Sharpshooter, then?' she said. 'That's impressive.' Sharpshooter was the second highest accuracy ranking, based on the forty targets on the range. Probably no more than five per cent of students achieved that level.

'And you?'

'A little better.'

Ed raised one eyebrow.

'The last time I missed a target was quite a few years ago.'

They sat in silence for a while. Traffic was moving on the M4, but slowly – they would have very little time at the airport. Ed appeared to have been suitably impressed by Nadia's shooting skills and she was definitely pleasantly surprised by the new Ed. She no longer needed to worry about travelling around Lebanon with no-one to have her back – they were just there to poke around, but the country was volatile, a mess of conflicting factions, multiple religions and lots of guns. An unpredictable mix of the world she remembered – filled with love and security – and Unicorn's world – filled with violence and vengeance.

From everything she'd read, anything could happen in the new Lebanon – and frequently did.

Ed broke the silence.

'So. What did David have to say for himself?' he asked. 'He was being a bit cagey when I spoke to him.'

Nadia didn't like the idea of secrets between partners – trust was essential when the pressure was on and there was no time for nuanced thinking when lives were at stake. She would talk to Ed before they landed in Beirut. She trusted him.

'I'm still trying to figure that out myself,' she said. 'It makes no sense at all. Give me a few hours and we can work through it together.'

'OK,' he said. 'We have time. In the meantime, tell me what you know about Sidon.'

For Nadia, thinking about her mother's home town brought back feelings of anger and regret – conflicting loyalties and hidden memories, many of them painful. She would have preferred to avoid the subject completely but, as that was the main reason why she'd been chosen for the mission, it wasn't really an option.

'I've not been since I was ten,' she said. 'And what I do know is complicated. Do you mind leaving the serious conversations until we're on the plane?'

Ed nodded, smiled and settled back into his seat without pushing the point. He was a frustratingly easy-going man. Did he not understand the risks involved in poking around on Unicorn's home turf? Or was the coolness all an act?

# 13

Being MI5, Nadia's assignments had always been UK-based and she'd never had any reason to fly abroad for work. She was already walking towards the BA check-in desks when Ed tugged on her sleeve.

'We're this way,' he said, pointing towards a set of double doors at the end of the concourse. 'Have your ID ready.'

A press on a buzzer and they walked into a small room half-filled with armed police, drinking coffee and chatting. Their ID's were checked and then they walked out through a set of double doors to find themselves facing a brightly lit row of duty-free shops.

'Is that it?' she said.

Ed nodded. Was that a note of James Bond smugness on his face? Apparently he was just as childish as the rest of them underneath?

As they walked towards the gate, Nadia couldn't help thinking about the ease with which people accepted and tolerated the inconveniences of life: commuting to work on sweaty tube trains; trying to buy a drink in a busy pub jammed three-deep and desperately trying to make eye contact with the barman; queuing in long lines at an airport for check-in, then security, then passport control.

It was only when some dark magic allowed a glimpse of an

alternative that the inefficiency of civilisation was thrown into sharp relief. She knew those daily hurdles were much higher in other places, but that only served to reinforce the point.

Someone from Ed's office had phoned ahead and BA was holding the plane for them. A stewardess was standing in the gaping doorway, hopping from one foot to another as they arrived. She managed a smile, but only just – and that was the moment when the VIP treatment came to an end. Nadia heard the door closing behind them as they turned right and made their way through a gauntlet of glares all the way to the back of the plane. Normal life was resumed.

Ed waited until they had a drink and a pathetic packet of pretzels in front of them before turning to face her.

'So. Sidon?' he said.

'Yeah ... Sidon,' said Nadia, feeling a familiar emptiness fill her. She couldn't talk about Sidon without thinking about her mother and grandmother. They were bound together by curling vine tendrils. 'I don't remember much about the place I'm afraid. The last time I was there, I was only a kid. But I can tell you a bit about my family and who I know is still there...' She sipped her tomato juice – which she only ever drank on planes – and turned to face him. 'And afterwards, you can tell me a bit more about yourself. It's only fair if we're going to work together.'

Ed nodded his agreement and settled back in his seat.

Nadia took a deep breath and opened her mind to those distant and painful memories. 'My mother was born in a small suburb to the north of the city, close to the fields and not far from the sea. She had one younger sister, Leila, who lives in New York now. They always talked about the place as a paradise before the civil war. I never knew that paradise and, in 1982, when the Israeli army came, things apparently went from bad to much worse.'

'So your mother and sister left after the Israeli invasion?' said Ed.

'Not straight away. My grandfather collapsed with a stroke after their house was bulldozed to the ground; my mother and sister stayed at home to help my grandmother look after him.' Nadia had always loved the photograph of the grandfather she'd barely known. It had sat above the small table in her grandmother's kitchen – a simple black and white portrait of a handsome, proud man with laughter wrinkles around his eyes and a carefully trimmed moustache. 'Anyway, he died a few years later and by that time my mother had already left to marry my father – he was a French doctor working with Medicin sans Frontieres in the Palestinian refugee camps.'

'That must have created a few waves.' said Ed, raising both eyebrows. 'And after you were born, you used to go back with your mother and visit family?'

'Yes. Things became a little easier after the PLO left in the early nineties and we used to go out to spend time with my grandmother and Auntie Taz once or twice a year until I was ten.'

'Auntie Taz?'

'Tazeen. She was my grandmother's neighbour and part of the family since Mama was a child. She's the one I'm planning for us to visit.'

'And you think Tazeen might know something about Unicorn's family?'

'It's possible,' said Nadia. 'It's not such a big place and she was always one of those women who knows everything there is to know about everyone. If she doesn't remember the family, there's a good chance she knows someone who does.' Nadia shrugged. 'I'm not sure how much use that will be, but we have to start somewhere.'

'Agreed,' said Ed. 'We're clutching at straws here.'

'What about your contact,' said Nadia. 'Can he connect us with anyone useful?'

'I'll ask, but I doubt it,' said Ed. 'He's not been back in Lebanon for long and he lives in Beirut. Ali's a great guy though, we've been friends for years. I'm not sure how I'd have coped in Pakistan without him … or since for that matter.'

'So that's where you met him?' said Nadia. 'During your time in Karachi.'

Ed nodded. 'Ali used to drive me whenever I needed to go up country,' he said. 'He combined the roles of interpreter, bodyguard, driver … and friend, of course. We're almost exactly the same age and Ali studied psychology, same as me.'

'I'd forgotten you were a shrink before you became a nerd,' said Nadia, laughing.

'Anyway,' Ed continued, ignoring her comment. 'I've not seen him since his wedding over a year ago and he's just become a dad. It makes me feel old.'

'Becoming a parent's a huge deal,' said Nadia. 'That's when life really changes.'

'I guess,' said Ed. 'As we both know, it's never easy in our business … although things seem to be going well for you and James?'

'The flowers?' said Nadia.

Ed nodded.

'He actually sent those because we had a huge fight last night,' said Nadia. 'But we've been doing pretty well apart from that, I guess.' She felt strangely disloyal talking about James with Ed. 'And there's no Mrs Ed?'

'No,' said Ed sharply, turning to face the window.

The blunt finality of his response left Nadia lost for words and they sat in silence for a few moments as the awkwardness grew between them. Eventually Ed coughed and shifted around in his seat.

'So. You said you stopped going back to Sidon when you were ten,' he said. 'What happened? Did your grandmother pass away?'

'No. My parents did. They were killed in a car accident in Brittany. I was in the car.'

'God, I'm sorry,' said Ed. 'That must have been terrible.'

Nadia nodded. She never told people about her parents for good reason. It was too easy to go back in time and remember the sense of helplessness and failure which had never really left her. Running to get help before the tide came in, running as fast as she could, but not making it in time. It was still the recurrent theme of most of her nightmares. Never quite fast enough.

She suddenly felt the weight of the previous twenty-four hours pressing on her from all sides. The fight with James, David's shocking revelation and the fact that she was in a plane back to Lebanon for the first time in so many years. She knew she was resilient enough to deal with it all, but she needed a chance to think.

'Can we pick this up later?' she said. 'I could use some sleep.'

When Nadia woke up, the plane was cruising calmly, her drink had disappeared and someone had tucked a pillow under her head. She looked at her watch; she'd only slept for an hour, but it had made all the difference.

Nadia looked at Ed, head lolling back against the headrest, lips slightly apart and breathing in a slow steady rhythm. Each exhalation was accompanied by a gentle rasping rumble, not quite a snore, more like the purring of a large leopard.

Why had she never told James about her parents, but she'd already told this virtual stranger? It had seemed important to be open with Ed and, for some strange reason, she trusted him viscerally. She also trusted James, of course, and would make a point of telling him about the accident when they were back. Their relationship had been burdened with too many secrets already.

But, before that, she would have to tell Ed what David had revealed to her. Maybe he would be able to make some sense of it.

Her boss and mentor had been unusually restless when she'd walked into his office, pacing up and down like a newly caged bear.

'Close the door,' he'd said. 'Sit down.'

'What's going on, David?' said Nadia as she sat at the small coffee table. 'Why am I learning about my future from Ed Bailey?'

'Sorry about that.' The sunlight had been behind him and it was only when he sat down that she noticed his loose collar and the stubble on his chin. David wasn't dull or straight by any means, but he always wore a tie in the office and he was always clean-shaven. 'The truth is, Nadia,' he said. 'I'm not sure I know what's going on. What Ed just told you is true – your investigation was officially closed yesterday and we want you to make yourself scarce for a while – but there's something else.'

'Something else?'

'Yes. And that's the real reason why I've changed my mind about allowing you to work with Six on the Unicorn project.'

Nadia looked at him and shrugged her shoulders. Why wasn't he getting to the point? His behaviour was beginning to make her feel anxious.

'I've had a piece of intel from someone I'm close to inside Homeland Security,' he said. 'An unofficial channel. For my eyes only.' He sat down opposite her. 'After they took that photo in New York, they traced Unicorn's route on CCTV – back to a flat on the

Lower East Side.'

'Ed told me … And?'

'They were able to access the broadband router details and use those to crack some elements of the VPN he was using. He made two VOIP calls. One to a burner phone in Brooklyn and the other to an office in London.'

Nadia was well known for her intuition and warning lights were flashing everywhere.

'What office?' she asked.

'I think you've guessed,' said David. 'Apparently, Unicorn spoke to Liu Janlin three days before you saw him sending out that package … right before he attacked you.'

'Bloody hell,' said Nadia, feeling the sharp pain of her fingernails digging into her palms. 'But why?'

'I have no idea. We've been running all sorts of scenarios, but none that fit with anything we know about Unicorn. The most likely one is that Unicorn bribed or blackmailed Liu Janlin into stealing a bunch of 5G prototype chips. What he intends to do with them is the big mystery. He could use them to set up secure, un-jammable communications for a small army, but that seems unlikely.'

Nadia began to have a sinking feeling. How long had these discussions been going on?

'When did you find out about the call?' she said.

'A couple of weeks ago,' he said, looking down at his hands. 'I didn't know what to do. Homeland should have been sharing this through the usual channels, but they still haven't. I have no idea why.'

Nadia stood up and walked over to the window, placing both palms on the cold glass and breathing heavily. She counted to ten before turning back to David, but couldn't keep the anger from her voice.

'You should have told me earlier, David,' she said. 'How could you not say anything? Especially after what happened to me.'

'Well, I'm telling you now,' he snapped back. 'There's some sort of connection between Unicorn and Shan-ding. I don't know what it is, but it seems you may be well positioned to help me find out. I'm assuming you're happy with my decision to assign you to work with Six?'

'You know I am,' she'd said, still standing by the window with her arms wrapped tightly around her chest. 'You may be my boss, but I want to have a proper discussion about communication when I'm back. OK?'

'OK,' he'd said. 'It's a deal.'

They'd talked for a while longer, but all the information David had was vague and nothing was consistent with the way they knew Unicorn had operated in the past. They both agreed that the attempted rape must have been opportunistic, a consequence of Nadia being caught in the wrong place at the wrong time by a man who was accustomed to taking what he wanted.

But the risk of terrorists getting their hands on 5G technology was, of course, part of the reason Nadia had been placed at Shan-ding in the first place. The fact that the Unicorn should have been the one communicating with Liu Janlin was such a bizarre coincidence that Nadia shivered when she thought about it. She couldn't help feeling that fate and destiny were driving her towards the Unicorn at every turn.

David was clearly shaken by the fact that the Americans had decided not to share the intel with the UK. The call had been made to Shan-ding's London office and Unicorn had masterminded a major terrorist attack on British soil just eight months earlier. The UK agencies should have been in the loop from the start.

She adjusted the pillow behind her head and closed her eyes. The next few days were likely to be busy, and it was always a smart move to store up sleep before a mission. Nadia had learnt to snatch moments of rest wherever and whenever she could, but it seemed she was out of practice. Thoughts and questions swirled around in her mind, each one generating more questions with no answers.

Why would Unicorn want 5G chips? What was he planning? If David had told her about the call to Liu Janlin as soon as he'd found out, maybe she could have found some clues in those thousands of emails she'd been ploughing through.

Nadia couldn't believe someone of Unicorn's background was going to swap his sword for a keyboard. Anything was possible, of course, but gut feel and instincts were important, and leopards didn't change their spots.

On the subject of leopards, the sound of purring next to her stopped abruptly and she watched Ed as he sat up and rubbed his eyes.

'Hey there,' he said. 'Did I drop off?'

'Just a bit,' said Nadia. 'Anyway, I'm glad you're awake. I want to tell you what David told me, but I need to go through a bit of context first.'

Ed looked at her blankly for a second.

'Give me a minute to throw some water at my face,' he said, unbuckling his seatbelt and standing up. 'Back in a bit.'

By the time Ed got back to his seat, Nadia had managed to beg two cups of coffee from the stewardess and his eyes lit up as he sat down.

'Just what the doctor ordered,' he said. 'I'm back on Planet Earth now. Tell me.'

'I know you're more up to speed on cyber stuff than me,' said Nadia, 'but bear with me for a couple of minutes.'

Ed nodded his agreement.

'The next big battleground won't be in the world of guns and explosives, but in the world of data and cyber-warfare. Agreed?'

'Yes,' said Ed. 'You only have to look at the last few major elections around the world to see that media manipulation and information theft is the new front line.'

'But that isn't Unicorn's world?'

'Absolutely not,' said Ed. 'I've been studying him for years and he's not a techie. He's intelligent and well read, but Ibrahim Abdel-Hak is a soldier at heart. It wouldn't surprise me if he's beginning to feel like a dinosaur.'

'But the dinosaurs aren't quite extinct yet, which is why they still need people like us?'

'Also agree,' said Ed. 'But going back to cyber-warfare for a sec, the bit that frightens me most is if – or when – hostile parties gain access to centralised control systems in the private sector. Have you read the Johnson Report on supply chains?'

'Yes,' said Nadia. 'That's the one where he claims most major cities are less than forty-eight hours away from serious food shortages if essential supplier's core technology is compromised. Every stage of the distribution process is now completely reliant on data communications. I worked on contingency planning for it a couple of years ago with the Army and was shocked. The genie's out of the bottle and there's no putting it back.'

'And that's one reason why you ended up being a cleaner again, I guess,' said Ed. 'Even if 5G offers huge efficiencies, it brings new vulnerabilities. Apart from anything else, it'll be a while before we learn to hack it properly.'

Nadia nodded. After Phil's description of a world where data attacks were combined with a major global pandemic, she was even more afraid of the myriad of silent enemies facing security services across the world.

'I'd forgotten you started out as a GCHQ boy,' she said. 'Anyway, this all brings me neatly around to my conversation with David …'

# 14

'So much for the Five Eyes partnership and the special relationship,' snapped Ed when Nadia had finished telling him about David's bombshell revelation that Unicorn had been in touch with Shan-ding and that Homeland Security weren't sharing that intel through official channels. Ed spat out the words through clenched teeth and even bothered to use his fingers to put sarcastic quote marks around 'special relationship'.

Nadia hadn't known Ed long but, in that short time, she'd seen him worried, stressed, and plain terrified. She'd not seen him angry and was taken aback by the strength of his reaction. 'Bloody Americans,' he continued. 'Full of buddy-buddy smarm, but ready to stab you in the back given half a chance.'

'Whoah,' said Nadia. 'Tell me what you really think ... And we never sit on intelligence for a few weeks? Really?'

'Stop being reasonable, Nadia,' said Ed. 'I don't feel like being reasonable.'

He turned to her and smiled, neatly countering his unjustified outburst. While his boyish charm was infectious, Nadia couldn't help thinking that a woman couldn't easily use that puppyish soft underbelly tactic and get away with it. A woman would either be seen as coy, flirtatious or weak.

'Glad you got that out of your system,' she said. 'I'll put it down to waking up on the wrong side of the headrest.'

'Sorry,' he said. 'I'm just fed up with the one-way street.' The moment of fury had passed, but Ed was still tapping his fingers nervously on the tray table. 'I've been on the wrong end of playing catch-up too many times. One of our officers in Pakistan was picked up by the Taliban a few years ago because of just that sort of selective sharing. They always expect more from us than they're prepared to give.'

'I wouldn't really know,' said Nadia. 'David seems to be involved in all sorts, but those inter-agency problems don't reach down to my level. I've only ever worked on domestic targets until now.' She put her hand on top of Ed's to calm the drumming finger. 'Did you get your colleague back safely?'

Ed turned to look out of the window. 'No,' he said. 'He was the star of that video beheading which was blasted all over the internet about three years ago – right before the social media companies started to apply some sort of controls.'

Nadia could see that Ed had been really marked by the experience and she worried – not for the first time – about her own lack of emotion. The last ten years seemed to have left her numb and hardened to the myriad terrible things that people were prepared to do to each other. During her first real field operation, she'd been part of team tasked with bringing down a Glasgow-based drug operation. It was run by a family of three brothers and a clean beheading would have been merciful when compared to the way the three of them dealt with anyone who got in their way. In the years since then, she'd seen more of the same, and worse. Strange how that kind of common domestic viciousness almost never made the news while a single Jihadist execution was prime time viewing.

'God, that's horrific,' she said in a soft voice.

'Yup,' said Ed. 'And the Americans probably weren't actually at fault. It's just easier if there's someone to blame.'

The unmistakable voice of a British Airways stewardess chose that moment to tell them they were making their descent into Beirut and should check their seat tables, seat backs and seat belts. It was well timed as Nadia had nothing to say in response to Ed's revelation.

Everyone in the office had been obliged to watch that awful video clip and, as the plane tipped downwards and her ears started popping, she couldn't stop thinking about that poor man. What must have been going through his mind in those final moments as he stared into the infinite black pupil of the video camera lens? She shivered. Maybe she wasn't quite as hardened as she feared.

The plane taxied to a standstill in a dark, remote corner of the airport and Nadia sat idly wondering what the rules were for deciding which flights got priority landing rights. What were the criteria for having a slot next to the terminal and leaving via an air-bridge? She wasn't a huge traveller, but any reasonable law of averages would have dictated that her plane shouldn't always be as far away from the landing gates as possible. Someone must be out to get her.

She tucked her headscarf into her collar and followed Ed down the steps to the waiting bus. An icy wind sent needles through her thin blouse and left her shivering. She zipped her jacket up to the neck as she stepped into the bus. What was the point of flying to the edge of Africa? Beirut was colder than London.

Ed's super agent airport skills didn't seem to stretch to Lebanon and passport control took forever, even for Nadia with her national passport. She'd been following the anti-government protests closely and knew the government was paranoid about Lebanese citizens coming from abroad to support the movement and agitate for regime change.

Paranoid with some justification; there were hundreds of thousands of Lebanese spread around the world, many of them wealthy and powerful. Perversely, that was just like Israel. Both countries had huge diaspora populations, generation after generation leading normal lives far away, but never losing that umbilical tie to one of two small pieces of dirt at the far eastern edge of the Mediterranean.

Even Leila, with all her glitz and glamour, was a daughter of Lebanon at heart and, for Nadia, the sense of coming home was almost overwhelming.

Ed's travel agent performance improved soon after they'd walked out into the crowded arrivals hall. The noise was that of a meat market, over-bright lighting casting stark shadows which highlighted the sense of total chaos and anarchy. Finding a taxi was not going to be an issue – they were accosted by at least a dozen drivers before they reached the exit. Finding a trustworthy one would be more of a challenge.

'Shall we try and find the official taxi rank?' she shouted to Ed.

'It's OK,' he said. 'Ali should be meeting us.' He looked around and then lifted his hand in greeting.

The young man in the shabby black suit folded the piece of cardboard he'd been holding and half ran towards them, his face split in two by a huge smile.

'Ed,' he said, wrapping Ed in a big hug. 'It is very good to see you, *habibi*.'

'And you, Ali,' said Ed, extracting himself from the hug. 'You're looking well.'

Ali rubbed his expansive stomach with both hands. 'You know what we say about this in Lebanon? I am a strong man.'

'And a little stronger every time I see you,' said Ed, laughing. He turned to Nadia. 'This is my colleague, Nadia. Her family's originally from Sidon.'

Ali's eyes lit up. 'Very good,' he said. 'My cousin also lives in Sidon. *Ahla, Nadia.* Welcome home.'

'*Shukrun,*' replied Nadia, enjoying the feel of the word on her tongue.

'*Afwan,*' said Ali, as he picked up Nadia's backpack. 'Come along. The car is this way.'

The two men walked slightly ahead, leaning close and talking in urgent whispers. Nadia couldn't pick up any of the conversation, but Ed seemed to have something he needed to get off his chest. Ali appeared to be reassuring him, fingers and thumb squeezed together in the universal hand signal which punctuated so many conversations across the Middle East. *Shwaya shwaya* – take it easy, slow down.

She liked the new Ed more than the nervous analyst she'd first met six months earlier, but he wasn't easy to figure out – especially as the infuriating man held his cards so close. It couldn't only be because of his field training – he was hiding something darker and deeper. Perhaps he was trying to impress her by showing how professional he had become? Or maybe he just didn't feel at ease around her? There had to be a reason why.

She wondered for a second whether the two young men's relationship had been something more than just friends. Ed's eyes had lit up when he'd first started talking about Ali and she couldn't help noticing the way they were walking together with linked arms and shoulders touching. Definitely unusual for two straight men in the UK, but not so much in the Middle East. In any event, why should she care and what business was it of hers?

Although Nadia had probably not spent more than four or five months in Lebanon in her life, the chaos of the airport was comfortable and familiar. The place was a part of who she was and her feelings of coming home were inextricably linked to memories of her mother – whose regressive transformation into an excited chattering teenager had amazed Nadia each time they'd stepped off the plane in Beirut.

Lebanon had been her mother's true home, and Nadia believed she'd sacrificed a part of her heart when she'd left to start a new life with the crazy, charming French doctor who was to become Nadia's father. It felt as though those feelings of belonging and sense of place had been passed down to Nadia through some kind of genetic osmosis – which, like so many things in life, made no rational sense.

As they walked out to the car park, the icy wind funnelled down the covered walkway, even colder if anything. Travelling two thousand miles south should have made more difference. Ali had pulled ahead, threading his way through the crowds with practiced ease. Nadia pulled her headscarf tighter and looked at Ed, who had both arms wrapped tightly around his chest.

'Enjoying the balmy Mediterranean climate?' she said.

'I should have brought my shorts,' said Ed. 'Seriously, though. You never said anything about the cold.'

'I've never been here in the winter,' she said. 'Glad I brought my warm coat though.'

Ed glared at her and turned to follow Ali through the car park.

'How did Ali end up in Karachi?' said Nadia, speeding up to walk alongside him.

'He grew up there,' said Ed. 'His uncle worked as a chef at the Deputy High Commission and, when Ali finished school, his uncle got him a job as a driver and Ali started taking me up to Peshawar. We spent weeks at a time up there, just the two of us, which was how we became close. He was a master at dealing with guards at checkpoints – always finding the right balance of humour and obsequiousness. I'm sure he saved my life more than once without me even knowing we were in danger. Then, about a year before I left Pakistan, he was introduced to a family friend from Beirut and six months later left to marry her and start a family. The other drivers were useless in comparison.'

'Sounds like a great guy.'

'The best,' said Ed. 'He's actually asked me to be godfather to his son … which is a huge honour.'

'Ali must think a lot of you,' said Nadia.

Ed's response was cut off by their arrival at the car, a battered blue Peugeot 504 which looked as though it had been round the clock at least twice. MI6 obviously travelled in style.

Ed opened the back door for her and then climbed into the passenger seat next to Ali. The serious talk seemed to have finished and once they started driving, the two men launched into a stream of animated banter, laughing and joking as though she wasn't there. Nadia knew they hadn't seen each other in a long time and wanted to be understanding, but Ed didn't even register the way he'd been ignoring her, or offer any sort of acknowledgement. It was another reminder of how women seemed to be sidelined in most Middle-Eastern cultures – often treasured, but mostly ignored.

She had quite a reputation for standing up for herself in England and it was good to be reminded that everything is relative; London was a feminist paradise in comparison to Lebanon. The place was home in some fundamental way, but that didn't make it perfect.

She was tempted to say something to Ed, but the drive from Beirut airport to Sidon took less than an hour and it was after midnight. She chose to close her eyes and store up a little more sleep – just in case.

Nadia woke from a strange, distant dream to find Ed reaching through the open car door and shaking her gently.

'Come on,' he said. 'We're here.'

She got out of the car and stood blinking in the streetlights while her brain cells rearranged themselves. They were standing at the entrance of the Al Qualaa Boutique Hotel, which was to be their accommodation. It looked smart and not at all what Nadia had expected. The Sidon she remembered was much more broken and crumbling.

'It used to be a crusader church,' said Ali. '… And was falling down stone by stone until one rich man from Beirut decides to build this hotel. It is a very nice hotel and …' He pointed over Nadia's shoulder. '… The best view in Sidon.'

She turned and there, right in front of her, was the famous sea castle, floodlit stone walls reflecting yellow in the bay. Memories came rushing back – walking along the Corniche after dinner, sandwiched between her mother and grandmother, half-listening to their incessant chatter, but mostly just happy to be there, wrapped in the warm evening air and surrounded by what had seemed to be the entire population of Sidon.

'I will see you in the morning,' said Ali, snapping her out of the daydream. 'I have asked the hotel to make some food for you.' He then got back in the car, waved and drove away.

Nadia and Ed picked up their bags and walked up the steps to the hotel entrance.

'He was in a hurry,' said Nadia. 'Where will he sleep?'

'With his cousin who moved back here about ten years ago,' said Ed. 'His family are probably all waiting up for him. I said he should stay in the hotel, but he wouldn't hear of it. Although we really are friends, there's always been a certain distance between us. It feels like some sort of weird colonial deference. It took me more than a year to stop him calling me Mr Ed, for Christs's sake.'

Ed had lived in Pakistan for years and Nadia was surprised he hadn't picked up a better understanding of the nuances of Middle-Eastern culture – but she didn't feel like opening that can of worms.

'... And you don't think it's because you reminded him of that talking horse on the American TV show?'

Ed laughed. 'No, Nadia. I really don't think that's why.'

The hotel was even more impressive inside than out. Exposed stone walls were cleverly mixed with modern fabrics and designer furniture which oozed money. Those stone walls would have kept the place cool and fresh in the summer but, in the middle of Lebanon's short winter, Nadia could almost see the tendrils of cold air snaking out into the room.

The young woman on reception gave them their keys and pointed towards a low table covered with plates of dips and vegetables.

'There is a small snack for you,' she said. 'And I will bring some tea.'

'That would be lovely,' said Nadia. 'Is there some heating in the rooms?'

'Yes,' said the young woman. 'But it's difficult to keep them warm when the weather is cold like this. We do our best.'

'Thank you,' said Nadia, before turning to Ed. 'I'm just going to pop upstairs to give James a call before it's too late. See you down here in ten minutes?'

'OK,' said Ed. 'I'll be here.'

Her room was a little warmer than the reception, but not by much, and Nadia's first task was to search for blankets. Luckily there were plenty, and she wrapped one around her shoulders before dialling James.

He answered on the second ring and Nadia pictured him sitting on the blue living room sofa, watching Designated Survivor – which wasn't a shared pleasure. His phone would have been sitting on the cushion next to him, waiting for her call. She smiled at the thought.

The line was awful, which kept the call short and sweet. James pointedly didn't ask anything about what Nadia was doing or where she was, which should have pleased her, but perversely only reminded her of how obnoxious she'd been at that dinner. Maybe the drink could be blamed, maybe he'd deserved it somewhat … the reality was, whichever way you cut it, she'd behaved like a total bitch.

As she put the phone back in her bag, Nadia felt a warm glow in the pit of her stomach. She liked the idea of her man sitting in a warm flat, waiting for her to come home – and she knew just how she'd make it up to him when she got back. But, until then, she had a job to do and needed to focus.

The downstairs lounge felt even colder than before. Ed was huddled over the low table scooping up hummus with a piece of flatbread. Two cups of black tea were steaming in front of him.

'Any chance of a cold beer,' said Nadia. 'I'm parched.'

Ed shook his head and grunted, pointing to his mouth and

chewing theatrically.

'No joy,' he said, once he'd finished his mouthful. 'It's a dry hotel.'

Nadia scowled before sitting down and picking up her tea. Nothing could compete with a cold beer after a day's travelling.

'Apparently the restaurant opposite serves beer,' he said. 'They're closed now, but we can go tomorrow.'

'It's OK,' she said. 'I shouldn't be so needy, anyway.'

They sat in silence as Nadia attacked the food. The tabouleh wasn't as good as her grandmother's, but it wasn't bad at all. That was something she could thank Leila for – her aunt had always insisted on speaking Arabic at home and most of their food had been Lebanese. From the local deli, of course, but Leila had ensured that Nadia never completely lost that link with her roots.

'Ali will be here at eight,' said Ed. 'I persuaded him to join us for breakfast. After that, we'll try and track down your grandmother's friend and take it from there. If that doesn't lead anywhere, I've got introductions to a couple of local newspapers and the mayor's office. My colleague already went through their records, but we might pick up something he didn't.'

'This may end up being a short trip,' said Nadia. 'I've not been able to speak to Tazeen as she doesn't have a phone – all I know is she moved into my grandmother's house after she died. According to my office, she's still living there. I hope their info's up-to-date and Tazeen is still as sharp as she used to be. She seems to be one of the last of that generation still around.'

'And you knew her well?'

'Yeah. When I was young. We saw her every time we came. Everyone used to call her Auntie Taz. She never had children of her own and was like a second mother to Mum and Leila. You know the type?'

'I do,' said Ed, standing up and brushing breadcrumbs from his trousers. 'I grew up with an Auntie Doreen living next door. Hopefully Auntie Taz can give us something to get started with, however small. Apart from the Palestinian camp, Sidon's not such a big town and Unicorn must surely have left some sort of trail.'

They began to walk up the stairs to their rooms and then Ed suddenly stopped.

'I completely forgot,' he said. 'Ali said that we were lucky to arrive so late. The anti-government demonstrations have picked up again. There might not be so much going on in Sidon, but getting around – at least in the centre – could be difficult.'

'Yet another opportunity for false hope,' said Nadia, sadly.

'A longer conversation for another time,' said Ed, as they reached Nadia's room. 'Sleep well. I'll see you for breakfast at eight. It'll be a long day and we need to be ready for anything.'

# 15

Once they started driving, the smart, newly renovated hotel and the floodlit castle were soon revealed to be rule-proving exceptions – poor attempts to window dress reality – tourist Disneyfications which didn't bear much scrutiny. The real Sidon hadn't changed from Nadia's memories – if anything there were more wild dogs, more potholes, more abandoned buildings and nothing to indicate that life was improving for ordinary people. Even the bright winter sunlight and unblemished blue sky didn't help.

Ali had joined them for breakfast, but refused to eat anything, claiming he'd already had a huge meal with his uncle's family. Nadia could see the frustration in Ed's eyes; whatever their actual relationship might have been, it was hard to have a close friend who sometimes treated you as though you were somehow different and special. Even after five years living in Pakistan, Ed didn't seem to have understood the nature of class and status in that part of the world. Ali wasn't treating him with deference because he was English – it was because of his job status, the fact that he was relatively wealthy and because Nadia was there. That was how his world worked.

The Sidon traffic was predictably awful, and they crept southwards. As they moved further into the residential areas, Nadia had a growing sense that something wasn't right. The skyline was different, but she hadn't been to Sidon for almost twenty years and couldn't work out what was confusing her.

And then it was clear.

'I know what's wrong,' she said. 'The Makab. It's gone. I read they were taking it away, but I can't believe it's actually gone.'

'What's the Makab?' said Ed.

'It was a mountain of rubbish,' said Nadia, pointing out of the window. 'Over there. You could see – and smell – it from miles away. It was huge. A real mountain.' She continued to stare as though expecting it to reappear. 'It was Sidon's shame.'

'My cousin works there,' said Ali. 'They have recycled all the rubbish and opened the first green park already. In five, maybe ten years it will be finished and the sea will be clean again. We will go and look at the park afterwards, if you want.'

Nadia sat back in her seat. Maybe not everything was doom and gloom. If Lebanon could solve a problem as massive as the Makab, there was still hope.

'Auntie Taz?'

The old woman stood in the shadowy doorway, blinking in the bright morning light. She shaded her eyes with one hand and bent forward.

'Nadia?' she said. 'Nadia? Is it you?'

She reached out and held Nadia's face in both hands, fingertips digging into Nadia's cheekbones with surprising strength.

'Let me see you, *habibi.* Is it really you?' She stared at Nadia and a smile of pure joy transformed her wrinkled face. 'You are even more beautiful than your mother,' said Tazeen. 'Although I'm not surprised – your father was very handsome too.'

Nadia pulled the hands gently from her face and wrapped the old woman in a hug, hiding her tears in the rough cloth of Tazeen's hijab. Underneath the inevitable acrid smells of old age and poverty, she imagined she could still pick out the signature rosewater scent remembered from hundreds of childhood hugs.

'I was so sorry I couldn't come to your mother's funeral,' said Tazeen. 'I lost my passport in '82 and never bothered with a new one. They told me it would take two months …'

'I understand,' said Nadia. 'You wrote to Leila, and we got your flowers. They were beautiful.'

She released Tazeen from the hug and they went inside. When she introduced Ed, Nadia saw the old lady running her eyes over him like an antiques dealer and she suddenly remembered something her mother had said during one of their last visits – 'You are growing so tall, my angel,' she'd said, bending over her daughter. 'When the time is right, Auntie Taz will find you a good husband. No-one has a better eye.' Nadia remembered wondering why Auntie Taz had no husband of her own if she were such a good judge of men, but she'd been ten year's old and the thought hadn't lingered long.

It appeared the assessment was positive as Tazeen raised a questioning eyebrow and pulled in her chin. Nadia smiled and shook her head.

'Ed's a colleague, Auntie,' she said. 'Nothing more. I have a boyfriend in London. His name is James.'

'I see,' said Tazeen, turning to the two-ring cooker where the coffee was already coming to the boil for the third time. 'If you say so. We can talk about this James in a minute.' She poured the coffee into three small cups with a steady hand and carried them over on a small bronze tray.

Nadia reached forward to touch the tray, stroking the cold metal with the tips of her fingers.

'You recognise it?' said Tazeen.

Nadia nodded.

'It was your grandmother's,' said Tazeen. 'Your grandfather gave it to her on their eighth wedding anniversary. I think she used it every day until she died.'

They were speaking in Lebanese and, although Ed spoke some Arabic, Nadia stopped to translate.

'I know you haven't seen Tazeen in ages,' he whispered, 'but can you ask her whether she knows anything about Unicorn? It's a long shot, but we may not have a lot of time.'

'Auntie?' said Nadia. 'I wanted to ask you about someone. He goes by the name of Ibrahim Abdel-Hak, but he may have been called Mohammed Assam back then. He must have been about the same age as Mama.'

Nadia could tell straight away that her seeds had fallen on fallow ground. Even though Tazeen was clearly in full control of her faculties, she shook her head slowly from side to side, no spark of recognition lighting her eyes.

'What about Fathi Aoun?' said Ed, leaning forward.

The old lady laughed.

'Now that's a name I've not heard for a very long time,' she said. 'If we're talking about the same boy, he was the reason why your mother and I had a falling out. He wasn't Fathi Aoun though. His family went by Oun.'

'You knew him?' said Nadia.

'Of course I knew him. He was always around – like a fly on a bowl of dates. Completely besotted with your mother.'

Nadia flinched as though pricked by a needle. Her mother had known Unicorn? The strong coffee turned acid in her stomach.

'Tell us what happened,' she said, her body tensed rigid as she listened to Tazeen's memories unfold.

'Fathi was a nice enough kid when he was little,' said Tazeen, staring into the distance. 'It wasn't his fault he went wrong. Most of his family were killed when an Israeli shell hit their house. He can't have been more than twelve or thirteen at the time. I felt sorry for the poor boy, but that didn't make him good enough for our Amal.'

'Were they seeing each other?' said Nadia.

'For a while,' said Tazeen. 'Your grandmother could see the rage boiling inside the boy just as I could and she was beside herself with worry. But your grandfather had already had his stroke by then, so it was just us women. Amal was seventeen and in love. Nothing we could say or do meant anything. We were left waiting for the terrible day when he would come to ask for her hand.'

'And did he?' said Nadia.

'No,' said Tazeen. '*Hamdullah*. I introduced Amal to a certain French doctor, and the spell was broken.'

Nadia was struggling to take everything in. Her mother had never mentioned any of this. Not about Tazeen being *her* matchmaker, and certainly nothing about anyone else. And if her mother's teenage boyfriend really had been Unicorn, that would be an impossible coincidence. They would need to find some harder evidence, but somehow Nadia knew it would turn out to be true. The entire revelation had a sick inevitability about it.

She took a moment to make sure Ed was following the conversation, although his expression was enough to show that he'd understood the important parts.

'And what happened to Fathi?' she asked Tazeen.

'Your mother breaking up with him gave him one more reason to be angry,' said Tazeen. 'We were afraid he might do something stupid for a while, but when your mother left to marry your father, Fathi went off to fight in Afghanistan. I think he wanted to die a martyr … and I heard he did.'

Nadia looked at Ed. Another piece of evidence which matched Unicorn's background. There was no need to tell Tazeen that Fathi Oun was actually very much alive and one of the world's most wanted terrorists. Ed leaned over to her.

'We have to call this in straight away,' he said. 'My office might be able to confirm we're talking about the same guy and use this intel to chase down more leads. If the analysts had his surname wrong before, it may have been leading them down some blind alleys.'

'Auntie,' said Nadia. 'We have to speak to some people from work now. Can I come back tomorrow so we can talk more? I can tell you what Leila's up to.'

The old woman smiled.

'That would be nice,' she said. 'Don't worry. I'm not going anywhere.'

They stood up to leave and Nadia leant forward to hug Tazeen goodbye.

'It's his poor brother I feel sorry for,' said Tazeen. 'Stuck alone in that big villa.'

Nadia leapt up and heard Ed's sharp breath from behind her.

'What brother?' she said, feeling the adrenaline coursing through her. 'You said all his family had been killed.'

'I said most of his family had been killed,' said Tazeen. 'You should wash out your ears. Fathi and his younger brother, Omar, survived, although Omar's back was broken. He's been in a wheelchair ever since. Amal used to say that Fathi blamed himself for what happened to his little brother, although I never understood why. It's not as though he dropped the bombs, after all.'

'And he still lives here?' said Ed.

'Yes. Alia Haddad looks after him,' said Tazeen. 'Alia and I see each other from time to time, and she tells me he's become a bitter, lonely man. Spends most of his time behind a computer screen or playing those video games.'

'That's very interesting,' said Ed. 'You've been very helpful. Can you tell us his address?'

'I told you already,' said Tazeen, although Nadia knew she hadn't. 'In that big villa just along from the Saray Nasib Basha. I think he's very rich. Does something with computers.'

'Do you think he'd be prepared to meet with us?' said Nadia.

'How would I know?' snapped Tazeen. 'I've not seen him since he was a teenager.' She stood up and moved toward the door. 'It's been wonderful to see you, Nadia, but I'm tired. Come around the same time tomorrow and we can talk more.'

'Of course, Auntie,' said Nadia, steering Ed outside. 'See you tomorrow.'

'And I'll be asking the questions,' said Tazeen as she closed the door behind them.

The battered blue Peugeot was sitting at the end of the narrow lane. When Ali saw them, he raised a hand in greeting and dropped his cigarette to the ground, crushing it surreptitiously underfoot like a guilty teenager.

'So much for the MI6 research team,' said Nadia, grabbing hold of Ed's arm for balance. She felt as though she'd just stepped off a cross-channel ferry and the small scar next to her left eye was throbbing, sending stabbing jolts of pain into her skull. 'How could they have missed the fact that Unicorn had a brother still alive?'

'I don't know,' said Ed. 'But I intend to find out ... Are you OK?'

'I'm fine,' said Nadia. 'Just got a bit of a headache – and finding out my mother was once Unicorn's girlfriend has come as a bit of a shock to put it mildly.'

'I can see how that might happen,' said Ed, half smiling as he reached into his pocket and took out a plastic strip of tablets. 'Here,' he said. 'Have a couple of paracetamol. Have you got water?'

Nadia nodded and took the pills. As she gulped them down, she wondered if Ed was one of those boy scout guys who always had the necessary to hand: a pack of needles and thread; an emergency toothpick; a tiny knife with nail scissors; a small finger plaster in the side of his wallet.

'So. What do we do now?' she said.

'I guess we pay Omar Oun a visit,' said Ed. 'I'll update the office on the way and we'll see if they can redeem themselves.'

'OK,' said Nadia. 'But we need a reason. I think we'll have to tell him who I really am. Say I'm trying to find out about my mother's family. You can be my husband.'

'How kind,' said Ed, taking her arm and walking towards the car. 'Does that mean I get a kiss?'

Nadia smiled and slapped him gently on the hand. 'Enough messing about,' she said. 'This is a better lead than anything we could have hoped for and we can't afford to be turned away at the door.' She stopped a few meters from the car. 'Seriously, though. We need to be careful. If Omar is involved with his brother, we might be better off calling for back up.'

'I'd be really surprised,' said Ed. 'The researchers at my office haven't exactly covered themselves in glory, but they wouldn't have missed that. I'll run our plan by HQ anyway, though. Just to be sure.'

Ali had somehow sourced two iced coffees, which were miraculously still cold. Ed slipped into the back seat next to Nadia and, for a few minutes, they sat quietly, sipping their coffees. They were medium sugar coffees, *ahwa mazbut* meaning 'perfect coffee' in Arabic, but the course-grained Nescafe granules still managed to overcome the sweetness of the sugar and leave a familiar bitter tang on the roof of Nadia's mouth.

Coffee was the only thing which Leila had bothered to make herself when Nadia was young. Everything else had been bought in from local delicatessens, but Leila had insisted that coffee was never as good as when it was home made. Nadia tended to agree with her aunt, but right at that moment, as the initial shock wore off and the paracetamol kicked in, the coffee in her hand was about as perfect as she could imagine.

The area they were driving through was unfamiliar, less built up and with more green spaces in between and around the apartment blocks. Clearly a more upmarket part of town, although there were still plenty of abandoned plots and broken buildings. Ed was tapping furiously away on his phone – this was an MI6 operation and Nadia had no reason, or authority, to update the MI5 office directly.

They pulled up in front of a set of imposing metal gates and a security guard stepped out of a small cabin set into the high wall. He was dressed in black, full-bearded and had the confident swagger of an ex-soldier.

'Can I help you?' he said, bending forward to look into the car.

'I hope so,' said Nadia. 'We're looking for Omar Oun.'

'And who is looking for Mr Oun?' said the guard.

'My name is Nadia Davis,' said Nadia. 'This is my husband, Ed. My mother was Amal Fawaz. I think she and Mr Oun were friends.'

'Wait,' said the guard and disappeared into his cubicle.

As the minutes ticked away, Nadia could see Ali tapping his fingers on the gearstick. His shoulders were rigid and the nervous energy was filling the car like poison gas.

'What's wrong, Ali,' said Ed. 'You're always Mister Cool.'

'I don't like this,' said Ali. 'He's taking too long … and he's a dangerous man. Trust me.'

Before Ed had a chance to reply, the guard came back out and leant through the open window.

'The two of you can go up to the house,' he said to Nadia. He then turned to Ali and pointed. 'You park the car over there and wait.'

As Ed and Nadia made their way in silence up the long drive, they saw a second guard walking down from the house towards them. He looked even more fierce than the first one and Nadia felt the hairs on her arms rising as her body filled with adrenaline.

There is a moment in most police or spy thrillers when the audience is desperate to shout at the screen. 'Why are you going in there unarmed and without support? You're not supposed to be that stupid. Wait for backup.' Nadia's antenna were telling her this was one of those moments, but the reality was that it was usually impossible to be sure if a situation was dangerous until it was too late. As the approaching guard reached them and turned to lead them towards the house, Nadia couldn't help thinking that it was definitely too late.

The guard opened the ornately carved doors and gestured for them to go inside. The entrance courtyard was spectacular and took Nadia's breath away; she didn't even hear the heavy doors closing behind her. The villa was modern, but once inside they could have been in a sultan's palace from the middle ages. Towering palms, exotic scents and the sound of splashing water had turned the space into a magical oasis. She turned to Ed, who was nodding in appreciation.

'Pretty incredible place,' he said.

'I'm glad you like it,' said a voice from behind Nadia. 'I took many years over it.'

His wheelchair rolled silently towards them over the marble slabs and he held out a hand to Nadia.

'I heard Amal had a daughter,' he said. 'But I never dreamt I would meet her. Welcome, Nadia.'

He looked nothing like Unicorn – a lifetime trapped in a chair hadn't been kind to him – although there was something about the intensity of that gaze.

'Come. We have mint tea,' he said. 'I promise you will never have tasted better.'

They sat at a small round table and sipped their tea from thimble-sized glass cups.

'This is incredible,' said Nadia. 'I've never tasted anything like it.'

'It can't be rushed,' said Omar. 'So many things in today's world have to be rushed. A good mint tea can take an hour to make. Heating, reheating, pouring and pouring back, over and over … The Bedouin knew how it was done, but they are harder and harder to find.'

Nadia nodded and put her empty glass on the low table. 'Can you tell me about my mother,' she said. 'Please.'

'It was a long time ago,' said Omar. 'And I was two years younger than the others, always the hanger on. Amal was the most beautiful girl in Sidon, maybe in Lebanon. I was very sad to hear of her accident. It must have been terrible for you.'

Nadia shrugged. There was nothing to add.

'The four of us were inseparable for a while. Me, my brother Fathi, Amal and Dounia Haddad. Even more so after the Israelis came … All of us had been affected in one way or another.' He waved a hand over his wheelchair. 'Me most of all. So we took solace in each other's company. The Israelis allowed us to go swimming, and we spent our days at the beach. The three of them would help me into the sea and I learnt to swim without using my legs. I could float on my back and almost forget what had happened – for a while.'

'They must have been tough years,' said Ed.

'They were,' said Omar. 'Living at the beck and call of the people who murdered one's family. No-one should have to experience that. But we were kids, and we somehow managed to shut ourselves away from what happened. Until Fathi and Amal fell in love. That ruined everything. They wanted to be alone all the time and you can imagine that Dounia didn't want to spend her days babysitting the crippled little brother. On top of that, she'd always loved Fathi herself.'

'… And then my mother met my father,' said Nadia.

'… And then Amal met your father.' Omar looked straight at Nadia, bulging eyes unblinking. 'I can't describe how angry that made my brother. Fathi was a good boy, a decent boy, but I believe he was very close to killing that thieving Frenchman.'

'What happened?' said Ed, before Nadia had a chance to defend her father.

'I convinced my brother to do nothing. To wait until she came back to him,' said Omar. 'But she never did. And then when the two of them suddenly ran off to France, Fathi blamed me. Things were never the same between us – he left for Afghanistan after just a few weeks.'

‘Mujahideen?’ said Ed

Omar nodded, his bulging eyes unfocused.

‘He sent money home for two or three years, and I got the odd letter or message telling me he was OK. Then, one day, the letters – and the money – stopped coming. Luckily I was able to look after myself by that time. My legs might not work, but my brain does, and I’m very good with computers.’ He swept his arm around the courtyard in an expansive arc. ‘That’s how I have all this.’

‘And you think Fathi died in Afghanistan?’ said Ed.

‘I’m sure of it,’ said Omar. ‘That was why he went.’

# 16

Ibrahim wrapped the woollen scarf around his face in a vain attempt to block the biting wind which was shearing off the ice-bound Oslo fjord. Tempting as it was to stay curled up in his warm apartment, he needed to keep his body and mind strong; he hadn't once allowed himself to miss his daily twenty kilometre walk, whatever the weather.

Ibrahim couldn't remember the last time he'd spend an entire month in one place and had to admit he was sad to move on. He often took his walks around the coastline of the Fornebu peninsula, where the old airport used to be. It was now filled with luxury offices and apartment blocks but, unlike those fool Saudis, the Norwegians were spending their oil money well. Every building or road that was built was balanced by huge areas of gently landscaped park land – places to breathe freely and live a good life. Fornebu was also the last place anyone would expect to find someone like him.

He was alone apart from a few young mothers pushing prams, which gave him peace and solitude to think. Winter's horizon-hugging sunlight made diamonds of the hoar frost which coated every twig and branch, and even the ground shimmered under his feet. The place was beautiful and blessed by God – if only it hadn't been so relentlessly cold.

Rare to see any dark skin or a headscarf in areas such as this, though. Just as in every city of the world, refugees and immigrants were corralled into their own ghettos where they could keep themselves to themselves and not interfere with the privileged lives of the indigenous population.

Ibrahim smiled as he turned back towards Lysaker train station. 'Give them time,' he mouthed the words silently, watching the icy vapour spelling out the letters in the freezing air. 'Give them time.'

There were still ghettos in New York, but the lines between them were becoming less and less obvious every year. The slow crusade continued to inch forwards and, although he regretted the fact that he and Omar would set that progress back a few years, it would recover soon enough.

He might have been happier to leave Oslo if he'd been going somewhere hot and sandy to escape from this unnatural cold, but the forecasts said New York was going to be just as wintry. Just as cold, and scarred by dirty heaps of frozen and refrozen grey slush – quite unlike the ethereal beauty of Oslo in winter.

It was almost time to call Frank. Thinking back to their previous conversation reminded him that he needed to be even more careful than usual in New York. Who would have thought that they could pull DNA from inside the barrel of a Yale lock? What with that, the growing number of video cameras and face recognition technology, the spotty adolescents of the NSA were winning the war.

He was still angry that he'd allowed the FBI to trace his call to Liu Janlin. That was his error, and there was too much at stake to make any more last-minute mistakes. He'd tried to call the Chinaman again to warn him to say nothing, but he really had disappeared into thin air. The last time he'd called, the woman on reception had transferred him to security and Ibrahim had hung up. Definitely something fishy going on – although, if he couldn't find Liu Janlin, maybe the Americans wouldn't either.

In any case, the 5G chips were safe and sound with Omar and they'd been hand delivered so there would be no trace. The spies would be desperately trying to figure out what he wanted them for, but Ibrahim doubted they'd work it out in time. Let them waste their days guessing.

Before making the call to Frank, he had one more thing to do. A necessary act which filled him with dread. After ten minutes pacing up and down outside, he walked into the building on Bygdøy Allé and sat in the offered chair. Then he pointed at his beard, swallowed twice and told the barber what to do.

He hadn't shaved since the day he'd first left Sidon, a lifetime before. He'd promised himself he would wait until Amal was his. But then there had been five long years of fighting in Afghanistan's Panjshir valley. By the time he'd got back home, Amal and her Frenchman were long gone. Fathi Oun had been too late, he'd become Ibrahim Abdel Hak, and the beard had remained untouched.

'Hi Ibrahim. How's it going?'

'I'm well. Thank you, Frank.' Ibrahim had learnt that the quickest way to move forward was to indulge Frank in his social niceties. 'What do you have for me?'

'The first thing is hot off the press,' said Frank. 'The Brits have sent a couple of agents to Sidon in the Lebanon. You said you'd want to know if anyone started sniffing around.'

'I did indeed,' said Ibrahim. 'Who are these agents? Do you have names?'

'Yes,' said Frank. 'They're both senior field officers. Quite young. Ed Bailey from MI6 and Nadia Laroche from MI5.'

Alarm bells rang in Ibrahim's head. Why did he know that name?

'This Nadia Laroche,' he said. 'Is she from the Lebanon?'

'I don't know,' said Frank. 'That's all I have.'

'Thank you,' said Ibrahim. 'I will find out. Now, tell me what else they've found in their search for me?'

'OK,' said Frank. 'The second phone number they traced turned out to be the number of a senior executive at Shan-ding in London. A guy called Liu Janlin … but I guess you knew that?'

Ibrahim said nothing. Frank would generally take the hint after five or six seconds.

'Anyway,' said Frank. 'Liu Janlin has disappeared. No-one in Homeland can find any trace of him – not in London and not in China. But I guess you knew that too?'

So the Americans assumed that he had dealt with the Chinaman. That wasn't such a bad thing.

'Anything else?' Ibrahim said.

'They've found a link between the missing guy and some prototype 5G chips which were stolen around the same time. They believe he gave the chips to you, but no-one can figure out why you might want them. Cyber-terrorism isn't exactly your thing, is it?'

Ibrahim was tempted to try to take Frank down another false trail, but there was no certainty that the call wasn't being recorded. He could fool Frank easily enough, but no-one could be sure of fooling modern voice analysis software.

'OK,' Ibrahim said. 'There's one more thing I need to know …'

He heard the insistent ringing of his new cellphone from across the room. Who could be calling him? He'd only had the phone for a couple of days and only one person knew the number.

'Hold on, Frank,' he said. 'Stay on the line. I'll just be a minute.'

It was Omar.

'We need to talk,' said Omar, panic in his voice. 'Now.'

'*Omar. Calme-toi,*' Ibrahim said. 'Just hold on for a minute. I'm on another call.'

He walked over to the bed and picked up his laptop.

'Frank,' he said.

'Yes. I'm still here.'

'We're going to need to do this another time,' said Ibrahim, and hung up.

'I'm back,' he said, picking up the cellphone. 'What's the panic?'

'You'll never guess who's just been to see me?' said Omar.

'Two British agents, Ed Bailey and Nadia Laroche,' said Ibrahim, secretly pleased to be one step ahead of his genius little brother.

'Why didn't you warn me?' Omar was almost screaming. 'She said they were married and gave me a different name. I thought they were dodgy, but spies? You told me they'd never trace you back to me.'

'I would have warned you, but I only found out two minutes ago,' said Ibrahim. 'And I don't know how they could have linked the two of us. I'm sorry, brother.'

Ibrahim couldn't remember the last time he'd apologised to anyone apart from Omar. He carried his sibling responsibilities as a heavy weight and he would never forgive himself for what happened on the day the Israeli bombs fell.

'That's all right,' said Omar, already much calmer. 'I know you do your best.'

'Will these two spies be a problem?'

'I don't think so,' said Omar. 'They were asking after you, but I told them you were dead.'

'And they believed you?'

'Yes,' said Omar. 'Not that you were dead, but that I believed you were.'

'Well done, little brother,' said Ibrahim. 'Not easy to handle a surprise visit like that.'

'That's not the surprise.'

'No?' Ibrahim saw the nervousness in Omar's eyes and shivered. 'And what is?'

'Nadia Laroche is Amal Fawaz's daughter,' said Omar. 'If I hadn't been strapped into my wheelchair, I swear I'd have fallen out when I found out.'

The pieces of the jigsaw fell into place in Ibrahim's head. That was why the name was familiar. Of course … How many nights had he fallen asleep, curled up on stony ground, cursing the name 'Laroche'? And Amal's grandmother had also been called Nadia. He should have joined the dots at the moment he heard that name.

He wasn't shaken by the co-incidence – after all, everything was ordained and what appeared to be impossibly unlikely was nothing more than *Quadar*, a part of the great plan. Even so, the idea of Amal's daughter walking the streets of Sidon was enough to fill his mind with bittersweet memories. What might have been. Who he might have been.

'I have to think about this,' said Ibrahim. 'Will they be back?'

'I don't know,' said Omar. 'I asked Mohammed to have them followed.'

'Good. Who is he using?'

'He said he'd asked the El Khoury brothers.'

'Not so good,' said Ibrahim. 'They can't be trusted. Tell him to find someone else.'

'OK,' said Omar. 'I'll make sure he does that first thing tomorrow.'

'I must go,' said Ibrahim. 'You've done well. Let me know if anything changes, otherwise I'll call you when I arrive in New York.'

# 17

The guard opened the metal gates and shouted to Ali, who jumped out of the car and rushed round to open the door for Nadia, a big smile splitting his face.

'I am very pleased to see you both,' he said, once they were in the car. 'You were gone a long time and I was worried.'

'We were fine,' said Nadia. She turned and looked back at the two guards who were standing in front of the gate. 'Is it normal for a private house to be so well protected? I remember the big houses often used to have an old gatekeeper who slept by the entrance, but those guys are carrying automatic weapons and they look like they know how to use them.'

'Unfortunately, it is necessary these days,' said Ali. 'Times have changed and people no longer have respect. Our policemen are either too afraid, or no good and, even with the new wall, the Palestinians from Ain al-Hilweh are causing more and more trouble.'

Nadia thought about pointing out that, having been stuck in a refugee camp and treated as second-class citizens for almost three generations, it wasn't such a surprise that they were creating problems. But she took a deep breath and kept her opinions to herself – her upcoming thirtieth birthday was a major life milestone and she'd made several resolutions, one of which was to think before she spoke.

That had never been an issue with confidential intel and both Ed and Nadia knew better than to compare notes about their meeting with Omar until they couldn't be overheard, even by Ali. They sat in silence and, as the car drove away, Nadia could sense the gaze of the bearded guard following them down the street as though his eyes were painting crosshairs on her back. It was only after they'd turned the corner that she allowed herself to breathe again.

Was Omar telling the truth? Could he really not know that his supposedly dead brother Fathi was now Ibrahim Abdel Hak – The Unicorn – alive and well and spreading terror across the globe? Nadia had always found it easy to smell a lie and if Omar was playing them for fools, he was a master.

Ali dropped them off at the Saida Rest House restaurant opposite their hotel – one of the few places in Sidon which served beer and wine.

'I will come back for you at three o'clock,' he said. 'We can visit the new park … And don't forget we are busy at six o'clock.'

Ed and Nadia watched him drive away before walking towards the restaurant entrance.

'What's happening at six o'clock?' she said.

'Sorry. I forgot to tell you,' said Ed. 'I've arranged to meet Ali for a drink. Just the two of us. I need to talk to him … godfather business and some other stuff.'

'OK,' said Nadia, noticing how Ed was mumbling and avoiding her gaze. He was hiding something.

'We'll only be an hour or so,' said Ed. 'You'll be all right?'

'Of course,' said Nadia. 'You guys need a chance to catch up.'

The restaurant entrance led out onto a wide terrace. The views of the sea and the castle were postcard perfect, the midday sun was warming, and they were sheltered from the breeze. Two other couples were sitting at the far end of the terrace, but that was it. They ordered a beer each and sat back to enjoy the moment. Nadia glanced at Ed once or twice, but the shifty look of a few minutes earlier was gone completely.

'Do we have time to sit around enjoying lunch and a visit to the park?' said Nadia. 'Shouldn't we be trying to find out more about Unicorn?'

'We should wait until my office gets back to us,' said Ed. 'I don't want to end up flailing around aimlessly before we know more … and we might accidentally do something which lets Unicorn know we've found his brother. And, besides, we need to eat something.'

'OK,' said Nadia. 'We definitely don't want to scare either of them.' She watched a small fishing boat puttering out into the harbour. 'Ali was actually worried about us back there, wasn't he?'

'Yup,' said Ed. 'I'm surprised. He was always the level-headed one, even when things were difficult – something definitely spooked him at the villa.' He took a sip of his beer. 'Did you notice the jacket the second guard was wearing?'

Nadia shook her head.

'Spetznaz,' he said. 'Russian special forces. The Mujahideen would wear them as a badge of pride, like a trophy or a scalp. That guy must have been in the thick of it back in the day.'

'Unicorn using his top guys to look out for his little brother?'

'Maybe. I still can't figure out whether Omar was lying or not.'

'Me neither,' said Nadia. 'And, once again, how could your people not have known that Unicorn had a brother? Still alive and living in his home town, for Christ's sake.'

'I don't know,' said Ed. 'But we only figured out where Unicorn came from last year and we had the surname wrong.'

'Even so,' said Nadia. 'Someone seems to have dropped the ball big time. The surnames are very similar.'

Ed shrugged and Nadia realised it probably wasn't constructive to blame him personally for the failings of MI6, or the CIA for that matter.

'Sorry,' she said. 'I didn't mean to give you a hard time. I'm grateful you managed to get me involved in this trip. I'm good at my job and this ...' she waved her arm expansively across the horizon. '... This is what I am supposed to be doing.'

Ed smiled. 'No worries,' he said. 'I couldn't have hoped for a better partner.'

They sat in silence for a few moments, embarrassed by gratitude and compliments in that uniquely British fashion. Nadia felt a twinge of guilt because she hadn't thought about James all day. Her mind was racing, fully immersed in the thrill of the chase and trying to make some sense of the few pieces of intel they had to work with. She knew they were on the right track, though.

Ed was scrolling through messages on his phone.

'So. What news?' she said. 'Is Omar for real? Where does his money actually come from?'

'The analysts have been working on that since we left Tazeen's house and it seems he's legit. Omar has his own software development company, mostly working as a high end security consultant. Our guys pulled the accounts and he's definitely minted. That part of the story checks out.'

'And there's no way of finding out if he's been in touch with his brother?'

'For the time being, no. They're still digging, though. And my boss must be talking to the Americans by now. We should know more later today.'

At that moment, the food arrived and Nadia realised how hungry she was. They'd ordered a starter selection, half a dozen hot and cold *mezzes* and, as the small plates were laid out one-by-one, Nadia was transported back in time. There were hundreds of Lebanese restaurants in London, but the food was always missing something – the tomatoes and herbs in the *tabbouleh* were flavourless, the *labneh* wasn't fresh or the aubergines weren't smoky enough. The Saida Rest House was very different – a reminder of how to do things properly.

'You should see your face,' said Ed.

'Smell that,' she replied, pointing at the dishes in front of them. 'That's proper Lebanese cooking.'

Ed leant forward and breathed in. 'Point taken,' he said. 'I've not seen food like this in ages. Reminds me of Karachi. The restaurant round the corner from my house was Lebanese and I went there most days.'

He picked up a piece of bread, tore it in half and scooped up some *tahine*. 'Come on, Nadia,' he said. 'No point standing on ceremony.'

Nadia felt her shoulders sag as she reached over to the bread basket. The morning had been hyper-stressful and full of shocks which were only just beginning to sink in. It was going to take time to wrap her mind around the way her personal and work lives had become intertwined, but life would be pointless if she forgot how to enjoy a cold beer and great food on a seaside terrace … and the company wasn't too bad either.

'Do you want to talk about it?' said Ed, once they'd both had a chance to fill their empty stomachs.

'About my mother and the Unicorn?' said Nadia. 'Not really … I'm not sure what there is to say. On the one hand, it's an impossible co-incidence, on the other I feel as though I've always known there was some sort of connection between us. Even from the moment we met and you put his photo up on the screen.'

'That sounds a bit far-fetched.'

'Of course it is – and you know I don't actually believe in any of that bullshit,' snapped Nadia, annoyed that Ed had taken her so literally. 'Look. It doesn't matter anyway. All that matters is that we find him in time and stop him.'

'Of course,' said Ed. 'And we'll get on with doing that as soon as we hear back from my boss. In the meantime we wait. You've been doing this much longer than me. Aren't you used to waiting by now?'

'You never get used to it,' said Nadia.

'That makes me feel much better,' said Ed. 'Great motivational speaking.' He checked his phone before leaning towards Nadia. 'Tell me more about your parents. You said they died when you were young. What happened?'

Nadia had just taken a huge mouthful of bread and hummus and could only manage a grunt in response.

'Of course. If you don't want to talk about it, I understand,' he said, mumbling and avoiding her eyes.

Nadia guessed Ed was in his early thirties, but there were times when he still had something childish about him, shifting seamlessly from a complex, confident and professional man to awkward and self-conscious boy.

She gulped down the food and wiped her lips with a napkin.

'No. It's fine,' she said. 'I've not told many people, but I'm OK telling you seeing as you know the basics anyway. Although I guess there's not so much to tell.'

Ed took his beer glass and leant back in the chair.

'Well, you already know how they first met from Auntie Taz,' said Nadia. 'Most of that stuff was actually news to me as well … Anyway, they died when I was ten and my memories of them are a bit confused. I don't know what's a real memory, what I've invented from photos and what comes from the stories Leila told me.' She looked up at Ed to see if he understood what she meant. 'As I remember it, my mother was beautiful and kind, a little conservative perhaps, but she had a mischievous side to her … along with the most infectious giggling laugh you've ever heard. She was the best person I've ever met – I can't believe that Unicorn could have been her first love. It seems so wrong.'

'What about your father?'

'I know I sound like I'm idolising them both, but my father was my hero – dashing and brave, full of energy and intelligence, always joking and teasing me. I'm sure they must have been very much in love. I just wish I'd been able to see them with older eyes. Ten-year-olds don't tend to notice much that doesn't involve them directly.'

'And then they died?'

'Yes,' said Nadia. 'We were on summer holiday in Brittany when the accident happened – our car went off the road and rolled down some rocks to the edge of the sea.'

'You were in the car?'

Nadia nodded, suddenly surprised by how quickly the memories and emotions came flooding back.

'That must have been terrifying,' said Ed. 'And you weren't badly injured?'

'No,' said Nadia. 'None of us were – but the tide was coming in, the car was upside down and both my parents were trapped in the front seats. I managed to climb out the window to go for help …'

Nadia felt the familiar nagging reminder that she'd been too slow, too late and her mind filled with the sound of a ten-year-old girl screaming as she watched the men with the tow truck trying to pull the half-submerged car from the waves. She turned away and looked over the harbour towards the castle.

'Sorry, Ed. Can we talk about something else,' she said after a few seconds. 'I thought this would be easier.'

'Of course,' he said. 'I understand completely … in that case, let me tell you about the Maqab – your famous rubbish dump. I did some research while we were stuck in traffic.'

Nadia could tell she was about to get a geeky lecture, but was grateful for Ed's sensitivity, the way he'd instantly tugged her away from the dark hole she'd been tipping into.

'That would be great,' she said. 'I'm very pleased you know more about my ancestral home than I do.'

Ed smiled. 'That's just the beginning,' he said. 'Before we left the UK, I also read up on the castle and its role in the Crusades. People never bother to learn about their home towns. That's what tourists are for.'

He then pulled his sunglasses down to the end of his nose and peered over them before launching into a detailed history of the Maqab, from its origins as a dumping ground for all the rubble left in the wake of the Israeli invasion, to its growth into the polluting monster Nadia remembered from her childhood visits, all the way through to the inspirational project which had led to its current transformation into a public park. The facts were astounding – at its height, the mountain of rubbish had been higher than a four-storey building, it had covered an area the size of Hyde Park and had contained six hundred thousand cubic metres of rotting garbage and medical waste.

Not only had Ed read the blurb, he'd memorised all the facts and made it entertaining despite the subject matter.

Nadia was also happy to stop thinking about Unicorn for a short while.

Ed's mini-lecture probably lasted less than five minutes but, by the time he'd finished, Nadia felt refreshed and ready to get back to work. The story of the rubbish dump could be seen as the story of her mother's Lebanon and the fact that it was ending on a positive note reminded her once more that, in the midst of misery and gloom, there was always hope. There would always be destroyers like Unicorn and there would also always be people like Hamzi Moghrabi, the engineer who pioneered the Makab restoration. The destroyers didn't always win.

She saw Ali standing discretely outside the entrance and beckoned him in.

'Come on, Mr Tour Guide,' she said to Ed. 'Let's go and visit this park of yours. If the guys in your office manage to redeem themselves and find us some useful new intel sooner, we can get on it straight away.'

'Sounds like a plan,' said Ed, pulling his wallet from his pocket. 'Let me just settle up …'

'The bill is paid,' said Ali. 'We can go now if you're ready.'

As they got up and walked out to the car, Ed leant towards Nadia and whispered. 'That's the Ali I remember,' he said. 'Always one step ahead, calm and in control. I don't know what came over him earlier.'

It was mid-afternoon, and the streets were deserted. Nothing moved except for the odd lonely dog as the Peugeot zig-zagged through dusty back streets between crumbling walls of bullet-scarred concrete. Even the graffiti looked tired and old.

'Looks like we're taking the scenic route,' said Ed, turning back to Nadia who had been relegated to her lonely back seat again.

'It's much quicker,' said Ali, shouting over the car noise. 'No traffic lights.'

He drove well and managed to avoid most of the worst potholes, although there were places where the tarmac was no longer even a memory and the ridged washboard surface rattled Nadia's teeth and left her waiting for one of the wheels to fall off, or worse.

'That was the worst part,' said Ali, as they turned off the broken surface into a narrow concrete lane. 'It's much better from here.'

Nadia settled back in her seat with a sigh. The constant vibration had left her anxious, and she was worried about the newly mended bone in her left temple.

But, after a few scant seconds of relaxation, they stopped sharply, crabbing sideways on the sandy surface and throwing Nadia forward into the back of the driver's seat.

'What the hell,' she shouted. 'That nearly broke my nose.'

'Shit,' said Ed. 'This is not good.'

The car suddenly lurched backwards and Ali's face appeared from between the seats, twisting round and staring wide-eyed out of the rear window as he reversed back down the lane, engine screaming and pot holes ignored.

'What's happening?' shouted Nadia, leaning to the side so Ali could see where he was going.

'Some sort of militia in a pickup,' said Ed. 'They don't look friendly.'

'Are they following?' she said.

'Of course they're following,' snapped Ed. 'They weren't there by accident.'

Nadia could almost taste the adrenaline as it surged through her, heightening her senses. She looked over her shoulder. They were almost at the end of the lane. Once they were out, they'd have a good chance of getting away.

She stretched up and peered over Ali's left shoulder. The truck following them was very close, two men in the cab and one standing in the back, all of them wearing balaclavas. She couldn't see any weapons, but they would be there.

Guns or not, real-life car chases weren't like those in the movies. It was very hard to hit anything when firing from a bouncing vehicle. In training, even Nadia had only managed two hits from ten in a simulated kidnapping. And, if they could get to the road, the Peugeot would be faster.

She turned back. Almost there … just another twenty metres … and then the bonnet of a second pickup swung into view, blocking the exit. Ali hit the brakes, and they skidded, fishtailing back and forth until they bounced off the wall and stopped in a huge cloud of dust less than a metre from the second vehicle.

For a moment, there was silence, those seconds after an accident when everyone involved stays frozen in place, checking for injuries and trying to process what just happened.

Nadia glanced up and saw the three men with balaclavas were now standing in front of the car, two holding AK-47s and the third pointing a pistol at the windscreen.

'Let me speak to them,' said Ali. 'Make sure they can see your hands. Don't worry. It will be OK.'

Ali pushed open the car door, taking care to keep his movements slow and his arms raised.

'Hello, my friends,' he said, his accent slipping seamlessly into the local dialect. 'What can we do for you?'

The man with the pistol was in front of the others; he looked over-excited and jittery, pacing from one foot to the other and waving his gun from side to side like a conductor's baton.

'Who are these people?' he said, speaking in a guttural accent which Nadia didn't recognise. 'Where are you taking them?'

'They are tourists,' said Ali. 'I am taking them to the new park. To show them how we are making Sidon a better place.'

'She is not a tourist,' said the man, staring at Nadia and pointing his pistol for emphasis.

'You are partly right, friend,' said Ali. 'Her mother came from Sidon, but she lives in London and hasn't been here since she was a child. She is on holiday with her husband.'

The man spat on the ground and laughed as he looked back at his friends.

'Liar,' he said. 'I know who she is, and I know she is not here on holiday.'

Ali took a step forwards, hands open in supplication.

'Look, my friend,' he said, almost whispering. 'I'm sure we can find a way to come to an arrangement … something beneficial …'

The man's eyes opened even wider, and he spat again, right between Ali's feet.

'I … am … not … your … friend,' he said. '… And I don't want your filthy American dollars.'

And then he lifted his pistol with a steady hand and shot Ali in the face.

# 18

The moments after Ali's shooting were a blur of noise and confusion. From the reaction of the other attackers, no-one had expected it and the three of them stood over the body shouting and gesticulating. Ed was locked in place for several seconds and then Nadia saw him reaching for the door handle.

'Ed. No,' she said firmly, reaching forward to grab his shoulder. 'Don't be stupid. Let me handle this.'

He pulled away from her, pushed open the door and leaped out of the car, barging Ali's murderer aside before crouching low over his friend's prone body. She froze as she watched him frantically checking for a pulse before dropping his head forwards in apparent despair. Their attackers were still shouting and screaming at each other, more out of control every second.

And then the gunman was up again, pistol pointed at Ed's back. Nadia started to open her own door. She couldn't just sit there and watch him be executed.

Before she could get out of the car, there was a barked command from behind them and all three of the attackers froze in place. Nadia turned and watched as a fourth man – presumably the driver of the second truck – strode past, walked up to Ali's killer and backhanded him across the face. He didn't bother to wait for a reaction before moving over to Ed who was still crouched low, glaring up at him like a crazed animal.

The man grabbed one of the AK-47s and, as Ed jumped to his feet, sidestepped and rammed the butt into the side of Ed's head, knocking him to the ground where he lay in a crumpled heap.

Nadia leapt out of the car, but, before she could get there, she felt strong hands grabbing her from behind and she was slammed against the car bonnet, all the air driven from her lungs. She gasped and choked, struggling to find her breath and then, before she had time to recover, a hood was pulled over her head and her wrists and ankles were pulled together. She tried to break free until she felt the blood running down her wrists, but it was a waste of time – they must have used plastic cable ties.

She stopped struggling and forced her breathing back under control – at least she was alive and Ed might still be all right. Like a swimmer caught in the vicious pull of a rip tide, she knew that struggling further would be a futile waste of precious energy. Better to gather her thoughts, let the current take her and wait for a better opportunity to escape.

In spite of the fact that they'd just murdered someone in broad daylight, her attackers didn't seem worried about any imminent arrival of the authorities and Nadia was left slumped on the sandy concrete while the men shouted at each other for at least twenty minutes. From inside the heavy hood, it was difficult to hear what was being said, but she understood enough to know that shooting Ali had not been part of the plan.

Eventually, the talking stopped, and she felt herself being lifted up and thrown into the back of the pickup truck like a sack of potatoes. The men were laughing as they drove off and Nadia had no idea whether they were leaving behind one dead body or two.

'Do not turn around.' The man's voice came from behind her left ear. He sounded educated, in control, but definitely not happy about something.

Nadia tensed as she felt rough fingers at her throat and the coarse material of the hood scraping her cheeks as it was yanked from her head. A hand reached around and fed her water from a small plastic bottle. She finished every drop; it tasted so good that she almost said 'thank you'.

'Do not speak. Do not turn around,' the man repeated. Then a door slammed behind her and she was alone again, tied to a chair in a room without windows.

Alone except for a pair of halogen lights, a video camera and a blank TV screen. The red light on the front of the camera glared at her and the black iris of the camera lens was a chilling reminder of Ed's colleague who'd been captured by the Taliban.

Her mind was racing as she blinked in the bright lights and tried to focus. If they knew she was British Intelligence, they surely wouldn't kill her? None of the terrorist groups operating out of Lebanon would dare risk bringing down that level of international retribution. They were all making money and stockpiling weapons – as a result of a macabre state of equilibrium between the various factions, aid agencies and global governments. She'd read an up-to-date briefing on the plane and the situation seemed clear; no-one had an interest in rocking the boat.

Unless these guys were unknown rogue players …? That would change everything.

Nadia dug her nails into her palms and squeezed her knees tightly together. No point in allowing her mind to take her down those dark alleyways. She was well trained and well briefed, her status protected her, she would be all right.

But the camera lens kept on staring at her.

Was Ed safe? That guy had hit him hard and, as far as she knew, they'd left him there, crumpled over Ali's body. Luckily it was only December and the sun had no real bite – in the summer he'd have been in trouble within hours. Then Ali's beaming face flashed in front of her eyes; he was dead – there was no question of that. Nothing could prevent his newborn son being orphaned and his young wife a widow.

She'd lost track of time, but several hours must have passed. MI6 would surely be looking for her soon. Whether or not Ed had made it back to the hotel, there was a call-back protocol in place for overseas missions. If neither of them made contact, alarm bells would start ringing and Special Forces would probably be scrambled out of Akrotiri in Cyprus. She moved her right arm back and forth as much as the bindings allowed. No pain, so the tracking device under her right armpit hadn't been found and removed. Even if her kidnappers had found the secondary transponder in her phone, she would still be easy to find.

Thinking about rescue was the only way to hold back the terror which was beginning to rise in her belly, scratching and screaming like a banshee. She could feel the sweat beading on her forehead as she fought to push the fear back down – no amount of experience or training was enough to completely suppress such primal emotions.

Why was nothing happening? All she needed was a chance to speak to someone, to explain that they were making a huge mistake, that they'd already made a huge mistake, and that every second which ticked away was making their predicament worse.

Then, as she wondered if she could take any more waiting

without screaming out loud, the screen in front of her flickered into life, bars of white dots drifting upwards like an upside-down snowfall until …

… the snowflakes began to clear, and a face materialised, pixel-by-pixel.

It was him – Ibrahim – the Unicorn. His hair was shorter and the beard was gone, but those green eyes were burned into her mind from the first time she'd seen a picture of him. Nadia jerked forwards, straining against her bonds as a complex cocktail of icy terror and white-hot anger surged through her.

'Hello Nadia,' he said. 'Are you all right?'

She spat on the floor and sat upright, looking at the face on the screen with disbelief. 'I've felt better,' she said. 'How do you know my name?'

'I make it my business to know what is going on in Sidon,' he said. 'I still have many friends there …'

'… And a brother,' said Nadia.

'… And a brother,' said Ibrahim. 'Although he thinks me dead for many years … It is better that way.'

Nadia couldn't tell if he was lying. 'What of my colleague?' she asked. 'Do you know if he's alive?'

'Yes,' said Ibrahim. 'He will have a headache, but no more. I believe he is back at his hotel – organising a rescue for you, I would imagine. Your driver, unfortunately, is dead. The group that took you are known for their volatility – their drug taking. You were unlucky.'

Nadia had known Ali must be dead. She could still picture him walking towards their assailants, hands held open by his sides. Such bravery … and then that crazy idiot had shot him in the face at point blank range. For no reason. It was all wrong. Everything was wrong.

'And why take me?' said Nadia, trying to appear calm and confident, but desperate to know if her life was now dependent on the narcotic-fuelled whims of a group of unstable young zealots.

'Your captors are fools.' Ibrahim dismissed Ali's murderers with a wave of his hand. 'They think they will help their cause by beheading a traitor – a daughter of Lebanon who works for the British intelligence services. They want to make an example of you, to plaster videos of your beheading around the world. To remind people that generation after generation of Palestinians continue to suffer. The world has forgotten about the refugee camps and they want to change that. Unfortunately they don't understand they're wasting their time, nor do they know what the consequences would be.'

'So. They intend to kill me?' Nadia felt the floor shifting. Was her life really going to end in this room, brutally murdered for no reason?

'Their intentions are not important,' said Ibrahim. 'They will do whatever I say. Tell me, Nadia Laroche. Why should I tell them to let you go? Will you continue to betray your country and your faith?'

Nadia felt a pulse of anger flush into her cheeks.

'My mother's country and my mother's faith,' she said. 'Not mine. And if you're asking if I will carry on doing my job, the answer is "yes". I will do everything I can to find you and stop you.'

'Spoken like Amal's daughter,' said Ibrahim, nodding his head.

Nadia stared at him, feeling the anger growing.

'How dare you pretend to know who my mother was?' she said, spitting out the words. 'She would have detested everything you have become … and everything you stand for.'

Ibrahim smiled. 'I have no doubt of that,' he said. 'Amal was a sweet, gentle girl and it was clear even back then that she would become strong as well as kind … My life would have been very different if she had stayed true to me … I would have been very different.' His smile disappeared as though never there. 'But Amal made her choice and, as a result, I have become who I am. It is *Qadar* and not for mortals to question.'

Nadia bit her lip. The bastard dared to suggest that her mother was responsible for who he'd become and the horrific things he'd done, but there was nothing to gain by just venting her fury. She needed to concentrate on getting released or, at the very least, buying enough time for a rescue team to reach her. Maybe he had a point about Qadar, though. The string of extraordinary coincidences which had led her to this exact place and time felt to difficult to explain without the involvement of some machiavellian deity playing puppet master.

She took a deep breath.

'I was there, you know.' she said.

'Where?'

'At the Museum. I'd been investigating Hassan Qureishi for six months. I watched him decide not to go through with it …and then you detonated the bomb, anyway.'

'Ah,' said Ibrahim. 'That boy turned out to be even weaker than I'd expected.'

'Who? Hassan?' said Nadia. 'He wasn't weak. Quite the opposite. His conscience prevailed, and he stood against you at the end.'

'In times of war, a conscience creates indecision,' Ibrahim said. 'And indecision costs lives.'

'This isn't a war.'

'And there we must again disagree, Nadia.'

Nadia looked at that hard arrogant face and realised he was toying with her as a cat might a mouse. He didn't care about anyone unless they could be useful to him. When he had finished tormenting her, the others would come and finish what they'd started. Nothing she could do or say would change that.

'Is that why you're here?' said Ibrahim. 'You and that young man from MI6. You think you'll learn something about me in Sidon? You think you'll find out how to find me and stop me?'

'Yes. And we will,' said Nadia, spitting out the words. The longer she kept him talking, the more chances he would let something slip. He was already behaving out of character by showing his face. Maybe he would make another mistake? She shivered as she looked at the cruel face in front of her. Unicorn's mistakes wouldn't matter if she was destined to die in that chair.

'I'm afraid you're looking in the wrong place,' said Ibrahim. 'And you're running out of time.'

'We'll have to see about that,' said Nadia, struggling to control the tremor in her voice. She leant forward. '...Will you tell them to kill me?'

'Kill Amal's only child?' said Ibrahim. 'No. I will not do that. When we have finished our conversation, you will be released. These people will not dare to cross me ... and the man who killed your driver will be punished.'

'That won't help his widow,' said Nadia. 'Or his son.'

'They will receive compensation,' said Ibrahim. 'Lebanon is a dangerous country. This is the way.'

Gving Nadia no chance to respond, Ibrahim continued talking. He clearly saw himself as in control of the discussion and Nadia – tied to a chair and facing a TV screen – wasn't in a great position to challenge that assumption. In any case, she was too busy trying to decide whether to believe him. Was there still a chance she might make it out alive?

'I never believed I would have the pleasure of meeting Amal's daughter,' he said. 'But, before we talk, I need you to ask MI6 to put on hold any rescue missions. For the sake of a few minutes, it would be better if no-one else was hurt.'

'I don't know if I can do that. Or if I should.'

She could feel the intensity of Ibrahim's gaze as he lifted his right hand and held it over his heart.

'I give you my word you will be released. Tell me your partner's telephone number and I will connect you. Tell him that, if you are not back at your hotel in forty-five minutes, he can continue. There is nothing to stop them finalising their preparations during that period, after all.'

Nadia nodded her head. 'All right. I agree.'

She gave him the number. Seconds passed and then she heard Ed's voice. 'Nadia? Are you there?'

'Yes,' she said. 'I'm fine, but this is not a secure call. I repeat, this is not a secure call. Assume your phone is burned.'

'Understood. Now tell me what's going on.'

'I'll tell you later, but for now, hold any extraction plans. If I'm not back in forty-five minutes, come and get me and kill every one of these bastards.'

'Do you want me to call James?'

This was their agreed method to signal if she was speaking under duress.

'Just send him a text, please. I'll call him later.' That meant all was (relatively) fine and he should do as she asked.

'Will do. I can't wait to see you safe, Nadia.'

Ibrahim ended the call and his face reappeared on screen.

'We have just over twenty minutes, Nadia. What would you like to talk about?' He bowed his head and closed his eyes for a few seconds. 'I am sorry. Before you start, I must offer my sincere condolences for the loss of your mother. Whatever the choices she made, she was always my hope and inspiration and I never stopped loving her.'

'Even though she would have hated you for what you've become?'

'Yes,' said Ibrahim. 'Even so … But what exactly have I become?'

'A thoughtless, indiscriminate murderer, filled with hate and revenge, making life harder for all ordinary, decent Moslems.'

'Thoughtless? Indiscriminate? I would argue with that. I have considered each of my actions for many years … and, at the end of the day, the choice of target is not always mine.'

'So. It's even worse. You're just a puppet?'

'I prefer to think of myself as a soldier, fighting for a cause I believe in. All armies have chains of command. There are many ways to protect the faith – ways of words and of the sword. I have been chosen for the sword.'

'That's just self-delusion,' said Nadia. 'As I see it, you're only interested in revenge. The Israelis killed your family and crippled your brother … then my mother left you and you allowed your anger and bitterness to define who you became.'

'It's not so simple,' said Ibrahim. 'It's true that I will never forgive Israel for what they did, but the war to defend the faith is a greater and never-ending mission. Maybe I would have been chosen for another path if Amal had stayed with me … but she didn't.'

'The Israeli invasion destroyed my family as well,' said Nadia. 'And those of many others. They didn't all become terrorists.'

'As I said,' said Ibrahim. 'Each of us has our path and we must follow the ways that have been chosen for us.'

'More abdication of responsibility,' said Nadia. 'But why are you telling me all this? What's the point?'

Ibrahim stared at her and, for the first time, Nadia saw something human and vulnerable in his eyes.

'I have been fighting this war my whole life,' said Ibrahim. 'Not once, in all that time, have I ever explained myself to anyone. I would have bared my soul to Amal, but that was not to be. Perhaps you are as close as I will ever get?'

'Would you have stopped your war if Amal asked you to?' said Nadia.

'It's possible,' said Ibrahim. 'I don't know.'

'Will you stop if I ask you on her behalf?'

'No.'

'Then what else do we have to say? I'm not interested in your self-justifications and you won't find forgiveness here.'

'Maybe there is nothing more to say,' said Ibrahim. 'Although I am pleased to have met you this once, Nadia, daughter of Amal ... Go with God.'

And the screen went blank.

Nadia didn't know why she believed Ibrahim would keep his word, but she did. Her heart only gave the slightest flutter when she heard the door open behind her and the same man's voice telling her not to turn around.

The hood went on, the ties were cut and strong hands helped her to stand. The feeling of blood rushing back into her hands was a welcome agony, and she managed to shuffle forward as the numbness left her legs. Nadia had always hated being hooded, even in training exercises, but every stumbling step away from that video camera seemed like a step back to life.

The man guided her into the seat of a car and closed the door. He leant through the open window and spoke in a low voice.

'I am taking you back to your hotel,' he said. 'I will not tie your hands, but do not touch the hood or try anything else foolish. Understood?'

'Yes,' said Nadia. She just wanted the nightmare to end.

'… And the Haj Ibrahim has a message for you. He says he hopes your paths never cross again. He releases you today, but you should know that, if ever you stand in his way in the future, he will not hesitate to kill you. Is that understood?'

Nadia nodded and sat still in her seat. The gloves were off. So be it.

They drove away and, less than twenty minutes later, the car stopped. She heard the car door open and the man helped her out onto the road.

'The hotel is very close,' he said. 'Count to twenty – slowly – before you take off the hood.'

# 19

As Nadia walked into the Al Qualaa Boutique Hotel lobby, a part of her was still expecting some kind of macabre, sadistic twist – Ibrahim would be sitting on one of the red sofas, laughing. 'Did you really believe I would let you go ...?'

But there was Ed waiting for her, flanked by two hard-looking men. He immediately ran across the room, wrapping her in a smothering hug which would have made a boa constrictor proud.

'Thank God,' he said. 'I've been going out of my mind.' He pulled back and stared at her with red-rimmed eyes. 'Ali's dead.'

'I know,' said Nadia. 'I'm so sorry, Ed.'

'I have to go and see his wife before we leave,' he said. He looked over his shoulder at the two men. 'But they say it's too dangerous. What am I going to do?'

'I don't know,' she said, suddenly feeling her stomach churning. 'Ed. I need to go to my room ...'

'God. I'm sorry,' he said. 'I'm such a selfish bastard. Go. Go.'

By the time Nadia had reached her room, her breath was already coming in deep rasping gulps. She threw herself onto the bed, bit into the pillow and screamed, every muscle in her body locked tight. Her mind was still in denial, but her body knew that it needed to expel something toxic; a poison or an evil spirit.

She screamed until she was exhausted, hollowed out like a poorly trained marathon runner. Then she twisted into a foetal position and lay curled up on the bed, hands over her head, sobbing gently.

She must have fallen asleep as the next thing she registered was the sound of knocking at the door.

'Miss Laroche,' said a stranger's voice. 'I'm sorry, but we need to go. We have your bags.'

Nadia got up, threw some water on her face and, five minutes later, she was sitting in a dark-windowed SUV separated from Ed by one of the silent, hard-faced men. They drove in convoy to a small airfield north of the city where a helicopter was waiting for them, rotors already turning. An hour later, they were landing at the British military base in Akrotiri, Cyprus.

Nadia tried to speak to Ed during the journey, but the soldier nursemaid had other ideas.

'I'm sorry, ma'am. We have orders that you not communicate prior to debriefing.'

And so she sat, staring forwards, focused only on keeping a lid on the mess of emotions swirling inside her. Memories of the video camera and Ibrahim's face flashed before her eyes and the musty, sandy taste of the hood still lingered at the back of her mouth. Nadia focused on her breathing, remembering one of the yogic mantras she'd been taught. *Soh Hah, Soh Hah* – I am that I am – in out – in out …

She was in Cyprus for a week. The first couple of days were brutal as she was forced to dredge up her memories and report back every detail of what had happened. Again and again, the same questions and each time she remembered something more. The experience was even worse than after Liu Janlin as the debriefing team kept digging away at the relationship between Nadia's mother and the Unicorn. For the first time in her life, Nadia felt her loyalty was being questioned.

The initial questioning was brutal, but surprisingly cathartic and, on the second day, she began to exercise, which seemed to be exactly what was needed. Gently at first and quickly building up to a punishing daily routine of running, weights and cycling. With each stride, bench press or turn of the pedals, she felt her mind washing away the fear and shame of everything she'd been through.

It was her decision – up to her whether to allow these evil people to define her or not. Nadia felt a quiet fury growing within her. How dare Ibrahim talk about loving her mother? He had no right. Anyone who had done what he had done was incapable of love. His feelings were no more than twisted memories and Nadia knew how distraught her mother would have been to hear him speak about her in that way.

She called James every day, loving the sound of his voice and the tenderness behind it. She could hear that he was desperate to have her home and drifted off to sleep each night imagining his strong arms wrapped around her. As far as she'd been told, they'd be flying her back after a few more days and the embrace would no longer be imaginary.

As for Ed, there had been no sign. She didn't know him well enough to predict how well he might be dealing with what happened. Ali's death had understandably hit him hard and, unlike Nadia, he had almost no field experience to fall back on. They should have let her speak to him. It might have helped. But, whenever she asked anyone about him, she found herself talking to a stone wall … and both his phone numbers went to voicemail.

Her office flew out Sheila Pinker, the psychiatrist she'd been seeing, on the fifth day. It was good to see a familiar face and, in place of a consulting room, the two women sat on a small terrace overlooking the Mediterranean, sipping cold beers. Nadia had just finished a fifteen kilometre run and was still dressed in her running gear. Not perhaps an orthodox counselling session, but 'normal' seemed to have no part in Nadia's life any more.

'How have you been?' said Sheila.

'Surprisingly well,' said Nadia. 'At least for the past few days. I seem to have found a way over some sort of hurdle and back to myself. To be honest, I feel better than I have since the museum bombing.'

'That's good to hear,' said Sheila. 'Do you know why?'

'I think so,' said Nadia. 'I think it started with the feelings of helplessness I had after I arrived too late to stop the bombing at the museum. We've talked before about how my parents died …?'

Sheila nodded.

'Well. It may all be part of the same problem. I've never dealt well with not being in control … which is probably why I tend to jump into most situations feet first.' Nadia grimaced as she remembered a few of the myriad occasions when she'd acted first and thought later. 'Anyway. With everything that's happened, the fears and doubts running around in my mind seem to have reached a kind of critical mass and that's triggered a change. Ibrahim talking about my mother made me angry and I've been thinking about what she would have wanted for me. Obsessing about having been too slow to save her from drowning would not have been high on her list.'

'Of course not,' said Sheila. 'No mother would wish that for her child.'

'I've realised I can't be in control of every situation – all I can do is try my hardest to do what I believe is right and accept the rest.

Obviously, it's normal that I'm affected by the things that have happened to me recently, but I've trained for these scenarios and I can handle it … to answer your original question again, I'm OK. Better than I've been for a long time.'

Nadia knew she wasn't only saying these things to please Sheila and get a positive report. She had changed and, although she'd never forget those feelings of helplessness, she was no longer going to allow them to define who she was.

'And the fact that Unicorn was your mother's childhood sweetheart?' said Sheila. 'You really had no idea?'

'Of course not,' said Nadia, sharply. 'How could I have known? I only found out he came from Sidon a few months ago. The whole connection seems impossible and I get angry even thinking about it.' She glared at Sheila. 'The fact that everyone seems to think I'm hiding something really doesn't help.'

'That wasn't what I meant,' said Sheila, glaring back. 'I suppose you were assigned to partner Ed Bailey in the first place because of your connections with Unicorn's home town. That does narrow the odds.'

Nadia nodded. 'But still …'

'But still …' said Sheila. 'You might not like it, but I think you should assume your office won't stop digging into that. No-one likes an impossible co-incidence.'

Nadia nodded again. She'd known that her unasked-for connection with Unicorn wouldn't be easily brushed aside, but there was nothing she could do to change that. After all, she still found it hard to believe herself.

The two women sat there for another hour as the sun sank behind them. Nadia could feel the glow from the beer mixing with the residual endorphins from her run – Sheila probably asked her more questions, and Nadia probably answered, but everything blurred into a general sense of grateful well being which Nadia was more than happy to embrace.

Nadia was due to join the meeting at eleven o'clock, but was told they were running late. She was sent off to one of the smaller sixth floor meeting rooms and sat nursing her third cup of coffee, wondering if Ed would be there. She'd been thinking about him a lot. The way they'd been separated after Lebanon had been painfully abrupt and she needed to see him. He was the only other person who'd been there, after all. They would understand each other.

The executive offices were decorated for Christmas in a tasteful, half-hearted way. Silver and white might be more designer cool than red and gold, but against predominantly grey walls, the effect was less than festive. On the second floor, where Nadia was still working, someone had gone completely overboard, and it was hard to move without becoming tangled in garish tinsel and baubles. There were also two real Christmas trees, one at either end of the office. Much more fun.

She'd been back in the London office for a week and most of that time had been spent preparing for her presentation. She was expected to update the senior teams from MI5 and MI6 on both Shan-ding and Lebanon. Hopefully, they would want her to stay for the follow on discussions. She'd dug up an interesting email thread involving Liu Janlin and discussing missing 5G prototype chips, but not much else.

David had been deliberately vague about next steps; she didn't know if she would be continuing to investigate Unicorn or if this was where she was going to be cut out of the loop again. There was no indication of a UK threat – all the chatter was in the US – so it was clearly an MI6 matter.

It was almost twelve when she heard a knock at the door. David's assistant.

'Sorry for the delay,' she said. 'They're ready for you.'

The room was full. Five people from the office, including David and Phil, and four others who she didn't recognise, bunched together on the other side of the room. Presumably they were from Six. David indicated that she should go to the head of the table where her first slide was already up on the screen. He introduced her, but it quickly became clear that the strangers had no intention of introducing themselves. Ed was nowhere to be seen.

The presentation was twenty minutes long, covering the background to her time at Shan-ding and the trip to Lebanon. It seemed a little pointless as they would all have received the detailed reports and there were only a few elements which might be useful. Nadia had included those on her summary page.

'In conclusion,' she said. 'I believe the following uncertainties are material and deserve further investigation. Firstly, are Unicorn and his brother in touch with each other and, if so, is Omar involved in Unicorn's plans? Secondly, what happened to the missing 5G chips? And finally, was my abduction really just bad luck and does anything Unicorn said to me help us to understand what he is planning?'

'Thank you, Nadia,' said David. 'We'll deal with any questions during the discussions.' He looked at the most senior-looking of the MI6 contingent. 'We have Ed Bailey scheduled next. Is he on his way?'

As if by magic, the door opened and Ed walked in. He smiled at Nadia and half raised a hand in greeting before walking around the table and sitting with his colleagues.

'Sorry I'm late,' he said. 'I was waiting for one more piece of intel from Lebanon.'

'Not a problem,' said David. 'Tell us what you've found out.'

'There's remarkably little,' said Ed. 'Omar is almost too clean. His company's legit, he pays his taxes on time and we can't find anyone or anything to support the theory that he's lying about his brother. None of our guys can even make a dent in his IT security, but that's not so surprising given that's what he does for a living. The only thing that's unusual was in the report I just received … Apparently he had a delivery of three large generators six months ago.'

'What's special about that?' said Phil. 'Presumably there are frequent power cuts in Sidon – he would need independent power as back up for his IT systems if nothing else.'

'And to power any hoists and lifts he needs to manage daily life as a paraplegic,' said Ed. 'Having a generator, or even two isn't the issue. It's the size of them. Each of these units is able to deliver over a hundred kilovolt amps – a normal large house wouldn't need more than ten – and these machines retail at over fifteen thousand pounds each.'

'And no idea why he might need that sort of power?' said the nameless MI6 suit sitting next to Ed. He was skinny with square-rimmed glasses and a nervy, twitchy manner which led Nadia, probably unfairly, to pigeonhole him as a techie of some sort.

'No,' said Ed. 'My sources are looking into it, but I was told not to expect too much.'

They took a break for coffee, naturally splitting into two muttering groups. Although Nadia and Ed shared glances every few minutes, there was no opportunity for either of them to split off from their teams. He looked well, a little thinner, perhaps more lines around his eyes and there was something different about him – a restless energy she didn't remember from before.

Once they were back seated around the table, David stood up.

'Now we're done with the presentations,' he said. 'I wanted to share something. It's hot off the press and only came in a few hours ago.' He looked around the room. 'I know we've all been wondering why Homeland have been unusually bad at sharing intel recently. More than the usual arrogant older brother attitude.' He looked across the table, apparently seeking confirmation from the others. 'Even the back channels have gone silent. It hasn't made any sense.'

Nadia leant forward. She'd never heard of field operatives sitting in on meetings at this level and she could hear her pulse pounding in her ears. This was the real thing. This was the place where strategies were cooked up and decisions were made. She looked across at Ed, who seemed equally engaged.

'I just found out why,' said David. 'They've had a leak. Someone on the inside.' Nadia could almost hear the sharp intake of breath around the room. A traitor on the inside was the biggest fear for all intelligence services. 'They brought him in last night and have just confirmed he's been talking with Unicorn. So far, he's claiming to know nothing about the transponders.'

'Bloody hell,' said Phil. 'That explains a lot.'

'What transponders?' said Ed.

'I briefed the group earlier,' said Phil. 'We don't have details yet, but in the past two weeks there have been three recorded incidents where passenger jet pilots have reported an override of their flight systems – they were unable to control their planes for a few minutes – a bit like what happened with those two 737 MAX crashes.'

'And they think it's a similar fault?' said Ed.

'That was the initial assumption,' said Phil. 'However, the third time it happened, a few days ago, Homeland Security impounded the plane on landing. They found a suspicious object in a suitcase. Some sort of transponder, but we don't know much more for the time being. There's a possibility that someone has found a way to hack into the avionics and take control of the planes.'

'… the worst case assumption is that we are looking at a possible repeat of 9-11, but with remote takeover of the planes,' said David. 'One way or the other I think we should stick to what we agreed earlier. Ed and Nadia should go to New York as soon as possible and do what they can to help Homeland Security explore the Unicorn link. At the very least they can keep us in the loop.'

Nadia couldn't believe what she was hearing. It was Christmas Eve, and she was getting her presents from Santa a day early. She would be right at the heart of everything. Were they supposed to go straight away? Even though she was over the moon to be involved, there was one nagging doubt which wouldn't leave her. If she had any common sense at all, she would just keep her mouth shut.

Her mouth had other ideas. 'David,' she said. 'Obviously I'm happy to go to New York and help however's needed, but are we absolutely certain that the US is the target? There are still a lot of loose ends in Lebanon. And we don't understand the Shan-ding connection. What if Unicorn is working with his brother, after all? What if the target is Israel? The two of them have reason enough to want revenge.'

Phil laughed – the snorting, scoffing laugh which was his speciality. 'Israel?' he said. 'There's a reason why no major terrorist attack has been successful there for decades. Their defences are too good. Iron Dome and their other missile defence systems are impregnable and they can scramble jets in less than three minutes … Added to that, they have no compunction about shooting anything out of the sky and worrying about consequences later. That's why the Palestinians and Hezbollah have mostly stuck to suicide bombings and short range rockets in recent years.'

Nadia looked at the nodding heads around the table and realised she was wasting her breath. These men had been spoon fed the accepted wisdom for years and none of them looked likely to go out on a limb and challenge the status quo. That didn't mean they were right, though – her instincts were screaming the complete opposite – they were all missing something, and Omar was at the heart of it.

David smiled at her. 'Nadia,' he said. 'I agree that your trip to Sidon has thrown up some important questions which will need to be dealt with in due course. However, apart from the transponders and the bombshell that Unicorn has been running an agent inside Homeland Security, we have a number of other reasons why we're confident the US is the target. You'll receive full briefings after this meeting and I think you'll agree once you've read them.'

He knew her well enough to see she wasn't convinced, but Nadia could see that the idea of a mole in the FBI was too big for him to ignore. She nodded and pressed her lips firmly together. Insisting wouldn't achieve anything. They would hopefully pick up some useful intel in New York, but in the meantime she would try to convince Ed to get MI6 to keep digging in Sidon.

'When do you want us to leave?' said Ed.

'I don't think anything's going to get done today or tomorrow,' said David. 'We'll arrange flights for Boxing Day. I suggest you both get some rest between now and then. You're going to need it.'

# 20

Nadia checked the turkey for the umpteenth time. It was her first attempt at cooking a traditional Christmas lunch and, against all the odds, she was beginning to believe she might pull it off. Christmas with Leila had always involved something pretentious and exotic like oysters or caviar and after she left, there was even less reason to bother. Nadia usually enjoyed the pre-Christmas buzz and the nightly drinks with friends and colleagues but, when the day itself arrived, she'd always been happy to curl up alone on the sofa with a glass of red.

The lunch needed to be very good as the previous day's conversation with James had been very horrible. They had agreed to be off work between Christmas and New Year and he'd agreed with his parents that they would spend the holiday apart for the first time in his life. The news that Nadia was flying to New York on Boxing Day had not gone down well.

She'd tried to explain how important the trip was for her career – what a big deal it was that she was at the heart of such a key investigation. James wasn't having any of it. Unlike Nadia, James cared a lot about Christmas … and she'd ruined it. He hadn't exactly slammed the phone down on her – tricky with a mobile – but it had felt as though he had.

James' petulance had been badly timed. Nadia was already irritated by David's lack of support during the meeting. At first, she'd been genuinely excited to finally be in the room and consulted when key strategic decisions were being made. But that experience had turned out to be a huge disappointment – those decisions weren't the result of careful thought and incisive intelligence and no one from senior management had seemed remotely interested in her opinions. The famed 'centre' was nothing more than a group of middle-aged men who'd somehow made their way up the ladder nodding and agreeing to take safe courses of action which wouldn't reflect badly on them.

She should have known better than to expect real insight and decisiveness. It wasn't the first time she'd seen politics and bureaucracy get in the way of what needed to be done. She'd always assumed that government was to blame, but now knew the problem lay much closer to home. David and the other directors had grown up during the Cold War and Nadia imagined them sitting in leather armchairs, reminiscing about the old romantic days of 'proper' espionage. Meanwhile the real threats grew and multiplied around them like the plague.

To make it worse, she still hadn't been able to catch up with Ed. He'd left with the MI6 team after the meeting and then texted her to say that he was leaving London to be with family and would see her at the airport. What family? Where? She still knew next to nothing about his background.

But it was Christmas. The turkey was ready to come out and rest, the expensive red wine was breathing, the champagne was in the fridge and the presents were under the Christmas tree. All that was needed now was for James to turn up and to have got over his sulk. Nadia stirred the bread sauce and breathed in the scent of cloves; she was beginning to understand Leila more and more –

relationships were hard work.

Nadia's prayers were answered. James breezed into her flat carrying bags full of presents and other goodies. He appeared to have forgotten completely about the fight and, helped along by a beautiful plate of canapés from Fortnum and Mason, it wasn't long before the bottle of champagne was sitting upside down in the ice bucket.

They'd agreed to open gifts after dessert and, even half way through the main course, Nadia could see that James could hardly contain his excitement. He was an only child like Nadia, but growing up with Leila had clearly been very different from life in the Barclay household. Nadia could picture the tastefully decorated living room and the happy, slightly chubby little boy sitting expectantly on the edge of the sofa waiting for his father to hand him the next of many perfectly wrapped packages.

As James got up and took up his natural God-given position under the tree, Nadia realised she couldn't remember a single Christmas spent with her mother and father. There were photos and the odd bit of video but, as far as she was concerned, they may as well have been put together with Photoshop. She couldn't connect them with real memories – smells, tastes, the feeling of being hugged – all those precious sensations had faded away.

But the bittersweet thought came and went like a butterfly in June – Nadia didn't dwell on that sadness as she might have done just a few weeks earlier. After all, there were presents to open and, although Christmas wasn't such a big deal for her, she did love presents.

The ritual of handing out the packages was a complete success with each of them seemingly delighted at the thought and effort the other had put into each gift. A complete success until right until the end when James handed her a smallish box, wrapped in silver paper and tied with a soft black ribbon. Nadia felt the weight of it in her hand and her heart sank. She knew what it would be.

Her mind was racing as she took off the ribbon and peeled back the wrapping paper. She was right – it was a beautiful top-of-the-range iPhone, sitting like a work of modern art in its exquisite packaging. Beautiful, but useless to her.

James couldn't have known that personal phones were strictly forbidden for all MI5 field officers. She'd not thought to tell him. Why would she?

She couldn't say anything. Not on Christmas day. She'd speak to the IT department at work and see if something could be done. Until then, she would need to draw on her acting skills.

'It's wonderful,' she said as she took the shining silver phone out of its cradle. 'So beautiful.'

'I'm glad you like it,' said James, face beaming as he looked up at her. 'You're always banging on about your phone being crap – now you can FaceTime me. It's so much better than WhatsApp.'

Nadia took a deep breath and knelt down on the floor next to him, took his face in her hands and kissed him, feeling his body start to strain towards her and her own immediate response.

She stood up, pulling him after her with one hand, and led him into the bedroom. They'd both had just the right amount to drink – not enough to deaden the senses, but enough to dampen thoughts and allow sensations to dominate.

James was always a measured, gentle lover – which Nadia loved about him. But the growing passion she sensed in him as they fell onto the bed on Christmas Day was quite different and matched her own intimately, breath-for-breath and heartbeat-for-heartbeat. For their own private reasons, they were each in thrall to an unfamiliar urgency, with no time for lengthy foreplay – and no need.

Afterwards, they lay without speaking, holding each other tight as if afraid to let go. Nadia revelled in the warm glow which filled her from fingers to toes; there'd been no question of faking anything – the issue had never had anything to do with James and, now she had moved forward, would be a thing of the past.

James had insisted on taking Nadia to the airport. She knew it was in the hope of meeting Ed and didn't see what harm it could do. James would see that Ed was nothing more than a colleague and it would put his mind at rest.

They checked in her bags and went to join Ed, who was waiting at Carluccio's.

'Don't you need to go through security now?' said James. 'Your flight leaves in ninety minutes and it looks busy.'

Nadia smiled. 'One of the perks of the job,' she said. 'We get to use a shortcut.'

For some reason, James scowled. He was clearly on edge and she wondered if introducing the two men was such a great idea, after all.

Half an hour later, as she and Ed walked through the back door into the customs area, Nadia had concluded that it would have been better if the two men had stayed apart. Although they'd both behaved themselves on the surface, underneath there had been the sense of two wolves circling one another, sizing up the opposition. She'd expected a little posturing from James, but Ed had been as bad, if not worse.

What was it about men? There was nothing between her and Ed. Why did he feel the need to show off to James? And, as for James, Nadia could already imagine the phone conversation she would have that evening, full of jealous innuendo and insecurity.

Still, there was nothing she could do about it and there was work to be done. She and Ed would be able to talk about what happened in Lebanon for the first time. She'd read all the briefing notes, but they were dry and factual and did nothing to capture the reality. She was impatient to talk it all through with Ed – he would understand.

But Nadia would have to wait. As soon as they walked out into the relative anonymity of the Duty Free shop. Ed turned to her and hugged her.

'It's great to see you properly,' he said. 'You look good … I really don't know how you do it. You're like one of those toys that keep bouncing back up, however many times they get knocked down.'

Nadia looked at him. There were dark rings under his eyes and his skin was waxy. There were no signs of the familiar laughter lines around his mouth.

'What about you?' she said. 'Are you all right?'

'I will be,' he said. 'I just don't seem to bounce back as well as you do.'

His voice was shaking and Nadia reached out to touch his arm.

'I'll be fine,' he said sharply, pulling away and starting to walk towards the gate.

Nadia grabbed him by the shoulder and pulled him back and around.

'Ed,' she said. 'If we're going to work together, we need to be able to talk. You can't just brush me aside.'

He pulled away and, for a moment, she wondered if he might hit her, but then his face softened and he managed a half smile.

'I know,' he said. 'And I'm sorry. I really will be OK … but I've got a favour to ask.'

‘Of course,’ she said. ‘Whatever you need.’

‘Can we not talk about what happened in Sidon?’ he said. ‘Not yet at least.’

Nadia hadn’t expected that and, for a moment, didn’t know how to respond. She felt as though the perfect chocolate eclair had been sitting on a plate in front of her before being whisked away with no explanation.

‘Sure,’ she said. ‘There’s no hurry.’ She saw Ed’s shoulders sag and realised he’d been dreading talking about the kidnapping almost as much as Nadia had been looking forward to it. It was different for him, of course. Nadia’s traumatic experience had ended with her being released unharmed and she was keen to understand what had really happened and to learn from it. From Ed’s perspective, he’d watched his close friend being shot and killed in a seemingly random act of violence – nothing was going to change that.

She touched his shoulder gently. ‘Of course there’s no hurry,’ she continued. ‘I’m afraid I’m not good at thinking about anyone apart from myself these days.’

They stood like statues as ordinary travellers flowed around them, smiling and laughing in their innocent bubbles, completely unaware of the evil and danger lurking in the deep.

‘But we do need to talk about Omar,’ said Nadia. ‘There’s something wrong there. I know it.’

‘Yes,’ said Ed. ‘He was a little too hospitable for my liking … and as for those guards … What you said about Israel in the meeting. Do you really think it’s a possible target?’

‘Why shouldn’t it be?’ said Nadia,’ I can see David’s point about the US, but it’s not enough.’

‘So you’re still not convinced?’ said Ed.

‘Far from it,’ said Nadia. ‘I think they’re wrong. The thing is …

when I was strapped in that chair, I got this feeling that Unicorn wasn't really the great warrior for Islam he makes himself out to be. I wonder if it's all window dressing. He might even have convinced himself, but my gut tells me he's driven by something much more basic. He wants payback for what happened to his family and, as a consequence, to his life. I'm sure he blames Israel – with good reason – for everything bad that has ever happened to him … and, if he is actually working with Omar, you can imagine how that hatred could grow and grow.'

Ed nodded. 'And, as for Israel's defences, that part of the world is littered with the ruins of castles which were famed for being impregnable … until it turned out that they weren't.' He looked at Nadia and smiled slowly. 'On a separate note, that bloke Phil is a real tit, isn't he?'

Nadia laughed, pleased to see the old Ed coming to the surface. 'Oh yes,' she said. 'An arsehole of the first order. But, to be fair, I was underwhelmed by all of them. Your lot as well. Even David. They know Unicorn must be planning something. How can they ignore the new intel about his brother? It's like they're so full of schadenfreude that the Americans have been compromised this time, they can't see anything else.'

'I agree,' said Ed. 'At the very least, I would have expected a full team to have gone to Sidon on the next plane.' He picked up his bag and slung it over his shoulder. 'Anyway. Let's go to New York and learn what we can. In the meantime, I still have a couple of guys in our office trying to figure out what those massive generators could be for and looking for evidence that Unicorn has been in touch with his brother. If they find anything, we'll be the first to know.'

# 21

Everything was going to plan. They were so close. Just a few loose ends to tidy up.

Ibrahim stood in the hallway of the small flat he'd rented, looking at the fist-sized dent in the door. He couldn't see what might stand in their way and that worried him. Complacency had always been the enemy of success.

The fiasco in the Lebanon had come out of nowhere, and could have brought everything they'd worked for tumbling down around them. The last thing they needed was for the intelligence agencies to be sniffing around Sidon and investigating Omar. If anything had happened to Nadia, the UK secret services would probably have asked Mossad for help and that wouldn't have led anywhere good.

Ibrahim had only just arrived at the New York apartment when he'd heard what those idiot El Khoury brothers had done. He'd been tired and grubby after a delayed flight and two hours in the infamous JFK immigration queues. All he'd wanted was a shower and a good night's sleep.

Fortunately, he'd checked his messages first … Ibrahim liked to believe that he was in control of his emotions, but that day was an exception. His fist was still throbbing from where he'd punched the door.

They'd killed Nadia's driver and kidnapped Nadia. The drug-addled fools had only been told to follow her, but apparently they'd decided Ibrahim would be grateful if they took their own initiative. Apparently they were actually pleased with themselves when they told Mohammed how they'd captured the British spy.

Ibrahim was still furious with Mohammed for not thinking things through … and with Omar for taking field action without consulting him. He realised he was becoming angry again, just by thinking about what had happened. Didn't they know what they were up against? Did they think all this was some sort of game?

Luckily he'd found out what had happened just in time to stop things becoming disastrous and, as far as he could tell, any investigations into Omar had been put on hold while the agencies focused their resources on the threat to America.

He'd decided to give up Frank earlier than planned – a nice Christmas present for Homeland Security and another reason to keep their attention where Ibrahim needed it. Frank had served his purpose, and they'd learn nothing from him. Nothing that mattered, at least.

The last thing Frank had told him was that Nadia was safely back in London. Letting her leave unharmed had been the smart move, although he had to accept that speaking to her on video link had been unnecessary and indulgent. The dark cloud of incompetence and thoughtlessness in Sidon had come with a silver lining – he'd been given the chance to meet Amal's daughter. It had been a risk to show her his clean-shaven face and to talk for so long, but it had been worth it.

Nadia didn't look much like her mother, but there was something in the eyes and the smile … It brought all those memories flooding back.

Nadia had been right that Amal would have hated who he'd become … and what he was about to do. She would have looked at him with imperial disdain, turned her back and walked away. He closed his eyes and pictured the scene.

But it was her fault. She'd made him what he was. If she hadn't chosen the Frenchman over him, everything would have been different. He would have put his anger aside and been happy to live a simple life, fishing or working in construction, providing for children and grandchildren.

Ibrahim opened his eyes wide and leant against the damaged door, unable to suppress the bitter laughter which rose from his belly. Who was he trying to fool? He could never have been that weak sheep, bleating in quiet complacency as life became harder and harder and less and less fair. The rage which burned inside him had always been a part of who he was; Amal would never have been able to change that.

The cold wind bit into Ibrahim's freshly shaven skin, and he pulled his hood tighter, rubbing his cheeks until the circulation returned. The smoothness under his fingertips still felt alien – as though he was wearing someone else's face.

He looked around the abandoned factory yard. Sheets of rusty corrugated-iron banged in the wind and dust swirled in eddies around the wheels of the truck parked in the far corner. The dust was probably laced with asbestos from the factory roof, but the cost and regulations involved in removing it were prohibitive and so the site remained unused – wasted space in the middle of the city.

He had arrived early, but Karim shouldn't be much longer. The mechanic had proven to be reliable up to that point and Ibrahim saw no reason for that to have changed. Karim had bought the generators in Kentucky, loaded them onto the truck and driven them to the abandoned yard. The remote management system he'd installed had worked twice without issues, but Ibrahim wanted a final check made. Just to be sure.

He heard the screech of rusty metal hinges and saw Karim walk through the gate.

'*Salaam Alaikum*,' said Karim as he approached Ibrahim and the truck.

'*Walaikum Salaam*,' said Ibrahim. 'Sorry to bring you out in this cold, but I wanted to double check things hadn't frozen up.'

'The set-up should be fine as long as the temperature doesn't drop below minus thirty,' said Karim. 'I've used silicon grease everywhere and the diesels have block heaters, battery warmers and fuel additives. It's the same configuration we use on oil rigs in Alaska.'

Ibrahim nodded, shrugged his shoulders and pointed to the truck.

'Happy to make sure it's all still good, though,' said Karim, walking over and loosening the straps on the canvas tarpaulin.

Ibrahim watched carefully as Karim worked his way methodically through the system checks. He was good at what he did and took pride in his work – both admirable qualities.

When Karim had finished, he strapped the tarpaulin back in place and walked over to Ibrahim.

'Do you want to give it a try?' he said.

Ibrahim nodded and took out his phone. The remote control app used a simple graphic interface and, as he pressed on each red image, the corresponding diesel engine roared into life in front of him and the image turned green.

'Best to leave them to run for ten minutes now they're going,' said Karim, shouting above the noise of the huge engines. 'Too much stop-start isn't good for them.'

Karim walked over to the truck, apparently listening to make sure each engine was running smoothly. Ibrahim slowly took the gun from his pocket and followed him. He liked Karim, but there was no place for loose ends and some sacrifices needed to be made.

Exactly ten minutes after he'd started the engines, Ibrahim pressed the three green images one-by-one, and the engines stopped. Peace returned to the yard as Ibrahim walked out, locking the heavy padlock on the gate and mouthing a silent prayer for Karim's soul.

'Omar?'

'Yes. I can hear you now. There was too much background noise before. Is everything all right?'

'Yes,' said Ibrahim. 'I've just checked the generators and they're ready to go whenever you want.'

'Good,' said Omar. 'And the transponders?'

'All five have been delivered,' said Ibrahim. 'I've recruited baggage handlers to place them, so security won't be an issue. And at your end?'

'Everything is ready and tested,' said Omar. 'I can't see what can go wrong.'

'That's my worry,' said Ibrahim. 'There must be something we haven't thought of. We still have a few days. Go through everything again, just in case.'

'I will,' said Omar, laughing nervously. 'If nothing else, I need the distraction.'

'Good,' said Ibrahim. 'What about the El Khoury brothers?'

'They won't be causing any more problems,' said Omar. 'Mohammed has seen to that … I'm sorry, big brother. I know I screwed up.'

'That's all right. You are forgiven. You were under pressure and no-one could have guessed what those fools would do. It is forgotten.'

'Thank you,' said Omar. 'Will we speak before?'

'No,' said Ibrahim, feeling a shiver of anticipation run through him. 'I won't call again until it begins. Go with God, little brother.'

# 22

It was almost midnight by the time their cab pulled up outside the New York Palace Hotel, a building which had definitely seen better days. Nadia sighed at yet another reminder that real life in the secret services was nothing like the movies. Both she and Ed were exhausted, and they staggered off to their rooms like zombies.

They'd been told someone would meet them in the hotel lobby at eight o'clock and both wanted to make a good first impression. They were sitting on a low corner sofa at a quarter to eight when Nadia saw a familiar face coming through the revolving doors.

'Danny?' she called across the room. 'Over here.'

'Hi Nadia,' he said, leaning forward to give her a kiss on the cheek. 'And this must be Ed Bailey. Pleased to meet you.'

The two men shook hands while Nadia stood back, hands on hips.

'Do you know how much shit you got me into last time?' she said to Danny. 'Why did you have to make such a big deal of a simple question?'

He had the grace to look sheepish. 'I had no choice,' he said. 'You now know why, I assume?'

Both Nadia and Ed nodded. There was no need to spell it out. There must have been a massive witch hunt once it became clear the

FBI had a leak. No one would have been above suspicion.

'How did you catch him?' said Ed. 'It's unlike Unicorn to make a mistake like that.'

Danny shrugged. 'The truth always comes out,' he said. 'Every time. It just depends how much damage gets done before it does.' Ed's question was completely inappropriate and Nadia breathed a sigh of relief that Danny hadn't said as much.

'I guess,' said Ed, before sinking back into his seat and starting to pick at some loose skin around his thumb.

'Come on. Let's go,' said Danny. 'We can catch up later.' He turned to Nadia and smiled as they walked out to the waiting town car. 'At least I came to pick you up.'

The Homeland Security meeting was nothing like the briefing they'd had in London. This was no cosy chat between senior operatives around a polished table – there must have been fifty people in the brightly lit room, lined up on folding chairs and facing a huge screen.

Danny handed them paper cups of murky brown coffee from a folding table and they found seats near the back of the room. Nadia took a sip and almost spat it back into the cup – how had America reinvented itself as the global home of great coffee? It beggared belief. At least the growing number of artisan coffee shops in the UK were evidence that not everyone had fallen for the Starbucks puff.

The first hour consisted of a montage of video clips covering a seventy-two-hour period – the star was a man being interrogated in a faceless grey room. His hands were handcuffed to the table and, as the video progressed, his fear and exhaustion became more and more obvious. Despite that, his answers never changed and Nadia would have sworn he was telling the truth.

The video stopped, leaving a frozen image of the man's anguished face, staring at the camera with red-rimmed eyes. A tall, thin figure stood up and walked to the front of the room.

'That's Andy Chalmers,' whispered Danny. 'He heads up the Science and Technology Directorate.'

'You've been looking at Frank Kowalski,' said Andy. 'Many of you know him and, for those who don't, he's a twenty-year FBI officer with a spotless record. We've been questioning him for three days and he's not deviated from his original statement once. Apparently our person of interest, Ibrahim Abdel Hak, AKA, the Unicorn, threatened his family. Frank claims he would have followed protocol and called it in but, as the Unicorn was only looking for information to help him avoid capture, he didn't want to take the chance. Kowalski consistently denies any knowledge of an upcoming act of terrorism or a plan to hijack aircraft.'

He signalled to the control desk at the back of the room and the haunting image on the screen changed to a picture of some sort of laboratory. Two men in white lab coats were standing next to a black cube about six inches square.

'This is the transponder we recovered from AA1742 last week,' said Andy. 'It was found in a suitcase in the hold. We have the owner of the suitcase in custody, but she's denying any knowledge of it.' He looked around the room. 'The flight recorder backs up the pilot's statements that, for three minutes, the plane's autopilot took over all flight controls and repeatedly denied him and his co-pilot manual access.'

He held up a white folder with 737 MAX written in bold letters on the front.

'The pilot's reports are very similar to recent black box recordings from the two Boeing 737 MAX crashes, Lion Air Flight 610 and Ethiopian Airlines Flight 302. In both those cases, the Manoeuvring Characteristics Augmentation System malfunctioned, taking over control of the plane. According to those reports, the pilots were pulling on the joystick with over a hundred pounds of force and were still unable to regain control.'

Nadia clenched her right fist as she imagined what must have been going through those pilot's minds as they realised they were powerless to stop their planes plummeting down.

'There is no suspicion of foul play in the 737 MAX crashes, but our initial assumption is that these transponders are designed to gain wider access by exploiting similar flaws in the automated safety software.'

Andy put the folder down and pointed to the screen.

'Have a look at the video,' he said, as he walked back to his seat, 'and we'll have an hour of open discussion before lunch. This afternoon, I'd like to break into smaller brainstorming groups.'

The video started to play and one of the two scientists gave an ongoing commentary as they ran a series of tests on the cube.

'… Sealed in resin … definitely contains some electronics, but we won't know what until we open it up … battery power must be limited by its size … I can't see how it could operate for much more than a few minutes …'

They went on scanning and guessing, but Nadia and the rest of the agents in the room were becoming restless. They could all see that the real information would only come when the scientists opened up the device.

Eventually the moment came, and the commentator placed the cube on a metal workbench in front of a large circular saw.

'We're going to take this easy,' he said. 'Shave off one millimetre slices at a time until we see some innards.'

The process was unbearably slow, with each slice taking over ten minutes to pare away. Everyone in the room was leaning forward, desperate to find out more about the device.

Then, as the spinning blade reached the half-way point of the sixth slice, there was a flash of orange flame, a loud bang and a cloud of grey smoke filled the screen.

'Shit. Shit,' came the voice through the smoke. 'It's booby trapped.'

The video stopped and Andy stepped forward again.

'And that was that,' he said. 'The lab is still trying to piece together what they can, but most of the chips inside were completely destroyed. We believe this device was used to take over the controls of AA1742, but we're no closer to knowing how.'

A grey-haired man in the front row raised one hand. 'Are you saying that putting one of these in the baggage hold would allow a terrorist to turn any plane into some sort of remote-controlled missile?'

'It's a possibility we have to consider,' said Andy.

'Then we need to ground all flights over US airspace with immediate effect.'

'For how long?' said Andy. 'Can you imagine what grounding flights would do to the economy? We're coming into an election year. This president would never sanction that.'

All discipline in the room evaporated as everybody began to talk at once, either calling out to the speaker or muttering to their neighbours. Nadia felt a shiver run through her. If Unicorn was behind this, what would he do with all that power? And how had he accessed the technology to build such a thing?

The lobby bar of the Palace hotel was empty apart from the three of them. Ed and Danny looked as exhausted as Nadia felt; eight hours trapped in a stuffy room with no windows was hard and, on top of that, the level of tension hadn't dipped all day. The NSA was picking up an increased level of chatter between terrorist groups and the consensus was that an attack on the US was imminent – probably before the end of the year. And, without more information, they were powerless to do anything to stop it.

'What are you having?' said Ed. 'If someone doesn't go to the bar, we'll be here all night.'

Nadia briefly toyed with the idea of ordering a Negroni, but one look at the half-stocked shelves and the scruffy, half-shaven barman was enough to cancel that thought.

'I'll have a beer please,' she said. 'And some nuts or pretzels or something.'

As soon as Ed was out of earshot, she turned to Danny.

'Can you get us in to see this Frank?' she said. 'Apart from him, I am the only person we know who's actually spoken with Unicorn. I might pick up something which others have missed.'

Danny shifted in his seat. 'I don't know,' he said. 'I don't think …'

'… You owe me,' said Nadia. 'Do this and we're even.' She glared at Danny, willing him to concede.

'OK. I give in,' said Danny, raising both hands in surrender. 'I'll try to set it up for tomorrow morning. Will half an hour be enough?'

'Plenty,' said Nadia, reaching forward to squeeze his hand. 'Thanks, Danny.'

Danny leant towards her and whispered. 'But you get your partner under control,' he said. 'No more questions about our internal housekeeping.'

Nadia nodded her agreement as Ed came back with the drinks,

grumbling as he put them on the table.

'That guy was totally useless,' he said. 'I thought the States was supposed to be all about service with a smile.'

They all laughed and picked up their glasses. Nadia couldn't remember enjoying a beer so much. It was some sort of craft IPA and the bitter tang at the back of her throat was just what was needed to make up for the long day. She would find a time to have words with Ed later.

'What are you two up to tonight?' said Danny.

'There's a drone fireworks display out on Long Island,' said Ed. 'A thousand of them, all flying in synch. I'm really into drones and this is supposed to be a top event. They're programmed to work as a swarm – each drone talks to all of the others directly to control the patterns and the timing. They have different-coloured LED lights and some are capable of launching actual fireworks.'

'Sounds fun,' said Danny. 'If you like that sort of thing.' He looked at Nadia and raised his eyebrows. 'Wrap up warm, though. When that wind comes in off the Atlantic, it's quite something.'

'I just had a message from my aunt,' said Nadia, as they sat in a yellow cab on the way out to Long Island.

'Leila?' said Ed.

'Yup,' said Nadia. 'She's invited us both to the New Year's party at the Cipriani. Apparently it's the hottest event in town.'

'Very kind of her, but I can't see us being able to go,' said Ed. 'Can you?'

'Not unless we stop Unicorn before then,' said Nadia. 'I just thought I'd mention it. You'd like Leila.' She turned to Ed. 'On another topic. Do you really fly drones in your spare time? I didn't have you down as that much of a geek.'

'Really?' said Ed 'I thought it was written on my forehead in flashing purple neon … I was a teenage hacker, I worked at GCHQ and I've been flying planes and helicopters on computer simulators all my life. Simulators are great, but it's still just graphics on a screen. Drones don't cost that much and you get to fly them in the real world.' He laughed. 'It's living the dream.'

'So. I guess you didn't have girlfriends growing up?' said Nadia, not wanting to drop the bone now she had it firmly between her teeth.

'Oh. You know. The usual,' mumbled Ed, taking out his phone and pretending to check for messages. 'I wasn't a complete loser … Speaking of romance, did you and Danny have a thing?'

Nadia looked at him. 'Why do you ask?'

'Just a feeling,' said Ed. 'A couple of glances between you. I don't know …'

'… But you do know it's none of your business,' said Nadia, secretly impressed that Ed had noticed. 'More importantly, my "thing" with Danny just got us half an hour with Frank, their mole, tomorrow morning.'

'That's the first good news I've heard all day,' said Ed. 'There may be nothing more to learn from him, but it's got to be worth a try. Especially after your conversation with Unicorn in Lebanon. I think we know a lot more about what makes that bastard tick than our American cousins do. It's typical of their arrogance that no-one has even bothered to ask you about your conversation with him.'

'You don't have much time for Homeland Security, do you?' said Nadia. 'But that's no excuse for poking your nose into their private business. I couldn't believe you asked Danny how they found their mole. He was really pissed off and I don't blame him.'

'Sorry,' said Ed. 'Ever since David told us about him, I've been trying to imagine what it must be like to be exposed like that. I knew I shouldn't ask Danny, but couldn't help myself.'

'Why so interested?' said Nadia. 'Are you working for the Unicorn as well?'

'Don't be ridiculous,' snapped Ed, looking Nadia straight in the eyes. He then turned to look out of the cab window, before muttering in a low voice. 'I was just interested. That's all.'

Nadia sighed. Ed was turning out to be quite different to the cheerful monochrome guy she'd originally thought him to be. The new version wasn't entirely an improvement.

'In any case,' she said. 'If we don't get something useful out of Frank tomorrow morning, we may end up going to Leila's New Years Eve party, anyway. Every lead we have is drying up and we both know we're running out of time to find Unicorn.'

Nadia didn't know what to expect from the drone display and would never have considered going if it hadn't been for Ed. He'd promised to buy her dinner afterwards to make up for it and anyway the whole drone-firework-geek thing wasn't going to last much more than half an hour.

As it turned out, the event was amazing. Nadia and Ed stood in a crowd of maybe five hundred people and watched as the dots of light lifted from the ground and started to form ever-more-complex patterns in the sky. The effect was uncanny – the robotic co-ordinated precision somehow reminiscent of a science fiction movie.

The music, which had been blaring from huge stacks of speakers, suddenly stopped and all the drone lights winked out. Then, as the Star Spangled Banner started to play, a familiar shape appeared in front of them, made up of tiny blue-green dots. The figure of the Statue of Liberty must have been fifty metres high and the whole crowd gasped in amazement.

The anthem reached a crescendo, Lady Liberty's torch lit in a plume of golden sparks, and she turned and strode gracefully out over the sea, gradually reducing in size until she faded away.

It was truly impressive. Nadia had never seen anything like it and, as the emotions of the past few days rose to the surface, she felt like laughing and crying at the same time. She turned to Ed and saw he was equally overawed. The simple childish pleasure of the display seemed to have had a cathartic effect on them both.

'Thank you,' she said. 'Thank you for persuading me to come.'

And then, before she realised what was happening, he leant forward and kissed her on the lips.

The kiss wasn't mentioned during the long cab journey back to Manhattan, it wasn't mentioned during their dinner and it definitely wasn't mentioned in the hotel lift as they made their way back to their rooms. Nadia didn't know what had come over them and decided the best thing was to forget all about it.

In any case, she had other priorities. They would get one shot with Frank Kowalski in the morning and, if that came to nothing, it would probably be back home to her analyst's desk. David wanted results and, apart from Omar, they had nothing. She knew that David wouldn't authorise another Sidon trip and she didn't really blame him. They had nothing.

But, as she felt the delicious coolness of her cotton pillow against her cheek and curled up in the warmth of her bed, she couldn't help thinking about the moment Ed had kissed her. She had definitely kissed him back, that much was certain. It had been tender rather than passionate, but dangerous enough. She started to list all the reasons why the kiss had been a bad idea and drifted off to sleep somewhere around number twenty.

Nadia had never jumped through so many security hoops. The FBI were understandably paranoid about their traitor and for a few seconds she thought she was about to be strip searched, hosed down and dressed in a paper jumpsuit.

After forty minutes of X-rays, document checks and form signings, they found themselves in the interview room they'd seen in the video. Frank Kowalski looked worse, if anything. It was likely he'd been denied sleep for the whole four days they'd had him and she knew how that could play strange tricks on the mind and body.

She and Ed had agreed that Nadia would ask the questions. There was, in fact, only one question which they cared about, but it was necessary to go through the motions. They sat down opposite Frank and introduced themselves.

'So Frank,' said Nadia. 'We know you've been through all this a hundred times and you must be exhausted.' She smiled at him. 'But my partner and I have become quite expert on this man and thought it might be worth seeing if we can pick up anything which might have been missed by your colleagues. Is that OK?'

Frank nodded. 'Sure. All I want is to help … and to keep my family safe.'

Nadia tried to appear friendly and sympathetic as she worked through the list of prepared questions even though she couldn't help feeling annoyed by the weak, servile attitude of the man in front of her. She could see how he'd fallen under Unicorn's spell, but people like him shouldn't be allowed to reach senior positions in the intelligence services. His answers were predictable and uninteresting and, as she reached the bottom of the list, she sighed as though disappointed. She then looked at Ed and shrugged before collecting her papers together and starting to stand up.

'There was one last question …' she said, leaving her words hanging in the air. '…Did Ibrahim ever mention someone called Omar?'

Frank shook his head. 'Sorry, no,' he said. 'He really avoided all conversation, much as I tried. He just wanted me to report information and answer his questions.'

Nadia stared long and hard at Frank willing him to tell her more, but there was nothing and, as she and Ed walked towards the exit, she could feel the weight of genuine disappointment pressing down on her shoulders. For some reason, she'd believed something more could be gleaned from this sad, broken man.

It was only when the guard opened the door that they heard the voice from behind them.

'Wait,' said Frank. 'I *have* heard that name before. One time a few weeks ago, I heard another phone ringing while I was talking to Ibrahim. He told me to wait and went to answer the call.'

'Go on,' said Nadia.

'He must have been listening to the caller for a while, before he said. "*Omar. Calme-toi*" in French.'

'And you're sure that was the name?'

'Yes,' said Frank. 'I immediately thought of Omar Sharif for some reason.'

'… And then what happened?'

'Nothing,' said Frank. 'He told me to wait for him to call back and hung up.'

'When exactly was this?' said Ed.

Frank rubbed his forehead with the heel of his hand. 'I was in the Bronx, so it must have been on the tenth or eleventh of December. You can check on the duty roster.'

# 23

It was four in the morning UK time when Nadia dialled the twenty-four-hour hotline and asked to be put through to David. He didn't complain about being woken up and listened patiently while Nadia told him about the meeting with Frank. She ended by saying she was convinced Omar was key to whatever Unicorn was working on, and that she needed to get back to Sidon and find out more.

'I still don't think it's enough,' David said, once she'd finished. 'What you've told me doesn't actually prove Unicorn's in touch with his brother and, even if he is, there's no evidence that Omar's involved in any of his terrorist activities. You're more valuable to me doing what you're doing in New York than you are following loose ends in the Lebanon. I'm also surprised you're so keen to get back there after what happened but, once this scare is over, I'm happy to agree that you and Ed go back to the Lebanon and dig some more.'

'I'm sorry, David,' said Nadia. 'I can't agree. The call where Frank heard Omar's name took place just minutes after we visited Omar. It can't be a coincidence.'

'I'm not asking whether you agree, Nadia. I'm asking you to do your job. Am I being unclear?'

'No,' said Nadia, 'But if we don't act immediately, I know it will be too late. This is happening now.' She felt the hard edges of her phone pressing against her finger and took a deep breath. 'I actually rang to tell you I'm about to get on a plane to Beirut. Ed's boss saw things differently and felt Ed should get back there ASAP. I can't leave him to go on his own. I really am sorry.'

As she hung up and switched off her phone, Unicorn's words were ringing in her ears 'It's true I will never forgive Israel for what they did'. This would probably be the final straw which ended her career, but Nadia knew she was right. Everyone else was looking in the wrong direction – just as Unicorn intended. Despite all the evidence to the contrary, they all – even people as smart as David – continued to underestimate Ibrahim Abdel-Hak.

There was no Ali to meet them as they walked into the arrivals hall at Beirut International Airport. Nadia pictured his beaming smile as he'd walked across the crowded hall just a few weeks earlier. Then memories of the shooting pushed their way into her mind – the sound of the gunshot and his body crumpling to the ground like a discarded doll.

She looked at Ed who was standing still, staring at the exit doors; his lips were pressed tightly together and his fists were clenched. He would be having the same thoughts, but it was so much worse for him. Ali had been his friend. Hopefully he would have a chance to visit Ali's widow before they left but, before then, there was work to be done. The clock was ticking – Nadia could feel it in her bones.

She rested one hand on his shoulder and steered him outside.

'What's the plan?' she said.

'I'm waiting for a text,' he said, taking out his phone. 'I couldn't get a signal before.' The phone beeped twice. 'There we are,' said Ed. 'We're in Car Park 1. Bay 213.'

The airport concourse was eerily quiet as they crossed the road –

it seemed that most of the usual taxi drivers and hotel hawkers couldn't be bothered to get out of bed at eight in the morning. The car was just inside the car park – a black BMW which was as dirty and scratched as most of the other cars they'd walked past. The people with new cars had drivers and wouldn't dream of leaving their shiny toys at the airport.

Ed reached under one of the rear wheel arches, muttering to himself.

'The text said I'd find the keys here,' he said. 'I don't understand.'

Nadia walked around to the other side of the car and squatted down. A set of keys was sitting on top of the tyre. She reached forward and took them before standing up and waving the keys at Ed.

'Looking for these?' she said.

'But the text said "on the left-hand side",' Ed said, a note of petulance creeping into his voice.

'This is the left-hand side,' said Nadia, throwing him the keys. 'You're completely knackered, aren't you?'

'We both are,' he said. 'Let's get to the hotel and grab a few hours sleep or we'll be no use to anyone. We can go and see your Auntie Taz after lunch.'

He looked around carefully before opening the boot.

'Come and look,' he said, lifting the floor panel. 'I'm thinking we might need these.'

The panel had been raised up by a few inches and the resulting space filled with weapons and ammunition. A Glock pistol each, two assault rifles and a selection of shaped charges and hand grenades.

Nadia picked up one of the pistols and checked the action. 'Your boss is definitely taking our gut feel seriously,' she said. 'Unlike David, who's probably having me fired as we speak.'

'I doubt it,' said Ed. 'He rates you too much. And anyway, I asked my boss to give David a call. They'll straighten it out.' He closed the boot and walked around to the driver's seat. 'Come on. Let's crack on.'

Nadia managed to suppress her memories of the last time she'd walked into that hotel lobby. She also felt much less like a potential victim with a loaded Glock tucked into the back of her jeans. She'd back herself against two, or even three, of those bastards with a weapon in her hand.

She didn't quite understand why, but her feelings of urgency were growing minute by minute. Something terrible was going to happen as the old year gave way to the new – unless she and Ed were able to figure out what was going on in time.

Nadia checked her phone while Ed was at the reception. There was one secure message from Danny. She read it twice to be sure, feeling her pulse quicken and the thrill of the chase fill her with energy.

'I don't think we've time for a rest,' she said to Ed as he handed over her room key.

'Why?' he said. 'What's happened?'

'I just had a message from Danny. They've found a truck in an abandoned factory yard in Queens. Someone complained about the engine noise a few nights ago and the police only just followed up.'

'Sorry. Not with you,' said Ed. 'What's so special about this truck?'

'Under the canvas, they found three huge generators and a two meter wide parabolic antenna.'

'Just like the generators delivered to Omar's villa?'

'Exactly,' said Nadia. 'The team working on the transponder have confirmed that the set up could possibly be used to track a plane and to transmit electrical power to a transponder in the plane's hold. It's called power beaming – the same microwave technology used in directed energy weapons.'

'Shit,' said Ed. 'And you still think all that was put in place to divert attention from here?'

'I don't know,' said Nadia. 'It sounds a bit far fetched when you say it out loud. Maybe they were planning a two-pronged attack? In any case, this means we're in the right place – Omar's involved and Israel is almost certainly a target.' Nadia reached out and squeezed Ed's arm. 'Are you OK to leave straight away? We need to find out whatever we can as soon as possible.'

'Of course,' he said. 'A quick shower, a coffee and I'll be fine … see you down here in twenty minutes?'

Her grandmother's old home looked shuttered and abandoned as they got out of the car and Nadia reached behind her to loosen the pistol in her waistband. They were travelling under fresh identities, but that didn't mean the Unicorn couldn't have set a trap. She knocked on the door, taking care to keep her body behind the breeze block wall.

Long seconds passed before she heard a rustling from within and the sound of Tazeen's voice.

'Hello,' said Taz. 'Who is it?'

'It's me, Auntie Taz … Nadia. I've come back with that nice man you liked.'

'Well. You took your time,' said the voice as the door was opened half way. Tazeen's face appeared in the crack, looking at Nadia, before poking her head out to check up and down the street. She opened the door all the way and beckoned, the whites of her eyes showing brightly in the darkness of the room. 'Come in quickly,' she said.

It was only after they were safely inside and the door was bolted that she calmed down.

'What's wrong,' said Nadia. 'You look terrified. Has something happened?'

Taz nodded. 'A few days after your last visit, two men came to see me. They asked me questions about you. What you wanted, why you were here, what I had told you. Many, many questions. They were not kind men and showed no respect. Before they left, they told me to remember that, when you were back in England, I would still be here, in Sidon … and so would they.'

Nadia bent down to hug the old lady. 'I'm so sorry, Auntie Taz. I had no idea they would link you with us. You must have been terrified.'

'A little,' said Tazeen. 'But it's you I'm worried about. I've had a longer life than I expected and most of my friends have gone ahead of me.' She held Nadia's hand and squeezed. 'They are very dangerous men,' she said. 'What have you become mixed up in?'

'I'm sorry,' said Nadia, 'but it's better if I don't tell you. These men might be about to do something terrible and we are here to try to stop them.'

'What can I do to help?' said Tazeen.

'Is there anything else you can tell me about Fathi or Omar Oun?' said Nadia.

Tazeen shook her head slowly. 'It's as I told you before, I've not seen Omar since he was a boy and, as far as I know, his brother Fathi went and got himself killed in Afghanistan years ago.'

'Is there anyone else we could speak to?' said Ed.

'You could talk to Alia Haddad,' said Tazeen. 'She's looked after that poor crippled boy for years. I could introduce you, but I don't think she'd tell you much. She's cared for him for most of his life, after all.'

'No-one else?' said Ed.

'Her daughter, Dounia, might see things differently,' said Tazeen. 'She's been helping her mother with Omar for the last couple of years and I don't think there's any love lost there.'

'Why not?' said Nadia.

'There was jealousy between Dounia and Amal at the end,' said Tazeen. 'You see, Dounia also loved Fathi, but he only had eyes for your mother … and then once your mother and Fathi started to walk out together, Dounia was left babysitting Omar. She resented having to do that, but would do anything for Fathi. Her mother told me once that Dounia blames Omar for driving Fathi away after Amal ran off with your father.' Tazeen nodded her head. 'Yes. Dounia won't have any problem telling you about Omar. I'm sure of it.'

Although Tazeen had known exactly where Dounia lived, her ability to explain that to people from out of town was proving challenging. It was only after Nadia asked in the nearest bread shop that they received clear instructions. They'd been very close all along, but without a house number, very close hadn't helped.

Dounia's house was small and run down, tucked away in a narrow side street. Nadia knocked on the door, looking at Ed and noting the anxiety in his eyes. If no-one was in, they didn't have much of a Plan B.

The door opened to reveal a woman in her early fifties, attractive except for the way the wrinkles around her mouth pursed her lips. This wasn't a woman who had embraced life and seized every moment; this was someone who had spent too much time complaining about the raw deal she'd been given.

'Yes?' she said, looking at the pair of them suspiciously. She leant forward and peered closely at Nadia. 'Do I know you?'

'No,' said Nadia, suddenly feeling like a nervous child. 'But, if you're Dounia Haddad, you knew my mother, Amal.'

The woman's mouth dropped open. 'Nadia?' she said. 'Are you little Nadia? I don't believe it. I haven't seen you since you were a small girl.'

Dounia wrapped Nadia in a bosomy hug before dragging her inside and putting the kettle on. Ed followed and closed the door behind him. When Nadia introduced Ed, she could see Dounia sizing him up in exactly the same way Tazeen had. The country seemed full of matchmakers.

Fortunately Dounia's friendship with Amal had been stronger than any rivalry over a boy and they'd kept in touch until Nadia's parents died. She was obviously delighted to see her best friend's daughter again and, over home-made cakes and mint tea, she launched into a full-scale interrogation; Dounia insisted on knowing all about Nadia's life and what Leila was doing. No detail was too trivial.

Nadia knew she needed to be polite, but she also knew the clock was ticking and could see Ed shifting around on his chair across the room. She took advantage of a tiny break while Dounia was pouring more tea to jump in.

'Dounia,' she said. 'Ed and I have some work to do this afternoon and we need to leave soon. Would you like to join us for dinner tomorrow night?'

'That would be wonderful, *habibi*,' said Dounia. 'It's so good to see you. I feel like a sixteen-year-old girl again.'

'Before we go,' said Nadia. 'I wanted to ask you about Omar Oun. You were all friends, weren't you? With him and his older brother.'

Dounia nodded. 'I still see Omar from time to time. I help my mother when she's not feeling well. He lives in a huge villa by Saray Nasib Basha.' She scowled. 'I don't know why he deserves to be so rich while I have to live like this.' She waved a hand around the small room. 'He hasn't changed. Still a spoilt brat.'

'So you know the villa well?' said Ed. 'You clean the whole place?'

'Yes,' said Dounia. 'Apart from his private offices. Even my mother isn't allowed in there. I guess one of his security guards cleans them.'

'Do you know his guards well,' asked Nadia. 'How many does he have?'

'Why do you want to know all this?' said Dounia, her eyes narrowing.

'This is highly confidential, but we're part of an international team investigating him,' said Nadia, almost whispering as she leant forward. 'Omar is suspected of banking fraud. Using illegal software to siphon off small amounts from millions of private bank accounts.'

'I knew he was no good,' said Dounia. 'All that money doesn't come from honest work.'

'Maybe,' said Nadia. 'At the moment, it's just an investigation. We need to find proof.'

'I can help you,' said Dounia, her eyes narrowing. 'There are two guards and they're not allowed to speak with us. I remember one of them, Mohammed, from when we were kids, but now he doesn't even smile at me.'

'And you've never been inside the private office?' said Nadia.

'No,' said Dounia. 'Although I did get a peek once – from the end of the corridor. It's a huge room full of screens and computers and what-not. I think poor little Omar just sits there and plays video games all day.'

'Sorry to ask all of these questions,' said Ed. 'You're being very helpful … Where exactly in the villa are these offices?'

'They're down the end of the long passageway to the left of the entrance,' said Dounia. 'The wall at the end is actually a secret door. How childish is that?'

By the time they got back to the hotel, the sun was already low on the horizon. Nadia was jumpy with adrenaline, but she knew that she and Ed needed to be methodical and work through their options. Panicked, shoot-from-the-hip decisions could be just as bad as turning up too late.

Preparations for the New Year celebrations were visible everywhere. A big banner sat above the hotel entrance and the restaurant opposite appeared to be hosting a party. As she got out of the car, Nadia saw two men wheeling stacks of massive loudspeakers onto the terrace; she and Ed would be glad of the hotel's triple-glazed windows and solid stone walls later on.

Ed had the larger room, which became their improvised operations centre. Nadia was surprised to notice his clothes were all neatly unpacked and his suitcase tucked away out of sight; she hadn't taken him for the tidy type. He'd even managed to persuade the woman on reception to dig out a small flip chart, which he set down in front of the television.

Ed had been short tempered and twitchy since they'd left New York, but the man standing in front of the blank paper with a marker in his hand was calm and in control. Impending danger, urgency and fear tended to have one of two effects on a person;

either the resulting adrenaline slowed time and created the space for calm, rational decision-making, or it turned the person into a panicking imbecile, frozen into indecision. Although Nadia had expected Ed to fall into the first category, one could never tell until the chips were down.

'Let's think this through,' he said, pulling the cap off the marker. 'What do we know? Or think we know?'

'First of all,' said Nadia. 'I think we're both sure Omar is working with his brother. It also seems to make sense to assume he's behind the technology for the transponder.'

'Agreed,' said Ed. 'Unicorn isn't a techie, but together with Omar, they make a hell of team.'

Nadia continued. 'And the activity in the US was either a distraction or a back-up for the main attack on Israel. In either case, finding that generator truck should have blocked the US attack.'

Ed nodded and updated the list on the flip chart.

'The remaining attack will involve taking over the controls of one or more passenger jets?' he said. 'And then mounting a 9-11 style attack on targets in Israel?'

'Based on what we learnt in New York and what we know of Unicorn and Omar, that has to be the assumption.'

'Do we think the control centre is here, in Omar's villa?' said Ed. 'And he's going to fly the planes?'

'Makes sense to me,' said Nadia. 'Especially if he's the one who developed the technology.'

Ed drew two more horizontal lines under the numbered list.

'So what don't we know?' he said.

'We still don't know how they intend to bypass Israeli defence systems.'

Ed sat on the edge of the bed, repeatedly spinning the marker pen up in the air and catching it.

He caught it a final time and pointed it at Nadia. 'Could they just be planning to embarrass Israel by forcing them to shoot down passenger planes?'

'I don't see that,' said Nadia. 'It's too weak a vengeance and Israel has shrugged off worse in the past. I'm convinced there'll be a plan to get through the defences. Almost certainly targeting Tel Aviv.'

'And the 5G chips?' said Ed. 'Where do they come in?'

'I don't know,' said Nadia. 'But, one way or the other, your office has to send an infiltration team to the villa. And that's got the potential to be a political minefield. I think we have to go out there and get the lay of the land. The more info the team has, the less chance of a screw-up.'

'That makes sense,' said Ed. 'There's a laser-targeting scope and a camera in the car.'

'OK,' said Nadia. 'We should aim to be there before dawn, find a spot and update them from there. Will you report our current status now? I'm not sure David will want to hear from me.'

Ed nodded. 'And we'll meet here at oh-four-thirty,' he said. 'Try to get some sleep if you can.'

# 24

The water shimmered oily black as M.S. Habibi motored slowly out of the harbour. Nothing unusual about a fishing boat leaving before dawn, before the first pink streak on the horizon. For more than twenty years, the fish had been moving further and further out to escape a seabed which had been dragged and scraped into a desolate moonscape. The distant lights of drilling rigs to the north and south were harbingers of more desolation to come. An early boat stood a chance of making it home with half a catch at least.

In another twenty years, Ahmed doubted any boats would be left working out of Sour harbour, but that was no longer his problem. After a lifetime of living and working in Tyre, this would be Ahmed and Habibi's last voyage; Ahmed's wife was dead and both his sons had been taken from them many years earlier. The avenging angel with the green eyes had promised him retribution. Maybe he had been lying, maybe not. God would decide.

They were not looking for fish and had taken no crew for this final journey, only the foreign boy with the strange accent and the dozens of cardboard boxes piled high on the gutting deck. Ahmed could see him bent over like a demon in the glowing red bubble of his head torch. He was unpacking the boxes, one-by-one and taking out what appeared to be huge spiders. Ahmed had no interest in the boy devil and his evil familiars. He would take the boat south to the agreed location, drop an anchor and then go below to his tiny bunk.

He may not have been interested in other people's affairs, but couldn't stop himself from turning to look as he opened the hatch which would take him down below. They had reached their destination; the anchor was holding, and the boat had settled downwind in the gentle breeze.

The morning sun was biding its time, but there was enough light for Ahmed to see the boy, still hunched over, placing the strange spiders onto floating boards, each connected to the next by short ropes. There were already ten or twenty on the water, stretched out behind Habibi in an evenly spaced line, red eyes blinking back at their master. Ahmed shivered as he turned and climbed down the ladder to his waiting bunk. Not his business.

He couldn't sleep. The images of that infernal string of blinking eyes had burned themselves into the backs of his eyelids and he wondered what kind of devilry he'd allowed himself to become involved with. He'd lived a simple life, worked hard, loved his God and looked after his family. Had he now, of all times, allowed Shaitan to worm his way under his skin with tricks and deceptions?

He pushed the hatch open as quietly as he could and climbed out. He could now see the long row of floating spiders stretching out behind the boat, glinting in the first rays of the sun. With the benefit of daylight, he realised his imagination had been twisted and distorted by the darkness and shadows of the night – these were not some evil creatures spawned from the bowels of hell. They were machines, made of metal and plastic, and their glowing eyes were nothing more sinister than small lights like the ones on his radio and depth finder.

He walked down the steps towards the boy who was standing on the lower deck talking into a telephone. As Ahmed approached, the boy lifted one hand, palm outwards, commanding him to stop. Who was this child to be issuing orders to him? And on his own ship? But Ahmed found himself stopping, nonetheless.

The boy picked up a black box from the deck and pressed a button. As though by magic, all the machines rose up in the air, before pausing and hovering high above the boat. There must have been at least a hundred of them. The boy pressed another button and the floating armada split into smaller groups, each making V-shaped formations like ducks flying North for the summer. A final button press and all the phalanxes jerked forward in unison, before shooting off to the South.

They were out of sight in seconds. The boy smiled and reached down to put the controlling device into a black holdall at his feet.

It was only when he straightened up that Ahmed saw the gun in his hand.

# 25

It hadn't taken long to find a suitable building with a view over Omar's villa, although the only access to the roof seemed to be from a neighbouring office block behind it.

Nadia and Ed stood at the back of the car and prepared in silence, strapping on combat vests, checking gun mechanisms and ammo clips and tucking explosives and flash bangs into secure pockets.

'We'll take the ropes,' said Ed, picking up two coils of smooth grey-black cord. 'In case we need to get down in a hurry.'

The roof of the first building was easily reached via a metal staircase, but the only way across to the other rooftop was via a narrow beam, maybe five metres long. Nadia watched as Ed walked calmly across it, apparently unaware of the twenty meter drop. She'd never been a big fan of heights.

Just as she stepped out on to the beam, Nadia's phone started vibrating, causing her to wobble and drop to one knee. This was stupid. She'd managed much more difficult things in training. She struggled to control her panic until she heard Ed's voice through the pounding of blood in her ears.

'Come on Nadia,' he said. 'You're halfway. Just stand up slowly and keep your eyes on me.'

The phone continued to vibrate as Nadia stood up and completed the last few steps to where Ed was waiting, crouched low and stretching out his right arm. They locked wrists and she felt his strength as he guided her onto the roof.

'You OK?' he said, maintaining a tight grip as Nadia steadied herself.

'I'm sorry,' she said. 'That was pathetic.' Her phone continued to vibrate, and she laughed nervously. 'I suppose I'd better answer that.'

It was David, and Nadia braced herself for the inevitable tirade.

'Nadia. Where are you?' he said.

'On the roof of a building overlooking Unicorn's brother's place with Ed,' she said, handing one of her earbuds to Ed. 'He's listening in.'

'OK,' said David. 'Well I'm in the ops centre at MI6 and everyone's here. You're an insubordinate nightmare, Nadia. But it seems you were right. We've been looking in the wrong direction.'

'Well. There's a thing.' said Nadia. 'What is it? What's happened?'

'Two passenger jets have just dropped communications and changed course.'

'Where?'

'The first left Cairo Airport an hour ago, and the other took off from Larnaca in Cyprus at five-fifteen.'

'Changed course to where?' As she spoke the words, Nadia realised she already knew the answer. Unicorn had dressed up a lifetime of murder and terror in words of principle and a fight for God's justice, but that was nothing more than a cloak. He wasn't more principled than anyone else – he and his brother wanted vengeance for their family. Nothing more.

'It looks like they're heading for Tel Aviv,' said David. 'Israel has scrambled jets and Iron Dome is at full alert, but something smells wrong. Unicorn must know there's no way past their defences. The planes won't get through, so why is he trying? What are we missing?'

Nadia thought back to her argument with Phil. He was always so certain about everything – people seemed to embrace that certainty and believe him. But nothing was ever black and white, especially not in a world where technology moved faster than anyone could imagine. The perceived wisdom was that it was a waste of time to attack Israel. Did that make it true?

'There's more, Nadia,' said David.

'Tell me.'

'As you recommended, we've had satellites monitoring Omar's villa,' he said. 'The whole place lit up like a roman candle about two hours ago. The heat signature is off the scale. It can't be a coincidence. He must be controlling the planes from there.'

'I knew it,' said Nadia. 'The way Ibrahim made those kidnappers release us. He was never going to do that just because he'd been in love with my mother. It made no sense.' She rapped her knuckles against her forehead. 'He had to let me go to stop anyone looking at Lebanon. He wanted us to stay focused on the US.'

'And we did just what he wanted,' said David. 'Except for you. I'm sorry, Nadia. I should have listened. How long until you can be on site?'

'About fifteen minutes,' said Nadia, looking at Ed who nodded in confirmation. 'But the place is well guarded and there's just the two of us. Ed's people sorted us with weapons, but I don't know how long it'll take us to get in.'

'You'll need to do it fast. A Special Forces team have already left Cyprus, but they won't be there in time. We've identified a skylight in the north-west corner of the main building as the best entry point. That's also where the radio signal's concentrated. In any case, Israeli defences will be engaging in the next fifteen minutes. They won't mess around.'

'And if they fail? How long until the planes reach Tel Aviv?'

'The first one is about forty-five minutes out, the second a couple of minutes behind.'

'Shit. That's not enough time, David. What about an airstrike?'

We've got open comms with the Israelis and the Americans and at least two missile-carrying drones are in range. We could take out Omar's place in plenty of time, but that won't help if the planes are locked on autopilot. We need you to get in there somehow and take control.'

'Great,' said Nadia, watching Ed who had already attached the two ropes and was throwing them off the side of the building. 'No pressure then. Do we have confirmation on how he's controlling the planes?'

'Yes. He's tracking them with an ultra-high power directional microwave like the one found on that truck in New York. They must have planted transponders on the planes. If we break the beams, we have no way of knowing if the transponder batteries will last long enough to get them to the target.'

'All right,' said Nadia. 'We'll be in position in fifteen minutes. I can see the skylight you mean and we'll aim for that.'

'OK,' said David. 'Call me when you're in place at the skylight. We'll know by then if the Israeli fighters have engaged successfully. If the passenger planes are down and the primary threat is neutralised, you stand down and wait for Special Forces. Is that clear?'

'As crystal,' said Nadia. 'I've got no desire to cross swords with Unicorn's Mujahideen mates. Remember, we don't have combat comms, so we're going dark for now. Message me updates as they come in. Wish us luck.'

Ed was already half way over the edge of the building, ready to abseil down. Nadia ended the call, not waiting to hear David's reply, and ran over to him.

'You go ahead,' she said, checking her assault rifle was strapped on tightly and picking up her own rope. 'I'll be right behind.'

They'd identified a large tree overhanging the compound wall, which allowed them to reach the garden at the back of the villa without triggering any alarms or security lights. The compound seemed deserted, but they could see cameras dotting the building walls at ten metre intervals.

'I don't think w've got a choice,' said Ed, looking at his watch. 'We'll have to just run for it and hope they're too focused on flying planes to look at the camera feeds.'

Nadia nodded. 'There's a staircase in the corner. Let's aim for that and go straight to the roof. I'll cover you from the top while you scope out the skylight.'

Before they'd covered half the distance, the entire area lit up in a blinding burst, dozens of halogen security lights sending stark shadows streaking across the lawns. Nadia was up the steps first, crouching behind the low parapet as Ed followed her up. She rested her assault rifle against the wall and placed two clips of ammunition next to it. Ed had already disappeared behind her.

Seconds later, the lights went off as abruptly as they'd come on and Nadia closed her eyes, counting slowly to ten to allow her vision to recover. There was a night vision scope on the rifle, but that wouldn't be much use if she couldn't see where to point it.

The sound of a twig breaking underfoot drew her attention to the tree they'd used to climb over the wall. A dark shape was moving very slowly underneath. No. Two dark shapes. As she brought the night vision into focus, Nadia saw that the man had a dog with him. She hoped she wouldn't have to shoot the dog. The poor creature hadn't done anything to deserve it.

Ed came back and squatted down next to her.

'What's happening?' he whispered.

'A hostile with a K-9 in the far corner,' she said. 'He'll be coming this way shortly. I'll need to engage unless a miracle happens.'

'OK,' said Ed, unstrapping his rifle and focusing the sight. 'Yup. I see him.' He gave a thumbs-up sign. 'I've found the skylight and rigged it to blow. We're ready to go if David gives the all clear.'

'You cover him, said Nadia. 'I'll call David. The Israelis should be engaging right about now.'

'David,' Nadia whispered. 'We're in position, but they know we're here. We'll need to engage in the next couple of minutes one way or the other.'

'Nadia,' said David, a note of panic in his voice. 'You need to get inside there now. The F-16s haven't managed to engage. You're all we have.'

'What?' said Nadia. 'Why not?'

'Each time they've tried, a cloud of drones has materialised around the targets, each one projecting a fake radar signature. The missiles haven't been able to lock on. The same goes for the ground-to-air systems. Tel Aviv is on Red Alert and people are going to the bomb shelters.'

'Jeezus,' said Ed. 'Drones. That's what the 5G chips were for.'

'… Not following you,' said Nadia

'Intelligent, autonomous drone swarms like the ones we saw in that firework display. And, if the drones are communicating using those prototype 5G chips, none of the existing jamming systems will have any effect.'

'Shit,' said Nadia. 'OK, David. We're on our way.'

She took three long breaths, allowing the fear and tension to meld into a measured, adrenaline-fuelled focus.

'Ed, blow the skylight,' she said, seeing him turn and run as she picked up her rifle. Then she focused her night sight on the figure walking towards them and flicked off the safety catch. Just a target – a shadow – not a man. A textbook double-tap, chest and head, and the shadow crumpled to the ground. Nadia turned and ran after Ed.

The skylight looked down into the long corridor which connected the villa with the office annexe. They agreed Nadia would cover the corridor while Ed set charges to blow Omar's secret door. There was no time to figure out how it opened.

Nadia was through the hole and on the floor before the last shards of glass had finished falling; if the shots outside hadn't brought any remaining guards running, the explosion was going to. She set her rifle to semi-automatic and dropped to one knee, facing down the long passageway. Seconds later, she heard Ed land lightly beside her. He tapped her on the shoulder and signalled he was moving towards the secret door.

Nadia struggled to find that all-important balance between full alertness and over-concentration. If she focused too hard on the target zone in front of her, she would tire quickly and her reactions would actually end up slower. She'd always found it easy in training, but this was different from anything she'd yet experienced in the field … and the stakes were unbelievably high.

'Fire in the hold,' said Ed as he sprinted back and crouched down behind her, covering his head and sheltering Nadia with his body.

She heard the double whoomph of the two shaped charges detonating, followed by a crash which must have been the door falling inwards. She wanted to look behind her as Ed moved off to enter Omar's secret room, but her job was to cover the corridor.

A man's scream followed by the sharp crack of gunfire set her pulse racing. Three pistol shots. What was happening? Should she be pulling back to support Ed?

'How many?' she shouted. 'Is the hard Mujahideen with the Spetznaz jacket inside?'

'Negative,' shouted Ed. 'It's just Omar with a pistol. Work your way back here slowly, but keep covering the corridor. I've got this.'

Nadia slowly edged towards the doorway without taking her eyes from the bright rectangle at the end of the passage. If the other guard wasn't inside with Omar, he would be coming from there. It was only a matter of time.

'All OK?' she called back.

'Under control,' said Ed. 'I have the pistol and there's no longer a threat in here.'

At that moment, Nadia saw a shadow move across the rectangle and suddenly there was the second guard, running at her full pelt, rifle set on automatic. Nadia was a great shot, but she wasn't a soldier and had no experience of being under fire. In that game of chicken, the battle-hardened guard was always going to be the winner.

She dived into Omar's office and rolled sideways, not even managing to pull the trigger of her own rifle once in her instinctive desire to escape the hail of bullets.

'Take cover, Ed,' she screamed.

The rest happened in slow motion. The Mujahideen warrior burst into the room, rifle still spraying bullets. He spotted Ed and turned towards him, bringing his gun around. Ed dived for cover behind the nearest shelter as the guard fired a burst of three, maybe four, bullets.

Nadia saw the look of horror and anguish on the guard's face even as she lifted her own rifle. He turned towards her and she watched the barrel of his gun swinging round in her direction. This wasn't a moment to be trigger shy and Nadia felt her training kick in at last. Before he'd completed his turn, she shot him twice, once in the chest and once in the head. He dropped to his knees and fell forwards.

She turned back to check on Ed and immediately saw the reason for the guard's look of horror. Ed had taken cover behind Omar's wheelchair and Omar was slumped forward in the chair, blood gushing from what looked like a fatal head wound. He'd been caught in the crossfire.

Ed seemed unhurt as he stood up from behind the wheelchair and Nadia felt her heart skip a beat. She'd started to care about the man and, apart from that, they needed him. He was the expert on remote flying systems – she didn't have a clue.

Ed reached over and pressed one of the buttons on the electric wheelchair, making it lurch backwards and out of his way. Omar's head lolled to one side, bulging eyes staring glassily straight at her. Nadia felt nothing. It was a shame they couldn't have taken him alive, but she wasn't sorry he was dead.

In front of Ed were two huge computer monitors sitting on a big metal desk. The rest of the room was filled with blinking computer racks and shelves of electronic equipment, most of which she didn't recognise. She ran over to stand next to Ed.

'We don't have much time,' he said. 'Those jets will hit Tel Aviv in less than twenty minutes.' He leant over the desk. 'Now, let's see what we've got here.'

Each screen held a perfect replica image of an airplane cockpit, down to the last detail. The windows were blank but, apart from that, they might as well have been sitting in the pilots' seats.

'He was controlling the planes by mapping in a standard cockpit from X-Plane,' said Ed. 'It's a gaming company which has simulators for pretty much every airport and airplane in existence. I have this software at home. Give me a second to figure it out. I don't tend to fly passenger jets. I'm looking for a button called Flight Director Mode … or maybe just Flight Dir.'

Nadia leant forward and scanned the screens. There were hundreds of buttons. How long was it going to take to find the right one? The letters on the buttons started to float in front of her eyes, forcing her to blink again and again.'

'We're never going to find it,' she said, panic edging into her voice.

'Hang on. I'll try Googling the manual,' said Ed, taking out his phone. 'It'll be quicker.'

'Wait!' shouted Nadia, pointing at a blue button in the centre of the screen. 'Is that it? There.'

'Brilliant,' said Ed. 'Well spotted. He tracked the mouse across the screen and clicked on the button twice until the display indicated 'OFF'. He then did the same thing with the other control panel.

'Nadia. Call David,' he said. 'Ask him if the pilots have manual control again.'

Nadia didn't hear him. She'd spotted Omar's laptop, which was sitting on the desk. The screen had suddenly filled with Ibrahim's face. He must have been on live video link to his brother and would have seen everything as it happened – Nadia had never seen such anger and hatred in someone's eyes.

She stood transfixed as if by a snake charmer until Ed slammed the laptop screen shut and shouted at her. 'Call David. Now!'

Nadia snapped out of her trance and dialled David's number. Ed grabbed the phone out of her hand.

'David,' he said. 'We're in Omar's office and we think we've disabled the autopilots. Do the pilots have manual control? Yes or no?'

Nadia watched Ed's face for clues. He was clearly waiting for a reply and she could see the hope and doubt rippling across his features. Then his head dropped, and she knew David's answer.

'Thanks David,' he said. 'We've still got a few minutes. I'll try something else.'

Nadia looked at the screens frantically, but had no clue what she was looking for. There were two small black boxes on the table, one next to each screen and each connected to thick wires snaking across the room. A single red button sat in the middle of each box.

'What are those for, Ed?' she said, pointing at the boxes.

He looked for a second and then his eyes lit up.

'Of course,' he said. 'Omar needed to isolate the computers from the transmission beam. Too much power and potential interference.'

He pressed one of the red buttons and a whirling circular symbol appeared on the screen. Five seconds later the symbol was replaced by a message – 'settings synchronised.'

'Yes,' said Ed and pressed the other button. When the message appeared on the second screen, Ed picked up Nadia's phone and handed it to her.

'You call him,' he said.

David put her on hold and she waited, counting the seconds as time ebbed away.

David's voice was almost a screech when he eventually returned. 'You did it,' he said. 'The planes have pulled up and the pilots have control again.'

Nadia couldn't believe it. 'Are you sure, David? The attack is aborted?'

'Yes. With maybe five minutes to spare. You saved a lot of lives today ...'

Nadia put the phone down and looked at Ed. She was on the point of hugging him when she heard voices from outside. She grabbed her rifle and signalled for Ed to cover her.

'Stay back,' she shouted in English and Arabic.

'Hold your fire!' The Welsh accent was enough to freeze Nadia's trigger finger. 'We're friendlies.'

# 26

Ibrahim stood in the faceless Manhattan apartment, staring at the cuts and bruises covering his knuckles. There was also an ugly gash on his forearm which was slowly oozing more blood. He felt nothing – not the pain of his wounds, nor the pain of Omar's death. He knew he'd failed, but still couldn't believe it. The plan had been foolproof. What devil-driven impulse had made him let Amal's daughter leave that room alive?

Just twenty minutes earlier, he'd been sitting at the low table hunched over his laptop. The breeze from the open window had been icy enough to speckle goosebumps onto his forearms, but he'd barely noticed.

The end had finally been in sight. Israel had taken Ibrahim's family from him and condemned his brother to half a life. For almost four decades, he'd nurtured his dreams of revenge like tiny seedlings until, at long last, the moment of truth was within touching distance.

For too long Israel had sheltered behind twin pillars of military superiority and a cold-hearted willingness to impose swift and disproportionate retribution for any attack. No longer. In less than half an hour two passenger jets would smash into the centre of Tel Aviv and the myth of impregnability would be shattered.

After that, if they managed to find either him or Omar, they could exact whatever retribution they wanted. It would have been worth it.

Finding them wasn't going to be easy, though.

Losing the New York generators had been bad luck, but they were always designed to be as much a distraction as anything else. In a post 9-11 world, the chances of any rogue flight reaching its destination without being shot down were slim at best.

Israel had always been the goal and with every nervous breath, he and Omar had been closer to finally taking their revenge. Almost forty years of waiting and the final twenty minutes would feel like an eternity. Using the drone swarms to spoof Israel's notorious air defence systems had been inspired. It had been Omar's idea of course – Ibrahim had never stopped marvelling at his brother's extraordinary mind.

He'd remained silent as he sat in front of his laptop, watching Omar at work. He hadn't wanted to disturb his brother's concentration and, besides, he had no need to ask for updates – Omar had provided a continuous commentary, seemingly without drawing breath.

'Both planes still locked on target … Already flying above populated areas … The Israelis must have started engaging over ten minutes ago … the drones are working.'

Ibrahim had found it easy to picture the Israeli command centres. Teams of professional and well-trained soldiers, swollen with confidence and arrogance as they went through the motions of foiling yet another futile attack. No need to ask permission to shoot down a passenger jet. There was always a standing authorisation in place.

Then the first reports of missiles failing to engage would have started flashing up on the screens. Additional reports appearing one after another as the clock ticked down and the two rogue flights moved through the safe kill zone and over population centres. Faces and voices shifting from calm efficiency to uncontrolled panic as the truth dawned on them – they didn't have a Plan B to deal with this threat.

Ibrahim's pleasure had been cut short when he'd seen the high windows behind Omar light up on his screen, followed by what sounded like the noise of a door slamming.

'What was that?' he'd said.

'It's only the security lights,' Omar's reply had been too nonchalant. 'It happens every couple of days. Normally when a cat comes over the wall. I would show you, but I can't look at the camera feeds and monitor the planes at the same time. Don't worry. Mohammed and Said will check it out.'

'Have your pistol ready,' said Ibrahim. 'We're so close. Nothing can be allowed to stop us now.'

'I have the gun right here,' said Omar, smiling. 'Relax, big brother. We still have four more drone groups on the flight path. Those planes will reach Tel Aviv. Now shut up and let me do what I need to do.'

Ibrahim hadn't been able to relax. His mind had never gifted him that luxury.

'... And Mohammed has everything ready for afterwards?' he'd said. 'You'll get out of there as soon as the planes hit?'

'Yes. Yes,' said Omar. 'I'll be on the boat before the dust has stopped rising ... now stop distracting me. This last bit is tricky.'

Ibrahim had seen the windows darken again – the guards must have switched off the security lights. He'd looked at his brother. Omar's eyes were flicking between the two screens and his fingers were flying over the keyboard. He'd been totally absorbed in his task and Ibrahim could see the pink nub of his tongue poking out from between his lips. Omar had always hated being teased about that – it had become a family joke – back in the days when they'd been a family.

He'd barely started to feel his heart rate slowing when there'd been a loud crash and the sound of falling glass. He'd looked around the small apartment and reached for his own gun, thinking for a moment that Homeland Security must have tracked him down. Then he'd seen the look on Omar's face. The explosion was there. In Sidon. His brother's eyes were wide and bulging white as he stared across the room at the entrance door.

'Ibrahim,' Omar had shouted, apparently forgetting about the screens and the planes. 'Something's happening. What do I do?'

Ibrahim had been tempted to punch his laptop. He should have been there. How could he help his brother from the other side of the world?

'Take it easy, Omar,' he'd said. 'Remember to breathe. Pick up the gun.'

He'd watched impotently as his brother took the pistol, held it high and started to wave it from side to side as though chasing ducks at a fairground.

'Calm down.' Ibrahim had done his best to exude self-control although his own nerves were screaming. 'Keep hold of the gun, but rest your hand on the table until you have something to aim at. Then, if anyone comes through that door, aim and squeeze the trigger. Take your time and make each shot count.'

'All right,' said Omar, beginning to breathe again. 'I'm ready.'

But he hadn't been. Of course he hadn't been ready.

Another explosion and what sounded like the entrance door

crashing to the floor. Ibrahim had been blind, completely reliant on what he could hear and Omar's reactions to whatever was happening. His poor brother had been wrapped in cotton wool all of his life and Ibrahim had trained enough inexperienced boys to know what would happen next.

Panic quickly became hysteria as Omar had picked up the gun and started firing. He probably wouldn't have been able to see anything through the smoke and dust and the chances of him hitting anyone were negligible. Ibrahim heard voices – speaking English – and then the shape of a man had appeared at the edge of the screen, grabbed Omar's gun and punched him hard. Omar had sagged back in his chair.

Ibrahim remembered reaching forward to put his thumb over the laptop camera. There was no point in letting anyone know he was watching. The man leant forward, examining the two large screens in front of him. It was Nadia's colleague from MI6. How had they got there so quickly?

Fortunately, the interfering fool would soon realise it was too late to stop the planes. They were locked on autopilot, the drones were preprogrammed and there was no time to stop them. But they had Omar …

What had happened to the guards? He'd picked up his phone and started writing a text to Mohammed.

It was hard to type one-handed and, before he'd written two words, Ibrahim heard the roaring of a man's voice and the sound of automatic rifle fire. Ibrahim had recognised his fellow warrior's berserker battle cry and put down his phone. The die was cast and, when the chips were down, he would back Mohammed nine times out of ten. These wet-behind-the-ears agents didn't stand a chance.

A woman's voice had screamed out a warning and Nadia's friend had dropped to the floor, desperately hiding from the bullets which ricocheted around him. But Mohammed's cry had transformed into a horror-filled scream and Ibrahim saw the red dot materialise in Omar's forehead like a Hindu bindi. It was only as the blood began to flow down his brother's face that Ibrahim truly understood what he was seeing.

Omar was dead. They had murdered him. He clenched his fists and tried to send his thoughts across the thousands of miles to Mohammed. 'Now, brother-in-arms. Now. Take your fury and kill them both. Omar is dead because of their meddling. Avenge him for me.'

The sound of gunshots. One. Two. A grunt and the clattering of a rifle dropping onto the marble tiles. It couldn't be. Ibrahim had felt the rage filling him like boiling water as he watched the man callously move Omar's body out of the way.

He'd taken his thumb away from the video camera. Let them see him. Let them understand their victory would be short lived. First the planes were going to crash into Tel Aviv, and then he was going to find them both. Let them see his righteous fury and know the truth.

He'd uncovered the camera and, in the same instant, she'd appeared – face filling the screen, and eyes wide with shock as they locked gazes. Nadia had been in his power and he'd let her go. Now Omar was dead because of his weakness. As he'd stared at her, he'd been forced to accept that it really had been weakness. Keeping attention away from Lebanon had been important, but the real reason why Ibrahim had let Nadia go was because he'd allowed the memory of Amal to find a way back into his heart.

He'd made a weak and foolish decision and his baby brother was dead.

Her colleague was talking to her, but Ibrahim had known Nadia wasn't listening. She and Ibrahim were joined by an invisible umbilical cord, each of them fighting to impose their will on the other. Did this girl really believe she was a match for him? He would not be distracted by weak sentimentality a second time.

And then Nadia's partner had reached out and slammed the laptop closed, the link had cut and Ibrahim had been left blind, screaming his anger and frustration into a blank screen.

But at least Omar's death hadn't been for nothing. The agents had arrived too late. Ibrahim remembered how a surge of savage euphoria had run through him as he'd reached for the television remote. He would watch the world wail in despair as the smoke and flames rose over Tel Aviv and they would all realise that nowhere was truly safe.

After that, he would have all of the time in the world to think about Nadia Laroche.

But there'd been nothing. The news channels had been full of pictures of drunken revellers in Times Square, but nothing about planes, nothing about Israel. It was impossible, but those meddling devils must have restored pilot control somehow.

And then, as Ibrahim played and replayed those final moments in his mind, the pain arrived. First in his battered hands and arms and then deep in his stomach and heart. Omar was dead. He'd failed him again and for the last time.

The truth of his brothers death was like a massive hand pressing down on his shoulders and Ibrahim felt the strength wash out of him; he sank to his knees, bowed his head and wept for his loss.

# 27

Nadia lowered her rifle to the floor and slumped forward as the Special Forces soldiers entered the room, moving to fill the space like well-rehearsed actors covering their marks before the first curtain. Ed was collapsed over the keyboard next to her, shoulders gently shaking. Was he laughing or crying? Or both?

A man wearing captain's bars walked up to them and saluted. 'Sir. Ma'am,' he said. 'It seems you made it here just in time. Well done.' Nadia looked up and smiled at him, feeling the lump in her throat and unprompted tears wetting her eyes.

'We need to get you out of here, pronto,' said the captain. 'You've been making a bit of a racket and none of us are exactly invited guests.' He turned towards the door. 'Follow me, please. My lads will be right behind us.'

He made no attempt to introduce himself or call them by name. Standard practice for Special Forces soldiers since the Northern Ireland conflict.

Nadia turned to Ed and smiled, resting one hand on his shoulder. 'Come on,' she said. 'Let's do what the man says.'

As they left the room Nadia turned and took a final look. The bodies of Omar and his guard had already been searched and laid out next to the computer racks, two soldiers were busy removing the last hard drives from the system and at least a dozen RDX charges were spread around the room, countdown timers flashing red warnings. Anyone trying to figure out what had happened in Omar's control centre was going to have a hard time of it.

The metal door by the front gate was open and a standard-issue black-tinted SUV was waiting outside. They climbed into the back seat and then they were away, leaving behind what already seemed like a surreal dream.

'We'll need to hang around an hour for the chopper,' said the nameless captain from the front seat. 'The lads will be making their way on foot.' He turned back to face them. 'Don't worry, though. It's a secure location.'

Nadia suddenly realised they may never be able to return to Lebanon, or at least not for many years. She leant forward and whispered in the captain's ear. She could see him thinking for a few seconds, before he nodded.

'OK, Ma'am,' he said. 'I'll see what we can do.' He then leant forward and started talking quietly into his radio.

'What was that all about?' said Ed.

'Nothing,' said Nadia, turning to face him. 'Can you believe we really did it? You were amazing with those simulators.'

'… And if you hadn't taken out that crazy mujahideen, things would be looking very different.'

Nadia didn't reply. She was too busy thinking about the way she'd frozen and then run when the man had first started firing.

'Listen to this,' said the captain, turning up the car radio.

'… to confirm, we have just received reports of two planes making emergency landings at Tel Aviv airport. Details are still emerging, but it appears that Egypt Air flight MS764 from Cairo to Rome and Easyjet flight EZ768 from Larnaca to Gatwick were caught in a freak magnetic storm in the Eastern Mediterranean. Early indications are that the storm caused malfunctions in both planes' avionics and navigation units and, despite the numerous safety and back-up systems which should prevent any interference, the pilots were forced to use emergency radio transceivers to call for support. Fortunately, the Israeli airforce were able to respond within minutes and scrambled eight F-16 fighters to identify the planes and to guide them to safety.' The newsreader paused for a few seconds. 'This just in,' he said. 'We can confirm that both planes landed safely at Tel Aviv's Ben Gurion airport and no injuries have been reported. The airlines and the aircraft manufacturers have so far refused to comment …'

'Hah,' said Nadia. 'Is anyone actually going to believe that bullshit?'

'Of course they will,' said Ed. 'People believe what they're told … and what they want to believe. I'm sure a few of the passengers will upload blurry photos of missiles exploding and drones zipping around, but it was a dark night and those images will soon become written off as the work of conspiracy theorists. I used to work with some guys at GCHQ who dealt with stuff like that full time.'

'Dealt with?' said Nadia.

'It's easy enough to discredit any social media posting,' said Ed. 'Make a couple of comments about the photos being Photoshopped, share the original posting with a bunch of paranoid nutter groups and, after a while, no serious person believes a word of it.'

Although Nadia had strong feelings about the brave new world of fake news and the associated loss of trust in authority, it was easier to believe that the agencies responsible for conscious, focused manipulation were on the other side of the geopolitical fence. The stream of idiotic drivel and denial coming out of the White House wasn't part of some devious strategy, it was just the random ramblings of a serial narcissist. She preferred to assume that the Russians, the Chinese and the North Koreans were the ones weaponising social media and she wasn't happy to be reminded that her own side wasn't entirely blame free.

She looked at Ed who appeared to be ready to launch into a full lecture on GCHQ's social media strategy.

'OK. I get it,' she said. 'Nothing is real or true any more and we're all just stupid sheep. I'm sure you're right, but it's depressing, isn't it?'

'Maybe,' he said. 'But better this way than terrifying the whole world by telling them we were minutes away from another 9-11.'

The captain's voice chipped in from the front seat. '… And having to explain what two British agents and a squad of Special Forces soldiers were doing in a foreign country without authorisation.'

'I know all that,' said Nadia. 'But where does it stop?'

It appeared no-one had an answer to that and they sat in silence until the car pulled into a walled compound on the edge of town. The electric gate whirred closed behind them, the engine was switched off and the pre-dawn silence settled over them like a woollen blanket.

'Feel free to get out and stretch your legs,' said the captain. 'We'll be here for forty minutes.'

As Nadia stepped out of the car, the events of the previous hour began to flicker through her mind in a series of disjointed flashing images. She felt a familiar sagging feeling as the adrenalin left her system and she leant against the SUV for support while she focused on controlling her breathing. Recapturing the euphoria of their success eluded her; all she could think about were the two bodies stretched out on the floor and the anger and hatred on Unicorn's face. Ed was pacing up and down a few metres away – Nadia suspected that, like her, he was lost in post-adrenaline shock and wanted nothing more than to be left alone.

Had speaking to the captain been the right thing to do? She hoped so.

Nothing much changed over the long minutes which followed – Ed's pacing slowed somewhat, Nadia no longer felt close to collapse and the first hints of dawn began to appear in the East.

The captain had disappeared into a small hut at the edge of the compound and Nadia watched nervously as he opened the door and walked towards her.

'She's here,' he said, nodding his head towards Ed. 'Have you told him?'

'Not yet,' said Nadia. 'I'll do it now.'

As she approached Ed, she felt a wave of affection wash over her. They'd spent such a short time together, but those hours had encompassed many of the most significant moments of her life. They were bonded together in ways she couldn't explain or understand, even though she felt further from understanding him than ever. Her request had been made with the best of intentions, but would it be appreciated?

'Ed?' she said, tapping him on the shoulder.

'Oh. Hi Nadia,' he said, eyes struggling to focus on her. 'Sorry. I was miles away.'

'Yup,' she said. 'It's all a bit surreal, isn't it?' She looked up at him. 'Look Ed. I did something. I thought it was a good thing, but right now I'm not so sure.'

'What is it, Nadia?' he said, eyes showing white in the darkness. 'What's wrong?'

'Nothing,' she said. 'It's just that … Look. I asked our anonymous captain to track down Ali's widow.'

'What? Why?' Ed's mouth was hanging open.

'I knew seeing her was important to you and neither of us are likely to be coming back here for a long time. If ever.'

'Sorry. I'm confused. I did want to see her. Of course I do. But I still don't get it.'

'She's here, Ed,' said Nadia. 'Waiting outside. You've got about twenty minutes.'

Several seconds passed – Ed's face remained blank and expressionless and Nadia began to sense that she'd crossed an invisible line by interfering in something so raw and personal.

'Where is she?' he said, at last.

'Just outside the small gate,' said Nadia, pointing across the compound.

Ed turned stiffly, robotically, and took a step towards the gate, before turning back and looking at Nadia. 'Thank you,' he said, voice tight with emotion. 'This means a lot.'

As Ed walked through the gate, Nadia felt her phone vibrate in her pocket. It was David.

'Hi Nadia,' he said. 'How are you holding up?'

Nadia took a moment to think before replying. She had no idea how to answer. All she felt was an overwhelming sensation of numbness, both physical and mental, but that probably wasn't a constructive thing to tell her boss.

'I'm OK,' she said. 'Everything's seeming like a dream right now. I can't really believe what just happened.'

'That's understandable,' said David. 'If you're not suffering from shock, I'd be surprised. At some point you're going to appreciate the enormity of what you two just did. All those lives you saved, not to mention the short and long-term consequences of Israel's inevitable reprisals if the planes had crashed. Not many people will ever know the truth, but a few of us will … and we'll never forget.'

The phone went quiet for a while. Nadia didn't trust herself to speak and leant against the SUV, shivering in the cold pre-dawn mist.

David broke the silence.

'I'm proud of you,' he said. 'Thank God you're so insubordinate and headstrong. It drives me crazy most of the time, but it made all the difference last night. I was wrong and should have listened to you.'

'Thanks, David,' said Nadia, suspecting this was a one-off, never-to-be-repeated admission. 'I'm looking forward to getting home and seeing you … after a shower and change of clothes, I hope.'

'Don't worry. There's no stress. Just travel safe and try to get some rest,' said David. 'You should be transferring directly at Akrotiri and back here late afternoon. Let's speak again when you land.'

As she hung up the phone, Nadia saw the small side gate open and the squad of Special Forces soldiers jog into the compound, followed by Ed. He walked towards her, but was only half way when she heard the rhythmic clattering of a Chinook helicopter as it flew low over the compound wall and settled quickly onto the sand.

It took less than two or three minutes of military efficiency to have all of them loaded, helmets and headsets in hand. The loading ramp was raised and before it was half way up, they were away, speeding low over farmland towards the coast. Nadia was strapped in towards the front of the helicopter next to the gunner and navigator. They both had their doors wide open, facing out with their feet dangling over the edge.

One of the soldiers tapped her on the shoulder. He looked at his watch and then pointed out of the window, his index finger wagging slowly from side to side like a metronome.

'Should be about …. now,' he said.

The sound of the explosion reached Nadia over the thumping of the helicopter rotors and then she saw red gouts of flame burst into the sky. Omar's control centre was no more.

# 28

As she watched the villa explode, Nadia felt as though a switch had been thrown inside her head. It was over. They'd done it. Against the clock and all the odds, they'd won. Her shoulders slumped and she sagged into the webbing harness, the heavy helmet pulling her head forwards. Her lead-lidded eyes closed and she could see Unicorn's face filled with shock and anger but, for the first time, she found it easy to sweep that image aside. He was still out there, licking his wounds and would need to be dealt with in due course. But that was tomorrow's problem – Ibrahim Abdel Hak could wait for another day.

That state of half-sleep, half-catatonia endured until the Mercedes limo pulled up outside Nadia's London flat. She could barely remember getting on the plane at Akrotiri, nothing about the flight and little about their arrival at Brize Norton airfield in Oxfordshire.

Ed was sitting next to her, smiling.

'I've never seen anyone sleep like that,' he said. 'Impressive.'

'You didn't sleep?'

'Oh, I slept plenty,' he said. 'But not while I was walking.'

Nadia stretched and reached for the door handle. As she got out of the car, the driver handed her the wheelie bag which had miraculously found its own way from the Al Qualaa Boutique Hotel.

She turned to say goodbye to Ed and he was right there, arms reaching out to wrap around her.

They hugged for a long time – no words needed to express their relief and shared pride.

'Will I see you tomorrow?' she said. 'David told me I didn't need to come in until the morning.'

'Yes,' he said. 'I'm debriefing with my boss first thing and then they want us all to get together.'

'Good,' said Nadia. 'I'll see you then.'

She walked up the familiar steps to her flat. Familiar, yet seemingly from a different world. Nothing was real, nothing made sense, but a long shower would help. She checked the telltale hair above her door – more a reflex action than anything else – and stepped into her empty flat.

There was nothing to eat in the fridge apart from a chunk of dry cheddar and some out-of-date yoghurts. There was, however, a cold bottle of Chablis which James had given her as part of his ongoing project to educate her about wine.

Nadia didn't care what side of the hill the vines were planted on, nor how they were picked, crushed or fermented. She loved wine though, and had a good idea of which types were her favourites. Chablis was one of them and, combined with some nuts and tortilla chips, would make for a perfect, healthy supper.

She hadn't bothered to dry her hair and could feel its dense weight swinging against the back of her dressing gown as she pottered around the kitchen. An evening of normality, sitting alone in front of a few episodes of Better Call Saul was what she needed. Then an early night – alone, wine-dulled and uninterrupted – would finish things off nicely. She could get back to the real world in the morning.

She settled into the sofa, took a sip of wine – delicious – and picked up the remote. The title sequence was barely over before Nadia realised she would need to call James before being able to relax. She couldn't tell him they were back as he would insist on coming over straight away, and that wasn't part of the plan. More lies were needed, but nothing new there – that seemed to have become the basis of their relationship.

'Hi Nadia.' James sounded so happy, it made her heart skip a beat.

'Hello sweetie,' she said. 'I'm sorry I've been so rubbish at calling. I've really not had a chance.'

'That's OK,' he said. 'You're calling now. When are you coming home?'

'Tomorrow or the day after, but it's not confirmed yet.'

'They really mess you about, don't they?'

'It's not always this bad,' she said. 'Anyway. How are you? Anything exciting going on?'

'Unless you call annual audits and lonely takeaways exciting, I've not got much to report, I'm afraid … I've missed you so much.'

'I've missed you too,' said Nadia, reflecting that she'd hardly had a moment to miss anybody or anything since she'd left for New York. 'But I'll see you very soon. I'll let you know when I'll be back as soon as I know.'

'OK,' said James. 'And what about you? Good trip? Any excitement?'

'Not so much,' said Nadia, noticing she was actually crossing her fingers. 'Sitting in airless rooms listening to dull investigators drawl on and on. It's typical. We dropped everything to jump on a plane and then everything slowed to a snail's pace. A bit of a wasted trip really.'

'And no time to call your boyfriend …?'

'You know what it's like,' said Nadia. 'Everyone wants to go for a drink after the sessions, then there's dinner, and what with the time difference …'

'I know,' said James. 'I'm not trying to give you a hard time. Are you on a coffee break?'

Nadia panicked for a second. He thought she was in New York. What time was it there?

'Yup,' she said as her brain joined the dots. 'And I need to go back in now. I'll try and call you tomorrow.'

'OK,' said James. 'I can't wait until you're home. I love you.'

'I love you, too,' said Nadia, hanging up. A little too abruptly, perhaps.

Peace and quiet were wonderful for less than an hour. The bottle of wine was half empty – probably more than half with an honest eye, but allowing the drinker to maintain that uncertainty was surely why the bottles were shaped that way in the first place.

Nadia struggled to concentrate on the TV. Although she was still exhausted, it was way too early to go to bed, and even finishing the bottle wouldn't be enough to put her to sleep. Her left leg was itching and she couldn't get comfortable on the sofa however much she moved around.

She should have talked to someone on the way home. It would have been cleansing to get a few things off her chest, rather than sleepwalking through the entire trip. There was only one person she could have talked to, of course. Only one person in the whole world who would really understand.

Maybe she should ask him to come over? Just for a chat. Although he might well misinterpret the late night invitation. That immediately brought back memories of their New York kiss. Had it really only been a couple of days earlier?

It wasn't hard to remember that kiss, the softness of his lips and the urge to hold him tighter, kiss him harder, pull their bodies closer together. She knew he'd been guilty of making the first move, but who had broken away? That wasn't quite as obvious.

She couldn't figure Ed out. He was a closed book and she still knew almost nothing about him, despite everything they had shared. She wasn't even sure she liked him that much any more. He'd been moody and unpredictable even before that first trip to Sidon … and, after Ali's death, it was as though a lot of the fun had been sucked out of him. There was something eating away at him, but if he wasn't prepared to tell her what it was, he obviously didn't think that much of her.

Or was there another reason why he was being so cagey. Could he be? … Nadia sat upright as the possibility forced its way into her mind like an ice pick … Could he be living undercover for some reason? It wasn't that unlikely and, if Ed Bailey wasn't his real name, he would have to stick to a pre-fabricated background legend – maybe he felt uncomfortable regurgitating lies to her and preferred to remain silent.

He really was infuriating. Did he not want to lie to her because he cared? There had definitely been moments when she'd imagined there was something more between them. A momentary spark which vanished as soon as it appeared. Then again, until that New York kiss, she'd almost convinced herself that Ed was gay.

It didn't matter. If he was living under an alias, there would be good reasons and she should respect them. She and Ed were colleagues and nothing more. She loved James and he loved her. Life was complicated enough without making midnight phone calls..

Ed was probably happily asleep, anyway. Whatever was bothering him, he hadn't lost his natural calm and that cat-like easiness he had. He wouldn't be squirming around on his sofa, scratching at his legs manically. He'd be lying in bed, purring gently with his lips curled into a gentle smile.

Nadia realised she'd been holding her phone, ready to make the call. She put it back on the table and stood up. Enough was enough – a last glass of wine and she'd go to bed. Sleep would come or it wouldn't. Calling Ed would have been a very bad idea.

As Nadia walked into her second floor office, she could feel every head turn towards her. She moved towards her desk, keeping focused on her friend Jenny who was looking up at her with a huge grin on her face.

And then Jenny stood up and started clapping. Nadia felt and heard everyone in the room following suit, the applause joined by shouts and whoops of congratulation. She couldn't ignore it, much as she wanted to, and she turned to smile at her colleagues, half-lifting one hand in recognition of the applause. Nadia felt tears filling her eyes as she looked at the beaming faces surrounding her. They were all part of the same team, fighting the same fight. This was what it was all about.

One she reached her desk and sat down, the office began to return to normal, although she couldn't help hearing a continuous murmuring and people were shooting furtive glances in her direction. Jenny leant over as Nadia wiped her eyes with the back of her hand.

'How does it feel, Nadia?' she said.

'How does what feel?'

'Being the hero of the day?' said Jenny. 'Zero to hero in less than two weeks. That's good going, girl.'

'I'm not comfortable with stuff like this,' said Nadia, peeling the Post-It note from her computer monitor.

'They want you on the sixth floor ASAP,' said Jenny, who had, of course, read the note. 'Meeting Room One. No time to hang around with us plebs. You'll be moving on to bigger and better things I expect.'

Nadia folded the note and dropped it in the bin.

'Rubbish,' she said. 'They just want a debrief. I won't be going anywhere.'

Jenny raised both eyebrows theatrically and as Nadia stood up to leave, she couldn't help hoping that her friend was right. Foiling Unicorn's attack had to be good for her career and they owed her a juicy assignment in any case. She felt light and energised as she picked up her bag and walked back out to the lifts.

Nadia's reception on the sixth floor wasn't quite as demonstrative as it had been downstairs, but the looks were the same … and even Phil Castle made a point of coming out of his office to shake her hand.

She was beginning to absorb the significance of what she and Ed had achieved. The investigation and the chase had been so intense, there hadn't been time to think beyond the next action. And, in any case, the real details of what Unicorn had planned – and what had very nearly happened – hadn't become clear until those final minutes in Sidon.

She escaped into the meeting room as soon as she could. The adulation would die down quickly enough; she just needed to make it through the first couple of days.

Nadia was the first to arrive and sat quietly at the end of the long table, remembering the last time she'd been there. Everything was the same – sitting alone, trying to calm her breathing as she watched the digital time stamp wander around the huge black screen at the far end of the room. It had been just half a year earlier, right before the Natural History Museum bombing and a few minutes before she'd met Ed for the first time. That screen had been the first place she'd seen Unicorn's face – the menacing image which had haunted her dreams ever since.

He'd looked quite different on Omar's laptop screen, his clean-shaven face in total contrast to the bushy, tribal warrior look of before. But the eyes remained unchanged – piercing emerald green and filled with so much anger. It wasn't hard to imagine him firing deadly green laser rays from those eyes like some sort of Marvel superhero.

And she'd stopped his grand plan. Well … with a little help from Ed. Together they'd undone that monster's grand finale and, for the first time since Sidon, Nadia felt the pride and shocked euphoria which comes from a righteous victory against impossible odds – like the Spartans at Thermopylae, or a tiny, shivering David staring up at Goliath with nothing but a smooth pebble and a hessian sling.

The Unicorn was still out there, but he would find it more difficult to hide without Omar's technology. There must also be clues on one of the hard drives taken from the Sidon villa and they would track him down soon enough. And after they found him …

Nadia had plenty of doubts about the morality of what went on in places like Guantanamo or the numerous black rendition sites run by military and intelligence services around the world. In the case of Ibrahim Abel Hak, however, she would open a bottle of champagne on the day they threw away the key to his cell. He had forfeited any human rights he might once have had and deserved the worst that could be thrown at him.

She looked down at her hands – both were clenched in angry fists. What would her father have had to say about her feelings of hatred and revenge? Nothing good, she suspected. Ten years as a doctor for Medecins sans Frontieres were evidence enough of his humanity and compassion for his fellow man. On the other hand, he'd spent his days dealing with horrific war injuries and poverty and Nadia would never know if he'd reserved a private hatred for the greedy monsters responsible for all that suffering.

The door swung open and David walked in, followed by a sharply-dressed man with a long angular face.

'Welcome back, Nadia,' said David, shaking her hand and clasping her forearm in lieu of a hug. 'It's good to see you home in one piece.'

He turned to the long-faced man, who stepped forwards. 'Can I introduce Moshe Berman, the Israeli ambassador. He's been impatient to meet you.'

'Miss Laroche,' said the ambassador, taking her hand between both of his. 'I am honoured to be able to thank you, both personally and on behalf of a grateful nation. Your bravery, skills and …' He smiled and looked at David. '… single-minded determination have averted an enormous tragedy. I really can't thank you enough.'

Nadia shrugged her shoulders.

'I was just doing my job,' she said. 'And we got lucky.'

'The results are the same,' he said. 'I'm sure you understand how much the peace process would have been set back if the attack had been successful.'

Nadia nodded. She had her own views about the chances of any peace process being successful, but this wasn't the time or place.

The ambassador finally released her hand.

'I will leave you to your meeting,' he said. 'I have already taken up too much of your time.' He turned and opened the door. 'Thank you again for what you have done for my country.'

'Well. He was a bit unctuous,' whispered Nadia, after the door swung closed. 'I was wondering if he'd ever let go of my hand.'

'That's his job,' said David. 'Most ambassadors are like that in my experience.'

They both sat down and David looked at Nadia as though he couldn't believe she was really there.

'The ambassador told me they plan to award you and Ed with the Medal of Valor,' he said. 'It's Israel's highest decoration. A huge honour.'

'I know what it is,' snapped Nadia. 'But you shouldn't expect me to be overjoyed. My grandfather would turn in his grave.'

'So. You wouldn't accept it?' said David. 'The Israeli invasion of Lebanon was almost forty years ago. Long before you were even born.'

'But memories run deep,' said Nadia. 'You only have to look at Unicorn and Omar to see that.' She took a moment to calm herself. 'And look at Lebanon today. It's a mess and half the population are starving. Are you telling me that isn't the legacy of 1982?'

'If you're going to turn them down,' said David, 'I need to know.'

'Let's see if they offer me the medal first,' said Nadia. 'Then I'll have a think and talk about it with Ed.'

There was a knock at the door and Phil poked his head into the room.

'Are you ready for us?' he said.

David nodded and Phil came in, together with a geeky-looking guy who Nadia recognised from the IT department. They sat down on the opposite side of the table and Phil's companion started fiddling with the remote controller for the big display screen. A presentation cover image filled the screen, the MI5 crest shining brightly in the centre.

'I've asked Phil to update us on the first findings from Omar's hard drives,' said David. He turned to Nadia. 'I'm not going to ask you to go through what happened in Sidon. That can wait until after you've given me your debrief report.' He lifted one eyebrow. 'Which I'm guessing I'll have by tomorrow morning?'

Nadia nodded. She'd already written the report in her mind and it wouldn't take long to put down on paper.

'Right,' said Phil. 'You know Simon, don't you?'

Nadia nodded again, and Phil's companion smiled at her before turning to face the screen.

'OK,' said Simon. 'We've been working 24-7 on the hard drives and on Omar's laptop. He was extremely talented and, without access to the drives themselves, I doubt we'd ever have cracked his security systems. Having the physical drives in our possession, however, gives us a huge advantage and we think we've got a handle on most of it.'

He moved to the first slide and launched into detailed technical explanations of how Omar had controlled the drones and how he'd hacked into the plane's avionics. He was clearly in awe of some of the programming involved, but Nadia wasn't particularly interested in the details of how it all worked. Ed would probably be fascinated, but he understood enough about systems to follow the logic, whereas she'd lost the thread – and the will to live – after the second slide.

'What about Omar's communications with Unicorn?' she asked, when he came to the end of his monologue. 'We never figured out how he's been keeping off the radar. Were they using encryption systems designed by Omar?'

'Yes,' said Simon. 'I was coming to that. The laptop had an extremely ingenious VPN system installed. I've never seen one like it, so I'm guessing Omar designed it himself. Not only does it disguise the location of the user completely, but it also makes it appear as though the login is happening from a specific, different location. The software comes with a preloaded list of hundreds of these dummy locations all over the world. The user just needs to choose one.'

'You need to explain why that's important to us,' said Phil, smart enough to know that Nadia and David wanted something to get their teeth into, rather than more fanboy adulation of Omar's programming genius.

'Sorry,' said Simon. 'Assuming that Unicorn has the same software installed on his computer, we'll know if he uses it.'

'How,' said Nadia. 'Have you broken the encryption key?'

'Not exactly,' said Simon. 'A simple trick, really. We've given Omar's list of dummy locations to GCHQ and they'll automatically flag and record anything originating from any one of those IP addresses. We should then be able to use that to track back the actual location and decrypt any messages or conversations.'

'But this relies on Unicorn using the system.' said Nadia. 'Surely he'll assume it's compromised and find an alternative?'

'We don't believe so,' said Phil. 'Without Omar's help, he'll struggle to find any other system we're not already keeping tabs on.'

Nadia looked at David.

'What do you think?' she said. 'Is Unicorn likely to take that risk?'

'I doubt it,' said David. 'He's always been so cautious. I'm thinking he'll move back to burner phones face-to-face meetings. We only need him to let his guard down once though …'

'There's one more thing,' said Phil. 'We've managed to track back all of Unicorn's communications with Omar over the past three years. We don't have the content, but we do have the actual locations. Do you know where he was when the attack happened?'

Nadia shook her head. It was past time that Phil moved back into his default mode of being smug and irritating.

'He was in an apartment in Brooklyn,' said Phil. 'He was in New York.'

'Hiding in plain sight,' said David shaking his head. 'He's nothing if not ballsy.'

'And the New York apartment was clean, I suppose?' said Nadia.

'Squeaky,' said Phil. 'Homeland Security are still there. They don't think he'll have been able to leave the country, but we'll have some confirmation on that in the next day or so.' He turned to face Nadia. 'There is one bit of intel you'll enjoy, though.'

'What's that?' she said.

'The TV was totally destroyed,' said Phil. 'It seems that Unicorn threw it at the wall and then smashed it up with a marble table lamp.'

# 29

The expected meeting with Ed and his MI6 colleagues had been pushed back and, when Nadia went back to the office the following morning, she ended up presenting her report to David and Phil without an audience. The process of putting things down in black and white and then spending three hours talking through every detail had wiped away the patina of otherworldly mystery from the events of the previous few days. There were no further updates on the Unicorn's location and it seemed safe for Nadia to relax – at least for a while.

She was back home by mid-afternoon and took the chance to get a few hours extra sleep. It was after six by the time she got up and, after a long hot shower, Nadia felt grounded in reality again and looking forward to seeing James.

Deciding what to wear for dinner was a welcome real world dilemma – about as far as possible from deciding how to break through the skylight of a well-protected terrorist's lair. Not totally straightforward, though – she did need much more time than usual in front of her bathroom mirror hiding scratches and bruises. Luckily, nothing was too visible and she'd already told James they wouldn't be able to spend the night together until the weekend. Hopefully the massive bruise on her thigh would be fading by then.

The restaurant was another of James's surprises – he never seemed to tire of thinking up new ones – but at least Nadia knew where they were starting the evening. They were going to her favourite cocktail bar, Mr Fogg's Residence in Mayfair. Set in a backstreet behind Berkeley Square, it was an unlikely location for an expensive bar, hidden amongst the messy service areas of some of London's most impressive buildings – a world of wheelie bins, fire escapes and massive air conditioners.

Nadia took a tube to Green Park and walked. The bright lights of Mayfair disappeared as soon as she turned into the grubbiness of Bruton Street until, after a few short paces, Mr Fogg's came into view – two flaming torches flanking the shining black door which was guarded by a huge figure in top hat and doorman's tails. He smiled, doffed his hat and opened the door for her.

A door into another world. The world of Jules Verne and his globetrotting hero, Phileas J, Fogg. Nadia could still remember her father reading her the stories of Phileas and his sidekick, Passepartout, as they'd raced around the globe. The inside of the bar was a snapshot of that forgotten fictional world.

The hostess was asking if she had a reservation, but Nadia had already spotted James waving from across the room.

'I'm with him,' she said, pointing.

'Great,' said the hostess, handing her the cocktail list. 'Have a wonderful evening.'

James stood up and leant forward to kiss her, the final piece in the puzzle which returned her to normality. She was home and she was safe.

'You're looking well,' he said, standing back. 'Almost like you've been in the sun.'

'I wish,' said Nadia. 'New York was bloody freezing.' She'd almost forgotten to check the East Coast weather. It wouldn't have been good to be caught in another lie.

James offered her his glass. 'Taste this,' he said. 'It's one of their signature drinks. A Passepartout, I think it's called.'

Nadia took a sip. 'Mmmn. I'll have one of those.'

James signalled to the waitress. 'They make nice enough cocktails,' he said. 'But otherwise I don't know why you like it here. It's a bit naff, isn't it? Not your usual style.'

'And what's wrong with a bit of naff now and then?' said Nadia. 'I know the place is just a bunch of props pulled from a Victorian tat warehouse, but sometimes it's fun to suspend disbelief, even for a little while. I allow myself to pretend it's real and that makes me happy.'

'... Definitely worth spending eighteen quid on a cocktail for,' said James as Nadia's drink arrived. 'Cheers.'

They clinked glasses and Nadia leant forward over the table.

'So. Where's dinner, then?' she said. 'I haven't had a decent meal since Christmas Day. American food always looks amazing and then falls short on the taste front.'

'I was going to keep it secret until we got there,' said James. 'But I'm dying to tell you. I've got us a table at Dinner. You know? The Heston Blumenthal place at the Mandarin Oriental.'

'Are you serious?' said Nadia, lifting her glass in salute. 'I've been wanting to go there for ever. That's the best surprise ever.'

Dinner, the restaurant, was everything it was cracked up to be. Buzzy, not fuddy-duddy at all and serving the most amazing food. Even more amazing considering it was all based on ancient recipes, some of them from the fourteenth century. For Nadia, the tipsy pudding had been the killer dish – she'd actually found herself giggling when she took her first mouthful. It tasted that good.

Dinner with James was also a wonderful experience. Afterwards, she couldn't have told anyone exactly what they'd talked about – this and that, everything and nothing. Time had evaporated like the tingle of tipsy pudding on her tongue and James hadn't asked a single work-related question.

He was even the perfect gentleman after he'd walked her home and they were saying goodnight outside her front door. It wasn't difficult to tell how much he wanted her, but there was no attempt to push matters. Nadia had enjoyed the evening more than any for a long time and was hard pressed not to suggest he did come in – she could have found some excuse for the bruises.

Wisdom and caution won the day, however, and Nadia wrapped both arms tightly around herself as she watched James walk back up the road, fading in and out between the street lamps until he disappeared completely.

The next morning, Nadia decided to walk to work. It would take her an hour and a half, across Clapham Common and then along the river to Vauxhall Bridge, but she'd been awake since five-thirty and needed to move her muscles. The sky was an unblemished eggshell blue – rare for smoggy, grey London – and, although it was cold enough for her to see the fog of her breath, there was no wind.

In any case, memories of the previous evening kept her warm. James had been a different man – no more inquisitions, no more prickly jealousy. It was as though he had experienced some sort of epiphany – managing to put their break-up behind him and, just as importantly, accepting the unreasonable rules which her job imposed on their relationship. She gasped as she remembered how close she'd been to calling Ed the night they came back. What had she been thinking? That would have been such a huge mistake.

As she walked along the side of the Thames, Nadia realised that a part of her had begun to question whether she and James would make it. They'd been on shaky ground ever since they got back together and rebuilding broken hearts was delicate work. She'd found herself struggling to ignore the small doubts which had begun to niggle away like worms inside an apple, eating away at the core while leaving the shiny skin apparently unblemished.

Those doubts had been partly why she'd avoided calling James while she was away. She'd obviously been fully engaged with work, but she'd also been afraid he would say something stupid, which would make her say something stupid, and then …

There were limits to how much of that sort of sniping a relationship could take.

As she walked across Vauxhall Bridge, she smiled as she found herself imagining his reaction if she were to drop to one knee and propose to him. Would his male pride be deeply offended or would he be delighted?

Nadia stopped walking. Where had that come from? One great evening together and she was jumping from rotten apple to confetti. After the emotional rollercoaster of the previous weeks, it was clear that she needed to get a grip on herself and, above all else, avoid making important decisions.

She held her icy hands to her cheeks and took a few deep breaths. The office was just ten minutes away and it was only eight o'clock. She had time to take a detour up to Pimlico and grab a double expresso from The Roasting. They claimed to make the best coffee in London and Nadia had never found a reason to dispute that. Her meeting with David wasn't until nine and there was no point passing by her sad second-floor analysts desk first.

David had assured her she would be getting a 'great' field assignment which should meaning moving back to the third floor, or even the fourth. He'd then refused to elaborate, clearly enjoying her frustration and telling her she'd have to wait until their meeting. She snorted at the memory. He was too old to play that sort of petty power game … although there were many worse ways to abuse power.

Nadia had bought a coffee for David as well and his face lit up when he saw the extra cup.

'Thank you,' he said. 'Thank you so much. I've got a machine outside which cost about as much as a Range Rover and the best beans available, but that woman still presents me with the same luke-warm, brown water every time.'

Nadia smiled. David wasn't stupid or out of touch. He knew that many of the things he said made him appear like the treasurer of a Home Counties golf club in some seventies sitcom. 'That woman' was the maternity leave cover for his long-suffering and much-loved secretary, Jane. Her replacement was prim, proper and efficient … and hadn't stood a chance with David from Day One. Of course, the idea of stepping out of his office and making his own coffee never crossed his mind. He knew how he came across to people who didn't know him well, and it amused him greatly to play along – even at the price of undrinkable coffee.

'When's Jane back?' said Nadia.

'Two more long months,' he replied, motioning Nadia to join him at the low coffee table. 'I'm very pleased for her. And her little boy is delightful. But I do feel she could have come back a little earlier in the circumstances.'

Nadia laughed. 'The way you behave sometimes, you're lucky she's coming back at all.'

'I've noticed …' said David, leaning back in his chair and doing his best to look serious. '… I've noticed you tend to show a lot less respect for my seniority when you've done well at something. Do you think that's clever?'

Nadia glared at him over the top of her coffee cup, not wanting to dignify his comment with a reply.

'Any news on Unicorn?' she said. 'How worried should I be?'

'I'll get to that,' said David. 'But first I want to discuss your next assignment.'

David's face was deadpan and Nadia had no idea whether to expect good news or another cleaner's job.

'OK,' she said. 'Tell me what you've got lined up for me. You promised it would be something substantial.'

David smiled. 'And you know me and my promises …'

Nadia still couldn't quite tell if he was bluffing and her heart missed a beat as David slid a sheet of paper across the table.

It was a photograph of a man, early thirties and extremely handsome. He was standing at the wheel of what must have been a very big yacht, perfect white teeth gleaming. He was dressed casually, but expensive-casual and the watch on his right wrist might have been solid gold.

'Recognise him?' asked David.

Nadia shook her head. The man could have been any one of the hundreds of rich playboys bobbing around the Mediterranean.

'His name is Ozman Yildirim,' said David. 'Turkish parents. Born in North London, now based wherever it suits him. Mostly on his yacht. He's come a long way from helping out in the local newspaper shop.'

'And what's so special about this one?' said Nadia. 'Apart from the fact that he looks as though he grew up in a family of oligarchs or presidents, rather than a tiny flat on Green Lanes.'

'I'll give you a bit of background,' said David. 'We know he's been involved in gangs since he was a teenager. The Met have a massive file on him, but he's still got a squeaky clean record – never been directly associated with any sort of violence or criminal act – not even a punch-up at school. His teacher's reports talk about him having an "uncanny influence" over his peers and it seems other people have always done the heavy lifting for Ozman. He's clearly very smart, but there's more to him than that.'

'So. He's some sort of criminal Derren Brown, then?' said Nadia.

'Something along those lines.' David wasn't smiling as he handed Nadia a slim folder. 'We now think he may be responsible for all people-smuggling coming out of Turkey – and everything crossing the channel into the UK.'

'Surely not all of it?' said Nadia. 'There must be competition.'

'From time-to-time,' said David. 'But apparently never for long. Turkey has a long history of fostering monopolies and cartels, starting from the huge market share of state-owned businesses. In recent years, they've done a lot to change that in the legitimate sector, but the crime syndicates don't seem to have got the message … and Ozman Yildirim appears to be particularly persuasive.'

Nadia tried and failed to match David's description with the spoilt-looking young man at the helm of a yacht. She looked at the folder which had a single word in large letters on the outside – Dante – which seemed like an apt name for the operation. The inside cover page contained an infographic, detailing flows of people and money. She'd kept a close interest on everything that had been happening since the start of the Syrian war and she knew only too well those huge numbers were easily translated into desperate people and unimaginable misery.

'What do you want from me?' she said, struggling to stop the string of horrible images tumbling through her mind.

'The police want us and MI6 more involved,' he said. 'His operations are based out of the UK, but the business is, of course, international and there are undisputed links with terrorism here at home. What we know about this man is frighteningly limited and we need to know more.'

Nadia looked at her hands. Not brown, but not exactly white either.

'Are you suggesting I go undercover in his organisation?' she said, feeling the tremor in her voice. Fear or excitement? Probably both.

'Not this time, Nadia,' said David. 'This time, I want you heading up the operation. You'll have a team of six and you'll be working with MI6 and a number of international agencies. The refugee problem is a political hot potato and we need to see results quickly.'

Nadia couldn't believe what she was hearing. This was a huge promotion – at least two grades. The sort of work she loved – and working to fix a problem worth fighting for.

'Thank you, David,' she said. 'I don't really know what to say apart from that I won't let you down. You have my word on that.'

'I know you won't,' he said. 'I wouldn't be giving you the bloody job if I thought you would.' He took back the photo and the folder. 'You'll find you have new access rights and can get to everything you need online. I've given you the rest of the week to get yourself up to speed so you don't look like an idiot when you meet your team.'

Nadia held the folder between her fingertips, unsure if she'd misunderstood something. The job was way more than she had expected and she was waiting for the catch. She stood up to leave, but David motioned her to stay in her chair.

'Before you go,' he said. 'We need to discuss Unicorn.'

Nadia settled back into her chair. She'd almost forgotten about Unicorn for an instant.

'We still don't know where he is,' said David. 'We've been working with the Americans to try to pick up his trail from New York, but for now, he's done his usual trick of disappearing into thin air.'

'So he's out there,' said Nadia. 'And he's angry.'

'Yes,' said David. 'We have to assume he's more dangerous than ever – and he would have had other plans in the pipeline. He always has.' He leant forward and looked at Nadia. 'Which brings me to the other element of your new role. I want you to continue to co-ordinate our Unicorn search with Ed Bailey and Danny Carhew from the FBI. It shouldn't take much of your time until he rears his head and we get some new intel, but the Americans have requested it and I thought you'd want to stay involved.'

'Thank you,' said Nadia. 'We both know it won't be over until he's behind bars or dead.'

'And you're not worried?' said David. 'For yourself, I mean.'

'A little,' said Nadia. 'I'd be stupid to ignore the fact that I'm not his favourite person, but what more can I do? I follow standard personal security protocols anyway. The only way to completely remove that risk is to find him and stop him.'

'I agree,' said David. 'But I do worry about you. Keep extra alert and let me know if you need anything. Anything at all.'

# 30

By Friday afternoon, after a week buried in the dark world of the Turkish mafia, Nadia was ready for a breath of fresh air. There was so much information to absorb, but few really solid facts. The web of people-smuggling organisations seemed to be inextricably mixed up in cults and conspiracy theories and, like in so many other ugly chapters in human history, many of the victims themselves ended up working for their exploiters.

She was dying to tell Ed about her promotion. As far as she knew he wouldn't be working on the Turkish operation, but he did have the right security clearance. With no other friends who were authorised to hear her good news, he was her best option. And, whatever he was, friend or colleague, she realised Ed was the person she wanted to tell first of all.

He'd suggested they meet at Muriel's Cafe in South Kensington which Nadia felt was a curious choice – the restaurant had been a key location in their failed race to stop the Natural History Museum bombing. There was a good reason apparently, but Ed wanted that to be a surprise – life would be much simpler if men stopped bothering with surprises. As she saw the cafe in front of her, Nadia found herself rubbing the small scar above her left eye.

It was great to see Ed. He looked happy and well, although there was something different about the tiny wrinkles at the side of his mouth and the slight shadows under his eyes. Small changes which left him looking less boyish than before. Life had caught up with him a little more rapidly than usual, but that wasn't such a bad thing; he was always going to be one of those irritating men who became more and more attractive as the years passed.

After a long hug, they sat down at the corner table he'd managed to grab. As usual, the place was full of South Kensington yummy mummies together with a smattering of American tourists on their way to see the museums. Nadia imagined how Hassan Qureshi, Snowflake, must have stood out in Muriel's. The poor boy had been so nervous, he'd almost ended up leaving his suicide vest behind.

'I hear you've got a new job,' said Ed, grinning from ear to ear. 'Congratulations.'

'Thanks,' said Nadia, feeling her cheeks warming. 'I'm unbelievably excited about it, but it's challenging stuff.'

'Yeah. That Turkish guy has a hell of a reputation for nastiness.'

Nadia laughed. 'No. Not because of that. All our targets tend to be nasty bastards. My problem is that I'm terrified of managing a team. I've never done it before and I can't imagine anyone ever doing what I ask them to.'

'Don't be an idiot,' said Ed. 'You told me once that your colleagues are all terrified of you. You'll be fine.'

'Maybe,' said Nadia, not convinced that fear was the management style she was aiming for. 'Anyway. How the hell did you know about my new job? Are you guys actually bugging David's office?'

'Probably,' said Ed. 'But I only know because it came up at a team briefing meeting on Tuesday. I'm not going to be involved in Operation Dante, but I'm glad we're going to carry on working together to track down Unicorn.'

MI6 and MI5 were theoretically equally important members of the security services, but there were different kinds of equal. There was no way that Nadia would have been briefed on an MI6 operation unless she was specifically working on it, and certainly not given details of the individuals involved. The two services played by different rules … unless Ed was actually more senior than he made out?

'What about you?' she said. 'I'm guessing you're not full time on Unicorn?'

'No,' he said. 'And that's partly why we're meeting here. Let's talk about Unicorn later. I really want to show you something first.'

'All right,' said Nadia, seeing a glimpse of the boyish Ed return. He was clearly very keen for her to see whatever it as and she didn't want to rain on his parade. 'Let's go.'

They'd only walked a few hundred metres from the cafe when Ed turned into a narrow alleyway between two brick buildings, stopped in front of a steel door and pressed a few buttons on an entry keypad.

'We're up here,' he said, holding the door open for Nadia. 'Just a bit more security to go through first.'

They walked along a series of faceless, institutional corridors, passing two more code-locked doors and a lift which was accessed via a retinal scanner.

'Is this part of Imperial College?' she said, beginning to get a sense of where she must be.

'Yes,' said Ed. 'We've got a couple of joint-venture projects running with them. That's why there's so much security. It's just in here.'

They walked through a final door into a narrow room with a long row of screens facing a big glass wall. All of the chairs were occupied by earnest-looking young men and women who looked like they might be oozing excess brain cells into the air like pheromones. The place could have been a television studio control room, but staffed by geniuses.

The main event was on the other side of the plate glass. A huge room, maybe twenty metres square, surrounded by five metre high glass walls and open to the sky. The floor of the room was divided into small sub-zones with tiny trees, small lakes, sections of tall grass and fake buildings. It was like a miniature movie set.

It took Nadia a few seconds to realise that the birds flying around the arena weren't birds at all – they were drones of all shapes and sizes.

'It's like a dream, isn't it?' said Ed. 'This is actually now my job.'

'What exactly?' Nadia watched as a drone crashed into a lake with almost no splash, only to emerge a few metres later, spraying drops of water from its rotors. Just like a cormorant or a kingfisher.

'I've been put in charge of MI6's drone development division,' said Ed. 'Working with a lot of brilliant people designing drones to help us do our job … as well as building anti-drone systems to stop them being used against us.'

He walked over to a large desk at the back of the room and picked up what seemed to be a toy drone. It wasn't more than four inches long, but when he handed it to Nadia, she could see it had three cameras, was very hi-tech and looked expensive.

'This is the Black Hornet,' said Ed. 'Front line troops have been using these for a few years now. They've got a range of a couple of kilometres and allow forces on the ground to scout ahead without personal risk. Hornets have saved dozens of lives already, especially by spotting IEDs ahead of time … but they have one problem.'

'What's that?' said Nadia, still feeling as though she'd walked onto the set of one of the Terminator films.

'They're too noisy,' said Ed. 'Fine, if you're trying to recce an enemy position in a war zone, but not so good if you want to listen in to a private conversation in a quiet room without being noticed. Even if the manufacturers do claim they are "nearly silent".'

'People might mistake them for very noisy mosquitos,' said Nadia, laughing as she imagined the buzzing drone hovering over a restaurant table.

'Not a hope, unfortunately,' said Ed, selecting another drone, slightly smaller and even more delicate. 'Now this one, however ...' He put it back on the table and picked up a controller.

Nadia couldn't stop herself gasping as the tiny device, lifted from the table with no sound. None whatsoever.

'How is that possible?' she said, tempted to swipe her hand above it to find the wires.

'At sixteen grammes, it's half the weight of the Black Hornet. Every moving component is almost frictionless and it has a dynamic noise cancelling system as a cherry on the cake. It works a bit like noise-cancelling headphones.'

'And this is your project?'

'Yes,' said Ed. 'At least it is now. I can't claim any credit for getting it to prototype stage, but from here on in, I'm the main man.'

Nadia looked at him and then across to the silent drone which was still hovering noiselessly about three feet above the table.

'You're a lucky man,' she said. 'You've landed the perfect job as well. I'm so happy for you.'

Ed held her gaze for a few seconds before turning away and using the controller to land the drone gently, like a feather, onto the table.

'I guess they decided they owed us both something,' he said. 'You know … for risking our lives, for being unsung heroes or whatever. Fair enough, really.'

As they were making their way back out to the street, Ed stopped and faced Nadia.

'We need to talk about Unicorn,' he said. 'Have you got time?'

'Of course,' said Nadia. 'I need to be back by eight-thirty because James is coming round, but he's bringing Chinese, so there's no food to prepare.'

Ed's choice of pub left a bit to be desired, but the beer was good and they found a quiet corner table.

'So. Why do we need to talk about Unicorn?' said Nadia. 'I thought we'd been making a point of avoiding the subject.'

'Not really possible,' said Ed. 'We had some new intel this morning …'

Nadia looked at him and raised her eyebrows. She had limited patience for dramatic pauses.

'There's no easy way to say this,' said Ed. 'He's here … in the UK.'

The taste of London Pride soured in Nadia's mouth. How had managed to get to England so quickly? With all the services on maximum alert, she hadn't considered the possibility for an instant.

'Shit,' she said. 'That's not the best news. How do you know?'

'The Americans have confirmed footage of him boarding a BA flight from JFK the morning after the failed attack. He got out before we discovered he'd been in New York.'

'But you can't be sure he's still here?' said Nadia, knowing she was clutching at straws. 'He could have transited at Heathrow. He could be anywhere.'

'Afraid not,' said Ed. 'Once they gave us the flight details, we were able to go back to the CCTV recordings at Heathrow arrivals. We tracked him as far as the tube and then lost him.'

'Shit,' said Nadia again, unable to find a better way to describe her feelings. 'So he's been here for days already. Do you think he's here looking for us … for me?'

'I don't know,' said Ed. 'But he's bound to blame you for Omar's death. You know he will. You have to be extra vigilant, especially when you're close to Thames House. He may try and pick you up there and the last thing you want is for him to find out where you live.'

Nadia's thoughts were scrambling furiously. Had she seen anyone suspicious outside the office? Could Unicorn have already followed her home? She tried to replay mental images of the street, but it was an impossible task. There were so many people at that time of day and if she'd noticed anything unusual, she would have remembered it.

'Thanks, Ed,' she said. 'I assume David will know by now?'

Ed nodded.

'Maybe I should move to a safe house for a while?' she said. 'Or at least beef up my home security.'

'Probably,' said Ed. 'We don't know why Unicorn's here, but you have to start with the assumption that he'll come after you. Me as well, but with you, it's personal. Remind me to send you the images of the TV at his New York flat. The screen was totally pulverised and there was blood everywhere. He must have cut himself badly, but carried on smashing it up regardless.'

Nadia sat quietly for a couple of minutes, sipping her beer and absorbing what Ed had just said. There was nothing she could do straight away. She would speak to David and consider the options. She looked up at Ed and forced a smile onto her face.

'If he's here somewhere, it'll be that much easier to catch him,' she said. 'Let's take it as a positive.' She put her glass down on the table.

'I know what I wanted to ask you,' she said.

'What?'

'Have the Israelis talked to you?'

'Yeah,' said Ed. 'I had a visit from the Ambassador right after he'd seen you. Strange bloke, but very grateful. And I heard this morning that they're definitely going to give us the Medal of Valor.'

'And you'll accept it?' said Nadia.

'Why not?'

'Well, for me, it's simple,' she said. 'Israel was directly responsible for destroying my mother's country and driving my grandfather to an early grave, but even without my personal angle, you surely can't support the way they've inflamed the Middle East and poured fuel on a religious conflict which may not have even needed to exist. And, not wanting to confuse state and religion, it's ironic that the main conflict we're facing now is Islam vs Christianity and Judaism doesn't seem to feature so much.'

Ed looked at her with wide eyes.

'Take a breath, Nadia,' he said. 'I get that you've grown up with those tribal resentments in your DNA, but you're an intelligent, educated person and you know perfectly well it's not so clear. That conflict goes back to the Middle Ages and before – long before the State of Israel existed. In any case, you wouldn't have such partisan views about the Troubles in Northern Ireland would you?'

Nadia shook her head. 'I guess not,' she said. 'I'd probably have to say that both sides are now equally responsible and the real culprits were the imperial colonialists. You know? The ones we work for.'

'And the same for India and Pakistan?'

Nadia nodded again.

Ed clearly had his own strong opinions about that subject.

'That's a region I know pretty well,' he said. 'Most Pakistanis I've spoken to – and Indians for that matter – believe that all of the Hindu-Moslem conflicts in the sub-continent were deliberately orchestrated by the British as part of a divide and rule strategy.'

'That doesn't surprise me,' said Nadia. 'We were famous for it.'

'So why is the Middle East any different? We had our dirty paws into everything after the First World War. Broken promises, self interest, deals made by aristocrats sitting in their leather chairs at White's Club. The Balfour Treaty, Sykes-Picot. It's the same story. Once the initial imbalance is created, it's inevitable that each side will do what it thinks is necessary to defend itself.'

'I know all that,' said Nadia. 'And don't forget, despite my family history, I just risked my life to stop those planes hitting Tel Aviv. But that's my job. On a personal level, I don't have to stand up and accept a medal from the country which caused my grandparents so much pain.'

'Fair enough,' said Ed. 'And do you want me to refuse as well? Personally I quite like the idea of having a gong to show my grandkids.'

'Oh. I don't know,' snapped Nadia, annoyed that Ed was making her feel petty and vengeful. 'I can't see that I've got the right to ask that, but it would be strange if you went there on your own.' As the words left her mouth and she realised what she was saying, Nadia developed a sudden interest in the froth at the bottom of her beer glass. What did it have to do with her what Ed did?

'Let me think about it,' said Ed. He waved his hand under her eyes. 'Cheer up. We're supposed to be celebrating our new jobs.'

# 31

Ibrahim sat quietly in the sole chair which occupied the tiny room. Time was running out. If he didn't leave London soon, they would catch up with him for certain. Without Omar to help him cover his traces, he was vulnerable in any Western country. The cameras were everywhere and their computers were too powerful.

He had only left the damp flat once – to buy some food and to meet the private detectives. He was about to go out again, but that would be the last time. Then he would have to leave.

He knew he was living on borrowed time, but there was one last thing to do before he could disappear. He owed it to Omar and had made a sacred promise to the memory of his brother as he vented his anger and frustration that last night in New York. On a television set of all things. The first time he had truly lost control of his temper since he'd found out that Amal had gone off with the Frenchman. And he'd wasted that pure white-hot fury on a piece of electronics.

He looked down at his right hand which was throbbing under the bandages. Earlier that morning, he'd seen the telltale streaks of red running up his forearm and suspected the antibiotics he'd been taking weren't working properly. They were from an old field medicine kit and were probably out of date. Another ticking clock, but he needed to focus on the task in hand. He would find more antibiotics afterwards.

And then he would go back home and take that trip to the desert he'd been promising himself. No-one would find him there. But maybe he would be able to find himself again. Ever since the failed attack and the death of his brother, he'd struggled to understand the point of anything. The driving force of Ibrahim's life-purpose, which had always burned magnesium-bright for him, had been snuffed out as though plunged into icy water. The only thing keeping him going was the dull, black ache of vengeance which gnawed away at him like so many starving rats.

It had been easy enough to find out where Nadia lived. His locker at Paddington Station contained enough cash and weapons to last a long time and the private detective was greedy enough to see no reason to doubt his story – he was an angry husband whose beloved wife had left him. The heartbroken husband didn't know where his wife was living, but assumed she still worked at Tate Britain, next door to the MI5 headquarters. The roll of fifty-pound notes was convincing enough to deal with any uncertainties.

All the agency had needed to do was to post a couple of men armed with photographs of Nadia at strategically placed points on Millbank and wait. She would have to go back to the office at some point and they could follow her home when she left. After that they would use a team of four to watch her house around the clock and report on all the comings and goings.

The operatives had picked her up on the second day and were certain the faithless wife hadn't noticed them. Ibrahim had relied on her having her guard down so soon after what happened in Sidon. The bonus had been when they'd seen her hugging her boyfriend outside the house and sent half the team to follow him home. They would earn an additional fee for that. It was only money after all.

He got up from the chair and walked towards the kitchen. It was time to finish the surprise.

The idea for the vest had come to him during the flight over from New York. He'd already started to run a fever from his infected hand and didn't have any medication – which had led to some very strange dreams.

In one of those dreams, he'd found himself on the beach with Omar, walking hand-in-hand, laughing. They were both adult men and Omar was how he would have been – fit, strong and not burdened by a lifetime of struggle and bitterness.

Ibrahim thought they may have been talking about girls. There was something about the mischievous look in Omar's eyes. And then, without warning it happened.

He felt his brother's weight pull on his arm as Omar collapsed to the ground, legs suddenly withered and useless. He stared up at his big brother, imploring him to do something, to make it all different, and all Ibrahim could do was to watch as Omar's features twisted and morphed into the bitter, angry face of the man he'd eventually become.

Ibrahim had woken with a start. Everyone else on the plane had been asleep and it was then that he'd known what he must do.

He looked around the kitchen of the small flat. The holdall he'd collected from Paddington station was waiting for him on the table and, as he pulled back the zip with his left hand, he felt awash with a sense of clarity and purpose he hadn't felt since Omar's death.

It might be the fever messing with his head, but he doubted it. He'd been taking double doses of paracetamol since he arrived in

London and the antibiotics from his medical kit must have had some effect. For the time being his right hand was almost useless, but he'd survived multiple gunshot wounds, bombings and knife wounds in the past. He was strong and would get better.

It wasn't the fever. He'd lost his way before, but now the future was clear. Ibrahim knew what was required of him. He and Omar were going to be remembered for a very long time.

He took the pre-wired bomb vest out of the bag and laid it carefully on the table. Then he picked up a small block of C4 plastic explosive and sliced off a piece. He'd rolled some cardboard into a cone earlier that day and it took only a few minutes to mould the explosive around the card, leaving a hollow cone-shaped indentation at its centre.

Ibrahim had first learnt about shaped charges during a year spent working on oil rigs in the Kurdish mountains. The shaped indentation caused the explosive to focus all its energy out through the cone into a single plasma jet … with incredible results. The ones they had used on the rigs were only the size of an egg, but able to punch a clean hole through ten centimetres of steel, fifty centimetres of concrete and a metre of limestone.

Ibrahim took his homemade version, slipped it carefully into a canvas pocket at the back of the vest and eased in the detonator. He'd checked all of the wiring and the remote activation switch already; everything was ready to go. He checked the remaining contents of the bag one last time and then laid the vest on top. It was time.

Very few people were around as Ibrahim walked along the Uxbridge Road, carrying the holdall like a backpack. It was wet and cold and dawn was still an hour away. The sooner he left this miserable country the better.

The second taxi he hailed pulled over and switched off its yellow light.

'Little Venice, please,' said Ibrahim. 'Fifty-four Randolph Avenue.'

'Right you are,' said the driver. 'Shouldn't be more than half an hour this time of day. Lucky you're not going a bit later. It'd take you three times as long. Like a bloody car park this road, sometimes.'

'Yes. Lucky indeed,' said Ibrahim, quietly thinking that nothing much would ever have been achieved in his life if he'd trusted to luck.

'You all right, mate?' said the driver. 'You don't look great.'

'I'm fine,' said Ibrahim, holding up his bandage-swaddled right hand. 'I have an infection, but the antibiotics will begin working soon.'

'Good,' said the driver. 'As long as you've seen someone for it.'

Ibrahim managed to avoid further conversation by pretending to be asleep, only opening his eyes when he heard the taxi's door locks click open.

James lived in the basement flat which meant his front door was sheltered and private. It was just before seven o'clock and the private detectives had told Ibrahim that James left for work at seven-thirty exactly. Every day. He would be up and about, although he wouldn't be expecting visitors.

Ibrahim walked down the steps to the basement entrance and took a small brown cardboard box from his bag, before pressing the button on the video entry phone.

'Yes?' said the disembodied voice.

'Delivery for Mr Barclay,' Ibrahim said, looking straight at the camera and holding up the box.

'Can you just leave it there, please?' said the voice.

'Sorry,' said Ibrahim, making a squiggling motion with his hand. 'I need a signature.'

'All right,' said the voice, clearly annoyed. 'Hang on a second.'

When James opened the door, his hair was wet and he was wearing a dressing gown.

'Sorry,' he said. 'I was in the shower.'

And then he saw the gun in Ibrahim's hand.

Ibrahim needed less than five minutes to find out where James kept Nadia's keys and get her alarm code. The boy was spineless and disloyal, although he did give Ibrahim an incorrect alarm code to begin with. The correct code only materialised after Ibrahim had explained what would happen if he went all the way across town and the alarm went off.

With James tied and gagged and two sets of keys jingling in his pocket, Ibrahim left. He had two more stops to make and then everything would be in place. Taxis were a decadent luxury, but they kept him away from security cameras and he didn't need to spend much time in either location. One cab would do for the entire round trip.

# 32

Nadia and Ed definitely had one beer too many and Nadia was bursting to go to the loo by the time she got home. She fumbled the key in the lock and almost forgot to check for the hair which should have been stuck across the door frame.

It wasn't there.

Nadia examined the frame quickly – she really did need the loo – but there were no signs of a break in. James was the only other person who had a set of keys. Maybe he'd come early for some reason? She took the can of pepper spray from her bag, cradling it in her left palm as she unlocked the door.

'James,' she called as she pushed open the door. But there was no reply. She closed the door behind her and ran to the bathroom, locking herself in just in case. When she came out, the flat was empty and silent – she must have just forgotten to stick the hair on that morning. Or it had fallen off. No surprise that she was jumping at shadows, though. Unicorn was in London. The threat was real.

She walked cautiously through to the living room and it was only then that she saw the note sitting on the low oak coffee table. Written on a folded piece of A4 paper, the Arabic script was perfectly formed – beautiful, flowing and evenly spaced. Nadia stiffened and spun in a circle, holding the pepper spray out in front of her. The letter must be from the Unicorn. He had been here. In her home.

She didn't touch it, but took a photograph before leaning forward to read it.

*'Dear Nadia,*

*Please read to the end before doing anything stupid. You will understand why.*

*I have James.*

*I need you to follow these instructions exactly:*

*- Pick up the phone which is behind this note.*

*- Leave now and take the underground to Greenford station.*

*- When you are outside the station, call the last number dialled from the phone and follow the instructions.*

*If you tell anyone, set off any alarms or fail to follow any of the instructions, James will die.*

*I will be watching.*

*Ibrahim.'*

Nadia couldn't breathe. How had he found her so fast? And how did he know about James? Maybe he didn't actually have him? She dialled James's number and listened as it rang and rang before clicking into the cheesy answerphone message he found so funny. Perhaps he was on the tube, on his way to meet her?

She knew James wasn't coming, though. The Unicorn had him – there was something inevitable, inexorable about the way Ibrahim operated, like a glacier grinding through a mountain valley. He was a force of nature and he didn't bluff.

Nadia didn't take long to analyse her limited options. She was trapped and the only thing which made sense was to go along with the instructions and hope for a better opportunity to present itself. If she contacted the office, they would mobilise maximum resources to capture the Unicorn. James would be a low priority.

She picked up the mobile burner phone from the table and put it in her coat pocket. Then she took her own phone and sent the image of Unicorn's note to Ed with a short message. 'I'm leaving now. You decide what to do. I trust you.' And then she walked out into the night.

It was already getting late as Nadia left the underground station. Most people had finished work and had gone home for the day. She called the number on the phone, but there was no answer. What was she supposed to do? Was he waiting in the shadows with a gun or a knife?

A few moments later, the phone beeped and she saw she'd been texted a postcode. Not exactly detailed instructions, but the message was clear. She pulled up her collar against the icy wind and set off into the night.

The last few open shops were pulling down their shutters and, as she followed the phone satnav down a twisting warren of backstreets, she could feel the isolation pressing in on her from all sides. Looking at the broken windows and rusted padlocks on the gates, most of the factories and workshops in this part of town had been closed for years.

Should she have called for back-up? Unicorn's note had made it painfully clear what would happen to James if she didn't arrive alone. If Ed had picked up her text, he would hopefully figure out what to do. Always assuming he was checking his phone. She had a knife in the sleeve of her jacket and the pepper spray in her bag, but no other weapon. Ed would be able to track her location, but the Unicorn would know that.

Her destination was at the end of the road. A pair of massive steel gates in front of a low concrete building – long gabled roofs chequered with panes of reinforced glass. Nadia wondered briefly what they had made there when she saw the fading sign above the gates, bookended by two musical notes – Columbia Records. It had been a record factory, but not for a long time.

The heavy chain around the gates was hanging loose and she leant her weight against the iron bars, the tortured screeching of rusty hinges sending shivers though her already-trembling body.

In front of her, a single, weak lightbulb picked out an open door in the wall of the main building, the black rectangle standing out against the white paintwork like a missing tooth. She walked across and stepped inside – what choice did she have? – ears straining to hear signs of someone lying in wait. She checked her phone – no signal – either Ed was on his way, or he wasn't.

She waited just inside the doorway while her eyes got used to the darkness. There was only silence and no ambush, just a long walkway stretching out between the shadowy forms of what must have been the old record presses. Another single lightbulb at the end beckoned her onwards and the only sound was that of her echoing steps as she approached the glass-fronted door of a small office.

She opened the door, carefully, slowly, and walked into an empty room, glass-windows on all sides. There was no-one to be seen as Nadia turned around, body tensed in a fighter's crouch, aware of how exposed she was, her skin tingling with the anticipation of a bullet's impact.

She completed a full three hundred and sixty degrees before she heard a familiar voice coming from the far corner. It was the Unicorn.

'Hello, Nadia,' he said. 'You've taken a long time to get here. I was beginning to worry.'

Nadia peered into the shadows, but there was still no-one there.

'Over here,' he said. 'On the table.'

Of course he wasn't there in person. He was too clever for that. Nadia walked over to a small plastic table and turned the laptop to face her. She had wished so hard that the next time she saw that face was cold and lifeless on a slab, but clearly she hadn't wished hard enough. Ibrahim's mouth was curled in a nasty sneer, although his voice wasn't as strong and confident as the last time they'd spoken.

'I knew you'd come,' he said. 'The dashing damsel rushing to the rescue whatever the risk.'

'I want to see him,' said Nadia. 'Let me speak to James.'

'Of course,' said the Unicorn. 'Here you are.'

The image on the screen span around and there was James, strapped tightly to a chair, eyes staring madly from a bloodless face. He seemed unhurt, but was clearly terrified and there was a dark patch between his legs. He was gagged with a white cloth and she could hear him grunting as he strained against the straps and tried to call out to her.

'You said I could speak to him,' she said.

'And so you can,' said Ibrahim. 'I said nothing about him speaking to you.'

'James,' she said, willing him to take strength from her. 'I'm so sorry, but don't worry. It will all be OK. I promise.'

Before she could see if he'd believed her, the image on the screen swung back to the Unicorn. As he adjusted the camera position, Nadia saw there were angry red streaks on his neck and beads of sweat on his forehead. Something was wrong with him. He wasn't well. Maybe he had that new bat virus from China?

'… And it will all be OK for James,' Unicorn said. 'Providing you do exactly what I ask you to. If you don't follow my instructions to the letter, then his fears will prove to have been more than justified.'

Nadia squeezed her hands tightly together to control the shaking.

'I'm here now,' she said. 'What do you want me to do, you bastard?'

'You murdered my brother,' Unicorn said. 'You may not have pulled the trigger, but it was you who killed him.'

'You know exactly what happened,' said Nadia. 'I had to try to stop you. I told you I would.'

'I remember,' he said. 'And I made sure you knew what would happen if you tried – Amal's daughter or not. There is no longer any room for sentimentality; someone must pay the price.'

Nadia stared at the screen. Ibrahim was shaking and the window was wide open behind him. Whatever was wrong with him was burning him up. If she could hold on long enough, she might have a chance.

'Open the box on the floor,' he said.

Nadia looked down and saw a large cardboard box. She pulled open the loose flaps to reveal a bundle of black material. It looked like …

'Take out the vest and put it on,' he said. 'Just like so many heroic martyrs before you.'

What was Unicorn planning? He must know Nadia would never go through with a terrorist attack, even if it cost James his life. She lifted the vest out of the box between finger and thumb. Something wasn't right. The vest was much too light to be packed with explosives and shrapnel.

'Are you crazy?' she said. 'I'm not putting this on.'

Ibrahim lifted his hand and she saw the glinting coldness of a cutthroat razor dangling loosely in front of him.

'I will count to three,' he said. 'One … two …'

'All right,' Nadia shouted at the screen. 'I'm doing it.'

'Pull the straps tight,' said Ibrahim.

Nadia's fingers were moving by themselves. She couldn't bear it if he hurt James. He hadn't signed up for any of this. She needed to buy some more time. Hopefully Unicorn would make a mistake, give away his location, anything that might give her a chance.

'Now take the two red leads and clip them together.'

Nadia felt as though she was floating outside her own body, looking down at a stupid, doomed woman who was following the instructions of a mad terrorist. She hesitated and looked down as the disembodied hands pressed the connectors together. There was a loud beeping noise and a red light began to flash on one of the connectors.

'Good,' said the Unicorn. 'Now it is armed. Any attempt to remove it or tamper with any of the connections will immediately activate the trigger.'

Nadia had studied suicide vest construction and had been certain that would be the case. The men who planned the attacks sat safely in the shadows and made sure that a change of heart from the young, naive bombers wasn't an option. She could only hold on to the belief that her own sacrifice, in an empty warehouse, might save James. It had to be enough.

'Now,' he said, wiping the sweat from his face with a towel. 'Would you like me to tell you what happens next to my brother's murderer?'

'You may have wondered why the vest was so light,' Unicorn said. 'There's a reason for that.' He laughed, which started him coughing into the towel.

'Just get on with it,' snapped Nadia. 'Stop dragging out your sadistic story like some second rate James Bond villain. Do you really believe I'm going to walk into a crowd of people and detonate this? You can't force me to hurt anyone else, you know. You can kill me and that's it.'

'So impatient to die,' he said. 'Although it won't be quite that simple.'

Nadia glared at him. For a few moments her anger had been stronger than her fear, but it wasn't long before the reality of her predicament came flooding back in a rush of terror.

'Let me explain,' he said. 'The vest contains a small shaped charge and nothing more. Around twenty grams of plastique – probably not enough to harm someone standing right next to you.'

'I don't understand,' said Nadia. 'What's the bloody point, then? What's this vicious farce all about?'

'When the charge is detonated,' he said. 'It will generate a plasma jet with a single purpose. The explosion will sever your spinal cord, somewhere between the L3 and L5 vertebrae. Nothing more.'

Nadia felt the bile rising in her throat as his words sunk in.

'You killed my brother,' said Ibrahim. 'And you stopped me getting my revenge on the country that crippled him. The price you will pay is to live the rest of your life as Omar did.'

He knew she wouldn't be his tame suicide bomber, but this … she could picture Omar all too easily, with his muscles atrophied though lack of use and his tight-set lips oozing anger and resentment at the cards life had dealt him. She wouldn't cope with that well. She began to shake, clenching her teeth and hands and forcing herself to stay focused. She needed to think.

'You might as well just kill me now,' she said.

'Why would I give you the luxury of a swift end?' he said, shaking his head and holding up his mobile phone like a weapon. 'You have an hour to make your decision. James and I will be watching. If you leave the warehouse or if anyone else enters, I will detonate the charge, you will be paralysed and James will die. There is a manual switch in the pocket of the vest. If you don't press the button yourself before that hour is up, the charge will detonate automatically and James will die. And one more thing, Nadia. If James dies, he will die slowly …'

'You mean you want me to cripple myself.'

'Exactly,' said the Unicorn. 'Now you understand. Nothing can save you, but if you want to save him you must activate the detonator yourself. You must make the choice to live like Omar did. You are a brave girl, Nadia – truly your mother's daughter – but actions have consequences and my brother is dead because of you. Don't worry. I will call the emergency services as soon as you make your final decision. There will be bleeding.'

# 33

Ibrahim looked over to James who was cowering in the corner like the dog that he was. Amal would have been ashamed of her daughter if she'd seen Nadia with this worthless cur. He realised that, whatever Nadia decided, he wouldn't bother to torture this man. The infidel wasn't worth the effort. Maybe it would be best to just kill him straight away to stop the whimpering.

He looked at the screen. Nadia hadn't spoken for several minutes. She was staring into the laptop camera, eyes full of hatred … and fear. There was definitely fear there. She was smart and experienced enough to know that her options had run out. The final victory would belong to the Unicorn after all.

As he prayed silently that Omar was able to watch this small victory from the other side of Death's door, he felt a sharp, stabbing pain in his left bicep. A wasp or a bee – probably crawled inside to see out the winter. He slapped at it hard, realising too late that he was using his infected hand. The agonising jolt which ran though his right arm almost caused him to cry out loud and it took a couple of seconds for him to realise that he'd been stung by a creature much larger than a wasp.

And not a creature at all … He reached down and picked up the twisted bundle of plastic and metal. The device was tiny, not much longer than his thumb and weighed almost nothing. It was only when he saw the small plastic rotor and the needle protruding from one end that he realised what had happened.

Ibrahim let out a cry of anger and reached for his phone. They might stop him from giving James a painful death, but they would be too slow to save Nadia. The phone number for remote detonation was set on speed dial and he smiled as it flashed onto the screen. All he needed to do was press the green button and Omar's revenge would be complete.

# 34

Nadia watched with sick fascination as the tiny drone hovered behind Ibrahim and then dipped forward to strike. Ed must have got her message after all. Ibrahim slapped at his arm and she saw the grimace of pain as he moved out of range of the laptop camera, before looming back into shot, crushed drone in one hand and mobile phone in the other.

He was leering triumphantly as he pressed buttons on the phone. What drug had Ed used? Would it be fast enough? Did anything work that quickly?

Unicorn's finger was poised to strike and Nadia wrapped her arms tightly around her chest. It was too late. She didn't know how much the explosion would hurt, but she knew the damage would be permanent. There would be nothing left for clever surgeons to piece together.

She remembered Omar sitting slumped in his wheelchair. Could she ever find the inner strength to live like that? A part of her was hoping Ibrahim had overdone the explosive and she wouldn't survive the shock. Maybe that would be better than the alternative.

At least James would be OK. She hadn't put her head into the lion's mouth for nothing.

Ibrahim's face loomed large in the screen as his finger moved lower … and then …

Nadia gasped as she watched those heartless emerald eyes glaze over and the phone drop from his hand. She heard a fingernails-on-blackboard screech as the table slid away and then the clattering of both Unicorn and the laptop hitting the floor.

Once she was sure Ibrahim wasn't getting up, Nadia stood upright and relaxed her arms. She placed one hand on her stomach and reached behind her back with the other. Nothing, except for the soft material of the suicide vest and the murderous lump of the high explosive behind her. She had been granted a reprieve, but was still trapped.

She heard a voice from the laptop in front of her and there was Ed's wonderful face.

'Nadia,' he said, his eyes shining brightly. 'God, I'm pleased to see you. I nearly passed out when I saw your message.'

'Lucky you didn't,' she said. 'What's happening, Ed? I'm still not out of the woods here. There's a timer switch in this vest and, by my count, I've got less than half an hour.'

'Don't worry,' he said. 'Bomb disposal will be with you in ten minutes, we have Ibrahim in custody and James is going to be fine.'

Nadia felt a rush of blood to her head and turned away. It was too soon to be relieved. She wouldn't put it past Unicorn to have lied about the timer or to have extra booby traps in the vest. Too soon to be relieved, but she couldn't stop the waves of hope flooding through her.

She only half-heard Ed's voice coming from behind her.

'Just hang on in there, Nadia. They'll be with you in a few minutes.'

The next five minutes were an eternity and then she saw torches flashing at the end of the row of record presses and watched as the team moved towards her. They stopped about ten metres away and one soldier moved closer holding a blast shield in front of him.

'Evening, Ma'am,' he called out. 'Any danger of trip wires or booby traps?'

'No,' she replied. 'I came in through that door earlier. I'm pretty sure he was relying on his mobile phone trigger to keep me here.'

'OK, I'll take your word for it,' said the man, gingerly turning the door handle. 'I'm Sergeant Thompson – Joe – we'll have you sorted out in just a minute.'

He entered the room and walked towards Nadia.

'Could you spin around slowly, please,' he said. 'And tell me what you know about the device.'

'As far as I know, there's only a single charge,' said Nadia as she turned around, arms held high. 'Shaped plastic explosive, and at the back of the vest. It felt very light when I picked it up, so that fits. His plan was to destroy my spine so I'd be a paraplegic like his brother.'

'Sick bastard,' said Joe. 'Anything else?'

'I'm pretty sure the straps are all wired,' said Nadia. 'And there's a timer due to go off in ten minutes.'

Joe beckoned and the rest of his team came running into the room. He turned and issued some instructions which Nadia couldn't hear. The men knelt down and began unloading their backpacks while Joe turned back to face Nadia.

'We don't have a lot of time,' he said. 'So, here's what we're going to do.'

As he went through the next steps, Nadia felt the fear returning. His plan was a long way from just knowing whether to cut the red wire or the black wire and didn't fill her with confidence – but what choice did she have?

She stood like a statue as Joe gently felt around the vest to check for other charges, before slowly sliding a large ceramic plate between the back of the vest and her body and securing it with tape. He then pulled her hair forward over her shoulders, and wrapped an asbestos blanket around her neck.

'This will stop the plasma jet,' he said. 'It's rated to block an M2 50-calibre round.' He moved round to face Nadia. 'There will still be a hell of an impact, though … and you'll be thrown across the room.' He pointed to where the rest of his team were standing, arms locked like footballers facing a free kick. 'Face towards us, head down and arms crossed in front of you. Don't worry we'll catch you.'

He put a pair of soft headphones over her ears, before walking over to the other soldiers and joining arms with them. Nadia couldn't believe what was happening. They were just going to wait until the charge exploded. What sort of amateur hour had she got caught up in?

She counted the seconds in her head, but it did nothing to make time move faster. She'd estimated there were five minutes to go, but it wasn't until almost the seventh minute was counted away that it happened.

She felt as though a giant hand had swept her aside like a crumb from a table leaving her face down, unable to breathe as the bomb disposal team swarmed over her, tearing away flaming material and shards of red hot ceramic plate and spraying her with a cooling gel. She tried to push herself up, desperate for air, but they wouldn't let her move.

Joe pulled away the ear protectors and shouted at her.

'Stay still,' he said. 'You're all right. Just a bit winded, but we need to get all this stuff off of you pronto. Give it a sec and you'll be able to breathe.'

It was easy for him to say, thought Nadia as she gulped for air with no success. She could feel the men's hands brushing burning embers from her buttocks and thighs and the realisation came to her just as the first gasp of smoky air entered her lungs. She had feeling in her legs. Her spinal cord wasn't broken. Somehow the crazy plan had worked.

# 35

Nadia's back wasn't broken, but she was sore all over.

The hospital had discharged her before midday – plenty of scrapes and bruises and a few minor burns, but nothing broken and they'd given her some painkillers which left her feeling warm and fuzzy.

She couldn't quite remember how she'd ended up in the hotel room. Everything after the explosion was a blur. The room was comfortable and quite big – although not exactly a suite – and someone had organised some clothes and toiletries for her.

She could remember getting an emotional message from David, telling her to rest for a few hours and promising to visit her later on. It was hard to rest as the warm, fuzzy feelings only lasted until she remembered the suicide vest. Her memories were stuck at the moment when Unicorn's finger was poised to detonate the charge – the moment she'd imagined feeling the explosion tearing through her.

Every time her mind slipped into that loop, she would get up out of her chair and walk around the room – to remind herself that she could. Then she'd make herself a cup of hot sweet tea because everyone knew that was the best cure for shock.

No-one had given her any updates about James or Unicorn, nor how Ed had managed to find her, but she wasn't in a hurry to find out. Such patience and disinterest was unlike Nadia. She clearly wasn't herself – another cup of sweet tea might help.

The news channel was running on the TV, but there was no mention of the dramatic events of the past few hours. There probably never would be. The Unicorn wasn't destined to be the subject of a high-profile publicity announcement. His future would involve being silently spirited away to some rendition site or other … and then passed around between the various security services until he lost his mind or his heart gave out.

Nadia wanted to see him one final time before then, though.

Someone was knocking at the hotel room door. When she opened it, David swept into the room and gathered her up in an all-enveloping bear hug. Nadia noticed the woman police officer over his shoulder and suddenly remembered she'd been the one who'd brought Nadia to the hotel in the first place. Had the policewoman been standing outside the door the whole time? Protecting her from what?

'David,' she said through gritted teeth. 'Could you put me down, please. I've just been blown across a room and I'm quite sore.'

'Oh God. I'm sorry,' said David, releasing her as he pushed the door closed with his heel. 'I'm just so unbelievably happy to see you in one piece.'

'Not as much as me,' she said. 'Come in. Grab a seat.'

David sat in the single armchair while Nadia perched on the end of the bed.

'How are you doing?' he said. 'I can't imagine what it must have been like … and on top of everything else, as well.'

'To tell you the truth, I'm fine,' said Nadia. 'For a short while, I imagined the worst and that was awful. But I got lucky again thanks to Ed, and with Unicorn safely out of the way, I actually feel like I can breathe freely for the first time in a long while.'

'That's wonderful,' said David. 'I've always known you were a tough cookie – you have an incredible ability to take a dribble at the bottom of a glass and make it appear half full.'

Nadia laughed. 'Not always,' she said. 'While Unicorn was explaining his plan for avenging Omar by crippling me, my water glass was definitely bone dry.' Talking with David, she could feel some of the shock and numbness fading away, but slowly. 'What am I doing here, David? It's all a bit of a blur. I'm guessing it's the drugs they gave me at the hospital.'

'The medics do like their opiates, don't they?' he said, laughing. 'We had you brought here while forensics finished up in your flat – which was under surveillance by the way.'

'No. Are you serious?' said Nadia, leaning forward. 'By who?'

'It seems Unicorn employed a private detective agency to have you followed from work and watched,' said David. 'That's how they knew where you – and James – lived. The agency is now co-operating fully with our enquiries.'

'Bloody hell,' said Nadia. 'I'll bet they are … I should have spotted them, shouldn't I?'

'They were using a big team,' said David. 'But, yes. They've been watching your home for four days – you should have made them.'

The good thing about the morphine-induced numbness Nadia was feeling was that being criticised by David didn't sting like it normally would.

'What about Ibrahim?' she asked. '… And James? How's he coping?'

'Let's start with the easiest of the two,' said David. 'James is all in one piece. Still in shock – we're arranging for counselling, of course.

He did ask if you were OK, but has also asked that you don't contact him for the time being. I met him briefly earlier today, but I don't have much of a sense of how badly this is going to affect him long-term.'

So. Maybe Unicorn would have some revenge, after all. Nadia thought back to the images of James in the chair, terrified and powerless, desperate to be saved. How was he going to get past that and not blame Nadia? She would give him time and do what she could to save their relationship, but a part of her was already mourning what might have been her last chance of a normal life.

'I'm sorry, Nadia,' said David. 'He might come round in time.'

Nadia squeezed her eyes closed and dipped her head. She didn't believe James would be able to put this behind him and the loss sat like ice in her stomach. She didn't know what hurt most. Losing James or being forced to face her dwindling hopes of having a proper family. Maybe it was time to stop pretending. She opened her eyes and looked at David.

'Now, I need to tell you about Unicorn,' he said, his tone more serious and professional.

'What?' said Nadia, feeling her left leg start to tremble uncontrollably. 'Don't tell me he's escaped.'

'No,' said David. 'Not exactly … He's dead. His heart failed on the way to the hospital.'

'How could that happen? Surely what Ed gave him was only supposed to knock him out.'

'We don't know,' said David. 'Could have been an overdose, a rare side effect or it may have had something to do with the infection he was fighting. We might find out more after the autopsy, but I doubt it.'

Nadia wasn't sure whether she was pleased or disappointed. She'd wanted to look into Ibrahim's eyes as they took him away, but at least this way he was definitely never going to be a threat again.

'Shit, David,' she said. 'A lot of people are going to be really unhappy about that. Especially the Americans.'

'Tell me about it,' said David, standing and walking towards the door. 'That's why I need to get back to the office now. To listen to a string of sanctimonious Yanks shouting at me for a few hours. Again. It's great to see you looking so good. You get some sleep and we'll catch up properly tomorrow.'

As David left, Nadia couldn't help thinking about Ibrahim and the circumstances which had turned him into the monster he'd eventually become. She pictured the teenager struggling to look after his crippled brother – crippled by the same foreign invaders who'd killed the rest of young Ibrahim's family. The same adolescent boy whose perfect girlfriend had then been stolen away by a foreigner.

That was how these things worked. Ibrahim hadn't chosen his path alone. The truth was much more complicated.

Nadia assumed that sleep was going to be impossible and lay on the bed staring at the ceiling, resigned to counting sheep for hours.

The next thing she knew, she was being dragged out of a wonderful dream by the sound of her phone ringing. Why hadn't she switched it off? She'd never get back to sleep and the dream had been so warm and comforting. She found the phone with bleary eyes. It was Ed.

'Why did you wake me up?' she said. 'I just needed a little rest.'

'You've been asleep for twelve hours,' he said. 'I think that'll probably do.'

Nadia held the phone out in front of her. Eight in the morning. He was right.

'I'm in the lobby,' Ed continued. 'Join me for breakfast?'

Nadia smiled. 'Give me half an hour to grab a quick shower,' she said.

'No problem,' said Ed. 'I've got a coffee and a newspaper. See you in a bit.'

As the hot water cascaded over Nadia's bruised and battered body, she thought about Ed. Every time she believed she was getting to know him better, he showed a different side to his character and she was back at square one. His mercurial personality shifts were driving her crazy, but she knew she wasn't well placed to judge.

Why did she even care? He was just a colleague and he wasn't her usual type in any case. Having confused emotions was normal after everything they'd been through together. Ed was a good man and had proven more than once that he would be there for her when the chips were down. She owed him a huge debt, but the feelings that there might be anything more between them were nothing more than PTSD-induced ramblings.

They would soon be going their separate ways and that was as it should be. She would miss him and he'd turned out to be a great partner, but now Unicorn was dead there was no reason for them to carry on working together. Time to move on.

The lobby was crowded, but she spotted Ed straight away and found herself almost running towards him. There were tears in her eyes as she hugged him.

'Thanks for being there with your little drone friend,' she said. 'I knew I could rely on you.' She released him and brushed some imaginary fluff from his lapel. 'Come on. Let's find a table and you can fill me in on everything.' The effects of the morphine and the shock were long gone and Nadia was back to her normal impatient, inquisitive self.

Ed nodded his agreement – Nadia wondered if his eyes might be a little moist as well – and they walked down the spiral stairs to the breakfast room.

'OK,' she said as soon as they'd sat down and placed their orders. 'The first thing I want to know is how you knew where to find Unicorn. I've got GPS trackers in my phone and under my arm, but you had nothing to tell you where he was. It's been niggling away at me since I woke up.'

'We were lucky,' he said. 'Unicorn used Omar's VPN software to set up the video call between the two laptops. He must have assumed it would be more secure, but as soon as he entered one of the dummy IP addresses, all sorts of alarms started ringing at GCHQ. They were able to hack into the video feed and the locations, so we knew exactly what was going on about ten minutes after you arrived at the record factory.'

'So …' Nadia said, gulping as she remembered those final moments in the record factory. '… If he hadn't used that software, you wouldn't have known where to look?'

'Worse, actually,' said Ed. 'We'd already located you using the tracker in your arm, but we wouldn't have found Unicorn in time. If we'd come to you, we wouldn't have been able to do anything to stop him detonating the charge remotely. You'd have been crippled, James would have died and the Unicorn would have got away.'

David often talked about Nadia's cat lives and she wondered how many of them she had left – if any. She could all too easily picture what might have happened. Ed would gone straight to the record factory and been left watching powerlessly through his drone camera as the charge went off …

… But it hadn't happened that way. They were here, now, and

Unicorn was dead. Spilt milk and not worth a single tear.

The arrival of breakfast was a welcome distraction. Nadia had ordered the works – bacon, sausage, mushrooms, beans, tomatoes, hash browns and two eggs. She felt drained and emptied out on every level and fatty carbs washed down with mugs of strong tea seemed like the ideal solution. Ed on the other hand was being much more modest and on trend with his smashed avocado on sourdough.

The waiter, predictably, tried to give her the healthy option and Nadia watched Ed grinning as she made it very clear who was having what. She shrugged her shoulders.

'I'm hungry, OK?' she said as she picked up her cutlery. 'I feel like I haven't eaten for weeks.'

'I'm not judging,' he said. 'It's great to see how quickly you're bouncing back, although I probably shouldn't be surprised any more.'

He cut a small mouthful of his breakfast and lifted it to his mouth before putting the fork back on the plate.

'I'll miss working with you, Nadia,' he said. 'I don't think "fun" is the right word, but I can't remember ever experiencing as much as I have in the past few weeks. We made a good team.'

Nadia nodded. 'No doubt,' she said, fighting hard to keep the emotion out of her voice. 'I've loved working with you. But there is something which has been bugging the hell out of me.'

'What's that?' said Ed. 'Have I been picking my nose? I do that, apparently'

'No. Don't be stupid,' said Nadia. 'It's nothing like that. I just don't understand how I've ended up knowing so little about you. We've talked about me a lot, but whenever I've touched onto your private life – either family or relationships – it's been like getting hold of a freshly landed trout. You always find a way to wriggle free and change the subject.' She laughed nervously. 'To tell you the truth, I've decided you must have been working undercover the whole time and Ed Bailey is nothing more than a paper identity.'

'Really?' said Ed.'Seriously?'

Nadia nodded.

'Absolutely not,' he said. 'And I'm pissed off you could even think that. If we can't be ourselves with colleagues, that leaves us nowhere to hide, doesn't it?'

'Of course I agree,' said Nadia, surprised by how happy she was he hadn't been lying to her. 'I never said I wanted to find out you weren't real, did I?' She speared a chunk of sausage and dipped it her egg. 'So why do I know so little about you, then?'

'Well, for one thing, I don't really like talking about myself,' Ed mumbled, shrugging his shoulders. 'I never have, not since I was a kid. It's safer just to ask the odd question, lean back and listen. Most people are happy to fill the silences.' He laughed. 'If the films and magazines have it right, I'm the perfect guy.'

'There are limits,' said Nadia. 'It's no fun hanging out with someone who doesn't have their own values and opinions, their own stories and experiences. Everyone needs a bit of colour, and relationships have to be give and take.'

'Hang on,' said Ed sharply. 'Where did that come from? You know perfectly well I've got values and opinions,' said Ed. 'And my life hasn't been a total bore … Not as interesting as yours, maybe, but not dull.'

'Sorry,' said Nadia. 'That came out wrong. I'd just like you to stop shutting me out. It doesn't take a mindreader to see you've got personal stuff going on … and I don't think it's all because of Ali.' Nadia took a deep breath. 'Although you've also avoided talking about what happened to him completely. I was there as well. If I can't be a shoulder for you, who can?'

Ed looked at her. 'I'm not sure you really want to know,' he said. 'Apart from anything else, it's embarrassing.' Nadia could hear the emotion in his voice and wondered if she'd pushed too hard. She felt like a Peeping Tom.

'I'm sorry,' she said. 'I didn't mean to pry.'

Ed shook his head. 'No. Nadia. You're right. I've been building walls and it's not fair. Not to you. Not after everything we've been through together.' He cleared his throat and sipped his coffee.

'I was engaged,' he said. 'Or I thought I was. Her name is Amina and she worked at the Deputy High Commission with me.'

'Not a Pakistani national?' said Nadia, suddenly filled with a sense of dread. Surely Ed couldn't have been that stupid?

'No,' said Ed, half smiling. 'I'm not a complete idiot … And, before you ask, she wasn't a Moslem either. Amina was a Coptic Christian. Her family came from Alexandria, although she grew up in London. She worked in security and I'd already met her a couple of times while I was at GCHQ. First-language Arabic speakers are like gold dust at the Doughnut. When I got posted to Karachi at short notice, it was great to see a friendly and familiar face. The last thing I expected was to fall head over heels in love with her.'

'So what happened?' said Nadia, thinking about her previous assignment and another Egyptian femme fatale. Mona El Masry had been the reason why the National History Museum bomber had tipped into a downward spiral of anguish and despair. The whirlpool which had eventually driven him into the arms of the Unicorn.

'We were together for three years,' Ed continued. 'In-house relationships were strictly *verboten* and we had to see each other in secret. We both kept second phones, just for us. The only other person who knew what was going on was Ali.' Ed was gripping the edge of the table as though afraid he might fall out of his chair. 'Ali was our go-between and our look-out. He was the best of friends.'

'I'm sorry,' said Nadia. 'I know you miss him.'

Ed released the table from his grip and interlocked his fingers. 'Anyway,' he said. 'Just before they called me back to help with Unicorn I asked Amina to marry me and she accepted. I know you thought I was a total airhead when we first met, but I was on Cloud Nine and struggling to get my feet back on the ground.'

He looked up at Nadia, blinking. 'And then I met you, the bombing happened, you nearly died and they reassigned me to the UK. I assumed she'd be happy to come back with me. We'd get jobs in different divisions and tell everyone the truth.'

Nadia was happy for Ed to carry on talking – it allowed her to concentrate on eating – but there was a growing inevitability to his story. Things weren't going to end well.

'What happened?' said Nadia. She lifted one hand to cover her mouth. 'She didn't die, did she?'

'God no,' Ed looked shocked. 'Worse, in some ways. First of all, she stopped answering my calls to her private phone. I tried her once on her work phone, but that went to voicemail. Ali was already in Beirut and, as I had a flight to Karachi a couple of days later, I convinced myself it would all be OK.'

'But it wasn't,' said Nadia. 'She dumped you?'

'Not exactly,' said Ed. 'When I got back to the office in Karachi, I was called straight in to the Head of Security. He wanted to know why I'd called Amina's phone.'

'They'd found out about the two of you?'

'No,' snapped Ed. 'I'll explain if you stop butting in.'

'Sorry,' said Nadia, shocked by his anger.

‘I told them that I’d only phoned Amina to invite her to lunch,’ said Ed. ‘… Because I was leaving. They seemed happy with that explanation and then it all came out. While I’d been in London, Amina had just vanished. All her stuff was still in her flat, her phone was sitting on her desk, but she was gone.

‘They’d put the office on full alert for a few days, expecting to get a ransom demand or worse, and then they got an unexpected message from one of our people in Moscow. Amina had been spotted there. Apparently she’d been working for the Russians for years. Her family had connections to Nasser and they’d got to her when she was a teenager.’

‘Shit,’ said Nadia. ‘And you had no idea?’

‘Of course I didn’t have any idea,’ said Ed. ‘And I don’t think I ever spoke out of turn or told her anything I shouldn’t have, but she had the same security clearance as me. I probably wasn’t paying that much attention.’

‘A nightmare,’ said Nadia, trying to imagine herself in Ed’s shoes. ‘And no one knows about your relationship?’

‘Just you,’ said Ed, staring fixedly at his untouched breakfast. ‘And Amina herself, of course. I don’t see how it helps anyone if I commit career suicide by volunteering the information. I guess that’s why I accepted the Field Officer training, though. Partly to take my mind off things and partly because I felt guilty for not speaking up. I keep waiting for a call telling me they’ve found out.’

‘Now I understand why you haven’t been so keen to open up,’ said Nadia.

‘The worst part is that I don’t trust my judgement any more,’ said Ed. ‘You know when you’re absolutely certain about something? … About someone?’ He looked up at Nadia, seemingly searching for understanding. ‘And then you find out you were completely wrong.

You were a total idiot. The rug gets pulled out from under your feet and you find yourself falling with nothing to grab hold of.'

Nadia reached over and took his hand. 'That sounds absolutely shitty,' she said. 'And I understand that feeling of betrayal and helplessness all too well. Thank you for trusting me with it. And you obviously don't have to worry about me saying anything.'

Ed smiled. 'My rational brain knows I just need to move on from it and I'll be fine. To tell you the truth, apart from anything else, I'm also embarrassed I was such a fool.'

'I understand, but that's the last thing you should feel,' said Nadia.

Ed shrugged.

'One more question,' said Nadia. 'And then I'm done.' She leant forward and whispered. 'What really happened with Unicorn? He was tough as nails. It seems unlikely he would just keel over like that.'

Ed look at his cold plate of food, his lips pursed and his shoulders tensed.

'I don't know,' he mumbled. 'We used a curare-based compound. It's been well tested and that dose should have just knocked him out.'

Nadia had never seen Ed looking shifty. He was lying, but about what? Had he deliberately given Ibrahim an overdose? Surely not? Ed wouldn't do something like that.

She smiled.

'It isn't important,' she said. 'The world is a better place without that man and that's all that matters.'

Ed relaxed his shoulders and looked up to face her. They would never discuss what really happened to Ibrahim. There was no need.

# Sixty Minutes

## by Tony Salter

### Five different people. Five separate lives. Sixty minutes to bind them for ever.

Hassan, Jim, Shuna, Dan and Nadia come from very different worlds. If life were straightforward, their paths would never cross. But our lives are rarely that simple and, as the clock ticks away the minutes of a single hour on a July morning, fate draws all five together in a headlong rush towards disaster.

Who are the heroes and who are the villains?

Tony Salter's latest novel leaves us guessing right up to the last page.

---

**** "Addictive thriller! I thought I knew where this was going, but couldn't have been more wrong."

**** "Fascinating characters. Loads of tension."

**** "Made me think differently. On top of the cat-and-mouse tension, I was surprised to find myself questioning my own stereotypes along the way."

**** "Clever and beautifully observed. Each of the five characters has a role to play - although it isn't always obvious what that will finally be. Loved it."

---

**Sixty Minutes is AVAILABLE NOW in paperback or eBook format from Amazon and most booksellers.**

# Best Eaten Cold

## by Tony Salter

## The Bestselling Psychological Thriller you can't put down.

Imagine that someone wants to do you harm. Someone you once knew, but have almost forgotten.

Now, imagine that they are clever, patient and will not stop. They'll get inside your head and make you doubt yourself.

They'll make you question who you are, and ensure that everyone you care for starts to doubt you too.

---

***** "Fast-paced, terrifyingly believable, chilling at times... the kind of book that's hard to put down"

***** "I admire any author who can hold my attention so thrillingly from beginning to end"

***** "Much superior to Girl on the Train."

---

**Best Eaten Cold is AVAILABLE NOW in paperback or eBook format from Amazon and most booksellers.**

# Cold Intent

## by Tony Salter

### The Thrilling Sequel to Best Eaten Cold.

It was always too good to be true.

Finding her, arresting her, proving her guilt … that should have been enough.

It should have been, but a small voice, deep inside him, refused to be silenced. The voice which whispered the same words over and over – how even a jail sentence wouldn't stop her.

And then Sam looked at Julie, standing tall in the dock waiting for the verdict. He watched her smile and knew that it would never be over. She would always find a way to reach out for him and the nightmares would become reality once more.

---

***** "Sleep isn't an option. You have to know what happens next."

***** "Utterly compelling."

***** "A masterclass in page-turning - thrilling!"

---

**Cold Intent is AVAILABLE NOW in paperback or eBook format from Amazon and most booksellers.**

# Acknowledgements

Writing novels is a solitary task but I don't think I could enjoy it without some company along the way. Feedback, encouragement and patient support are essential emotional props, but so are the sweeping blows of honest criticism which help to remind me that I am writing for readers and not only for myself.

The Unicorn was a difficult book to write for many reasons, not least because of the sensitivity of the subject matter. The book was started and is set in 2019 and early 2020. During the time of writing, the world changed in ways that no-one could have imagined before March 2020. Lockdown should have been a great opportunity to focus on my writing – unfortunately. it didn't turn out that way, but that is quite another story.

I need to thank all of my friends and family for their help and encouragement – in particular, Sue Brown, John Cronley, Di Cronley, Aliki Radley, Paul Manson, Dana Olearnikova and my late father, Michael. Special thanks are also due to my agent Kathy Robbins and my editor, Claire Baldwin.

Finally, I must thank my wife of thirty years, Gro. Without her love, support, patience and tolerance, none of this would have been possible.

Printed in Great Britain
by Amazon

81709102R00205